INSIGHT

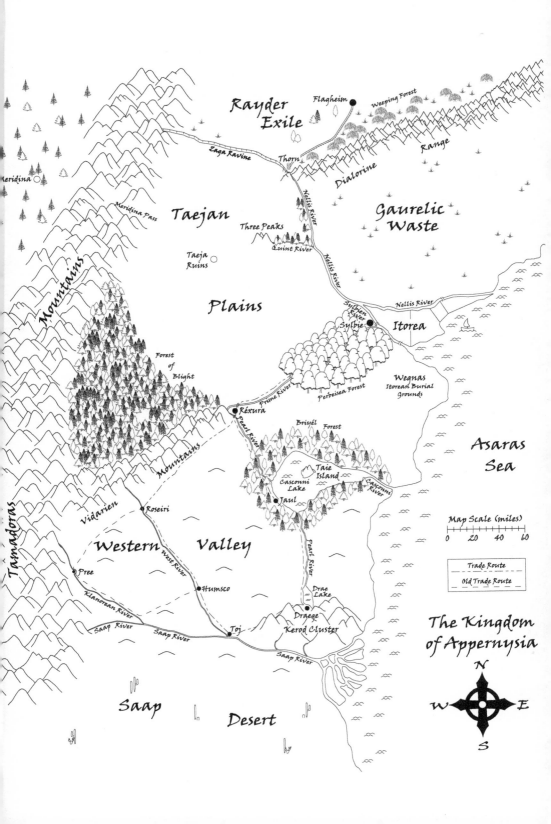

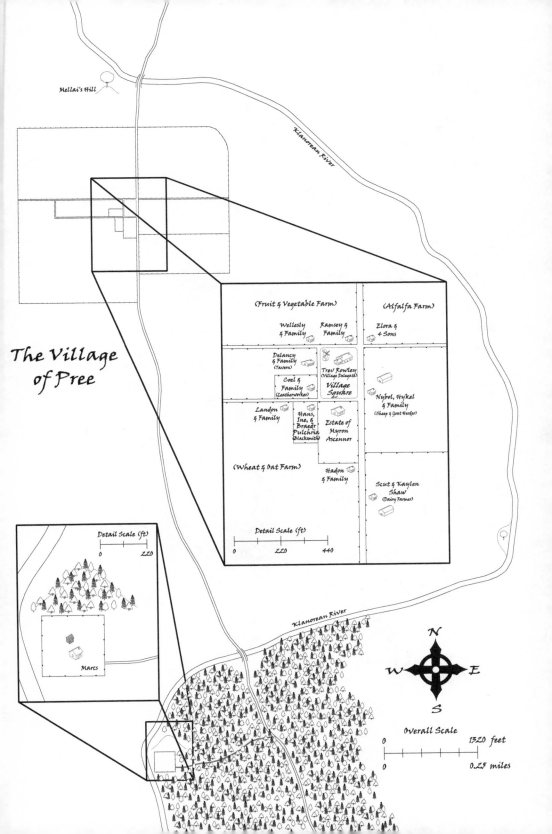

Mellai's Hill

Klanorean River

The Village
of Pree

(Fruit & Vegetable Farm)   (Alfalfa Farm)

Wellesly   Ramsey &   Elora &
& Family   Family   4 Sons

Delancy   Trev Rowley
& Family   (Village Delegate)
(Tavern)   Village
Coel &   Squire   Nybol, Hykel
Family   & Family
(Leatherworker)   (Sheep & Goat Herder)

Landon   Hans,   Estate of
& Family   Ine, &   Myron
                 Braedr   Ascennor
                 Pulchria
                 (Blacksmith)

(Wheat & Oat Farm)   Hadon
                       & Family   Scut & Kaylen
                                         Shaw
                                         (Dairy Farmer)

Detail Scale (ft)

Detail Scale (ft)

0   220   440

Detail Scale (ft)

0   220

Marcs

Klanorean River

N
W   E
S

Overall Scale

0   1320 feet

0   0.25 miles

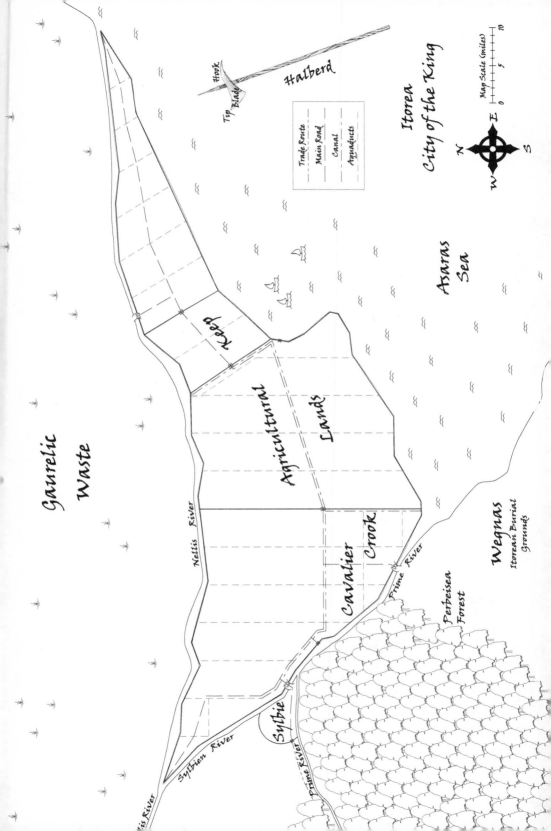

BEHOLDERS: INSIGHT

Text copyright © 2011 by Terron James
Maps copyright © 2011 by Terron James
Illustrations copyright © 2017 by Terron James

First edition published in July 2011 by Nypa Distributing, LLC
Tooele, UT

Second edition published in June 2013 by Jolly Fish Press, LLC
Provo, UT

This edition published in January 2018 by Nypa Distributing, LLC
Tooele, UT

Printed in the United States of America

ISBN: 978-0-9997400-1-9

0 9 8 7 6 5 4 3

For my big brother, Lonnie, the angel on my shoulder.
My love for telling stories began with you.

Acknowledgments

First and foremost, I grovel before Crystal, my wife and best friend, along with my sons, for their patience and understanding during the past five years. They have stood by me as I've squelched countless hours of their time to obsess over this book.

My dad, Allen, who first helped me brainstorm the concept of True Sight. Without him, I'd be another writer with only a blank sheet of paper.

Claude, Annie, and Marilyn, the most selfless and kind-hearted people I know, who have been nothing short of a miracle in my life. Scott, who donated years of his phenomenal ideas and talents to help build Appernysia.

Travis, my main muse, who always pushed me through my writing slumps with his positive attitude and enthusiasm.

Tyler, the world's most well-rounded fantasy reader, who selflessly shared his genius and encouragement over and over again.

Todd and AJ, engineering masterminds who helped design Itorea and Justice.

The League of Utah Writers, specifically those in my critique group.

My other insight-ful reviewers, including Melanee, Debbie, Angela, Val, Sharon, Erik, Tiffany, Mark, Connie, Chris, Amy, Emma, and Quinn.

Everyone who helped market Beholders for years before its official release.

My nieces and nephews, whose "fantasized" names appear throughout the maps and story of Insight.

Prologue

Shalán shielded her eyes with her free hand and peered over the river. "What's happening over there?"

"I don't know," Theiss replied. He yanked his arm free from her grasp and fled across the stout wooden bridge. A gust of wind tore through their small village. Theiss stumbled and fell sideways, nearly toppling into the deep current of the West River.

"Be careful," Shalán shouted, but her voice blew away only inches from her mouth.

Theiss regained his feet and, eight strides later, reached the safety of the opposite bank. He joined a large crowd of villagers who had gathered at the edge of a clearing. Shalán followed after him, anxious to see what held their attention. Her linen dress whipped sideways in the wind, and her braids fell apart. Black clouds had darkened the sky over Roseiri, and tiny spheres of frozen raindrops stung her careworn face.

The closer Shalán drew, the more animated the villagers became. They huddled together as they watched the northern pasture. Some were speaking emphatically and pointing at the large oak tree where Shalán's children always played.

Shalán forced her way through the crowd, fearing a cyclone had carried her children away. What she saw instead was just as unnerving. Her ten-year-old twins were kneeling under the tree playing stick-stack. Despite the howling wind and torrential hailstorm, they had managed to stack a narrow column of twigs over two feet high. The long grass surrounding them stood straight, while the reeds across the rest of the pasture bowed flat against the ground.

As Shalán marveled over what she saw, stranger things caught her eye. Her children's clothes hung loose on their bodies. Their hair didn't even twitch. The falling leaves and branches from the trembling tree stopped a few feet above the twins' heads and rolled away in different directions.

The villagers began questioning her. "What are they doing, Shalán? What sort of trick is this?" Despite how long they had trusted the Marcs family, some of the villagers suspected sorcery or witchcraft. Others argued fell spirits and demons.

Shalán ignored them all, for at that moment the wind hoisted a large bale of hay off the ground farther up the pasture and sent it tumbling across the field.

"Lon! Mellai!" Shalán screamed, sprinting desperately toward her children, knowing she would be too late. "Get out of the way! Hide behind the tree!"

Neither child responded. Shalán watched in horror, the wind driving her tears across her face, as the bale rolled forward. Just when it should have crushed the children, the bale blew apart, as though it had smashed into an invisible wall. Hay flew forward, forming a perfect dome of undisturbed space where the twins knelt.

Shalán stopped midstride, dumbfounded.

Lon and Mellai continued playing their game as if nothing was happening, until Lon knocked over the pile. Mellai laughed and Lon pounded his fists on the ground. Just then the wind penetrated the barrier. The grass surrounding them dropped flat. Their hair and clothes flapped and whipped wildly.

Shalán rushed forward again. Clutching her twins' arms, she turned and hurried home, ignoring her children's complaints and the villagers' wide-eyed stares.

"Aron?" she shouted as she burst into their quaint plank house. "Aron?"

"Right here," her husband replied from a chair next to the hearth. He looked up from his half-carved wooden bear, startled by her urgency. "What happened?"

Shalán glanced around the single-story cabin. "Where are my parents?"

"They're still eating dinner with the Arbogasts. With this weather, I wouldn't expect them home anytime soon. Why? What's the matter?"

Shalán sat her children in front of the fire, then took Aron's hand and led him into their bedroom. After closing the door, she relayed what she had seen.

Aron's lips and muscles tightened. Without a word, he grabbed a bag from the corner of the room and threw it on the bed. "Start packing, Shalán. We're leaving. Now." He opened the door and disappeared from the room.

Shalán pulled an armful of clothes from a nearby shelf and stuffed them into the bag. Tears of fear and confusion tumbled down her already soaked face.

Aron returned a few seconds later with a poker. Using it as a pry bar, he removed a floorboard on the far side of their room. Reaching down, he pulled out a sword. After setting it on the bed next to the bag of clothes, he took hold of his wife's shoulders.

"Look at me, Shalán." She lifted her gaze to his brown eyes. His expression was kind, but urgency poured through his scarred face. "There's only one explanation for what you saw tonight. We have to run."

Chapter 1

In The Dark

Gil wiped the blood from his dagger, then joined his four comrades around their small fire. "Keep your voices down, Rayders. Have you forgotten why we have traveled so far?"

"No, Lieutenant," his men whispered as they squinted at him through the light of the setting sun. They each saluted, touching two fingers to their right temples.

The four members of Gil's squad were young recruits, but his commander had ignored that fact. The rumors surging throughout Appernysia were too significant. A month earlier, every available scout had been dispatched from the Rayder Exile, their banished homeland, to find the Beholder and capture him.

Gil tossed a chunk of meat onto a large rock in the middle of the fire. "Do you know anything about this village?"

Gil knew their answer before they gave it, but it still angered him to see his men shake their heads. He never understood why his commander kept so much information to himself. As Rayders, the village of Pree played a significant part of their history and society. Their own weapon master was from that village.

"We Rayders have avoided Pree for ten years," Gil said, "because the last infiltration squad kidnapped a boy and murdered his family. That squad was arrogant and foolhardy. They did not think before they acted. Most importantly, they forgot the importance of stealth."

Gil drew his arming sword, pierced the sizzling meat, and flipped it over on the rock. "A decade has passed, but I guarantee these villagers will be on the lookout for us, especially after last night . . ."

He glanced pointedly at the butchered remains of a cow. They had run out of food on their month-long journey to Pree and were forced to steal a village cow for meat.

"We will be hard-pressed to keep our presence a secret."

One of his men leaned forward with obvious concern on his young face. "What is the plan, Lieutenant?"

"It is getting dark," Gil replied as he stood. "You four stay here while I search through town."

"What will you do if you find the Beholder?"

Gil looked west, ignoring the steady buzz of flies hovering over the cow carcass. "I will return to camp and give you further instructions . . . unless I am forced to capture him myself."

His four men glanced at each other with surprise.

"Is that even possible?" Drake, the boldest of the four recruits, asked.

"My heart tells me we will know soon enough," Gil answered.

"What if someone spots you, Lieutenant?" Drake pressed.

Gil sheathed his sword, tucked his tunic into his leather belt, and pulled the hood of his dark wool cloak over his head. "I will silence them. Permanently."

* * * * *

"Please leave her father out of this," Lon Marcs pleaded as he pulled his gaze away from Kaylen's log home and caught up to his sister. "It's been hard enough trying to convince him to let me court Kaylen without your interference. The last thing I need right now is you causing him unnecessary worry—especially with two of his cows missing. If they don't turn up soon, our whole village is going to feel it."

Mellai ignored him as they continued home. Her long linen dress hovered inches above the dirt road, jostling slightly with every stride.

Mellai turned her head and let the final rays of the setting sun soak her face, her brown curls tied casually behind her head with a red ribbon. A wolf howled in the distance, and a local dog immediately answered with a diatribe of furious barking.

When the twins neared the south bridge, they crossed paths with Myron Ascennor—an aged vagrant who had been wandering the village for more than ten years. They greeted him, but Myron only mumbled to himself and stared at the ground as he shuffled past on his bony legs; it was his typical response to any kind of social interaction.

"You just wait," Myron said. "I've set a trap. I'll kill you all. I'm faster than a chicken with a donkey and a fish. You just wait."

Mellai smirked, but Lon gave her a look of warning. He was tolerant of most of her inappropriate jokes, but making fun of Myron was something he wouldn't allow. His irritated scolding might have angered her, but because of their unique emotional bond, Mellai understood exactly where Lon was coming from. She couldn't imagine how it must have felt for Myron to lose his entire family in one day, nor could Mellai guess how she would react if the same thing happened to her. The sudden loss of her grandparents five years earlier had been hard enough.

Myron disappeared and the twins continued on. As they crossed the south bridge, a cow's lowing caught their attention.

"Sounds like we found one of Scut's cows," Lon said with a smile as he left the road, climbing down to the riverbank. Mellai stayed put and tapped her foot impatiently.

"Come down here, Mellai."

"Not a chance."

"I'm not playing, Mel. Get down here *now*."

Alarmed by the urgency in her brother's voice, Mellai followed his path carefully down the embankment to avoid tripping on foliage. When she reached the bottom, Mellai followed Lon's blue-eyed gaze to the opposite bank of the river. There stood one of Scut's missing cows, lazily munching on the high grass that tickled its belly. Cows had slipped out of Scut's corral before and usually ended up somewhere along the river's edge, so the sight was not unusual.

"You need to relax, Lon," Mellai scolded, "or you'll give yourself another headache. Why did you . . ." Her voice trailed off as she saw the thick hemp rope tied around the cow's neck. The other end was lashed to one of the bridge's beams.

Mellai's brown eyes narrowed and she looked up at her brother. Though they were twins, Lon stood more than a head taller than her short, five-foot stature.

"It must have been Myron," she said. "Remember what he said about setting a trap? He's not thinking straight, Lon, and besides us, nobody travels south of Pree. Who else would have tied the cow here?"

Before Lon could answer, a sudden dread fell over Mellai. She could see and feel the same terror in Lon. They froze, fear rooting them to the spot. They cast their gaze up and down the river, searching for the source of their unsettling suspicion. Just then, the wooden slats of the bridge creaked as someone crossed overhead.

The twins held their breath as the mysterious person continued across the bridge. Ten anxious steps, then on toward Pree, but the footfalls halted when the ignorant cow bellowed again. Lon pulled Mellai down into the thick undergrowth just in time. Peeking through the grass, Mellai saw a man step off the bridge on the opposite bank. He wore a heavy cloak with the hood pulled low over his face. As he slid down the embankment, Mellai caught sight of his hand wrapped around the grip of a hidden sword.

Mellai's heart skipped.

The man moved cautiously along the bank, glancing up and down the river for the cow's owner. As he stepped around the cow, it turned for another mouthful of fresh grass and knocked him into the deep river. He flailed around as his heavy clothes fought to drag him under, but he finally managed to catch hold of a large boulder and climb to safety.

The man paused on the riverbank, his wet cloak clinging to his face and body. Once he had regained his composure, the man walked up to the cow, pulled out a dagger, and slit its throat. The cow toppled over and thrashed in the yellow grass.

The man jumped back, nearly falling into the river again. He cursed and peeled off the wet hood.

A chill ran down Mellai's spine when she saw the right side of his face. "Is that a—" she started to ask, but Lon slapped his hand over her mouth.

The man's hand slid inside his cloak as he glanced in their direction. Mellai and her brother froze, afraid to even blink. After what seemed an eternity, the man turned away and walked to the cow. He kicked it hard, then stepped around it and continued east along the northern bank.

Mellai squirmed to free herself from Lon's grip, but he held her tight. Desperate to flee, Mellai sank her teeth into his arm.

Lon ripped his arm away, and Mellai leaped from her hiding spot. She clawed at the side of the embankment, struggling to find a good foothold. Lon caught up to her and helped his sister up the hill. Just as they reached the top, Mellai kicked loose a large rock. She turned and watched the stone bounce down the embankment and splash in the river.

The loud noise startled the intruder. He turned with a drawn sword in his hand. When he saw the twins standing atop the riverbank, he shifted his gaze between Mellai and her brother, took a few calculated steps in their direction, then seemed to change his mind. After sliding his sword into the leather scabbard at his waist, he turned back east, running at full speed along the riverbank.

"Come on," Lon urged, pulling Mellai to her feet and pushing her into a run. "We need to get out of here." They hurried down the dirt path toward their home; Lon took his sister by the hand to help her keep up.

"Did you see it, Lon?" Mellai asked. "I know it's getting dark, but please tell me you saw the marking on his face."

Lon only nodded, but that's all that was necessary. Mellai already knew Lon's answer before she had asked. She had felt his fear, which only added to her own.

"Why did he kill that cow?" Mellai panted as they fled.

"I don't know. It was probably just in the wrong place at the wrong time."

"Like us."

The further they pushed into the woods, the more Mellai's strength faded. Her legs struggled to keep up with her brother's long strides as they hurried along the dirt path through a thicket of juniper trees and wild grass. Yet, she knew if they continued just a little farther, they would be safe in their house; she forced herself to keep putting one foot in front of the other.

Lon eventually slowed his pace and gave her an encouraging smile. Although she knew her brother was just as terrified, she appreciated his effort to calm her. People rarely considered Mellai's feelings, mostly because she rarely considered theirs. Their parents and Kaylen, her only true friend, were the only people whom she treated with respect, and who respected her, apart from Lon.

They sprinted for half a mile until they finally reached the wooden rail fence surrounding their two acres of cleared property. The light of the setting sun had completely faded and the twins were both glad to be out of the dark woods. They paused outside the gate and leaned against the fence, gasping for air.

"That . . . was quite a run," Lon said between breaths, forcing a smile. "We should do this . . . more often."

Mellai ignored her brother. She was still shaking from their close encounter at the bridge. She placed her free hand on the fence and closed her eyes, inhaling deeply to calm herself while her short hair fell over her face.

When the twins were both breathing normally again, Lon opened the wooden gate for his sister. "C'mon. Mother and Father are waiting for us."

With fingers interlocked, they crossed through the gate toward their two-level frame house.

*   *   *   *   *

When the Marcs had originally arrived in Pree, the villagers were cold and unwelcoming—partially because the Marcs refused to divulge where they had come from or why they'd left. Rather than arouse resentment by demanding the village's respect, the Marcs built a small log house south of the Klanorean River at the base of a large hill. It took Lon and his father, Aron, two years of selfless service to Scut Shaw, the village dairy farmer, before their family gained the trust of the whole village. The Marcs were eventually invited to relocate their home inside the village boundaries, much to the delight of both Lon and Mellai. But their father had politely declined, pointing out that their new, frame house was nearly finished.

As Lon and Mellai approached the house, Mellai eyed the small donkey cart standing near the door. The image of a hammer and anvil had been etched into the side of the cart, which belonged to the village blacksmith.

Lon tightened his grip on Mellai's hand and pulled her toward the front door. "Mellai, only Mother and Father can know what we saw tonight. We just need to finish dinner with the Pulchrias. Pretend to have a good time—or better yet, pretend you're in one of your bad moods. Will you do that for me, please?"

"Lon, you know that I—" Mellai began, but her words turned to a squeak as Lon pinched her waist. Her look of shock transformed into a furious glare.

"There now, that's much better," Lon teased with a wink. "Thanks for your concerted effort, Little Sis." He opened the front door and entered their home.

The Marcs spent most of their time on the main level of their house. It was large and open, with a sitting area and fireplace on one side, and the kitchen and dining area on the other. Two small bedrooms also extended from the back of the house. Their parents slept in one and Mellai in the other. Lon preferred to curl up on a bedroll in front of the fireplace.

The aroma of roasted chicken and spiced potatoes filled Lon's nose. He loved having an herbalist as his mother. Not only was Shalán a skilled healer, she also knew exactly which spices would best complement the food she prepared. A meal at the Marcs home had become a coveted prize in Pree, but Shalán invited people over for one purpose only—to find a husband for her daughter.

Lon smiled at their guests, all sitting on wooden chairs near the fireplace. Hans Pulchria was an experienced blacksmith, with strong hands and broad shoulders. He said very little, though that might have been because his wife, Ine, hardly ever stopped talking. She was heavyset, bubbly, and the source of almost all the village gossip. Overall, they were pleasant company. Lon knew that even Mellai wouldn't have minded visiting with them for the evening—if it had only been the two of them.

Lon heaved a sigh when he saw their son, Braedr, slouched in his chair, a smug look plastered on his face. Like his father, Braedr was tall and muscular, but he lacked his father's respectful manner. Lon suspected he was too used to getting his way, perhaps because he was an only child. In Lon's eyes, there was no one more arrogant or selfish in all of Appernysia. Every decision Braedr made was calculated to build himself up in the eyes of the villagers so he could exploit them. He always had some sort of alternate agenda. Always.

"Good evening, Master Lon," Hans said.

"Good evening, Master Hans," Lon responded awkwardly—only a few days left before he turned seventeen, he wasn't old enough to be called Master—and ran a hand through his curly brown hair. He turned his gaze to Ine and smiled. "Good evening to you, too, Lady Ine. I hope your journey here was comfortable."

"Now look what you've started, Hans," Ine said as her cheeks flushed pink. "I won't have this turned into an intolerable evening of outlandish formalities. Address me for who I am, Lon—the wife of a blacksmith. I'm not, nor do I ever wish to be, a lady. Good gracious me, what a horrid thought."

"Well spoken, Ine," Shalán called from across the room. "What woman would ever wish to be a lady?"

"Perhaps one who wishes for an easier life," Braedr said as he rose from his chair, "free from suffering and toil. I'm sure Mellai agrees with me."

Braedr crossed the room to Mellai, who stood in the doorway with her mouth pulled tight in an unreadable expression. He took her hand and spoke in a voice too gentle for his stature.

"Hello, Mellai. I'm honored to be sharing supper with you tonight."

"Good evening, Braedr," Mellai said flatly as she pulled her hand free. "I assume your parents will be eating with us, too?"

"Of course, we will, my darling," Ine responded. "We mustn't let all of this wonderful food go to waste on just the two of you. What do you say we start eating, hmm?"

"Now Ine, we prefer our guests be honest with us," Aron teased. "If you wanted a sample of my wife's cooking, why didn't you just say so?"

Ine flushed in embarrassment, looking anxiously toward the front door. Shalán intervened. "You'll have to excuse my husband," she said, giving Aron a reproving glance. "He loves to make people uncomfortable. I keep telling him it's going to get him into trouble some day."

"Couple that with Hans' intolerable silence," Ine responded with a smile, "and perhaps our husbands will balance each other out. I'll see myself to the table." She got up from the chair and bustled over to the scrubbed wooden table.

"She balances him out just fine herself," Aron whispered to his wife.

"Oh, shush," Shalán whispered back, elbowing him away. "Go sit down."

Everyone joined Ine at the table. Braedr pulled out one of the wooden chairs for Mellai, but she merely sniffed at it, pulled out a different chair, and sat down. Undeterred, Braedr plunked down in the chair next to hers. Once everyone was seated, Shalán placed a plate of chicken and potatoes in front of each person, then took her place next to her husband.

"This is excellent," Ine commented as they ate. "It reminds me of the fancy meals we used to have with Myron and his family. He's such a sad case. It seems like he loses himself more every day. But I'm glad to be part of such a caring community, where people are sensitive to his situation and help him as much as he allows." She paused and looked at everyone around the table for emphasis.

"How long has it been?" Lon asked, knowing Ine was waiting for a response. He already knew the answer, but thought it best to keep her talking so everyone else could eat. The sooner the meal was over, the sooner he could tell his parents about the man at the river.

"Ten years," Ine replied, shaking her head. "It's such a shame. Myron was the best delegate this village has ever seen. If those Rayders had stayed where they belong, he never would have lost his family. He'd still be the same man I learned to respect when I was a little girl. Four innocent people dead in a matter of minutes. Such a shame."

"They never found Tarek's body though, right?" Lon asked.

"True, but he was the youngest of Myron's boys. Even if they kidnapped him, I'm certain he didn't survive. He was only eleven." Ine set down her fork and slumped her shoulders. "Poor Myron. He's never been the same since. I don't think he has even looked inside his manor. Now it's just an empty shell in the square, except for the young people who go in for a dare."

"Mumbling Myron's House of Spirits," Braedr added with a smile.

Ine shuddered. "Horribly disrespectful, if you ask me. Leave the dead to rest and they'll treat you the best. That's what I've always said."

Lon swallowed a mouthful of potatoes. "Is that why Trev never moved into the manor? Is he afraid of ghosts?"

"Hardly," Ine replied as she picked up her fork and resumed gorging herself. "He's no Myron, but Trev Rowley is a decent delegate who honors Myron's contributions to this village. He would never take Myron's home away from him. Besides, Trev's place off the meeting hall suits him and his wife—you know, since they have no children."

Ine paused to dig at a strand of chicken caught between her yellow teeth. "Well, we could continue on about poor, old Myron, but I expect it's stirring up unpleasant memories. After all, your family is no stranger to the brutality of the Rayders. Aron, your scar is proof of that."

Lon and Mellai eyed each other at Ine's mention of the Rayders, while Aron fingered the jagged scar on his right temple. "I wish there was more we could do for him."

"I should drown the old man in the Klanorean and end his misery," Braedr inserted after draining his cup. "I'd be doing him a favor, really. I'd beg for death if I were in his situation."

Silence fell over the table as everyone stopped to stare at Braedr. Ine finally swallowed her mouthful of chicken and scolded her son. "That's not for you to decide, is it? I'm especially surprised to hear such a remark from you. How could anyone murder an old man who has lost his family? Good gracious me."

Everyone else in the room continued to stare at Braedr. He obstinately returned their stares, but as the silence continued, he started shifting uncomfortably in his chair. Finally, he excused himself and slunk out the front door.

"I'm sorry for Braedr's behavior," Hans apologized. "I don't know what's gotten in his head."

"Don't worry about it," Aron replied. "He's as entitled to his opinion as the rest of us. I just wasn't prepared to hear it. I didn't know how to respond."

"We best be off anyway," Ine said. "Braedr's comment has spoiled my appetite." She and Hans apologized to Shalán for the unfinished meal, then departed.

As the sound of the cart faded, Mellai walked to the window and closed the oak shutters. "How could anyone be so completely heartless?" she said, then continued sarcastically, "Oh yes, Braedr, I'd *love* to marry you. It gives me great comfort to know that if one of our children is a cripple or an imbecile, you'd be compassionate enough to end his miserable life for him." Mellai blew out her breath. "This has got to be one of the worst nights I've ever had. When will your matchmaking obsession end, Mother?"

"Enough of that," Aron responded. "Even his parents were surprised to hear his opinion. He's usually very amiable. I wonder how long he's felt that way."

Lon only shook his head. He had always been amazed that his parents didn't seem to recognize Braedr's faults.

Shalán began clearing dishes from the table, obviously upset with the events of the evening. The only sounds in the room came from the soft crackle of wood burning in the fireplace, accompanied by the occasional clatter of plates and utensils being piled and scrubbed.

Lon moved next to Mellai and put his arm around her. "Listen, Father. Now that the Pulchrias are gone, Mellai and I need to talk to you. We saw a Rayder tonight by the south bridge."

A porcelain plate shattered as Shalán dropped it to the floor. Pale as a sheet, she gripped the back of a chair to steady herself. Both she and Aron turned their wide-eyed attention to Lon.

"We were close enough to see his face," Mellai added, her foul mood disappearing. "We saw the marking on his temple. He was a Rayder."

"Did he see you?" Shalán asked, her hands trembling on the back of the chair.

"Yes," Lon answered, and proceeded to give a quick account of what happened at the bridge.

Shalán gasped. Aron helped her sit down in the chair, then proceeded to clean the porcelain shards off the floor.

"What would he be doing in Pree?" Mellai inquired. "Do they think there's a Beholder here?"

"Perhaps," Aron answered as he glanced at his wife. "Those rumors have been floating around Appernysia for years, so there can't be many places left for the Rayders to check. It's all been a foolhardy attempt to bring magic back into their society, if you ask me."

"Rayders in Pree," Shalán whispered. "I hope no one else catches their attention."

"How would they know not to attract a Rayder's attention if they don't know he's here?" Mellai asked, angered by her mother's comment. "That's what happened to us."

"He only saw us because you were too impatient to stay quiet," Lon countered.

Mellai responded with a glare.

"What should we do about this, Aron?" Shalán asked.

"We'll do nothing," he replied as he sat in the chair beside her. "If we wish to avoid drawing attention to ourselves, we must act as we always have."

"I don't understand," Lon said. "How can our family be more important than the entire village?"

"We aren't," Aron replied. "If we warn the village, circumstances will become much worse for everyone. If the villagers refuse to leave their homes, the Rayders will take advantage of the easy access to crops and livestock. If we mobilize against them, they will take it as a challenge and start assassinating the villagers one at a time. By warning the village, everyone—including our family—would be in greater danger."

"Oh, great," Mellai grumbled. "If that happens, we'll probably have to pack up and leave again without a word to anyone."

Shalán stood up abruptly, knocking over her chair. Just for a moment, anger dispelled the fear in her eyes. "Despite what you may think, Mellai, your father and I didn't enjoy leaving Roseiri in the middle of the night, either. My parents still live there and I haven't seen or spoken to them for five years. It was a sacrifice we had to make to protect our family. I'm not about to have my family torn away from me. We've lost so much already—"

Shalán's voice caught and she left the room, sobbing into her hands. Aron stared after her for a moment, then picked up the wooden chair and sat down, inviting his children to join him around the table. He let out a long sigh.

"Your mother loves both of you more than you could imagine. Not a moment passes when she doesn't worry about you."

"Father," Lon said as he sat forward in his chair, "Mellai and I have tried to be patient and understanding since we left Roseiri, but it's hard to understand something that's never been explained. You've been putting us off for years. Why did we have to leave? What's Mother really so upset about?"

These questions piqued Mellai's curiosity and she also leaned forward.

Aron let out another long sigh. "Now isn't the time for a conversation like this. There's a Rayder out there, and he undoubtedly has a few of his friends with him. If what you told me is true, they'll be watching our family. We must be on guard."

"Another excuse," Mellai spat. "When will you ever trust us enough?"

Aron looked at Mellai carefully, then nodded. "We've been hiding the truth to shield you from our worries, but maybe it's been too long. I suppose it's time I told you the true history of our family. I must warn you though; it's not a happy tale. You'll have to deal with the same anxieties that haunt me and your mother. Do you really want to bring that on yourselves?"

"Of course," Mellai said at once. She tried to sound unconcerned, even a little impatient, but there was a tremor in her voice that she couldn't quite control.

Lon, on the other hand, sat staring down at his hands. "Mellai, why do you have to pretend to be so fearless? I know how you really feel. You're just as terrified as I am."

Mellai frowned at her brother, then nodded. "Fine. If we're all going to be more truthful tonight, I can start. Yes, I'm terrified. Now get out of my head, Lon."

Aron chuckled. "Since before either of you could talk, you've been uncannily aware of each other's feelings. Even when you were babies, as soon as one of you started crying, the other would join in. I'm actually somewhat jealous of the bond you share, although I would miss the privacy. Sometimes, it's nice to have a secret—even necessary."

"Yes, it is," Mellai responded, elbowing Lon in the arm.

"Now then," Aron said, "where to begin . . ."

Chapter 2
Hidden Truth

Aron ran his finger across the scar on his right temple as he sat in silence. "I suppose I ought to start with how your mother and I met," he finally spoke.

"You didn't grow up together?" Lon asked.

"I'm afraid not," Aron responded. "There are many things we've told you that aren't true. I apologize for the deceit, but you'll understand once I've finished my tale. Try not to interrupt until I'm done, or this will take all night."

Neither Lon nor Mellai responded, so Aron continued. "I didn't grow up in Roseiri. I met your mother during a . . . visit there about twenty years ago. I couldn't stay long, but I was so enchanted by her that I returned as frequently as I could during the following two years. We fell in love, and I asked your mother to marry me, but she refused. You see, I was a Rayder."

Mellai breathed in sharply and Lon looked as though he might be sick, but Aron continued, deep in reverie. "Honor and standing are very important to the Rayders. I lost both over the course of those two years because the Rayders became frustrated with my lack of . . . results. I didn't care, though, because I loved your mother and was willing to sacrifice everything to be with her. Unfortunately, it wasn't that easy. Rayders are never allowed to leave their society. If someone tries, man or woman, the Rayders will hunt them for the rest of their life. The penalty for desertion is always death—no exceptions."

Aron lowered his gaze to the floor. "I had quite the dilemma on my hands. Should I continue my life as a Rayder and lose the greatest love I'd ever find, or should I put both your mother and myself in constant danger by choosing her over the Rayders? I won't lie to you and say it was an easy decision. I wanted to be with your mother more than I valued my own life, but I couldn't justify putting her in danger. After a long struggle, I decided the choice should be your mother's."

"Did Mother know you were a Rayder during your courtship?" Mellai questioned.

"Of course, she did. Just like the man you saw on your way home tonight, every Rayder is permanently marked with the King's Cross on their right temple. You would never hear them call it that, though. Rayders just refer to it as the Cross."

"Why?" Lon asked.

"Rayders hate King Drogan as much as our king hates them. It's against Rayder law to speak of him."

Lon's mouth opened slightly with new understanding as he stared at his father. "So, that's how you really got your scar. How did you remove your mark?"

Mellai wasn't nearly as composed as Lon. She slapped the table with the palm of her hand. "Has our whole life been a lie?"

Aron tightened his jaw, his eyes slowly lifting until they were locked with Mellai's. "I'm not enjoying this conversation any more than you. Let me finish, then I'll be more than willing to answer your questions."

The three of them sat in silence listening to the soft crackle of the fire until Aron finally continued. "The King's Cross is permanent because it's branded into the flesh. I don't know where it came from or what it means, so please don't ask. The Rayders have been marking themselves with it for hundreds of years; they focus more on the traditional act than the reason for doing it."

Aron's chair creaked as he stood and walked to the fireplace. "I don't need to tell you that your mother chose to marry me, even though she knew it meant a life of unending danger for us."

"Is that why the Rayder's here?" Lon asked. "Is he looking for you?"

"I doubt it." Aron grabbed the iron poker and rearranged the burning logs. "As soon as I received Shalán's answer, I left the Rayders for good. They never knew about your mother, so I knew she and her parents would be safe—but I wasn't going to take any chances. We were married in Roseiri within a month, then Shalán and I hid in the Vidarien Mountains for a year. Although the Rayders never stop looking for a deserter, the manpower put into the hunt reduces significantly after a year or so. Only then did I dare take your mother from the protection of the mountains. I've never seen a Rayder since."

Aron paused again, eyeing his children for any signs of discontent, but found only a captivated audience. "We've told people my scar was caused by a Rayder I encountered while out hunting. In a way, the Rayders caused this scar by placing that cursed mark on me in the first place, but I created the scar myself. I had plenty of time to contemplate my life while we were in the mountains—and anguished over the monstrosities I committed as a Rayder. I mourned the manipulative and destructive upbringing every Rayder child experiences. I began to truly understand the corruption of the Rayder society. My mind and body were overwhelmed, and I became gravely ill. I only survived because of your mother's care."

"I'm glad Mother's good at what she does," Lon said.

"So am I," Aron replied with a nod. "When I finally had the strength to sit up on my own, I grabbed my dagger and cut the marking out of my face. Your mother was very upset with me, but she sewed up the wound and continued to care for me. Don't misunderstand me. The brand had to be removed in order for me to live among the Appernysians, but I should have allowed your mother to do it. I was lucky the wound healed with no infection. Either way, by removing that mark I purged myself of the Rayders' corruption."

Aron stowed the fire poker and dropped his chin to his chest, his shoulders gently shaking. When he turned around to face his children, tears filled his eyes. "Wise men will embrace correction while the foolish stubbornly cling to their pride. That's the best advice I've ever received. I was born a Rayder, and that life was all I ever knew. I even aspired to become the commander. What kind of man wishes to burn the King's Cross into a newborn's face with a branding iron?"

Mellai cupped her hands over her mouth and stared at her father in wide-eyed horror. "They really do that?"

"Absolutely," Aron replied, "on the day the child is born. Now you understand why I was so angry with what I had become. Shalán, on the other hand, saw me for something more. If it hadn't been for her . . . well, you both have a wonderful mother, and I hope you understand that. Your mother and I eventually returned to Roseiri to live the rest of our lives together," Aron continued. "In due course, the two of you were born. We lived together in peace for more than a decade, until—"

A loud crash shattered the silence of the house. Aron jumped to his feet, ran to the front door and cracked it open to peek outside before throwing the door open and rushing out. Lon stood, intending to follow his father, but by the time he reached the front door, Aron reentered carrying Myron, who was unconscious and covered in blood.

"Close the door, Lon," Aron shouted as he carried Myron to the table. "Mellai, go wake your mother. Myron needs her help. NOW!"

Lon slammed the front door shut, and Mellai hurried out of the room while Aron laid Myron on the table. Aron was just removing Myron's ragged tunic when Mellai returned with Shalán, whose eyebrows drew together when she saw the gaping wound in Myron's abdomen.

"Mellai, heat a pot of water and fetch me some clean rags," Shalán immediately began giving orders. "Aron, bring my satchel. Lon, keep watch out the window and make sure Myron didn't bring trouble with him. Hurry, everyone—he doesn't have much time."

Aron and Mellai dashed out of the room while Lon stationed himself at the window. He cracked opened the shutters and peered outside. As he searched the darkness, he noticed a slight haze obscuring his vision. He rubbed his eyes, but it continued to thicken and spread until he could see nothing but dense fog. It was as if a cloud had suddenly descended on their property.

Lon turned to warn his family, but the room was lost in the strange haze. He began to feel dizzy, as though the floor itself were bucking and heaving. His knees buckled, but it all seemed . . . distant somehow. The last thing he saw before blacking out was the glowing form of his father looking down at him with concern.

*   *   *   *   *

Lon cautiously opened his eyes. It was still dark outside, but the flames in the fireplace cast an orange glow, just enough for him to see. He was still in his home, but in one of the four extra rooms upstairs.

How'd I get up here? Lon thought as he closed his eyes again. His head swam.

A strange noise to his left caught Lon's attention. He turned his head and saw Myron lying on the neighboring bed, the man's breathing strained and raspy. A large bandage was wrapped around Myron's abdomen, soaked in his own blood.

Lon suddenly recalled what had happened. Myron had been attacked outside their home, there was the strange fog, then . . . nothing.

Where's my family?

One of the logs in the fireplace popped, startling Lon. He whipped his head around in search of danger. The quick movement caused a searing pain in his head, stabbing at the back of his eyes. Lon cried out in agony and squeezed his eyes shut.

Mellai came rushing into the room. Lon knew she had also felt his trauma—not the pain itself, but the emotional reaction of his body experiencing the pain.

"I never knew you were so squeamish at the sight of blood," she said, after seeing herself on the edge of the bed, a tremulous smile brushing her lips. "Mother hadn't even started cleaning Myron's wounds before you turned white and dropped to the floor. You must have really hit your head hard to knock yourself out this long. You've been asleep for a couple hours."

"Blood doesn't bother me," Lon whispered quietly. "It was another headache. My skull feels like it was trampled by a team of donkeys. Maybe Braedr slipped a drug into my drink before he left," he joked, attempting to lighten the mood.

"Not funny," Mellai responded. "Your headaches have been getting worse."

Lon didn't answer, more out of obstinance than agreement. He refused to let infirmity rule his life. Sliding his hands up on the bed, he attempted to push himself upright, but his arms were too weak to lift his body. He dropped onto the bed and pounded the straw mattress in frustration.

"You should relax and keep quiet, or you'll pass out again," Mellai said. She looked over at Myron. "I assume you've noticed your roommate. Mother kept him alive, but he's not doing well. I wish he'd wake up so we could find out who did this to him. Do you think it was the Rayder?"

"You just told me to keep quiet," Lon teased.

Mellai frowned. "Lon, this really concerns me. That could have been us tonight."

Lon nodded. "You're right, Mel. I'm sorry. Did Mother figure out what happened to him?"

"She said it was a clean cut, must have been from a tool or weapon. I've never heard of anyone accidentally cutting open their entire belly before—not even Myron. I think he was attacked."

Lon groaned. "Any other injuries?"

Mellai shifted on the bed and allowed her gaze to wander to the glowing fireplace. Gleaming tears flooded her eyes.

"What else happened to him, Mel?"

Mellai sighed. "His back was broken, and his skull cracked. Even if he survives, Myron will be a cripple for the rest of his life. I can't bear to think how he—"

"Water," Myron gasped, followed by a bout of violent coughing.

The twins flinched at his outburst, then Mellai grabbed a pitcher of water from the small table separating the two beds and filled a cup for Myron. She moved to his side and, tilting his head forward, helped Myron sip the water. The man took two swallows before pulling away with another fit of coughing.

Mellai looked pleadingly at her brother who only returned her gaze with a desperate shrug of his shoulders. Although Mellai's talent for healing was as natural as Shalán's, their mother had already done everything possible to save Myron's life.

Mellai dipped a rag in the pitcher of water and gently wiped the sweat from Myron's brow. He smiled up at her. Mellai stifled a sob as she dabbed some blood from the corner of Myron's mouth, then wiped the sweat from his face again.

"Revenge," Myron muttered. "Ten years . . . now I have revenge."

"What?" Mellai asked, surprised to hear him speak so coherently.

"The Rayder," he replied. "I saw him . . . and set a trap with the cow . . . but he ran away . . . and found his friends. I followed five . . . to your house . . ."

"Five?" Mellai asked, then her face fell. "Oh, Myron, how terrible it must have been, after all those years, to see Rayders return to Pree."

"Terrible for them," Myron shouted, but was subdued as his lungs filled with fluid. He turned his head to the side as he violently coughed up blood, then looked back at Mellai with an eerie smile. "They separated . . . waiting to ambush you. I caught them . . . one by one . . . killed four with my bare hands . . . fought with the last one . . . he cut me open . . . and smashed my head . . . through the fence . . . coward . . . I'll fix the fence . . ."

Mellai tried to smile as she dabbed at his face. "Forget the fence, Myron. You did more than enough for our family tonight."

Myron grabbed her hand. "Yes. One more Rayder . . . you must . . . be careful . . . both of you . . . protect your family . . ."

His gaze wandered toward the ceiling and he released his grip on Mellai. Although his body was trembling, his eyes remained calm as they glazed over. He drew a final breath and whispered, "My sweet Edis."

When the shaking in Myron's body stopped, Mellai lifted the blanket from his body and pulled it over his head. "He saved our lives," she said, returning to Lon's side.

Lon took her hand and together they mourned Myron's death. After starving in the streets for ten years, Myron had bested four armed Rayders with his bare hands.

The crackling fire had faded into the quiet smolder of glowing embers before a soft creak from the door broke the silence. Aron entered the room, but stopped after a few steps and stared at the outline of Myron's covered body.

"Your mother feared Myron wouldn't make it through the night," Aron said. "I'm sad to see she was right. Did he tell you anything before he died?"

Mellai gave a silent shrug, not daring to talk.

Lon pushed himself up onto his elbow. "He fought five Rayders, but one of them got away."

Aron nodded. "How are you feeling, Son?"

"I'm alive," Lon replied as he stared at the floor.

Aron crossed the room and tenderly hefted Myron's covered body. "I'd like both of you to get some sleep. We'll all talk in the morning."

Aron carried Myron out of the room and shut the door behind him. The sound of his footsteps faded down the hallway and stairs. The twins continued to sit together in silence until the glowing embers disappeared and darkness filled the room.

Chapter 3

Necessary Hardship

L on woke to the scent of breakfast seeping into his room. Aron had just slaughtered their pig a few days earlier—it had grown so fat that it couldn't even pull itself up to eat the slop from a trough—so their family had been enjoying daily supplies of bacon for breakfast. Lon imagined eggs topped with sizzling bacon, accompanied by chilled milk to drink. His stomach growled.

Lon draped his legs over the edge of the mattress and was pleased to discover his headache was gone. He stood up without so much as a tingle in his head.

On his way to the door, Lon glanced at the bed next to him. The linen was still stained with Myron's blood. Before the memories of the previous night could overwhelm him, Lon concentrated on the delicious meal awaiting him downstairs. Whatever unpleasant emotions destined to fill the day, he wasn't going to welcome them into his mind.

Just one step at a time, he thought as he made his way through the door toward the stairway.

When he reached the bottom of the stairs, Lon surveyed the room. Everything was unusually normal. Shalán was moving around the kitchen making breakfast. Aron sat at the table with his back toward Lon, sipping hot tea from a cup. Mellai wasn't there yet, undoubtedly still sleeping.

Lon crossed the room to join his father at the table.

"How did you rest, Son?" Aron said without taking his eyes off his cup of tea.

"Well enough, Father, considering all that . . ." Lon's voice faded as he drew closer to the table and noticed a sword lay out in front of his father. The sight of the sword disturbed Lon. As he stared at the King's Cross etched into the pommel, he imagined what atrocities his father had committed with that sword while in the service of the Rayders.

"It's called a falchion," Aron said, ignoring Lon's gaping mouth. "Its weight makes it harder to use than smaller one-handed swords, but it's still a lethal weapon ideal for wilderness survival."

Lon closed his mouth and licked his lips. "Can I hold it?" he asked as he motioned toward the sword.

"Of course. I'll teach you how to use it when we have the time. You need to learn how to defend yourself, especially now."

Lon wrapped his left hand around the leather-bound grip and lifted the sword from the table; it felt surprisingly lighter than he'd expected.

"Your ax weighs more than this," Lon said to his father. "How can it be so light when it's made entirely of metal?"

"Good question," Aron replied with a smile. "See the deep groove running parallel to the spine of the blade? That's called a fuller. It lightens the blade without weakening it."

Lon traced his fingers along the three-foot sharpened edge. The sword was a one-sided blade, but at about seven inches from the tip, the spine and blade curved together, both with sharpened edges. Holding a sword in his hand made Lon feel powerful. He stepped back from the table and awkwardly swung it back and forth, but stopped abruptly at the sound of a terrified squeal. Turning around, he found his sister cowering behind him with her arms wrapped over her head.

"I'm sorry, Sis," Lon apologized. "I didn't see you."

"Saying you're sorry wouldn't sew my head back on," Mellai snapped. "Where did you get that thing?"

"It's mine," Aron said, holding out his hand, "and I'd appreciate it if you'd give it back now, Lon."

Lon handed the sword to his father, then he and Mellai sat at the table. Aron slipped the blade into a leather scabbard hanging at his side and resumed sipping tea from his cup.

"How are you doing, Mellai?" Aron asked.

"She's terrified," Lon inserted.

"I can answer for myself," Mellai growled. "Besides almost being decapitated by my foolish brother, I'm very hungry."

"Your cure is served," Shalán said as she placed fresh bacon and eggs on the table. "Be kind to your father, you two. He's been up the entire night repairing the fence and burying dead bodies."

"Which is no easy task when it must be done quietly and with no light," Aron added as the four of them began eating.

"Oh," Lon said, jumping to his feet. "I forgot about Scut."

"Relax," Aron said. "Do you really think I'd let you sleep in if you had chores to tend to? I talked with Scut this morning. He's not expecting help from either of us until after your celebration tomorrow night."

Lon sank back into his chair. "Thanks."

"Where did you bury the Rayders?" Mellai asked.

Aron took another sip from his cup. "Up the hill in a thicket. It's well-hidden and deep enough to protect the bodies from wildlife."

"Myron, too?" Lon inquired.

"No," Aron said, shaking his head. "I didn't put him with the Rayders. I carried him to his estate and buried him next to his wife and sons. It was the least I could do in return for his sacrifice."

"That was a dangerous thing to do by yourself in the middle of the night with at least one more Rayder still out there," Lon commented, emphasizing each risk clearly.

"Rayders always travel in squads of five," Aron responded, then tapped the sword at his side, "and I'm perfectly capable of defending our family. There's no need to worry about our safety. Besides, the Rayder's tracks led away from the house. I tried to follow him, but lost his trail in the river. He knew someone would try to follow him."

Mellai dropped her fork. "He's probably on his way back to the Exile right now to report what he found."

Shalán placed her hand over Mellai's. "Your father said Myron spoke to you both before he died last night. What did he say?"

Without waiting for Mellai to speak, Lon recounted the details of their brief conversation.

"Myron is a valiant man," Aron replied. "I'm glad he was able to avenge his family before he died. I only wish I'd been there with him. I have my own score to settle with the Rayders."

"Didn't you hear what I just said," Mellai shouted as she pulled her hand free. "That Rayder is going to tell the rest of his people what happened here last night, then they're going to send their whole army to kill us and everyone else in this village."

"Calm down, Mellai," Shalán said sternly. "Don't worry about the village—they're safe enough for now while the sun is shining."

"Although that doesn't much improve our situation," Aron interceded.

"What do you mean?" Lon asked.

"Even if the Rayder was on his way back to the Exile right now," Aron said, "he'd have to cross all of Appernysia to reach them. It would be months before any retaliation arrived here. It doesn't really matter, though. He won't go home yet. He has a responsibility to fulfill first and that's his highest priority."

"What responsibility?" Mellai countered. "Rayders don't have responsibilities. They're just savages determined to see the world burn."

"What about your father?" Shalán asked. "Do you think he's a savage?"

Mellai's eyes dropped to the floor; she stuck out her bottom lip in a stubborn pout.

"This squad's assignment was to identify and capture the rumored Beholder," Shalán continued.

"And eliminate anyone who stands in their way," Aron added with a quick glance at Shalán. "The two of you obviously caught his attention. I'll search for him again a little later, but for now, all we can do is wait and see what answers reveal themselves."

"Is that really all?" Shalán asked.

"What else would you suggest, Shalán?" Aron answered, sounding irritable for the first time that morning. "We can't hide in our house—not with Lon's coming-of-age celebration tomorrow. We must continue on with our lives as if everything were normal. Until the Rayder shows himself again, the only other thing we can do is alert the village of his presence and send out hunting parties to track him down."

"So why don't we do that?" Mellai demanded.

"And put the entire village in a state of hysteria like you?" Lon teased.

"Drown yourself in a bucket of dung, Lon," Mellai snarled. "I'm talking about *our* lives. Do you really want to be killed by Rayders?"

"Mellai, that's enough," Aron commanded. "Calm yourself. I spent the first twenty-five years of my life as a Rayder and I know what to expect from them. In fact, we have a partial advantage because he doesn't know who I am."

"How can you be so sure?" Shalán nearly whispered.

"If he knew me, he'd have already broken down the door and charged in here with sword swinging. Also, it was our children who caught his attention, not me." Aron touched his wife's cheek with the back of his fingers. "Don't worry. We'll make it through this. We always have. There's strength unmatched in the blood of our family. The Marcs will always prevail."

Tears filled Shalán's eyes. She took her husband's hand in hers and kissed it. "Yes, we will."

The rising sun shone through the eastern window, bathing the room in light as the Marcs resumed eating in silence. Lon felt his sister's anxieties dissipate as the sunlight warmed her skin. She gave him a quick glance and he winked back at her.

Aron stood and beckoned Lon to follow him. The two of them went outside and followed a path that wound around the side of their home to their greenhouse. Lon noticed his father's hand covering the King's Cross marking on the hilt of his sword.

Good idea, Lon thought as he surveyed the trees beyond their property, *especially since the Rayder is probably watching us right now.*

When they reached the greenhouse, Aron disappeared inside and returned with two six-foot oak staffs that Shalán typically used to hang drying herbs and hides. The staffs were nearly two inches thick. Aron handed them to Lon, then led him past the greenhouse and up the steep hill.

"Where are we going?" Lon asked. "I don't think we should leave Mother and Mellai by themselves right now."

"They'll be fine for an hour," Aron responded. "Rayders are only out by night when they're in Appernysia—to remain hidden. He won't come back until tonight, especially since his squad is dead."

"Even so," Lon said, looking back at the house, "this feels wrong."

Aron said nothing, but continued up the hill.

Lon kicked a rock in frustration and followed his father. Their feet stirred up the dry soil, creating clouds of dust that reminded Lon of the haze from his misadventure the night before. He licked his dry lips. "Father, I want to talk about what happened to me last night."

"Oh?"

"After you brought Myron in the house, I was watching out the window and my eyes clouded up, like there was a haze outside. I thought it was fog, but when I turned to warn you, the haze was inside the house, too. Did anyone see what I saw?"

"If you're referring to the haze, no."

"It was strange," Lon continued. "I got weak, enough that I couldn't even stand."

"You also hit your head very hard on a solid wood floor," Aron added. "I'm not surprised you blacked out."

"I've been knocked out before, and I'm telling you that wasn't the reason I passed out. It felt like my mind left my body alone to try and think. Does this make any sense to you?"

"Last night was full of circumstances you've never encountered before," Aron answered. "No doubt you were scared and nervous, and it overwhelmed you. I can't tell you exactly what happened to you, Son. Focus on calming your mind if it happens again. Perhaps that will help."

"I'll try."

Aron looked back at his son. "Do me a favor; don't tell your mother or sister about this. Just tell me if it ever happens to you again."

They continued for another few minutes before Lon spoke. "I have another question. How did you get Mother to listen to you in Roseiri when she knew you were a Rayder?"

Aron chuckled. "Actually, it started the other way around. I was supposed to kill one of the men in her village, but she found out somehow and got to me first."

"Seriously?" Lon asked. "Why were you going to kill him?"

"He had been speaking out against the Rayders—which wasn't abnormal, but he was gaining a large crowd of followers. My job was to make an example of him."

Lon shook his head. "I can't believe Mother confronted you. Why didn't she get a man to stop you?"

"She wasn't afraid of me. In a way, she reminded me a lot of the Rayder women I knew. It was her courage, along with her beauty, that made me fall in love with her."

"So you didn't kill the man?"

"No, but I convinced your mother that he and his family had to leave—and stay hidden. There were four other Rayders waiting for me outside the village, and it was the only way I could protect the family and myself at the same time. As I expected, when I told my squad the family had disappeared, they wanted to keep returning to Roseiri until the family returned."

"Did the family ever come back?"

"No. Which means you don't know them."

Lon smiled. "I was just wondering. So, let me guess; you found Mother every time you returned, and eventually won her heart, right?"

"Correct."

"But that still doesn't answer my question. How did you convince her to listen to you when you returned the first time?"

"Just like your mother's courage impressed me, my compassion toward that man and his family impressed her. She was still angry at me when I first returned, but she recognized my ability to change, and knew I could become a better man if given the opportunity. She fell in love with the man she knew I could become—a man I didn't even know existed."

"Kaylen would love that story."

"I'm sure she would."

They continued climbing the hill until they were hidden from view by the trees. Aron unbuckled the sword from his waist and set it on the ground, then took one of the staffs from Lon and stood ready in a defensive position. "Let's see if you've got any talent with a staff."

Lon smirked at his father. "You can't be serious."

"I said before that you have to learn to defend yourself, and the best time to start is *now*. Attack me."

"But Father, I . . . I don't want to hurt you."

"I think I might surprise you."

Lon took a deep breath as he gripped the staff at one end with both hands, then swung it straight down at his father like a heavy ax. Aron easily parried the blow and knocked Lon hard on the side of the head with the opposite end of his staff. Lon staggered as flashing lights filled his vision, his head throbbing with each stabbing pulse of light.

When the pain subsided and Lon's vision returned, he squinted at his father. "Why did—"

Aron whirled his staff and smacked Lon on the side of his leg.

Lon fell to the ground. He put up his arm to ward off further attacks while rubbing his thigh with his other hand. "Stop it."

"Son, had those Rayders attacked us last night you'd be hurting much worse—if you had survived to feel anything at all. They wouldn't have shown mercy, so neither will I."

The reality of the situation sunk into Lon's mind. He stood up and mimicked Aron, taking hold of his staff in the middle with his hands shoulder-width apart. He planted his feet the same distance from each other and held the staff in front of him at a slight angle.

"Good," Aron said. "Now try again."

Lon tried to jab at his father with the end of his staff. When Aron deflected the attack, Lon used the momentum to snap the other end of his staff down against Aron's ankle with a loud crack.

After a moment of teeth grinding, Aron smiled. "Well done."

Lon and his father sparred for the next hour. Although Lon's skill improved significantly, every passing minute added to his frustration. For every attack he made, Aron had a counterattack that left Lon hurting, usually in more than one place. By the time they finished, Lon was bruised from head to foot and in a foul mood. After that first blow, he'd failed to land another successful strike against Aron.

"Your mother can mix a salve for the pain and swelling," Aron said as he strapped the sword around his waist again. "I want you to keep that staff with you at all times. A staff is a formidable weapon when handled correctly, but it should be subtle enough for you to carry without drawing too much attention."

Lon grunted in response and limped down the hill after his father. When they reached the front door of their house, Aron paused and put his hand on Lon's shoulder.

"We'll spar again later this afternoon, but you need to remember what we practiced today. I won't always be around. If there's one thing I know about Rayders, it's that they love surprise attacks. You might need to defend yourself at any moment, but more importantly, your mother and sister will rely on you for protection. Don't fail them."

Lon peered at his father through a swollen eye. "I'll do my best, Father."

"That's all I ask."

The two of them entered the house to find Shalán and Mellai busy scrubbing the remaining blood stains from the floor and table. Mellai gasped when she saw Lon. Shalán only frowned as she stood and left the room. Mellai barraged her brother with questions, searching for the source of his injuries. When she learned Aron had caused them, she burst into laughter.

"Father did that to you? You look like a squashed toad. You might want to reconsider before you decide to visit Kaylen. You'll scare her away for good."

Lon grimaced at his father.

"Don't worry, Son. Your mother's a skilled herbalist. I promise you'll be back to normal soon. She can't work miracles, though, so try to stay out of sight today."

"I refuse to stay trapped in this house," Lon countered. "Kaylen is expecting a visit from me today and I plan on being there."

"Then I'm going with you," Mellai said, still giggling.

"We'll all go with you," Aron inserted. "Your mother and I have some errands we need to take care of in town."

Shalán reentered the room carrying her healing satchel. "Not before I tend to those bruises. Sit down and take off your tunic."

Shalán hung a small pot of water over the fire while Lon placed his staff against the wall and sat on one of the chairs. He clenched his teeth as he removed his thick linen tunic.

Mellai stopped giggling when she saw her brother's body. His entire torso was covered in welts and deep bruises. "I'm sorry, Lon," she said after a soft gasp. She turned to her father. "How could you? I'm surprised he can even move." Her eyes flared with indignation.

"I'm going to be outside looking for any new signs of the Rayder," Aron announced, without so much as a word to Mellai.

Shalán continued to look at Lon with the same sad expression. "Your father is a good man," she said after the door closed, "and his past doesn't change who he's become. Your conversation with him last night had to come as a shock, but rest assured that you've both lived your lives with the true Aron. The Rayder part of him died in the Vidarien Mountains. He was hard on you today because he loves you. You're coming of age tomorrow and don't have time to be coddled. Understand?"

Lon shifted his gaze to Mellai. "It's true—he did what is best for our whole family. If they attack while Father is away, I have to protect you."

Mellai's lips tightened. "Our connection can be very annoying, especially when you abuse it like that."

"You think you hate it?" he gibed.

"I'm glad you appreciate your responsibility, Lon," Shalán interrupted, "but we aren't completely defenseless. I didn't survive a year in the mountains solely because of your father, and I'm certain Mellai would give anyone a difficult fight—especially if her life depended on it."

Shalán removed the hot water from the fire and poured some into a bowl. After adding a few powdered ingredients, she slowly mixed them into a thick paste.

"Ugh, that stinks," Mellai complained.

"Its virtue is worth it," Shalán replied. "Your brother will wake up tomorrow without a single bruise on his body."

"Smells great to me, Mother," Lon added, winking at Mellai. She sneered at him and covered her mouth and nose with her apron.

Using a wooden spoon, Shalán smeared the salve over Lon's torso, arms, and face. The paste stuck to his skin and, to Lon's astonishment, began soothing the pain at once.

"Where did you learn how to do this, Mother?" Lon said as the aching pain slowly faded. "Whatever it is, it's working."

"I've spent nearly my entire adult life trying to stay unnoticed, so I've had plenty of time to experiment with different concoctions. Not always successfully, though. At one point I thought I'd turned your father permanently green. The color didn't leave his skin for nearly a month."

"I wish I could have seen that," Mellai mused.

Lon smiled, but his eyes grew heavy with exhaustion. "I don't know how Father does it."

"Does what?" Shalán inquired.

"He was up the entire night repairing our fence and burying bodies; he finished my chores for me this morning, then led me up a steep hill and gave me a beating for nearly an hour. Now he's outside tracking down a Rayder. Father never stops. He's three times my age, and I still can't keep up."

"Your father has had a lifetime of training to do what he does," Shalán answered. "Don't discount yourself or your efforts. Very few people could ever match the pace your father sets for himself. I know I can't."

Lon breathed out in frustration as he stood up and limped to the window. "Yes, but . . . I only wonder . . ." His voice faded, unable to finish the thought that had constantly invaded his mind. Was his father proud of him? As Lon stood there, mulling over his sorrows, the strange haze from the previous night crept into the edges of his vision again. Remembering his father's counsel, Lon closed his eyes and took deep breaths. Despite his most desperate efforts, he could feel his mind slipping away.

"Lon, we should go and visit Kaylen right now," Mellai said. Lon knew she didn't fully understand what was troubling him, but his twin must have felt his mental anguish and decided to intervene.

"Father will understand. Kaylen's probably staring out her front window, wondering where you are. I think a short walk and a long visit with her are just what we both need."

It was the perfect cure to Lon's downward spiral—the thought of Kaylen. He quickly gained control of his mind and opened his eyes to see the haze disappearing, as if whisked away by a pleasant breeze. As he stood there smiling, Lon became aware of his reflection in the window. The paste covering his body and face had mostly dried, leaving him cloaked in a thin layer of dried mud.

Shalán went into the kitchen and returned with a cloth and a large basin, which she filled with the rest of the heated water. "The paste has lost its healing virtue by now," she said, "so let's clean you up. You'll still be sore for the rest of the day, but when you wake up, you'll be as good as new."

Using her fingers, she peeled the chips of mud free and wiped his skin clean with the wet cloth. Although there was still bruising scattered across Lon's body, he noticed the deeper welts had faded and the lighter bruising had disappeared. Unfortunately, his right eye remained swollen.

"You should change your clothes before you go," Shalán said, "And use the rest of this salve on your legs while you're at it. Leave it on until it's dried, then clean it off like I just showed you. We'll wait here for you. Your father should be home shortly."

Chapter 4

Discovery

Aron stepped out of his house and closed the door. He squinted into the sky, calculating how much time he had before he needed to be back for lunch.

An hour, he thought as he made his way to the front gate. *One hour of freedom from Mellai's incessant nagging. That girl's voice could chew the bark off a tree.*

With his six-foot staff in his right hand, and his left hand over the pommel of his sword, Aron searched his cleared property for any clues he might have missed during the night. Aside from six sets of fresh tracks leading through the woods from the east—five from the Rayders and one from Myron—Aron found nothing new.

They must have made a camp somewhere nearby to stash their gear and horses, he concluded. *If I want to catch the remaining Rayder, the best chance I have is to find him in his camp.*

Aron plunged into the woods and followed the tracks.

It appears Myron was telling the truth. I thought his wits would have escaped him after the loss of so much blood.

Aron continued to follow the tracks as they turned north, studying them as he walked. He realized from the length of the strides they must have been in a great hurry.

At the south bridge, five sets of boot tracks dropped down the embankment to the river and continued east along the northern bank, while Myron's bare feet followed the northern ridge of the embankment.

If Myron's path had kept him hidden from the Rayders the night before, following the same path would give him the best chance of remaining hidden from the survivor.

Aron traveled a half-hour until the river turned sharply north. As he studied Myron's path, he heard distant neighing. Horses, he knew, were only owned by soldiers, nobles, and Rayders—none of which were native to Pree. Nobles never traveled far from their cities of origin, and soldiers rarely appeared in that corner of the kingdom. The Rayder camp must be near.

Aron broke into a crouching run, abandoning Myron's tracks as he veered wide to approach the camp from the north. If the Rayder were in his camp, he would be looking south, where his squad had left an obvious trail in the soft riverbank the night before.

Using the horses' neighing as his guide, Aron crept toward the camp until he reached the edge of a low ridge, which dropped abruptly into a large grassy area by the side of the river. Four bedrolls sprawled beside a lone birch and the ashes of an extinguished fire. Five horses stood tethered to the far side of the tree. Sitting near the horses and gazing steadily south was the man he had been tracking.

He must have slept during the night, Aron thought as the Rayder picked up a stone and hurled it into the river. Aron noticed one of the horses was already packed and saddled. *Once nightfall comes, he'll make his move.*

Aron weighed his options. If he had a bow, it would have been easy for Aron to kill the Rayder where he sat, but that was not an option. He considered moving to the southern edge of the clearing to block the escape, but the Rayder would simply mount up and charge at him. The only other option was to cripple the poor beast.

As he pondered what to do, Aron remembered a sliver from his past; if a Rayder was challenged to a duel, he was honor-bound to accept.

Having made his decision, Aron rose and pulled out his falchion. "Rayder!"

Quicker than a snake, the Rayder rolled to his side and drew his arming sword, readying himself for an attack. He blanched at the sight of Aron standing upon the ridge with an oversized falchion in his hand.

"Coward," Aron continued, raising his blade in the air. "Fight me and see how you fair against a man with more than his fists."

To Aron's surprise, the Rayder ignored his challenge. With one running strike, the Ryder slit the throats of all the horses except for the saddled one, on which he climbed and fled south along the riverbank, disappearing downriver toward the bridge and the rest of Aron's family.

* * * * *

Lon and Mellai stood outside their home, waiting for Shalán to join them. She finally appeared around the back of the house, her healing satchel slung over her shoulder.

"Did you remember everything?" Lon asked.

"I believe so," Shalán answered, a little flustered. "I've brought livestock medicine to Trev several times, but I've never been able to guess exactly what he wants. I wish he would just make me a list."

"Can we go now?" Mellai said impatiently, turning and walking up the path toward the main road.

Lon and Shalán followed close behind her, enjoying the warmth of the sun contrasted by a cool breeze tickling their faces. The song of cardinals and the rhythmic thud of Lon's staff on the dirt road were the only sounds that reached their ears. Lon took a deep breath and let it out slowly, glad to be out of the house and on the way to visit his love.

They turned onto the main road and continued toward Pree. When the south bridge came into view, Shalán stopped.

"I've just remembered one more thing Trev will probably want," she said to Lon. "You two go ahead and I'll catch up to you."

Lon shook his head. "Father would kill me for leaving you alone."

"Just wait here with Mellai then," Shalán continued. "I'll only be a few minutes."

"All right, but hurry."

"What's going on?" Mellai asked, twenty paces ahead.

Lon didn't answer. His attention was focused on a strange noise in the wind, like the dull and rhythmic rumble of a distant storm. The sound concerned Lon, yet he didn't understand why. Perhaps it was because the blue sky was clear of clouds, or that he had never heard such a noise before. Dread filled his mind, as if an imminent doom accompanied the cloudless thunder.

Mellai looked up the road toward Pree, furrowing her brow. "It sounds like there's a waterfall somewhere nearby, but there isn't anything like that around here. Where's it coming from?"

"Quiet," Lon barked. "We need to get off the road."

Almost immediately, a huge beast burst onto the road a stone's throw in front of Mellai. It had an appearance similar to one of their village donkeys, but stronger, leaner, its shoulders towering over the top of Mellai's head. As it moved, its coat of short black hair cast a waving sheen under the rays of the overhead sun.

It was the first horse either of them had seen. Under a different circumstance, the sight of it would have been awe-inspiring, but its magnificence was overshadowed by the sight of the man sitting upon its back, a sword gripped in his hand. Lon recognized him as the same Rayder they saw the night before.

The Rayder's lips tightened in anger the moment he saw Mellai. He gave a terrifying shout and dug his heals into the horse's sides, causing it to spring forward with tremendous power.

For Lon, time froze when the Rayder and his horse entered the road. He reached for his sister, knowing the situation was hopeless. The dreaded haze appeared and instantly filled his vision, yet he could clearly see the glowing figures of Mellai and the Rayder through the dense fog.

Just as the Rayder raised his sword arm to slash at Mellai, something bright shot from Lon's hand. It connected with his sister, brightened for an instant, and exploded, throwing her off the road away from the charging horse.

The haze vanished from Lon's sight as quickly as it had appeared. The wide-eyed Rayder turned his galloping horse toward Lon and locked his eyes on him. Despite his own bewilderment, Lon instinctively widened his stance and tightened his grip on his staff to defend himself. He was surprised to see the Rayder sheathe his sword and reach out to grab him.

Lon dodged the Rayder's outstretched arm, then twisted his body around to catch the Rayder in the small of his back with the staff. The Rayder flew from his saddle, hurtling through the air. Lon heard a sharp crack as the Rayder struck a large birch tree and fell to the ground.

While the horse disappeared down the road, Lon kept his full attention on the Rayder and cautiously approached the motionless body. The enemy was facedown, so Lon rolled him onto his back with the staff. The Rayder flopped over like one of Kaylen's rag dolls, but his eyes were alive with horror.

"Why are you here, Rayder?" Lon demanded. "Why won't you leave my family alone?"

The Rayder's mouth barely moved. "I am sorry, Beholder."

Lon stepped back. "What did you call me?"

The Rayder's face lost what little color remained. He didn't answer. "Answer me!"

"Beholder," the Rayder repeated. "I called you Beholder." He looked up at Lon in terror.

Lon cocked his head to the side and stared at the ground. "Beholder?" he whispered, looking back at the Rayder. "You are mistaken."

The Rayder's expression changed from fear to confusion, then annoyance. "I am not a fool. I saw what you just did. Your secret is out."

Lon squatted down in front of the Rayder. "*What* did I do?" His voice shook.

"You tell me. I am no Beholder."

Lon slumped to his knees and dropped his staff.

Is that what just happened? Did I just use Beholder powers to save Mellai? Am I the person everyone's looking for?

His stomach churned, his head spun. How could this be? Why, after seventeen years, would he suddenly develop magical powers? It didn't make sense. The Rayder was playing a trick on him.

Lon grabbed the man by the front of his tunic. "You're lying." Once again, the uncanny mist blurred Lon's vision and intensified around the dying man.

The Rayder's fear returned. "Please, Beholder," he pleaded as he looked into Lon's eyes. "I beg of you. Let me die in peace."

Lon clenched his jaw and bared his teeth. "What about the man you murdered last night? What about my sister? What about me?" Tears filled his eyes as fury coursed through him. "Did you show us any mercy?"

The Rayder sobbed.

Lon dropped the man to the ground and sat back on his heels. A faint smile crossed his face as he thought of the irony of the situation. The Rayder's back was broken. He was helpless, on the edge of death, just as he had left Myron the night before—except Myron hadn't been acting under orders. Myron's actions were honorable. They were justified. If those Rayders hadn't shown up and murdered Myron's family . . .

As he listened to the dying Rayder's sobs, Lon had an idea—something that might help Myron's spirit rest in peace.

He grabbed the Rayder's tunic again. "I'll do what you asked, but only if you answer one more question. The man who attacked you last night—his name was Myron Ascennor. His eleven-year-old son disappeared ten years ago when a squad of your men killed the rest of his family. Do you know what happened to Tarek Ascennor? Answer me!"

"Yes," the man whispered. "He is still in the Exile . . . training soldiers."

Lon's stomach jumped. "How can I contact him?" he demanded.

"It is impossible . . . only Rayders are allowed."

As Lon ground his teeth in frustration, he felt a soft touch on his shoulder.

"Lon," said a breathless voice. "Let him go."

Lon's clouded vision cleared and he turned his head to find Kaylen standing behind him, her green eyes wide with shock and horror. Her long, sandy-blond hair followed the curves of her slender body.

"Kaylen, what are you doing here?"

"Put him down," she insisted, trying to maintain her calm.

Lon turned his gaze back to the Rayder and forced himself to release the tunic. He watched until the man's eyes unfocused and his body stopped fighting for breath.

Kaylen squeezed Lon's shoulder, reminding him that she was still there. He stood and wiped the tears from his eyes, then turned and threw his arms around her.

"Why had he come to Pree?" Kaylen asked with a trembling voice as she stared over Lon's shoulder at the dead body.

"I'm not—"

"Don't worry about me," Mellai interrupted from the other side of the road. "I'm fine, thank you very much."

Lon pulled away from Kaylen and went to his sister. She was sitting on the other side of the road, scowling and picking dry grass out of her hair.

"Are you all right?" Lon asked.

"Oh, *now* you care?" she complained. "I've only been sitting here for the last five minutes watching you argue with that Rayder."

Mellai continued grumbling as she stood up and brushed dirt from her dress. Lon was surprised to see that, besides a bit of dirt clinging to her clothes, she had escaped the blast unscathed. Not even her hair was singed. Lon shook his head in confusion. No one could survive such an explosion, much less come through without harm.

Mellai crossed the road with Lon and Kaylen and shuddered at the sight of the Rayder's dead body. "He tried to kill me, Lon." Her voice began to shake. "I shouldn't have been able to get out of the way in time. It felt like I was thrown off the road."

Lon stared at his sister in amazement—she hadn't seen the explosion. Question after question bubbled up in his mind, but rather than try to explain it all, Lon kept his thoughts to himself. Mellai was confused enough already.

"How else would you expect to feel?" Lon replied, forcing his voice to remain steady. "This was something you've never experienced before. Just focus on calming your mind. It will help."

"You're starting to sound like Father."

Lon grinned. "That's because he told me the same thing earlier today. It's really helped me. You should try it, Mel."

"Perhaps you're right," Mellai answered—her usual response when she had no intention of giving the idea a second thought. "I can feel how well that's working for you right now."

Lon shook his head and turned back to Kaylen, who stood dumbfounded.

"Kaylen, I don't even know where to start. You wouldn't believe what's happened since yesterday."

"I'm not sure I want to know," she responded as she touched Lon's swollen eye. "Did he do this to you?"

"This man? Hardly," Lon said before changing the subject. "What are you doing here, anyway?"

"You said you were going to visit me today, Lon. I was worried and decided to come find you. I'd barely left my house when I saw that man—that Rayder—burst onto the road at the bridge. I ran here as fast as I could."

"Did you tell Scut?" Mellai asked.

"No. I know it seems foolish now, but I panicked."

"It's probably better your father doesn't know, along with the rest of the village," Lon inserted, remembering his father's advice the night before. "How did you know he was a Rayder?"

"He was on a horse, like the Rayders who killed Myron's family. I remember that day as though it happened last week, even if I was only six years old. Everyone still talks about it, but in hushed voices in case Myron is around."

Lon and Mellai exchanged an awkward glance. They both knew the villagers would need to be informed about Myron's death, but they were unsure of how to relay the news. The truth could cause an uproar.

"What's wrong?" Kaylen asked.

Lon shifted uneasily, trying to think of a way out of answering her question.

Aron burst onto the road in a full sprint, breaking the uncomfortable silence. Without missing a step, he ran straight toward the three of them.

"Is your mother at home by herself?" he shouted between gasps for air. "How could you have been so—"

Aron stopped short when he saw the body of the dead Rayder. After catching his breath, he walked over to inspect the body. "Was he thrown from his horse?"

Mellai and Kaylen both turned to Lon with the same question on their faces. Ignoring the women's stares, Lon proudly looked back at his father.

"Yes—with a little help." He lightly tapped the side of his staff with his finger.

Aron nodded. "Well done. Were any of you hurt?"

"We're fine," Mellai replied, then sneered at Lon—warning him not to say anything about what had happened to her.

"Good," Aron said as he stretched his back. "I'm still upset you left your mother alone."

"We didn't," Mellai retorted. "She was just with us, but forgot something back at the greenhouse. She made us wait here while she went back for it. There was nothing we could do."

"That doesn't surprise me," Aron responded, "but you still shouldn't have let her go by herself."

Mellai's eyes darkened and she folded her arms across her chest. Lon didn't need to feel her anger to know she was on the verge of exploding, so he turned to Kaylen to change the subject.

"Is Scut expecting you?"

"Not until dusk, but maybe I should go home now. I don't want to be in the way." She eyed the sword hanging at Aron's side as she spoke.

"Are you serious?" Lon laughed.

Mellai unfolded her arms and placed her hands around Kaylen's elbow. "Come with me." She pulled Kaylen down the road away from Pree and disappeared around a bend.

"Looks like they left us to clean up the mess," Lon complained as he joined his father next to the dead body. "That's gratitude for you."

"Would you make Kaylen bury a dead body?" Aron asked.

"No, but they still could have offered."

"Do you offer to help with the meals your mother prepares every day?"

Lon blew out his breath. "All right, I get it. So what are we going to do with the body?"

"We'll carry him back to the hill and bury him with his companions. They can keep each other company."

Lon smiled in spite of everything that had happened. Leave it to his father to make jokes at such a time.

Aron reached down and unbuckled the sword from around the Rayder's waist. "Put this on," he said, handing the sword to Lon.

Lon folded his arms. "I don't want a Rayder's sword. Besides, I don't even know how to use it. I almost killed Mellai the last time I held one."

"Now," Aron commanded.

Lon hesitated, but eventually took it. After latching the belt around his waist, he pulled the sword out to examine it. It was a single-handed sword of about the same length and weight as his father's falchion, but the blade was straight and double-edged. The blade was slightly dull, but still sharp enough to pierce or slash through cloth and skin.

Lon noticed one side was covered with blood. "Myron's blood from last night."

"No," Aron countered. "That blood is from their horses."

"What? Why would he do that?"

"To keep me from following him."

"Savage," Lon growled.

As Lon scrubbed the blade with grass and dirt, Aron glanced around. "Where's this Rayder's horse?"

"He ran off down the road," Lon answered. He slid the sword back into the scabbard and turned to his father. "Now what?"

Aron dropped his staff on top of the dead Rayder and took hold of the man's ankles. "Grab his wrists."

Lon placed his staff next to Aron's, then the two of them picked up the body and began the arduous journey back to their house. A stretcher would have been more practical, but they had no material to string between their two staffs—unless they used their clothes and walked in the nude. The thought of a passerby seeing two naked men carrying a dead Rayder down the road made Lon chuckle, but his amusement dwindled with every step. He became so exhausted that he contemplated dropping the Rayder to the ground and helping Aron drag him by his heels.

By the time they reached the fence surrounding their property, both Lon and Aron were sweating profusely. At the gate, Aron turned and followed the fence as it angled north to the base of the hill next to their home. When they reached its southern face, they dropped the body and took a moment to rest before hauling it up the steep hill.

"And to think you had to do this four times last night all by yourself," Lon commented between gasps.

"I didn't have to carry them nearly as far, and I was a lot more rested then."

Lon winced at his father's statement, realizing that Aron hadn't slept for over a day and a half. Lon lifted the body by its arms and draped it over his back, then started up the hill by himself.

Aron laughed as his son trudged up the steep face. "Would you like to know where you're taking him?"

"Yes," Lon grunted, "and I'm sure you can catch up to lead the way."

After picking up their two staffs, Aron showed Lon where the rest of the Rayder corpses were buried. The sight was easy to recognize from the freshly-turned soil and a shovel leaning against a nearby tree.

CHAPTER 4: DISCOVERY ◆ 61

"I left the shovel here in good faith that we'd be bringing this man to join them," Aron mentioned.

"Too bad you didn't believe it enough to leave the bodies unburied," Lon groaned as he dropped the body to the ground.

"If I hadn't buried them, there would be very little of them left for us to find."

"Why would that have been a bad thing?" Lon retorted.

"Because I don't want a child to run across a mangled limb," Aron answered as he handed the shovel to Lon.

Lon began the unpleasant task of excavating the grave. He cringed at the thought of hitting a dead body with the shovel, so the process took a long time as he carefully shoveled the loose dirt. When a pale hand finally appeared, Lon rolled the last Rayder's body into the pit. He looked toward his father for guidance, but Aron had fallen asleep sitting against a tree.

The villages in the Western Valley of Appernysia had strict traditions of burial, believing them necessary to allow a person's soul to rest peacefully. Lon reflected on a funeral he had attended when their family still lived in Roseiri. Lon wasn't especially close to the family of the deceased man, but he had attended the ceremony with the rest of his family.

After the man's body was laid deep in the earth, the family had placed jars and baskets full of his favorite food and drink in the ground to comfort and strengthen him on his journey beyond. The grave was then filled with dirt, and the man's family had covered the fresh mound with various spices to ward off evil and protect the body from scavengers.

The funeral had ended with *The Song of the Dead*, a ballad sung by the man's oldest son. The poem was ancient to Appernysia and had been used at burials since their people first settled at the beginning of the First Age. Although Lon had heard it before, the song touched his heart. He hoped he could pay the same respect to his father, when the time came.

Lon thought of the five dead Rayders lying before him, imagining the unresolved sorrow of their oldest sons when their fathers never return home. Although he was certain his father wouldn't approve, Lon decided to pay what little respect he could to the memory of the fallen men. He glanced at his father to make sure he was still sleeping, then softly began singing *The Song of the Dead*.

> *Appernysia, jewel of light,*
> *Bolstered by unceasing might,*
> *Unmatched force and glory strong,*
> *No longer could your death prolong.*
>
> *I free you now from world-bound strife,*
> *And wish for you a better life;*
> *Release your pain, forget remorse,*
> *Continue on your ordained course.*
>
> *Go and find your resting place,*
> *Embrace no more this mortal race;*
> *Where pain and sorrow took their toll,*
> *Let joy and peace encase your soul.*
>
> *I will be watching for the day*
> *When my pains, too, are washed away;*
> *But 'til that time doth find me here,*
> *I bid goodbye, I'll shed no tear.*
>
> *Farewell, my friends, my time draws near.*

As Lon finished singing he felt unusually emotional and drained of strength. He forced himself to fill the large grave before collapsing beside his father. The reality of death finally sunk in, and Lon allowed his emotions to take control. Tears flowed down his face as he drifted into a peaceful slumber.

Chapter 5
Stick-Stack

L on awoke to the soft chirping of sparrows and the deep snoring of his father. His muscles were already beginning to tighten from the day's rigors, but otherwise his short sleep left him feeling refreshed and rejuvenated.

Lon climbed to his feet and surveyed the overgrowth surrounding him, frowning as he realized that even a child would recognize the fresh grave. He grabbed the shovel and dug up the nearby underbrush, spreading it around to disguise the terrain. He also relocated some rocks and kicked the dirt around to make everything look more natural.

It's definitely not perfect, he thought, *but it will have to do. Hopefully, nobody will wander onto our property. Not very likely, now that Myron's dead.*

As he waited for his father to wake up, Lon thought back to his encounter with the Rayder. Although it was just a few hours earlier, the circumstance seemed even more surreal than it had at the time. It couldn't be possible. He couldn't be a Beholder. He was just a peasant boy.

Even amid his doubts, Lon's curiosity still took control. He crossed his legs and concentrated, trying to summon the strange mist. He knew that somehow the mist and the blast of energy were connected. If he could only see the mist again, maybe he could do another magic trick. He squinted, grunted, groaned, and growled, but nothing worked.

"C'mon," Lon complained aloud. "Where are you, haze?"

"What's that?" Aron said, half-asleep.

Lon jumped to his feet. "I'm glad you're awake. Uh, we should probably head back."

"Agreed," Aron said as he stood up with a moan. "Even with the Rayders dead, it was foolish to leave your mother and sister alone. How long have I slept?"

"Maybe an hour or two, but I'm not sure."

"You've hidden the grave well," Aron said as he stifled a yawn.

"Thanks, Father."

As the two of them began their descent toward their home, Lon turned to his father. "Father, I'd like to continue the conversation we had earlier."

"I figured you might. Have you had more problems with your headaches?"

"Not really," Lon replied, "but I've seen the haze two more times. The first was in our house today, after you left to track the Rayder. I started feeling overwhelmed by everything that's been happening, but it only lasted a couple of minutes. The second time was very different."

Lon relayed his encounter with the Rayder, making sure to include every detail about what he had seen and done.

"Now that I think back on it," he added afterward, "when the . . . mist ball left my hand, I felt strange, like I was standing in the middle of a raging lightning storm and a bolt was about to strike. A shiver ran down my spine and I'm sure the hair on the back of my neck stood up. I don't know what to think, Father. Am I really a Beholder?"

"A Beholder, huh?" Aron stared at the ground in contemplation. "I know I told you to keep this information between the two of us, but I've changed my mind. Shalán might be able to help medicinally, and it's important that Mellai knows so that she understands what's going on inside of you. She should also know what happened to her."

"Fine, but what do you think?" Lon responded impatiently. "What's happening to me?"

"Wait until we get home; we shall discuss this as a family."

Lon sighed, frustrated. He knew arguing with his father was pointless. "What about Kaylen?" he asked instead. "She's probably still at our house. Should we wait until she leaves before I unveil my insanity to the family?"

"I'd hardly call it insanity," Aron replied. "It's your choice whether or not to tell Kaylen. If you intend to marry her, I believe she has the right to know, but I'd stop there. People generally don't respond well to things they can't understand. This I know for a fact." He tapped the scar on his temple for emphasis.

Lon remained reticent as he accompanied his father down the hill and into their house. Shalán was inside talking with Kaylen and Mellai, but when Aron and Lon entered, the three women fell silent and stared at each other with lips pulled tight.

Aron opened his mouth to inquire, but closed it when Shalán gave him a warning stare. He only chuckled as he walked into the kitchen and scavenged some bread and cheese from a cupboard. Lon joined his father and forgot about the women's peculiar behavior. The bread was partially stale, but they ate it without reservation.

Shalán finally broke the silence. "I've been talking to Mellai and Kaylen about your encounter with the Rayder . . . and his horse."

Kaylen snickered at Shalán's statement, earning a quick elbow from Mellai. When Lon glanced at them, Mellai gave him a nasty scowl and told him to tend to his own fields. Lon rolled his eyes and continued eating.

"I'm glad you were there to push Mellai out of the way," Shalán said.

Lon stopped chewing and searched the face of his mother. Her expression didn't show any hint of knowing the truth. Lon didn't want to put a damper on their cheerful mood—regardless of how odd it seemed—and hesitated to share his experiences with them.

"I'm not sure if I did. How could I?" he answered.

Aron raised his eyebrow at his son.

Lon shook his head. "I was twenty-five feet behind her, Father. There's no way I could have reached her in time."

"That's what I told Mother," Mellai added, "but I still can't explain how I was able to move out of the way before that savage sliced me in half."

"How do we know the Rayder was truly a terrible person, Mellai? He probably had a family at home that was just as important to him as we are to each other. Maybe he wasn't doing it out of cruelty, but for honor and duty. Father would know better. He changed, didn't he?"

"So, murdering Myron was honorable?" Mellai snapped.

"No," Lon replied, "but Myron attacked them, didn't he? I bet the Rayder thought it was self-defense. He wouldn't have hurt Myron if he hadn't felt threatened."

Aron pounded his fist on the table. "Use your head, boy," he shouted. "Those Rayders' intentions were about as honorable as a pack of wolves in a sheep pen. They corrupt and terrorize, kidnap and murder. Duty drives them, yes, but their intentions are never honorable."

"Lon, you're starting to sound like Braedr," Mellai added.

Lon recoiled. Although he didn't consider his comment to be anything like what Braedr had said the night before, the general message of her remark struck him to his core. He realized his opinion sounded somewhat irrational, but couldn't figure out exactly why he felt such a strong responsibility to defend his enemies.

"At least you're not proud of your words—I can sense that much," Mellai said. "I doubt Braedr feels any guilt over what he said last night."

Kaylen sat next to Lon and placed her hand on his cheek. "Lon, I'm terribly sorry—for you and your family. Shalán and Mellai spent the last few hours catching me up on everything that's happened since you saw that Rayder last night."

"Why did you tell her?" Lon asked Mellai. "Kaylen shouldn't have to worry about all of this."

Mellai rolled her eyes. "She has a right to know."

"It's fine, Lon," Kaylen intervened. "I don't blame you for what you said about the Rayder, either. I'm barely involved and I still can't deal with the complexity of the situation. If you had asked me two days ago whether or not I thought killing could ever be justified, I would have told you no—maybe in war; but even then I wouldn't like it. Now, after watching you defend yourself against the Rayder, I don't know what's right anymore."

Kaylen's tender words soothed Lon. He was glad she was there to share his burden. It felt good knowing he didn't have to face things on his own. Kaylen had a right to know about his personal struggles, but even more importantly, she wanted to know.

Lon took Kaylen's hand from his cheek and kissed it. "I've got news that's even more unsettling."

Kaylen stared unwavering into Lon's eyes. "Tell me."

Shalán looked at Aron, curiosity emanating from her face, but all he gave her was a slight nod. Mellai, on the other hand, breathed out in frustration and dropped into a chair near the hearth. "Out with it, Lon. We've been through too much for your annoying riddles."

"All right," Lon replied as he escorted Kaylen from the table.

They sat in front of Mellai and motioned for Shalán to join them on the floor while Aron lit a small fire with a flint set. Once the flames began licking the dry wood, he walked to the window and closed the shutters, then sat in a chair behind his wife and placed his hand on her shoulder. Aside from the flickering glow of the fire, the room was dark.

"Go ahead, Son," Aron said after he was settled.

Lon spoke carefully of his three encounters with the strange mist, omitting no details. No one interrupted. By the time he finished, tears were running down Shalán's face, and Kaylen's eyes were wide with amazement.

Mellai was the first to speak. "That makes no sense, Lon. You make it sound as if you used Beholder magic to throw me off the road—but that's ridiculous."

"I know," Lon agreed, "but that Rayder called me a Beholder after he saw what happened. Also, when he saw you fly off the road, he looked surprised, but not confused. Maybe I really am the Beholder everyone's talking about. I don't know."

"Even if it were true," Mellai continued, "that still doesn't explain the fog you've been seeing. This is madness." She turned to her parents. "Did you two know something about this?"

Aron ignored Mellai. "How would you explain your experiences, Lon?"

Lon contemplated his father's question in silence, staring into the fireplace. He watched the orange flames dance across the logs. Embers glowed brightly at the foothold of every flame.

As he watched the fire, Lon became aware of the intricate exchange of heat between the flames and the wood. He found an answer to his father's question.

"The best explanation I can come up with is that the haze I see is some sort of heat that floats around in the world. Somehow, I've learned to see it. I can't control when it happens, but I think anxiety causes it. When Mellai was in danger, I was able to use this . . . heat . . . and made it throw Mellai off the road. Still, I can't understand why it didn't hurt her."

Mellai furrowed her eyebrows. "You're insane."

Her words ignited something inside of Lon, something that had lain dormant his entire life. Never before had he allowed her loose tongue to affect him so personally, but she had called him insane—the exact word he used to describe his deepest fears to his father. Lon became infuriated and felt himself losing control. As anger consumed him, he looked at Mellai with utter disgust and the haze filled his sight.

The three women gasped in terror.

"Do you see it?" Lon asked as he stared at their glowing figures. "Can you see the haze?"

Only Aron remained calm as he took a small looking glass off the wall and held it in front of Lon. "No, but now they know you're telling the truth. Look at your reflection, then you'll understand why they're reacting this way."

Lon gaped. The natural color in his eyes had faded into white; blue and black alike were obscured, like a full moon behind a thin layer of clouds. The sight made Lon panic and lose what little control he still maintained. He grimaced as he felt his strength dissipate. As with the previous night, he fell to the floor and blacked out.

* * * * *

When Lon came to, he was lying on something soft and warm. He felt fingers running through his hair. Kaylen's sweet voice drifted to his ears—she'd cradled his head in her lap. He kept his eyes shut as he listened to her speak, reveling in her soft touch.

"Master Aron, do you know what's happening? He's been unconscious for nearly an hour."

"And I think you've nursed him back into awareness," Aron replied, no doubt at the grin forming on Lon's face.

Kaylen pulled back Lon's hair, then leaned down and kissed his forehead. Lon opened his eyes.

"I love you, Kaylen," he said without hesitation. Her flawless skin flickered with light from the glowing fire.

"And I you," she whispered.

"Thanks for establishing such an obvious fact," Mellai huffed from across the room. "He's awake now, Father, so please tell us what's going on. I'm as anxious as a cow in the slaughterhouse."

"As soon as your brother is up and ready to listen," Aron replied. "Lon needs to hear what I have to say more than anyone."

Mellai turned to her brother and glared at him. Lon responded to her impatience with a wink, then slowly lifted his head from Kaylen's lap. His arms shook as he tried to support himself. Kaylen sat forward to steady him.

"Take your time, Son," Aron said. "You're obviously a little weak."

"I'm not weak," Lon said, looking at his hands on the floor. "I just feel odd. It's like my arms aren't connected to my body."

"Perhaps it's best if you remain lying down," Shalán interceded. "I'm sure Kaylen won't mind acting as a pillow for a little while longer."

Kaylen smiled as Lon lowered his head onto her lap again. Aron stood and restocked the fire with a few logs that had been stacked next to the hearth. After stirring the coals with the iron poker, he sat in his chair and returned his hand to Shalán's shoulder.

"Father," Lon said, his eyes pleading, "no more secrets."

Aron nodded. "As you wish, Lon, but I fear this story will cause even more unrest than the one last night. There's a lot to share—most of which you won't like—but all three of you, listen patiently. Especially you, Mellai. Keep your temper and your tongue under control."

"Maybe I shouldn't be here," Kaylen replied with concern. "It sounds like you need to talk with Lon and Mellai alone."

"Kaylen," Shalán inserted, "we know how much you mean to Lon. Stay."

Kaylen squirmed and looked around uncomfortably, but she remained seated.

"Five years ago," Aron started, looking at Kaylen, "we lived with Shalán's parents in Roseiri. Our life was good and we had no reason to fear the Rayders. They hadn't been seen in the village since your mother and I returned from the mountains—although that doesn't mean they weren't around. For whatever reason, though, they left the village alone."

"We loved Roseiri and planned to spend the rest of our lives there," Shalán said. "My mother trained me in herb lore and I was going to take her place as the village healer when she grew old. But something happened that forced us to leave."

"The night of the hailstorm," Lon inserted. "You mean you're finally going to tell us what we did wrong?"

"I've told you many times," Shalán replied, "you didn't do anything wrong. Remember how terrible the weather was that night?"

"That wasn't the only terrible thing about that night," Mellai grumbled.

"You were so engrossed in your game of stick-stack," Aron said, "that you didn't notice what Lon was doing—he was using True Sight. He created a solid barrier around you that protected you from the wind—it even stood up to a bail of hay. You should've been crushed. Think about it. You had built up that stack of sticks over two feet high—a near impossibility by itself, even on a calm day."

"It isn't that hard to do," Lon said. "Mellai always had excuses for why she kept losing to me—the sticks were the wrong size, the ground wasn't level. That day, it was that the wind was picking up dust and making it hard to see."

"You were complaining, too," Mellai countered. "You knocked over the stack and tried to blame it on a gust of wind."

"A gust of wind," Lon repeated. "Oh, yeah. I remember now. It came out of nowhere. It did knock over the pile."

"You're wrong," Aron replied as he smiled at Mellai. "The wind didn't hit you until after you lost."

Mellai snickered. "Like I said, I wasn't the only one making excuses. I'm the one with the steady hands, remember? I always won, even when you made me play left-handed."

"When your mother came home and told me what happened," Aron continued, "I had only one explanation. Lon was a Beholder. I didn't wait for anyone to come around asking questions. It was too dangerous. If the Rayders discovered there was a Beholder in Roseiri, they would've taken to that village like flames to thatch. Everyone in the village—including Shalán's parents—would have been killed. We left that night without saying goodbye to protect our family, your grandparents, and the rest of Roseiri. I'd seen enough bloodshed in my life."

"After all these years," Lon said, staring up at the ceiling, "it's strange to know the truth." He looked back at his father. "Did I really use True Sight five years ago?"

Aron nodded. "Now you understand why we didn't tell you."

"I can't believe this," Lon said, shaking his head. "If I'm a Beholder, what does that mean? All I know about the Beholders is that they built Itorea, and that the Rayders murdered them. Am I some sort of magician?"

Aron nodded at his son. "I was just about to clarify that. You actually came very close to explaining it yourself earlier. Simply put, a Beholder is a wielder of True Sight, which is the ability to see the energies that bind the world together. A Beholder can see the world's energy and use it to do things, though I don't claim to know what a Beholder can actually do. I'm only familiar with a portion of their history, but I can tell you one thing for certain. You are much more than just a magician. For now, all you need to know is that the haze you've been seeing comes from True Sight."

"Wait a second," Mellai said. "Obviously we all know now that Lon was the one blocking the wind in Roseiri, but how did you know at the time that I wasn't the one doing it? How did you know I wasn't a Beholder?"

"Because Beholders have always been men," Shalán answered, "and for good reasons. Keep in mind, one man could repopulate an entire village if there were enough women to supply the need. The Jaeds wouldn't sentence Appernysia to extinction by sending our women into battle."

Mellai blew out her breath. "I can't keep track of all this new information. What in the world is a Jaed?"

"I had the same question," Lon inserted.

"Nobody knows for sure," Aron answered, "The only thing everyone agrees on is that Jaeds are ethereal beings who choose Beholders and regulate the use of True Sight. The Rayders also have historical accounts of Jaeds intervening when Beholders got too overzealous with their powers. Apparently, only Beholders can see Jaeds."

"So, they're like angels?" Lon asked, his eyes wide.

Aron nodded. "In a way."

Kaylen cleared her throat. "I'm sorry to interrupt, but how come none of us have heard of Jaeds before now?"

"Jaeds are usually only known to the Rayders," Aron answered. "When the Beholders were killed and the Rayders exiled at the end of the First Age, the knowledge of Jaeds was lost in Appernysia. However, the Rayders maintain knowledge of them, with the hope that a Jaed will bring another Beholder to the Exile."

"If Rayders killed the Beholders," Mellai said with a furrowed brow, "why do they want another one?"

"To take back Appernysia," Lon said. The answer seemed so obvious to him. Twelve-hundred years of exile will do that to a civilization. He rolled onto his side, his head still on Kaylen's lap. "Suppose I am a Beholder. Now what?"

"We're not just saying it," Aron replied. "It's the truth, whether you accept it or not. We all need to be extra careful—especially you, Lon. You're in great danger, not just from being discovered, but also from your new power. You've passed out twice today. Whatever it's doing to you, your body doesn't like it. If you don't learn how to control it soon, you might be a danger to yourself."

"I understand that," Lon said, "but what I don't understand is why now, so suddenly? If I used it five years ago, why haven't I had any similar experiences until now?"

Shalán shrugged. "It could be that you're coming of age this year, but I don't know. What happened in Roseiri was unusual. There have been subtle signs over the years, though. Where do you think your regular headaches come from?"

"And if anxiety is what summons True Sight," Aron inserted, "then we know Kaylen has played an invaluable role in helping you control it, although she hasn't realized it."

"I think she's done a better job at keeping Mellai calm," Lon teased. "I don't need nearly as much calming as my little sister."

Mellai glared at Lon. "My life isn't in danger."

"Yes, it is," Aron inserted. "Lon has had four . . . episodes in just one day. For all we know, Lon could kill us all just by blinking his eye. We're all in danger because of him."

"What am I supposed to do?" Lon asked, swallowing a lump in his throat.

"There's no clear answer to that question, Son," Aron responded. "I know very little about True Sight. Whatever I teach you could make your situation even worse."

"Can't you try?" Kaylen pleaded. "What other choice do we have?"

Aron leaned back in his chair and stared at the fireplace. "My mind is clouded—I've only had a few hours of sleep over the past two days. Let's have dinner and get a full night's rest, then maybe we'll find a solution in the morning. In the meantime, as we discussed before, continue to keep your mind calm—and by no means try to enable your power. It's much too dangerous."

"I promise," Lon consented.

"I hate to remind everybody," Mellai inserted, "but there are five dead Rayders on our property. How do we know there isn't another squad out there?"

"I've considered the same thing," Aron replied, "but Rayder squads have always traveled by themselves, to avoid unwanted attention. I believe we're safe for now."

"We'll just have to put our faith in the Jaeds to protect us," Shalán said as she stood. "After all, we have a Beholder amongst us now, so they're probably watching us as we speak."

As Shalán moved to the kitchen to prepare dinner, Lon looked around warily, wondering if he'd actually see a Jaed.

Mellai stood. "Are you coming, Kaylen?" she asked as she opened the door.

"No, thank you," Kaylen replied.

"Kaylen," Mellai said with more intensity, "you need fresh air."

"Oh, right!"

Kaylen jumped up, knocking Lon's head off her lap in the process. His skull bounced on the hard floor as Kaylen hurried after Mellai, shutting the door behind her.

"What's gotten into them?" Lon asked, rubbing the back of his head.

Aron glanced at his wife, but she gave him the same warning look.

"Women are one of the greatest mysteries you'll ever encounter in life," Aron answered, "perhaps even more than True Sight."

"I couldn't have said it better myself," Shalán said.

* * * * *

After dinner, Lon walked Kaylen home. When they reached the south bridge spanning the Klanorean River, Lon hesitated. He carefully looked up and down the river, searching for signs of danger, then asked Kaylen to wait on the road while he checked under the bridge.

Kaylen held onto his hand as he attempted to leave. "All you'll find under that bridge is a dead, bloated cow. We can't live the rest of our lives in fear."

It took all of Lon's concentration to keep his eyes from watching the river, but he stayed with Kaylen as they continued across the bridge and up the road toward her home. He thought about their future, and it worried him. He would be burdened with True Sight for the rest of his life.

Contrary to what Kaylen thought, Lon now feared any single moment of weakness or inattention might kill him. Where would that leave her? She would have to raise their children alone, acting as both mother and father to them.

When they reached Kaylen's house, Lon stopped and turned to face her. "This True Sight of mine isn't going to disappear. What you said earlier is true. I will always be a Beholder. I'll be hunted by the Rayders for the rest of my life. Even if they don't catch me, there's a chance True Sight might kill me anyway. I'll have to live every day like it's my last, never knowing what the next will bring."

Kaylen returned his gaze without wavering. "Which is why you'll need me. I'm not afraid of what the future holds. I love you and want to be with you." She brushed Lon's lips with hers. "Do you remember when we first met?"

Lon frowned. "How can I ever forget, but it's hard for me to think about it now"

"It shouldn't be. Our perspective on life all depends on how we choose to look at it. You might remember my mother dying, but I remember how you and your family worked so hard to take care of us. You and your father worked my father's fields so he could stay with my mother. Shalán did everything possible to save her. Mellai was a godsend to me. I miss my mother, yes, but I don't mourn her passing. It brought us together, which is exactly what she would've wanted."

"No one in this village likes Mellai except for you, and only because you can look past her rudeness to see who she really is inside."

Kaylen cupped Lon's face in her hands and kissed him passionately, while he wrapped his arms around her waist, holding her close, a scandalous behavior, even for a betrothed couple—which they weren't. Minutes passed before Kaylen finally pushed Lon away.

She turned and disappeared into her house, leaving Lon gasping in the middle of the road. It took a moment before he pulled himself back to reality and realized what just happened.

I can't believe I let myself get that carried away, he thought. *If anyone in the village saw what we just did and told Scut, he'd forbid our marriage.*

Lon searched the windows of Kaylen's house for her father. It was too dark to see anything so he turned and trudged home, quietly shaking his head.

Chapter 6

Coming of Age

S halán crept from her room with her healing satchel in hand. She pulled the bedroom door shut, taking care not to wake Aron. She crossed the room, put on her shoes and slipped outside.

She took a deep breath, relishing in the beauty of the sunrise lighting the eastern sky. The morning air was cool and crisp. She followed the path leading to the greenhouse and stepped inside. Once inside the door, she waited for her eyes to adjust to the darkness.

Shalán was in a dark storage room used to hold gardening tools and dry herbs. On the south wall was another door leading into the herb garden. Dual plank walls filled with mud insulated the room. Large sections of thick cubed-glass covered the three walls and ceiling. Sunlight poured through the glass into the enclosed herb garden, and the insulation kept the warmth inside, allowing the garden to grow year round.

A large space had been cleared in the storage room. Lying on the floor was a large, black horse. It took slow, deep breaths as it slept. Shalán crouched at its side and placed her hand on its neck, stroking the hair softly as she spoke.

"I'm sorry to keep you penned up, my friend, but I'm afraid you're just too big and noisy to keep awake. Please forgive me."

Shalán moved her hand to the horse's mouth and pulled back the upper lip, revealing a dark brown paste which she removed with her finger and flung to the ground. After pulling a few dried leaves from her satchel, she placed the new leaves against the horse's gums and let its lip hold them in place.

"These leaves taste awful, but they'll keep you quiet and safe. One more day of this, and I promise you'll have a new home. Be patient and you'll be gorging yourself on oats and hay."

Shalán left the horse and quietly returned to her home, smiling at Lon's sleeping figure as she tip-toed across the floor and reentered her bedroom.

*   *   *   *   *

Lon arched his back and stretched his arms high above his head; he threw off his blanket and stood up.

"I can't remember the last time I slept past sunrise," he said with a smile as he pulled on his tunic.

"Have a seat. Your breakfast is almost ready," Shalán said.

"Where's Father?" Lon asked as he sat down.

"Probably at the Shaw's. He went to clean up the mess by the river. Then he was going to make sure the fence around Scut's pasture is secure. He took a pack with him, so he most likely won't be back for the rest of the day."

"It shouldn't take that long to fix a fence and . . ." Lon's voice trailed off as he remembered the events of the previous two days. "Is he moving the cow and the dead horses?"

"Yes."

Lon frowned. "You know, it's strange. No matter how terrible things get, I always have to remind myself of them the next morning."

"You're lucky," Shalán answered with a weak smile. "Some people can't get to sleep, let alone forget their troubles."

"What's Father doing the rest of the day?"

"I wouldn't worry about him. You have something much more important to focus on today." As she finished speaking, Shalán placed a plate in front of Lon.

"Happy birthday, Master Lon."

Lon smiled. "I can't believe I've finally come of age. You know what? For my birthday, I want to stay home all day and do nothing."

"Nice try," Shalán replied. "You still have to declare your trade, and offer your services to each family in the village. It's not so bad, though. You're going to get a present from each family in return. And don't forget about your celebration this evening, either. You need to make sure you're in the village square by sundown." Shalán sat in the chair next to Lon and looked at him. "I wouldn't do anything rash until after your official acceptance tonight."

Lon furrowed his brow in confusion, so Shalán continued. "Scut is very protective of his daughter and he'll want proper protocol to be followed. Whether you like it or not, you have come of age. The entire village will judge your decisions and actions more harshly from now on. One of the quickest ways to destroy your reputation—especially with Scut—would be through impulsiveness. You'll marry Kaylen, but only if you use your head."

Lon looked down at the food in front of him and took a deep breath. "I'm afraid that *using my head* is what'll most likely get me into trouble, but thanks for your advice, Mother. I'll be careful."

"Are you sure you're even capable of that?" Mellai entered the room, her hair half-braided.

"Capable of what?" he replied without looking at her, then picked up his fork and poked at the eggs.

"Of being careful." Mellai finished braiding her hair and sat down beside him. "Happy birthday."

"You, too, Mel," he responded.

Mellai opened her eyes wide and feigned surprise. "Happy birthday wishes and no *Little Sis*, all in one sentence? I like this grown-up version of Lon much better."

"All right, Mellai, that's enough," Shalán interrupted. "I shouldn't need to remind you that Lon needs to stay calm. Let's try to avoid another episode. Actually, I was hoping you'd go with him into Pree today."

Lon spoke first. "The last thing I want is Mellai tagging along and jabbing insults at me."

Shalán returned to her cooking as she spoke. "Lon, you need support from somebody who understands what you're going through. Your father won't be around today and I have a lot of work to do to prepare for tonight. It would be inappropriate for Kaylen to go with you, so that leaves Mellai. You may not want her help, but you need it. You don't have a choice."

Lon slapped his hand on the table. "Of course I have a choice. That's what coming of age is all about."

Mellai leaned away from Lon, watching his eyes warily.

Shalán turned to her son. "I understand your frustration, Lon, and I wish what you said was true, but it's not. Coming of age doesn't free a person from responsibility. If anything, it does the opposite. As I already told you, everyone will judge you more harshly now that you're an adult. You have to consider the entire village when you make decisions. One wrong choice could cause a tremendous rift between families—maybe even a blood feud. Some of the villagers might even try to bait you to test your maturity."

Shalán placed her hand on Mellai's shoulder. "Take your sister with you. She can sense your state of mind. She'll be an invaluable companion who can intercede at a moment's notice to keep you from becoming too stressed."

"But I don't want to go," Mellai argued. "I've been of age for two years now. Doesn't my opinion matter?"

"Yes, it does," Shalán replied patiently, setting a plate in front of her daughter, "but not in this circumstance. Try as you might, you can't argue with logic and truth, Mellai. Lon needs you."

Shalán joined them at the table; the three of them ate their breakfast in silence. Lon was the first to finish. Getting up from the table, he rolled up his bedding, placed it next to the fireplace, and disappeared inside Mellai's room to change clothes.

"How is it?" Mellai asked in an excited whisper.

"He is just fine," Shalán answered quietly, "but he'll be upset for a couple of days once he wakes up. Horses are made for open plains and love to run more than anything else in the world. Hopefully, once he's had a chance to stretch his legs he'll be calm. Rayder horses are very well-trained."

"I wanted to help Father build the corral today. That's why I don't want to go with Lon."

"I know, but your brother needs you. Please put away your pride and help him. I know it's your birthday, too, but today will be stressful for him. We can't risk his exposure."

Mellai finally agreed, and when Lon returned with his staff in hand, they headed for Pree.

*   *   *   *   *

The twins first stopped at the Shaw homestead at the southern edge of Pree. At seven feet tall, Scut towered over the cattle in his pasture. He waved the twins to his fence with a long, skinny arm. They stopped at the wooden rail fence and waited for him to cross the field.

"Don't do it," Lon said in response to Mellai's coy expression. He knew she was up to no good. "Not today."

Before Mellai had a chance to respond, Scut started shouting in their direction "If it isn't Master Lon," he said as he closed the distance between them. "I've been waitin' for this day for a long time. Spill it."

Lon bit his lip and attempted to stifle his amusement. "Good morning, Master Scut. I'm sorry about your lost cows."

"Yeah, yeah. Don't you be worryin' none about that. Water under the bridge, if you ask me." His eyes suddenly brightened and he popped the fence with his fist. "That's a good one. Under the bridge . . . get it? Right where your father found the poor creature. Never did find the other one, though. Curse them wolves."

"I'll double my efforts to protect your herd, Master Scut," Lon replied.

Scut smirked. "You know, you and Aron are the only folks who speak to me like that. Apparently, cattle farmers don't deserve the same respect as the rest of this blasted village. I've been handlin' the verbal disrespect about my height and such, but this cow business has been pushin' me too far. If I ever run into that wolf pack, I'll—"

Mellai cleared her throat loudly. Scut flinched as he looked at her, then took a deep breath before speaking again. "Let's just say I'll get me some justice." He turned his attention back to Lon. "Anyway, enough of that. I already told you once, kid—spill it."

Lon nodded and pushed right to the point. "I would like to become your apprentice, Master Scut, if you'll have me."

"Yup," Scut immediately replied, "and here's a little somethin' to show you my respect in return." He pulled his other arm from behind his back, producing an intricately crafted stool. "Take it. My wife made it for milkin' my cows, but it's yours now. Do what you please with it."

"I'm honored," Lon said as he took the stool, "but are you sure you want to give this to me? This should be a family heirloom."

"Not too worried about that," Scut replied with a wink. "I'm gonna have to send you on your way, though. I got work to do, and my daughter's busy preparin' herself for the celebration tonight, just like every other maid in Pree." He smiled at the confusion on Lon's face and returned to his fields with long strides.

"What did he mean by that?" Lon asked as they started up the road. "Everyone knows I've been courting Kaylen, so why are all the other girls preparin' themselves for tonight?"

Mellai laughed at Lon's ignorance. "For the dance, of course! You have to dance with every eligible woman in Pree, whether they've just turned fifteen or they've got one foot in their grave. Lucky you!"

"Why do I still have to dance with all of them if I've already made my choice?" Lon asked, his anxiety growing.

"Try as you might, you can't argue with tradition," Mellai said, imitating their mother's voice.

Lon panicked at the thought of dancing with so many women, especially Elora—an old widow with four sons close to his own age. His breathing quickened, and True Sight overtook him. Mellai tried to speak to him, but Lon was completely distracted by his blurred vision. He collapsed in front of Scut's house, landing flat on his back, and blacked out.

*   *   *   *   *

Lon reopened his eyes to Mellai, who was kneeling over him and slapping the side of his face.

"I'm awake," Lon said, jerking his head back. He took a deep breath and glanced around. "Did anyone see?"

"No," she replied. "This new version of you is really going to foul up our relationship. Who am I going to harass now that you can't take it anymore?"

"That was a dumb thing to do, Little Sis."

"I know," Mellai said. "I wasn't thinking. I should've known better."

"Don't worry about it." Lon struggled to sit up. "Now that I think about it, I vaguely remember Kaylen telling me about the dance, but I forgot she wasn't the only woman participating."

"What are you going to do? You can't pass out every time something stressful happens to you, and it's unnerving to see your eyes cloud over. If anyone sees you, they'll think . . . well, I don't know what they'll think, but they won't like it. It's unnatural."

"I'm trying, but it's hard to control something that I don't understand."

"Maybe Mother can give you a drink to calm you down tonight."

"That's not a bad idea. Remind me to ask her when we get home."

Lon rested for a few minutes, then the twins continued north to visit the rest of the villagers. They stopped to see Nybol, the village sheep and goat herder. He gave Lon a pair of wool pants made by his wife. They visited Elora's alfalfa farm next. She gave Lon a large quilt and thanked him in advance for their dance that evening. Lon forced a nervous smile.

The twins left Elora's house and turned west onto a smaller road that looped around the village square.

"We should have brought a wheelbarrow," Lon grumbled, his arms already full of gifts.

"I wouldn't worry about it," Mellai returned with a smile.

The next two homes on their route belonged to Ramsey and Wellesly, the farmers responsible for the village's supply of vegetables and fruits. Both families had worked together to make Lon a small donkey cart. They offered to hold it until after Lon met with Trev Rowley, the village delegate.

When Lon and Mellai arrived at Trev's, he gave Lon a young donkey he had acquired during his annual trip to Itorea—where he paid the village's taxes and purchased any supplies they couldn't produce for themselves that year—along with all the leather trappings to hitch it to a cart. The donkey was young, about a year old, but still large enough to pull the new cart waiting at Wellesly's house. Lon thanked Trev and his wife for such a generous gift, returned with Mellai to strap the donkey to the cart, and loaded it with the other gifts he had received. After that, Lon and Mellai moved on to see Delancy Reed, the village brewer. When the twins knocked on his door, Delancy thrust a small cask of mead at Lon and closed the door in his face.

"It looks like he's still angry you chose Kaylen over his daughter," Mellai said with a smirk.

"Obviously," Lon responded, turning the cask of mead over in his hands. "He knows our family prefers Mother's herbal teas over his brew. What am I going to do with this?"

"Give it to your donkey," Mellai answered with a laugh, "but make sure I'm there to see what happens."

The twins continued south and met with Coel, the village leatherworker, who gave Lon a pair of thick leather gloves. Next, they met with Hans Pulchria, who had forged a small hammer for Lon. They visited the families of Hadon and Landon last, the farmers of wheat and oats. They had made Lon a long, twisted hemp rope and a large canvas tarp, both treated with pine tar.

"You ended up with quite a stash," Mellai observed as they led the cart east along the south end of the looping road.

"Yes," Lon agreed, "especially when you consider we've only lived here for five years. It makes me feel a little uncomfortable. I'm glad we don't have to see anybody else. I don't quite know how to express my gratitude."

"Make a noteworthy contribution to the village," Mellai suggested. "Just do your part and they'll know their gifts went to good use."

Soon, the twins came to Myron's abandoned estate on the south side of the looping road, opposite the village square. They both stopped and stared at the desolate house.

"We can't keep his death a secret for much longer," Lon said. "Someone is going to notice the new grave."

"I agree, but don't bring it up today," Mellai replied. "Wait until tomorrow, after our birthday."

Lon looked at his sister curiously. Just a couple of days before, Mellai had been grumpy and immature. She hadn't cared about the troubles around her or, if she did, she hadn't shown it. As he probed her feelings, Lon felt new, mature emotions inside her. The desire for solitude had almost completely disappeared.

"I guess everyone responds to stress in different ways," Lon said aloud.

"What does that mean?" Mellai asked.

"It means that . . ." Lon stammered, trying to think of a good lie. "That Myron hasn't fully avenged his family."

Mellai furrowed her brow. "I don't get it. What does that have to do with stress?"

"Everything," he replied, avoiding eye contact with his sister. "He avenged the ones who died, but what about his son, Tarek?"

"What about Tarek?" Mellai replied impatiently. "You aren't making sense. Besides, he's been missing for ten years. Tarek's dead."

Lon blinked with surprise. *She must not have heard.*

"Maybe, but what if he's not?" Lon had considered telling his sister the full truth, but he was afraid of dredging up the overwhelming emotions of the previous day.

"I don't know," Mellai said as she looked at the four graves next to Myron's house. "If Tarek's alive, he's been living as a Rayder. That thought is probably what drove Myron crazy. It would devastate me if you died, Lon, but I can't imagine how hard it would be if you just disappeared and I never found out what happened to you."

"Thanks, Mel," Lon said. He put his arm around Mellai and kissed her on the side of her head. "I knew you couldn't live without me."

Mellai rolled her eyes and shrugged out from under his arm. Lon smiled at his sister, then led the donkey and cart west, still thinking about Tarek. He wondered what sort of man Tarek had become and whether he had truly become a Rayder on the inside, or if he was only trying to survive.

Lon's thoughts drifted to the dead Rayders buried on the hill. Try as he might, Lon couldn't suppress his compassion toward them. He knew those men had to die to keep his family alive. Rayders were lawless savages, probably killed each other every day in the Exile; so, why did these five deaths bother him so much? He had only killed one of them, and it wasn't even on purpose.

Lon closed his eyes, trying to calm his mind, but the face of the terrified Rayder kept appearing in his head, painted on the black canvas of his eyelids.

Lon shook his head and reopened his eyes. *Brainless savage,* he thought. *Why did you have to be so foolish?*

"You all right?" Mellai asked.

"I'm fine."

The rest of the day passed slowly for Lon. When he and Mellai arrived back home, Lon tethered the donkey to the fence and took his gifts into the house. As he showed them to Shalán, Mellai disappeared and left Lon alone with his mother. He tried to help her with her cooking, but Shalán forbade it. Instead, he sat on a chair and quietly carved his staff with an old penknife he kept in his pocket. He had forgotten Mellai's suggestion about the elixir.

Mellai and Aron returned later that afternoon and Lon was finally allowed to help. They loaded up all the food Shalán had prepared in Lon's new cart, which he then led up the road toward the village square. Landon and his seven sons arrived just before the Marcs and helped move the food to tables positioned next to the meeting hall. The boys' ages ranged from seven to eighteen, and they all watched Mellai carefully as they worked. Lon found their behavior amusing.

Mellai glanced at Landon's sons, then left the square and walked up the main road. Lon caught up to her, hoping to stop her escape.

"Where you going, Mellai?"

"You know where I'm going," she said, "so please just let me go."

"Forget your hill, Little Sis. Today is your birthday, too, and you deserve to have a good time."

"I don't consider any part of this a good time," Mellai said as she stepped around Lon.

"Please, Mel," Lon pleaded. "I need you here."

Mellai ignored Lon's plea and continued walking north. Her sadness stung his mind, strong enough that he almost broke down where he stood. He watched her leave, but didn't follow her.

As the sun started to disappear behind the mountains, the rest of the village poured into the square—little more than an acre of cleared ground with a small windmill in the northwest corner. Oil lamps and candles had been scattered around the square. Everyone lined up at Shalán's food table, drooling over the feast she had prepared—fried chicken and cabbage, wild onion tarts, garlic potato pancakes, sausage soup, raisin pumpernickel bread, apple and butter cakes, and tea. Delancy Reed also supplied several barrels of his best ale and mead. Although he was less than cordial to Lon, Delancy still appreciated a good celebration.

"No party is any party without hard drinks," Lon muttered to himself as he watched Braedr raise an entire cask to his lips. "What does that even mean?"

Once everyone had filled their bellies, the dancing began to the flutes and fiddles of Elora's four sons. Elora insisted that she get the first dance with Lon and twirled him around until he was so dizzy he almost fell.

The celebration wasn't nearly as bad as Lon feared. Aside from his dance with the brewer's daughter, Sonela—who cried the whole dance—Lon had a fantastic time, even when he noticed Braedr sitting at one of the tables, gnawing on a chicken leg, glowering at him.

The pinnacle of the celebration came when Lon finally got to dance with Kaylen. She had been hiding behind her father while Lon gave all of the other eligible women their turn. Finally, Kaylen stepped out from behind Scut and grinned at Lon.

The full vision of Kaylen stunned Lon. She wore a chestnut-colored dress adorned with twisted gold piping along the hem, neckline, and wrists. It hugged her figure from shoulders to waist, then fell loosely to her ankles. As she glided toward him, the color of her dress cast a gentle glow in the shifting lamplight, setting off her green eyes, as well as an elegant, sage comb holding her long hair out of her face.

Lon returned her smile and took her hand in his. "You look lovely."

Kaylen blushed and leaned against Lon as the two of them moved together rhythmically with the music. The rest of the villagers stopped to watch the young couple dance together, though neither Lon nor Kaylen noticed. The night was theirs.

"I don't deserve you, you know," Lon whispered into Kaylen's ear as they danced. "Despite everything that's happened, you've never faltered. Why?"

Kaylen didn't respond until the music ended, at which point she leaned forward on her toes to give Lon an affectionate kiss on his cheek. "Because I love you, Master Lon."

"And I you," Lon replied with an embrace.

As the two of them stood in each other's arms, Scut walked to their side. "Master Lon," he said quietly enough that only Lon and Kaylen could hear, "I didn't like you much when you moved here. We're an old village and don't trust outsiders much, but when you finally earn it, nothin' in Appernysia is stronger. You're a hard worker with a good family, but what I like most about you is how you treat my daughter. I'd like nothin' more than for you to marry Kaylen and become my son."

Both Lon and Kaylen reeled with excitement at Scut's invitation and immediately announced their engagement to the whole village. Everyone cheered and made toasts in their honor, with the exception of the brewer and his daughter. Braedr said nothing, but stood up from his chair and walked away.

Despite the excitement, Lon followed his father's advice and focused on staying calm. He knew danger and anxiety would enable True Sight, but he wasn't sure how excitement would affect him. He kept Kaylen at his side and gripped her hand, regardless of the jostling and hugging going on around them. Kaylen had helped him stay calm before, and Lon hoped she would continue to do so.

In the middle of a toast—which silenced the entire village—Lon was overwhelmed with a sense of danger. The emotions were so powerful it took him a moment to realize they were coming from Mellai. Lon looked north for his sister, but save for the lights in the square, the village was dark. Luckily, the speech ended quickly. Lon excused himself from Kaylen and dodged the rest of the villagers until he reached the main road, then sprinted north toward Mellai's hill.

* * * * *

Mellai sat under the tree on her hill, facing away from the village, tears running freely down her face. When her family relocated to Pree, she had embraced the hill at first sight, falling in love with the large oak tree, the breathtaking view, and above all else, the isolation. A gust of October wind whipped about her. She pulled her knees up to her chest and gripped them with one arm, then hurled a pebble into the darkness with the other. Her hill was usually a place of solitude where Mellai could think, but now it offered little comfort to her.

"Lon didn't do anything wrong," she said aloud. "He deserves a party, and I hate attention anyway, so why am I feeling this way? What's wrong with me?"

"For one, you're out here by yourself, instead of down there, dancing with me," Braedr answered from behind the tree.

Mellai stood and wiped the tears from her eyes before walking around the tree to face him. "You should know better than to sneak up on people, *Master* Braedr," she responded. "It's rude."

"This is the only way I can get any time alone with you," he replied as he took a step closer to her. "Mellai, why won't you have me?"

Mellai recoiled at Braedr's tone and body language, but the lust in his eyes frightened her most. She took a step back and found herself against the oak tree.

"Braedr, I've never told you that I'm uninterested," she said in an attempt to calm him, "but I—"

"So, you will have me?" he interrupted as he took another step. "You know, I wish I'd known this before now. It would have saved me a lot of wasted time."

"Wasted time?"

"Yes, trying to win over other girls when all along you secretly wanted me." He placed his hand on the tree and lifted one side of his mouth in an eerie smirk. "So much wasted time."

Mellai stood her ground and squared her shoulders. "You don't scare me. Back away, Braedr, or else I'll—"

"You'll what?" he laughed. "Scream? Nobody will hear you. Everyone's at the square celebrating your brother's engagement to Kaylen."

"Oh, I get it," Mellai snapped. "Kaylen has officially rejected you so now you're out hunting for another—"

Braedr pounded his fist against the tree. "Such a naughty little mouth you have, Mellai. Someone should teach you to keep it shut before it gets you into trouble."

Sensing the real danger of her situation, Mellai tried to run away, but Braedr blocked her path. "No need to rush off in such a hurry," he said in a hoarse whisper. "We haven't finished our conversation."

Mellai screamed for help. Braedr wrapped his hand around her mouth and pushed her against the trunk of the oak tree. She struggled under his grasp, but Braedr held her firmly in place.

"Keep your hands off her!" Lon shouted from the distant shadows.

Braedr turned his head in Lon's direction and Mellai took advantage of the distraction. She brought her knee up as hard as she could and caught Braedr in the groin. As he fell back and doubled over in pain, a strange sound reached Mellai's ears. A burst of wind was roaring up from the south, bending reeds and shaking trees.

It took less than three heartbeats from the time Lon shouted until a burst of wind breached her hill. Mellai braced herself against the tree as the wind hit Braedr like a hammer. He stumbled sideways from the blow, tripped over an exposed root, and struck the side of his head against a rock. Mellai pounced on him, clawing his face and kicking his sides until Lon wrenched her away.

"Stop it, Mel," Lon said as he held her firmly by her shoulders. "Look what you've done to him."

"I don't care," she shouted, fighting to free herself.

Lon forced her to sit down. "Stay here. He might be dazed, but he's still a lot stronger than you. Let me handle this."

Mellai turned her head away in disgust and hugged her knees again. Lon watched her for a moment, then turned toward Braedr. Braedr was groaning on the ground with one hand between his legs and the other protecting his head, which was covered in fresh blood.

As Lon leaned over him, Braedr suddenly lashed out, swinging his fist wildly. Lon dodged the blows and Mellai jumped to her feet to resume her attack. She kicked Braedr hard in the side of his head before

Lon pulled her away again. Braedr grunted and rolled over to glower at them. Mellai screamed in anger as she fought to get past her twin.

"You better go," Lon said to Braedr, "before I decide to let her loose again."

Braedr rolled onto his knees and spit blood at the ground before standing up and limping away. Mellai picked up a rock and threw it at him, but it missed and landed in the dirt ten feet to his right. Braedr didn't even acknowledge the stone as he continued walking down the dark road and disappeared into the shadows.

"What was that?" Mellai spat as she pulled herself free of Lon. "You could've hurt me."

"What are you talking about?"

"The gust of wind you threw at us," Mellai whispered hoarsely.

Lon leaned against the oak tree. "I didn't do it on purpose. I got here just in time to see Braedr pin you against the tree."

"I know," Mellai said as she sat on the grass. "I heard you."

Lon sat next to his sister. "I was terrified you were going to get hurt. I couldn't stop myself. I was so afraid . . ." Lon's voice faded and he stared down the road after Braedr.

"I get it," Mellai said. "You were worried about me, so you used your stupid power."

"I already said I didn't do it on purpose," Lon replied. "When I shouted at him, a gust of wind shot out of my mouth."

Mellai furrowed her brow and looked at her brother. "From your mouth?"

"I know," Lon replied. "I watched the wind fly through the trees until it struck Braedr, then my eyes cleared and I saw you pounce on him. I never thought I'd have to rescue Braedr from you. I guess Mother knew what she was talking about. You can defend yourself just fine without my help."

Mellai shifted. "Actually, I would've been in real trouble if you hadn't shown up. You distracted him just long enough that I was able to knee him in the crotch."

"Seriously?" Lon laughed. "I hope you did it hard."

Mellai smirked. "I really did."

The twins sat quietly until the excitement slowly wore off—until the realization of what just happened finally seeped into Mellai.

"I can't believe Braedr," she said frantically. "I don't even want to imagine what he might have done if you hadn't shown up, Lon."

"I know."

Mellai stood up and paced back and forth on her hill. "What did we get ourselves into? Now that his pride's been hurt, he's going to want revenge."

"I doubt it," Lon replied. "I think his pride will prevent him from doing anything. There's no way he'd admit to you beating him bloody. He'll invent a story that makes him look like Appernysia's greatest hero."

"But what about us?" Mellai asked. "Should we tell Trev what happened?"

"You gave Braedr a worse punishment than a village council would. Unless he tries something else, let's just forget what happened and let him live his life. Nobody else needs to know about it."

"Well, I have to tell Kaylen," Mellai retorted. "I think my future sister-in-law should know about this, especially since Braedr still wants her for his wife. Your engagement really upset him, you know. Now she's officially rejected him."

"He told you we're engaged?"

"Yes."

"It's too bad you weren't there. You would've gotten a big laugh out of the whole thing. Scut proposed to me. So strange."

Mellai chuckled. Lon stood and put his arm around his sister. "Come back with me. I can't celebrate my betrothal to Kaylen without my twin sister there."

Mellai shrugged out of his arm, "You don't need me there to celebrate."

"I want you there. So does Kaylen."

Mellai reluctantly complied and the twins walked down to the square. As soon as they came into sight, the villagers cheered at their return. None of them questioned where Lon had gone, so he figured they must have thought he ran away to share the news with his sister.

After the cheering stopped, the villagers broke into a song traditional to Pree.

If time and pain run you down,
And gift you with an aged crown,
No more fretting, remove your frown.
Rejoice! You're part of this fine town.

Mellai squealed as everyone rushed at her, threw her up on their shoulders, and paraded her around the village square. She had never liked attention, not even during her own coming of age celebration two years earlier, but the tension in her was now finally beginning to dissipate. She blew a kiss at Lon and Kaylen as the crowd carried her past the couple.

The celebration continued long into the night. The food and drink had started to run out, and everyone was gradually leaving. As the night progressed, only the Shaws and Marcs remained in the square. Scut and Aron sat talking at a table; Shalán positioned next to her husband, her head on his shoulder, drifting in and out of sleep; the twins and Kaylen wandered together around the square, enjoying the cool night air.

The night was perfect, carefree.

But not for long.

Chapter 7

Dawes

L on was startled awake by a sharp jab on his side.
"Time to get up," Aron said as he poked his son in the ribs
again with Lon's staff. "We're already late."

Lon yawned, forced himself upright, and felt around for his tunic.
Once dressed, he guzzled a glass of milk and followed Aron out the
door, his walking staff in one hand and his new stool in the other.
They were silent as they walked up the dark road, entered Scut's cattle
pasture, and found him already at work in the barn. With his lanky
arms, Scut pulled the milking pails from a high shelf and shoved them
at Lon and Aron.

"No disrespect, Aron, but your boy ain't startin' his apprenticeship
off on the right foot. These cows follow a strict schedule. Bein' late
will mess 'em up for the rest of the day."

"I apologize, Master Scut," Aron replied. "It won't happen again,
I promise."

Scut eyed Lon for a moment, huffed, then led them out of the barn
with their pails and stools. Each of them found a cow and spent the
next fifteen minutes milking. Lon leaned his head against the side of
his cow, exhausted from the lack of sleep. It took everything he had
to keep his eyes open.

Once his pail was filled, Lon took it back into the barn and poured
the milk into a large saucer that slowly separated the cream. Scut and
Aron followed right behind him, then they all returned to the pasture

and followed the same cycle with three more cows. The sun crested the east and cast its light over the pasture just as they were finishing.

"I still don't understand why you keep comin' here every mornin', Aron." Scut said as he emptied the milk buckets. His foul mood had obviously disappeared. "Me and Lon can easily care for my herd. Oh, that reminds me. Any chance you've found clues about the two that went missin'?"

"Just this morning," Aron replied. "Looks like you were right. Some wolves caught them near the south bridge."

"I knew it." Scut spit on the ground. "Best be hopin' for heifer births in the spring then, else we'll all be in trouble."

"Indeed," Aron agreed. "About what you said before—would you prefer I stop assisting you with your cattle?"

"Don't be misunderstandin' me—I appreciate the help, especially when there's butcherin' that needs to be done. I just can't understand why you keep doin' it. Why not start your own trade?"

"Could you imagine starting a new trade at our age?" Aron replied. "I'm just fine helping you and anyone else who needs assistance."

"And it's a good thing everyone needs so much help," Lon added. "Mother's herb garden doesn't require nearly enough attention to keep him busy all day."

"Besides, you'll appreciate my help when winter arrives," Aron added.

Scut nodded. "You're good people, Aron. I'm gonna put in another good word about you with Trev."

"I appreciate that," Aron said. "We also need to visit Trev. We brought some bad news with us today."

Scut paused and eyed Lon. "About the engagement?"

"No," Aron replied.

"Good," Scut said. "What's the bad news?"

"We found Myron this morning on our way into town," Aron continued. "He must have died sometime last night. We carried him to his estate and buried him next to his family. That's why it took us so long to get here." He gave Lon a sharp glare.

"You should've said somethin' when you got here instead of lettin' me scold your boy," Scut said as he put down the last empty bucket. "That's too bad about Myron. I was startin' to worry about him. I hadn't seen him wanderin' around town the past couple of days. I thought he must've been holed up somewhere tryin' to get over some kind of sickness."

Aron nodded. "That's what I thought, too. My guess is that he finally decided to come ask for help from my wife, but never made it."

"Well, I'm glad he finally returned to his beloved," Scut said. "After ten years, I think it's about time he had some rest."

"I hope he finds it," Aron replied.

The three of them worked together baling hay that had been brought in the day before by Elora's sons, then Aron and Lon excused themselves and returned to the road.

"Are we really going to Trev's?" Lon inquired.

"Yes. The rest of the village should know what we found this morning."

"It doesn't seem right," Lon said, "robbing Myron of the honor he deserves for saving our lives."

"I agree, but it must be done. I told you before, if the village finds out five Rayders have been in Pree, they'd panic. Unlike myself, most Appernysians don't know Rayders always travel in squads of five. They'd assume more Rayders are prowling around. Remember what brought the Rayders to Pree in the first place. They attacked our family, Lon— suggesting one of us is a Beholder. Everyone here has heard rumors of the Beholder, so we need to avoid that kind of attention at all costs."

Aron and Lon found Trev outside the meeting hall on his way to the tavern for his morning drink. Their conversation was quick. Trev thanked them for burying Myron and promised to share the unfortunate news with the rest of the village, and plan a memorial.

Lon and Aron returned home in silence. They found Shalán and Mellai having breakfast. Lon looked at his sister with surprise. She was usually never awake that early—sometimes he even had to drag her out of bed—so he was suspicious when he saw her fully-dressed, a beaming grin on her face.

"Expecting someone?" Lon asked.

Mellai only smiled.

As Lon and his father joined the women for breakfast, Shalán placed a small box on the table and slid it to Lon. He picked it up and stared at his mother.

"What are you two so happy about?" Lon said as he opened the box. He looked down and gasped. Resting in the box was a pearl necklace.

Lon lifted the necklace from the box and dangled it in his hand. "Mellai, this necklace belongs to you. It's your inheritance—your dowry."

"It's for Kaylen," Mellai said.

Shalán nodded. "We both agreed it would fit her perfectly."

"But what about—"

"Please take it," Mellai insisted.

Lon sat speechless, looking back and forth at his mother and sister. After a moment, he carefully slid the necklace back inside the box and closed the lid. "Thank you both."

"Thank your father, too," Shalán said. "He gave them to me twenty years ago."

"And look what it's gotten us through," Aron replied. "Son, give that beauty to Kaylen and she'll be yours forever."

"She already is," Mellai teased. "Didn't you watch them together last night? Lon could drop a rock on her head and she'd still love him."

As soon as he finished his breakfast, Lon excused himself, walked to the corner of the room where he kept his bedroll, and secured the necklace inside it.

"Bring your sword with you," Aron said, belting his falchion to his waist.

"Where are we going?" Lon asked suspiciously, expecting another painful training session.

"Nowhere dangerous," Aron said while Lon searched for his sword, "or maybe I should say nowhere lethal."

Lon paused and looked at his father, who ignored him and walked out the front door followed by his mother and sister.

"You're coming, too?" Lon asked when he caught up to them. "I thought we agreed to stop keeping secrets."

Mellai gave him a huge grin, so exaggerated that Lon couldn't help but laugh.

Aron followed the trail to the main road and turned right, leading his family south, away from Pree. They had traveled for about half a mile when Lon stopped short. A strange noise reached his ears.

"What was that?"

Nobody answered, although Mellai laughed. They followed her for a few minutes as she led them toward the sound. The noise pierced the air again, but from much closer. Mellai laughed again and turned off the road in the direction of the sound.

"Do you know where you're going?" Aron called after her.

"Of course, I do," she replied.

"Mellai, wait," Lon called as she disappeared into the trees.

Shalán turned to face her son. "Lon, relax. You know your father wouldn't let her run away like that if she wasn't safe. Remember, you need to stay calm. Everything's just fine."

Lon took a deep breath as they followed Mellai through the woods for another hundred paces. He found his sister next to a rough wooden rail fence that stood eight feet high, lashed to four surrounding trees. Inside was a black horse, running in circles and bucking its hind legs into the air excitedly.

"That's the Rayder's horse." Lon said to his father. "Is this what you were doing yesterday?"

Aron picked up an ax from the ground. "Yes, after I cleaned up the Rayders' camp at the river. But the fence isn't finished. I'll need your help to fill in the gaps between the crossbeams. Horses are strong and fierce, but they can't protect themselves against an entire wolf pack."

"Do they normally make noises like that?" Lon asked. "It reminds me of the sound Grandfather used to make when he'd tickle us."

"It's called a neigh," Mellai said. "It's as common to a horse as a bark is to a dog."

"How would you know?" Lon asked.

"Mother knows everything about horses, and she's been teaching me. When this one was galloping down the road after you knocked the Rayder off its back, Mother was on her way back to meet us. She stopped it and was trying to calm it down when Kaylen and I found her. Anyway, we've been keeping him in the greenhouse until Father built this corral."

"Your mother is a natural horse-charmer," Aron added. "She didn't grow up with them, but she had plenty of practice with my horse while we were living in the mountains—not that she needed it."

"Dawes . . . I miss that horse," Shalán inserted. "I still don't think we should've abandoned him in the wild."

"We had no choice. We couldn't take Dawes back to Roseiri for the same reason we can't allow anyone in Pree to learn about this horse."

"Why didn't you hide him like we're doing now?" Mellai asked.

"He was my horse and it was my decision. I don't need to explain my actions to any of you."

Mellai grumbled something under her breath, but Aron ignored her and turned to Lon. "Listen to your mother, Son. She'll teach you how to handle your new horse, although I doubt he'll be ready to ride for awhile yet."

"My new horse?"

"Yes," Shalán answered. "It's our birthday gift to you."

"And to me," Mellai cut in.

"Thanks, but I don't want a Rayder horse," Lon said. "You can have it all to yourself, Mellai."

The thought of riding the horse made him shudder; the very sight of it brought images of the dying Rayder to his mind. He hated the idea of plundering from the dead. He might have taken the Rayder's sword, though reluctantly, but the horse was too much.

"Lon," Aron said, "accept this horse. Death isn't an easy thing to watch, and it's even harder to cause. You did what had to be done and you can't change it. But don't let guilt control your life. Consider caring for him as a way to repay what happened to his last master."

"How did you know?" Lon whispered.

"You're not the only one who has killed a man," Aron replied. "I've been through what you're experiencing. Trust me when I say that dwelling on it will destroy you. You must force yourself to move on."

Lon took deep, slow breaths in an effort to control his emotions. He nodded at his father but said nothing as he walked to the fence and peered at the horse.

Shalán stood behind Lon and placed her hand on his shoulder. "I'll teach you everything you need to know to care for this horse. You'll learn to love him, in time."

"Thank you, Mother."

Lon turned his head toward Mellai, who had been standing quietly nearby. She gave him a weak smile.

"I want you to name him," she said. "Any ideas?"

Lon watched the horse as it leaped around the corral, amazed by its size and power. The horse caught sight of Lon and trotted over to him. Lon immediately knew what to name him.

"Dawes," he said as he returned the horse's gaze. "How about I call you Dawes?"

The horse tossed its long black mane and nickered softly.

Mellai smiled. "He likes it. Dawes it is."

*　　*　　*　　*　　*

Lon and his father spent the day cutting down nearby trees and lashing them between the existing beams of the corral, while Shalán and Mellai led Lon's cart back to Elora's home to gather hay. The women came back with a large portion of it for Dawes, who had finally calmed down and was grazing in the small corral. Both mother and daughter watched him for nearly an hour before returning home again.

The men worked quickly and finished the fence by late afternoon. There were still small gaps between the slats, but small enough that a wolf's head couldn't slip through.

"Where are we going?" Lon asked when he saw his father angling up the hill into the dense foliage.

"To train," Aron answered.

"But we don't have our staffs with us."

"Astute observation."

"But the threat is gone," Lon said, afraid of another sparring session with his father. "We don't need to train anymore."

Aron stopped and looked at his son. "Your life is in greater danger now than it has ever been. I told you, Lon, True Sight could kill you if you don't know how to control it. Unfortunately, I can't teach you how use it."

"Why?" Lon asked. "You know all about it."

"I know about it, yes, but not how to use it."

"Then teach me about it," Lon said, frustration in his voice.

"I already have."

"You haven't told me anything except that I see the world's energy when I'm using True Sight."

Aron shook his head. "Sorry, but that's all I know."

"That's like telling a cow he's eating grass. It doesn't do me any good."

"I know. But I might be able to help you stop it. Keep your body and emotions under control, and you'll be able to prevent True Sight from surfacing. That's the best I can do for you."

"Any chance you'll take it a little easier on me today?" Lon muttered, doubting whether the training would do any good.

"No," Aron replied as he continued up the hill. "I know you're worried, but your engagement to Kaylen should give you extra motivation to figure this thing out. The most effective way to keep yourself and your family safe is to completely stifle True Sight."

Lon followed his father up the hill until they came to the same clearing where they had sparred two days earlier.

"So, are we just going to pummel each other with our fists?" Lon asked sarcastically as he sat on a rock. "I'm not going to fight you with a sword. Mother's good at what she does, but I'm quite sure she can't reattach body parts with herbs."

Aron smiled as he drew his falchion. "Not yet, Son. I have a couple of things I want to show you first. Draw your sword."

Lon's eyebrows drew together as he tried to process his father's request. With a shrug, he picked up a nearby twig and started drawing a simple sketch of his arming sword in the dirt.

Aron doubled over in laughter. In response, Lon broke the twig in half over his knee and threw the two pieces at Aron with defiance.

"I'm sorry," Aron said when he finally gained control of himself. "I wasn't making fun of your drawing. I only laughed because I forgot how little you know about weaponry."

"Are you saying I'm ignorant?" Lon fumed. "Don't forget, I defended myself from a trained Rayder on a horse, and I did it with just a staff."

"I'm not criticizing your skill—though it has plenty of room to grow. I'm talking about your knowledge, Lon. The phrase 'draw your sword' means pull your sword out of that leather thing belted around your waist—which is called a scabbard."

Lon flushed as he stood up and pulled the sword from its scabbard.

I should have known better, he mentally criticized himself. *How many times have I drawn a bowstring, or drawn water from the river? Now, I look like a complete fool.*

"You ready?" Aron asked. Lon nodded. "The first step to becoming a sword master is understanding how to use it against other types of weapons. Take my falchion, for example. What are the differences between it and your arming sword?"

"Arming sword?" Lon inquired.

"That big metal pointy thing you're holding in your hand. How's it different from my falchion?"

Lon lifted his sword to examine it more closely. "It feels lighter, and the blade is straight, and sharpened on both sides."

"Good," Aron replied. "Those are two very important things to remember. Assuming that we're both blademasters, how would those two differences affect how you fought against me?"

"My sword is lighter," Lon said after a brief pause, "so I'd be able to move more quickly, but you'd hit harder because the falchion is heavier. Wouldn't having two sharpened edges give me more fighting options, too?"

"Not necessarily," Aron answered. "Remember that although I might not be able to decapitate you with the blunt side of my falchion, I could still break your neck with a solid hit. Every weapon has its advantages and disadvantages in battle. The key is not only knowing how to use your weapon, but also how the enemy might use theirs against you."

Lon nodded as he contemplated his father's words. "How durable are these things? With such a thin edge, I wouldn't expect it to last very long in an intense battle."

"How long a sword lasts depends on who's using it and how it's being used. A weaponsmith does things to the metal to strengthen it, but it will still chip and dent. More importantly, there's a good chance you might break it. Imagine standing in the middle of a battlefield when your sword breaks. You can't call for a pause in the fighting, so you'll have to scramble for the closest weapon you can find. You see, it's also very important to know how to use everything as a weapon, including bows, axes, pitch forks—even a handful of dirt. If you can't pick up the closest thing and use it effectively, you'll be slaughtered where you stand. Do you understand?"

"Yes," Lon replied. "Speaking of multiple weapons, do you think we should unbury the Rayders' grave and take the rest of their swords? There's always a chance we might need them."

"There's no need. I stripped them of their swords before I buried them. The swords are all hidden in our house."

"Are you serious?" Lon said as he dropped his shoulders in exasperation. "Why didn't you tell me before you left me alone with Mother and Mellai? I could've used a sword to help protect them."

"After you nearly killed your sister with my falchion, can you blame me for keeping them a secret? Even now, a sword would be useless in your hands."

Aron sheathed his falchion and searched the ground for two sword-sized sticks. When he found a pair he liked, he tossed one to Lon and gripped the other in his hand.

"Shall we proceed?"

Lon shook his head. "Sure."

Aron showed Lon some basic skills he could use with his sword—mostly defensive moves—then proceeded to attack him with the same unreserved aggression he had used with the staffs. Although Lon did his best to defend himself, Aron continually bypassed all of his defenses and struck him repeatedly with the stick. After receiving a painful series of blows that ended with a hard whap on the side of his face, he lost control, his frustration elevating. It took only a moment before a veil of haze filled Lon's vision; a sharp pain pierced at the base of his skull. He grabbed his head and dropped to his knees.

Lon's initial thought was that his father had struck him, but Aron's glowing figure still stood in front of him. The pain was coming from inside his head, but he couldn't stop it, no matter how much he tried. He placed his hands on the ground and dug his fingers into the soil, screaming in agony as the pain consumed him. The stabbing became so unbearable that Lon began to wish for death. A hard thump hit the back of his head and the world went black.

Chapter 8

A Turn for the Worse

L on's eyes fluttered open to see his father sitting on a rock, the wooden sword still held loosely in his hand. Lon licked his dry lips and noticed a strange taste in his mouth—like he had been sucking on rocks. He spit onto the ground and tried to wipe his mouth with his hand, but his arm didn't respond. He felt weak and disoriented.

"How long was I out?" Lon asked hoarsely.

"Only a few minutes," Aron answered.

"That one was much worse. I couldn't control myself, and there was a pain in my head—it was terrible."

"There's no need to explain. Your screaming said enough."

Lon tried to wipe his face again, but his arm still wouldn't move.

"It's trapped under your body," Aron said. "True Sight."

Lon realized he was lying face down in the dirt with both of his arms underneath him. He rolled onto one side and moved his arms. They felt light and his fingers tingled, but he was able to wipe the spit away from his mouth. He touched the base of his skull where the pain had struck him, surprised that no matter how hard he probed with his fingers, the throbbing was completely gone. However, when he brought his hand up through his hair, he felt a large bump protruding from the crown of his head. It throbbed when he touched it.

"Strange," Lon said aloud as he gingerly felt over the rest of his head with his fingers. He ran through the events carefully in his head.

Nothing that happened should have caused such a bump. The overwhelming pain had been at the base of his skull, not on the crown, and he had landed on his face in the dirt. Lon looked up at his father, then remembered the blow he had felt just before he blacked out.

"It was the only way to stop it," Aron said, though not sounding entirely confident. "You were in terrible pain, Son. From what you've told me over the past couple of days, I can only think of two things that stop True Sight—at least without Kaylen around. Either you need to use it or you black out. I couldn't force the first option so . . ."

Lon brought his hand to his face and groaned. "I guess I should be grateful."

"You're getting worse, Lon. We're sparring to teach you self-control, so you can contain your power—but now I can't even train you without igniting it. This may be the first time it's physically hurt you, but we both know it won't be the last if you don't learn to control it."

"I'm trying," Lon replied as he slowly sat up.

Aron stared at the ground and scrawled circles in the dirt with his stick. "You're trapped in a loop, where every step requires a step before it. The best way to stop True Sight is to discipline both your mind and body. For that to happen, you must learn to overcome your physical pains and anxieties. The only way to overcome them is to confront them, which you can't do without activating True Sight. There's no practical place for us to begin."

"Mellai had an interesting idea yesterday. She suggested Mother should make an elixir that dulls my emotions enough to stop True Sight."

"Why not just carry your cask of mead around all day?" Aron replied dryly.

"I'm serious about this, Father. Do you think Mother will help me?"

"Probably, but that kind of tea won't just dull your senses. It will also sap your strength and hinder your reflexes. You'll take longer to learn self-control while relying on medicine to help you."

"At least it will help," Lon said. "Without it, I can't even try."

Aron paused before responding. "I'll talk to your mother."

"Thanks," Lon said as his thoughts drifted back to their sparring match. "It's no wonder you weren't afraid to challenge that Rayder to a duel. I was so busy trying to defend myself that I didn't have time to attack."

"That's an important lesson to remember about fighting. Never give your enemy an opportunity to strike. Hesitation and wrong choices will cost you your life—and you only get one." Aron dropped his stick to the ground, drew his falchion and whipped it sideways through the air in one fluid motion, cutting a nearby birch sapling in half. "Understand?"

"Completely," Lon answered with wide eyes.

"Just out of curiosity, why couldn't we have done this back in the trees by Dawes?" Lon asked as they walked down the hill.

"Because it would excite Dawes too much. He's a warhorse, trained for battle. Even if he couldn't see us, I'm certain he knows what fighting sounds like. For all we know, he might kick through his corral and join the fight."

"Could he actually do that?"

"Absolutely," Aron answered. "Aside from that, climbing this hill every day will build your stamina, which is a crucial part of your training. When two weapon masters of equal skill duel, the loser is almost always the one who tires first."

"Every day," Lon complained. "Great."

"Our sparring sessions will improve your swordsmanship," Aron continued, "but I want you to carry only your staff when you're in Pree. As with Dawes, a sword is something the villagers will never get used to seeing—especially if it's marked with the King's Cross."

"It seems like this keeps coming up," Lon said, "but I have to ask anyway. Why do I need to carry a weapon around at all? We're not in danger from anyone but me."

"Two reasons," Aron answered. "First, carrying a weapon makes you more aware of yourself and your surroundings. You'll pay more attention to your state of mind and maintain better control of it. Second, you'd be a fool to assume your encounters with the Rayders have ended. They'll eventually notice some of their men are missing and will want to know what happened to them. Rayders will come again to Pree, even if it's a year from now. You must be prepared for when that time arrives."

When they entered the house, Kaylen gasped at Lon's bruised face.

"Looks like the two of you have been playing with sticks again," Mellai giggled. "Did you actually hit him back this time, Lon?"

"We were practicing swordplay," Lon growled, "so of course I didn't. Father was just too fast."

"I'll get my satchel," Shalán said with a sigh as she stood up and left the room.

Kaylen frowned. "You did this to him, Master Aron?"

"Don't worry," Aron replied. "Shalán will have him back to normal in no time."

"It's true," Mellai added as she continued giggling. "Father gave Lon a much worse beating two days ago just an hour or two before we met you on the road. Most of the bruises were gone before we even left the house."

Kaylen nodded quietly. "I've been wondering where Lon's swollen eye came from."

"Kaylen," Aron said, "will you please step into Mellai's room while we apply the salve?"

"Come on," Mellai said as she took Kaylen's hand, "I'll keep you company."

"Trev stopped by while you were gone," Shalán said, reentering the room. "They are having a memorial for Myron tonight. I wish I'd known you talked with him today. His news caught me off guard."

"Sorry about that," Aron answered as Kaylen and Mellai disappeared behind the closed bedroom door. "When are they doing it?"

"After sundown. I told him we would meet them after you both returned and had something to eat."

Aron spoke to Lon while Shalán prepared the salve. "I'd like you to start following a regular schedule tomorrow. You need to start working on your house for Kaylen. I talked to Trev last night, and he agreed that since you'll be working your trade with Scut, the best place to build your house is on the south side of Scut's property. However, I suggest you visit Dawes first after we help Scut every morning. He won't like being isolated in the middle of the woods all night. He'll need a friend to calm his nerves. If you can convince Kaylen to wake up, you should take her along with you. She's fascinated by horses and would love you even more for including her. Shalán will also meet you there for a few days to teach you how to care for him."

Lon furrowed his brow. He wanted to build their house next to his parents', but he said nothing; he knew Trev's suggestion would make Kaylen happy.

"Can I really justify traveling a three-mile roundtrip every morning?" he asked Aron. "Why don't I just work on the house as soon as we finish at Scut's?"

"The weather's cooling and the days are shortening," Aron replied. "You'll want to wait until the sun has risen and warmed the air. You don't want to use saws and hammers with numb hands."

"Very true," Lon agreed.

"After you visit Dawes," Aron continued, "spend the rest of the morning and afternoon building your house. Kaylen should keep you supplied with all the food and drink you'll need, so don't worry about coming home for lunch. I'll stop by on my way to help Scut with the afternoon milking, then we'll spend an hour sparring before dinner every night."

Lon reluctantly agreed, and Aron turned his attention to Shalán. "Lon's burden has become worse. I had to hit him over the head today to stop his pain. Could you prepare an elixir that will take the edge off for our sparring sessions?"

"I'll see what I can do," Shalán replied with another sigh while she mixed the salve into a paste. "Take your tunic off, Lon."

Moving slowly and wincing at the aches, Lon took off his tunic to reveal the familiar discoloration on his skin. Shalán wasted no time in spreading the salve onto his face and body.

"Aron, maybe you should take it a little easier on your son," she said. "He can't endure this amount of abuse every day."

"Then he should learn how to defend himself," Aron responded as he pointed to his scar. "I had to endure twenty-five years of this kind of treatment, including the day I was born. Bodies can take it just fine. It's the mind that's weak. I won't allow my only son to die because he's afraid of a few bumps and bruises."

"Beating your son for an hour every day doesn't sound like an effective way to keep him healthy."

"I'm not trying to keep him healthy," Aron said. "I'm trying to keep him alive."

"Mother," Lon interrupted, "It's all right. I know I don't look like I'm benefiting from Father's help, but what we're doing feels right to me."

"Does this feel right?" Shalán argued as she dug her thumb into one of Lon's deeper bruises.

Lon jerked away and winced in pain. Both he and his father looked at her in shock.

Shalán broke into tears. "It's been so difficult to watch you leave your childhood behind, and now you have a horrible burden to carry. I just wish we knew more about True Sight so we could teach you discipline, rather than beat it into you."

Aron sat beside his wife. "Shalán, I wish there was another way, too, but there isn't."

Shalán leaned her head against Aron's shoulder, still weeping. "I know."

Aron took the salve from Shalán and smeared it over the rest of Lon's bruises. "You can take the rest of the salve upstairs and finish applying it to your legs."

"I'll be all right," Lon replied. "My legs don't hurt much, and I'm not strutting around Pree without pants."

By the time Mellai and Kaylen joined them for dinner, Aron had peeled off the dry mud flakes and removed the rest of the salve with a wet cloth.

"You're a miracle-worker, Shalán." Kaylen said as she reentered the room.

"But it still hurts," Lon said as he slowly sat down at the table.

"You poor baby," Mellai teased. "It was worse the first time."

They ate in silence. The excitement of Lon and Kaylen's engagement the night before was trumped by Lon's condition. The sun was setting outside when they left.

* * * * *

The Song of the Dead would have been sung by a direct male descendent of the deceased, but since Myron had no remaining sons, Lon stepped forward, anxious to fill the role Tarek should have been given.

The memorial was short—no one had much to say about Myron, though many tears were shed. After the song, Lon found himself walking Kaylen home since Scut had to hurry off to tend to his unprotected cattle. With his staff in one hand and Kaylen's hand in the other, Lon paced purposefully, his eyes focused on the horizon ahead.

"You have a beautiful voice," Kaylen said as they walked.

"I'll start on our house tomorrow," Lon changed the subject. "It will be next to your father's property so you can keep an eye on him."

"It's all really strange, isn't it?" she said. "Five years ago, I thought I was doomed to marry Braedr, but then your family moved in and I gained a new best friend and you—the man I love more than anything else in this world. I know we've been courting for three years, but now that we're getting married it all feels surreal. You're building us our own house, and as soon as you finish, we'll be married. Isn't it wonderful?"

Lon kissed Kaylen on the top of her head. "If you'd asked me a week ago, I would've completely agreed with you."

Kaylen looked up at Lon. "What do you mean?"

Lon took a deep breath and glanced around to see if anybody was nearby. "My control is getting worse, Kaylen," he whispered. "True Sight hurt me really badly today, enough that my father had to knock me out to stop my screaming. If I can't learn to stop it, it could kill me. My parents are doing everything they can to help me, but I don't know if anything will work. I love you, Kaylen—more than I can explain—but how can I justify bringing you into a relationship that's sure to end in tragedy?"

"I told you before," Kaylen answered softly, "I'll always be here for you and you can't convince me otherwise. Let's just take this one day at a time."

"You make it sound so easy."

"You should put more trust in your father. He's had plenty of struggles and impossible obstacles of his own, all of which he overcame. He's the wisest man I know."

Lon walked Kaylen to her front door and gave her a quick kiss, then helped Scut milk the cows, and returned home. He quietly unrolled his bedroll and laid it in front of the flickering embers of the fireplace.

What do you want from me? he silently asked, hoping the Jaeds would hear his plight as he curled up under thick blankets and stared into the fire. *Why me?*

Chapter 9

Solutions

One of the quickest lessons Lon learned was that horses are territorial and love to bite. He was standing next to Dawes while brushing his coat of hair, when Dawes turned his head and nipped at Lon's shoulder. Lon moved out of the way just in time, but the horse still caught his tunic and tore a large hole in it. Shalán smacked Dawes hard on the nose to show her disapproval, which took both Lon and Kaylen by surprise.

"If you want to stop bad behavior in a horse," she counseled, "you have to give immediate punishment. Wait even a few seconds and the horse won't associate the punishment with the behavior. I normally don't approve of such treatment, but Dawes was raised by Rayders. It's probably the only discipline he recognizes. With luck and careful treatment, Dawes will learn to trust you rather than fear you."

It took two weeks, but Shalán's hope finally came to pass. Dawes had grown accustomed to his new home, but much to Kaylen and Mellai's displeasure, he only allowed Shalán and Lon to ride him.

Shalán was first. She brought Dawes's tack from the greenhouse and began rigging Dawes.

"There are two very important things to remember when securing a saddle to your horse," she said as she wrapped the cinch strap of the saddle underneath Dawes, just behind his front legs, and buckled it on the other side of the saddle. "First, make sure to tighten the cinch slowly or else you might startle the horse and get kicked. Second, horses like to fill their lungs with air while you're tightening it, so take your time until you are sure it is snug enough that the saddle won't slip off his back."

After she tightened the strap, Shalán moved to Dawes's left side with her back toward his head and her left hand on the saddle's leather horn. She took a step back with her right leg, and with one quick motion, leaped forward, using her momentum to swing up onto the saddle. Dawes puffed air out of his nose, but he didn't seem to mind the extra weight on his back.

"Do we have to do that every time we get on him?" Mellai asked skeptically.

"No," Shalán answered with a satisfied grin. "I just wanted to see if I could still do it."

"Are you paying attention, Lon? You're next." Kaylen said. "Too bad those other four horses were killed. There would be one for each of us to ride."

Shalán leaned down and adjusted the length of the straps until the stirrups hung just above her feet, then slid her feet inside and took hold of the reins. She made a clicking sound in the back of her mouth and led Dawes slowly around the inside of the corral, testing his response to the reins and the tightness of the saddle. After a short time, she turned Dawes out of the corral and toward the road with the twins and Kaylen close behind.

When they reached the road, Shalán placed her hand on the side of Dawes's neck. "Want to stretch your legs?"

Dawes shifted his hooves and quivered with anticipation as he stared down the open road. Shalán gripped the reins and leaned forward before softly kicking Dawes in his ribs and shouting, "Yah!"

Dawes brought his front legs about a foot off the ground, rising onto his hind legs before sprinting forward. The twins and Kaylen watched in awe as Shalán and Dawes sped down the road. Lon would never have guessed that Shalán could stay on a horse traveling that fast; Dawes's back hovered smoothly over the ground as he galloped down the road and disappeared around a bend.

Lon listened to the soft rumble of Dawes's hooves as the sound faded into the low rumble of a waterfall. His mind shifted back to his encounter with the Rayder. Lon trembled at the mental image of the Rayder bearing down on his sister while on the back of Dawes. Before he realized what was happening, his thoughts overwhelmed him and True Sight filled his vision for the first time in two weeks.

"Oh, no," he said as he dropped to one knee.

"Not again," Mellai said. "Kaylen, do something before he kills himself!"

Kaylen kneeled in front of Lon, took his face in her hands and looked into his eyes. "Relax, Lon. No one's in danger. Our life is wonderful. Relax."

Lon shuddered, the haze began to fade, and Kaylen's face became clear again.

"What happened?" Mellai asked. "Your mind completely switched from ecstatic to panic in a second."

Lon stood and wrapped his arms around Kaylen. "That sound reminded me of your near-death encounter with the Rayder."

Shalán soon returned with Dawes at a calm trot. Her face was flushed and she was smiling brightly.

"All right, Lon," she said as she slid off the horse. "Now that he's worked off some of his excitement, it should be safe enough for you to ride him."

"I don't think that's a good idea," Lon countered; he explained what happened while she was gone.

Shalán's lips tightened. "Dawes is no longer a Rayder horse. You've already earned his trust. Now climb up there and stop whining."

"How?"

"Put your left foot in the stirrup and pull yourself up into the saddle by the horn."

It was awkward, but Lon succeeded. "This could be really dangerous for a man," he said as he eyed the large saddle horn in front of his pelvis. "This thing looks like a painful accident waiting to happen."

"Grow up, Lon," Mellai said. Kaylen only blushed.

"That horn should be the least of your worries," Shalán said as she untied the lead rope and attached it to the bridle. "Don't worry, though. We'll take it slow until you learn how to control your movements and keep yourself in the saddle."

Shalán walked down the road with the rope in her hand with Dawes following casually behind her.

"I feel like a kid on a donkey ride," Lon said impatiently.

"Dawes is no donkey," Shalán replied, "but if you insist, we'll try to move forward quicker. Take hold of the reins in your left hand and hold them so they're just barely hanging from the bridle. You don't want to pull back on Dawes's head or he might get mad and buck you off."

Lon did what Shalán asked. "I'm not completely ignorant, Mother. I've ridden a donkey before."

"Stop comparing him to a donkey. Dawes is a trained warhorse, Lon. If you're not careful, he'll throw you off and trample you to death. Understand?"

"Yes," Lon said. The thought of a man crushed by his horse disturbed him. He hoped he'd never have to witness such a horrific thing.

"Good," she replied as she tied the loose end of the lead rope to the saddle. "You can try riding him without my help, but be careful and don't do anything foolish. Keep your weight focused on your feet more than your bottom, and place your other hand on the horn to help steady yourself. Now, give him a *very* slight tap on his ribs."

Lon tapped his heels against Dawes, and the horse started walking. Lon pulled the reins to the right and to the left repeatedly to see how Dawes would respond.

"Horses are smart. Dawes knows if you're toying with him. Don't treat him like a brainless farm animal. If you respect him, you'll get respect in return."

* * * * *

After five weeks of following his grueling routine—the house building, the horse training, and sword fighting with his father—Lon realized his taxing schedule was killing him much faster than True Sight seemed to be. His eyes had become dark and sunken, and he was losing weight at a steady rate. He pondered over his predicament for many days until he came up with what he believed to be the best solution.

"I'm going to stop taking the elixir," he told his family during dinner. "I'm not getting enough sleep at night and I can't learn more from Father while I'm taking it. I'll have to stop at some point, and now is as good a time as any."

"Lon," Mellai replied, "are you sure you want to risk it?"

"Maybe Father's training has been enough that I'll be able to control it now. After all, that's why I'm training, right?"

"You're a man now and can make your own decisions," Aron replied, "but if you summon True Sight while we're sparring, I'll knock you out again. I won't risk you harming either of us. If you're willing to accept that, then we'll continue with your training."

Lon set his shoulders. "I accept."

Chapter 10
Failure

L on climbed the hill behind his parents' house feeling alive and excited. His father was in for a big surprise.

"We'll begin with you attacking me," Aron said. "I want to test your speed while you're sober. Don't hold back."

Lon smiled, eager for an opportunity to prove himself, as well as repay the bruises Aron had given him over the previous weeks. He paused for a moment, then unleashed a ruthless combination of attacks as quickly as his body would allow. Aron's eyes narrowed as he concentrated on defending himself. Lon tried every move Aron had taught him, mixing them up in an effort to catch him off guard, but Aron successfully blocked every attack.

He's been holding back before now, Lon thought as he fought, *but he also taught me everything I know about sword fighting. He knows what to expect from me. What if I try something new?*

Lon swung his stick at Aron, which Aron easily blocked. The exchange brought them close enough together that, on an impulse, Lon jabbed his fist at Aron's face. He made solid contact and blood shot out of Aron's nose as he staggered backward. Lon pressed the attack, raining blow after blow down on his father with the stick, until Aron fell onto his back and raised his arms up to protect his head. Realizing what he had done, Lon jumped back and stared at his father, his breath short, his heart racing.

Aron turned onto his side and reached up to feel his broken nose. He held his breath and clenched his jaw, then took hold of his nose and put it back into place with a pop. Lon had seen broken noses set before, but watching his father do it to himself made him squirm.

Aron opened his eyes and looked at his son. "If you're thinking to apologize, don't. You didn't do anything different than what I've been doing to you. I told you not to hold back. Well done."

Lon swelled with pride at his father's approval.

"This nose will take a few minutes to stop bleeding," Aron continued. "I'd like to take a short break from sparring."

Lon sat in the dirt next to his father. "Do you need me to get Mother?"

"I'm fine," Aron replied. "That punch was well-executed, Son. Obviously your head has cleared and allowed you a bit of improvisation. Had I been a true enemy, I'd be dead and you'd be walking away with your choice of plunder."

Lon frowned at his father's suggestion. "I'll never kill anyone again. I'll never steal anything off a dead body, either. I'm not training to murder or pirate, Father. I'm training to control myself and protect our family."

Aron stared at his son. "I hope not, Son, but life loves to throw dirt clods in your face. As a Beholder, you can count on running into a kill-or-be-killed situation. You need to be prepared to act because, when that time comes, there won't be any time to think about it."

Lon sat quietly contemplating his father's counsel until Aron was sure his nose had stopped bleeding. They picked up their sticks and faced each other again.

"You've proven your skill and speed," Aron told his son, "but now I'm going to fight back, so you'll need to strategize."

The two of them engaged each other again. They moved across the small clearing, but neither one could gain the advantage over the other. Lon felt himself tiring, but he didn't stop the match.

"C'mon, Lon," Aron shouted as they fought, "I'm an old man. You should've bested me by now. Don't tell me this is your very best."

Lon felt his frustration rise at his father's taunts. He tried to outwit Aron, but was unsuccessful in every attempt.

"It looks like you're getting tired," Aron added to his previous remark. "Do you need a minute to catch your breath?"

Lon's anger flared and he threw himself at Aron without reservation. Their sticks cracked, but Lon was still unable to best his father. He growled in frustration at Aron's smiling face and his vision began to blur.

Aron saw his son's eyes cloud. In a flash, he disarmed Lon and flung a handful of white powder in Lon's face. Lon coughed, collapsing to the ground.

*   *   *   *   *

Lon found himself lying on his back and staring up at the darkening sky, a familiar metallic taste suffusing his mouth. He blinked his heavy eyelids and glanced around the clearing. The two training sticks were broken in half and strewn on the ground. His father was nowhere to be seen, but Mellai sat nearby handling a wet cloth.

Lon licked his dry mouth, then forced himself to sit up and face his sister. "Where did you come from?"

"Mother sent me to check on you," she said quietly, "and wipe the remaining powder off your face."

"What was that stuff?"

"I don't know."

"Where's Father?"

Mellai only shrugged and looked toward their house. Lon pushed himself to his feet and staggered down the hill while Mellai followed close behind.

When he approached their house, Lon heard raised voices. He quickened his steps, thinking his parents were in trouble, but his fears proved baseless.

". . . won't make a bit of difference," Aron shouted. "I've been working and training him for five weeks, and the very first time he goes without your potion he summons his power. That boy hasn't learned a single thing. It's all been a waste of time."

"Even if that were true," Shalán retorted, "that doesn't justify your leaving him on that hillside by himself. I made that powder as a precaution, but it's dangerous. You should've cleaned it off, at the very least. He could have stopped breathing, Aron, or become prey to the wild animals prowling out there. What you did wasn't just irresponsible, it was inexcusable."

Mellai started crying. "I've never heard them shout at each other before," she whispered. "It frightens me."

Lon nodded and put his arm around his sister. "Me too, Mel. I don't know what to do. Should we interrupt them?"

"No. They didn't start shouting until after they sent me away to find you. Mother would be horrified if she knew we were listening."

"It makes you wonder how often this happens."

Mellai wiped her tears away with her apron. "I'm proud of you, you know? You've been so overwhelmed lately, with all your new responsibilities that I think you've forgotten about our connection. I've felt how difficult the past few weeks have been for you, but you haven't complained at all."

"It hasn't been easy," Lon replied, "but how could I give up? I'm doing this all for Kaylen, and we both know she'd never give up on me."

"Just remember you're no good to her dead. Don't push yourself too hard, Lon."

"She told me the same thing today. I guess I didn't listen very well, did I?"

*   *   *   *   *

That night's sleep seemed to brighten everyone's spirits. Lon slept better and felt refreshed for the first time in more than a month. On their walk to Scut's farm the next morning, Aron congratulated Lon on his advanced skill with the sword.

"Obviously, not good enough for you," Lon replied awkwardly. "It only took you a second to disarm me."

"There's a big difference between sparring and real fighting," Aron replied. "There are certain combinations you can make with the sword that are called kill strokes. You saw part of one of them last night. They are extremely effective and lethal, but I won't teach them to you. I don't want you accidentally breaking my neck because you're frustrated you can't hit me."

"Actually, I didn't *see* the kill stroke at all. I just felt my stick fly from my hands, and the next thing I knew, I was choking on that powder you threw in my face. What was that stuff?"

"It's a sedative your mother invented when we were first married. She used to give it to me to help me sleep, but in a lighter dose. What I threw in your face was undiluted."

"I noticed," Lon replied, then stopped and stared at his father. "Wait a minute. If she's known about the powder this whole time, why hasn't she given any to me to help me sleep? I've been exhausted."

"Because it's not compatible with the elixir you were taking. If you combine the two, they become lethal, but it doesn't really matter. Hopefully you won't need either of them anymore."

"Not likely," Lon grumbled as they started walking again.

"I wasn't just testing your skill with the sword last night, Lon. I was also testing your self-control. That's why I kept taunting you. I wanted to see if you could stay calm even during the most stressful circumstances. You let me get to you, and it provoked True Sight."

Lon took a moment to respond. "I'm sorry I've wasted your time."

Aron stopped walking and looked at his son. "You heard my conversation with your mother last night?"

"I'd hardly call it a conversation, but yes, we both did."

Aron shook his head. "I was frustrated and concerned for your safety, Lon. We can continue with your training tonight if you wish, but I won't handle the situation any differently if I see your eyes cloud over."

"I'd like to continue training."

Lon spent the rest of the day following his usual routine and reminding himself to stay calm, regardless of how frustrated or angry he got. During their sparring session that evening, Lon lasted about twenty minutes before Aron hit him in the face, causing him to spiral into True Sight. Again, it took Aron less than a second to disarm him.

The same pattern haunted Lon for the next week. He maintained total control over himself during every skirmish until Aron hit him hard enough to cause severe pain, after which he'd invariably lost control. Lon's head began to ache constantly, although he didn't know if it was the affect of True Sight or the white powder. The jarring strokes of the axe as he felled trees sent agonizing jolts through his head, so building his house became an impossible chore.

During one fight in which Kaylen had insisted she attend to provide Lon with whatever support he might need, Lon found himself trying too hard to impress Kaylen, leaving an easy opening for Aron to strike him across his back. Lon dropped onto his hands and knees in pain, squeezing his eyes shut in a desperate effort to control himself. He succeeded at overcoming the pain, but was concentrating so hard that the effort itself summoned True Sight. He didn't need to open his eyes to recognize its uncanny effects. Lon growled, disgusted that he had failed again, but it occurred to him that Aron couldn't see his eyes—and therefore didn't know.

Lon kept his eyes shut and attempted to eradicate True Sight. When that failed, he glanced at Kaylen, hoping she would give him the strength he needed. She was sitting on a log opposite Aron. The haze that obscured Lon's vision had spread from the air into the surrounding terrain. Trees and plants glowed with energy that bled into the soil and rocks. Everything was glowing.

Kaylen gasped, and Aron immediately reacted, rushing at Lon.

Lon looked up at his father, threw his hand forward and shouted, "Stop!"

A cloud of energy puffed from Lon's hand like hot breath on a cold morning. It surrounded Aron and solidified, stopping him mid-stride. Aron's eyes narrowed and his face turned red, but he was completely immobilized. Lon laughed aloud with excitement. He had discovered a new avenue to channel his power! He pondered the possibilities that would be available to him if only he could harness it.

"Lon," Kaylen screamed, "you're killing him!"

Lon realized Aron's eyes were unfocused and the expression on his face blank. The concentrated barrier encasing his father's glowing form was cutting off his supply of air. Aron couldn't breathe.

Lon leaped to his feet and tried to pull Aron free, but the energy barrier held his father firmly in place. Although Lon's vision was still hazy, he was unable to control the energy. As he yanked on his father's arm, the dirt underneath Aron's planted foot began winding itself up and around Aron's leg like a vine—hardening as it grew.

"What are you doing?" Kaylen screamed as the dirt neared Aron's knee.

"I'm not doing it on purpose," Lon shouted frantically. "I have no control over this!"

Kaylen ran up and pulled on Aron's other arm. "Do something!"

Lon knew the situation was getting desperate. If something weren't done quickly, his father would die.

"Knock me out!"

"What?"

"Don't argue with me, Kaylen! Hit me over the head and knock me out now or I'm going to kill my Father!"

Kaylen let go of Aron and picked up Lon's stick from the ground. "I'm so sorry."

A sharp pain racked the back of Lon's skull; bright lights flashed in his eyes and he collapsed into the dirt.

Chapter 11

Despair

Lon awoke to the same circumstance as the night Myron died. He was in the same upper room of their house with a similar glow coming from the cooling embers of the fireplace. He glanced at the bed next to him and thought he saw Myron's still form under the covers.

Lon blinked and stared at the ceiling. He was weak—a feeling he was getting rather accustomed to—but more than anything, his body screamed for water. His tongue felt fat and dry, enough that he thought he might have to peel it off the roof of his mouth. He leaned over, grabbed the pitcher of water off the nightstand, and guzzled from it in deep gulps.

"Why am I so thirsty?" he said aloud as he leaned back against his pillow.

"Because you've been unconscious for more than a day," Mellai responded groggily from the other bed. She pulled her blanket aside, sat herself at Lon's side and handed him a small loaf of bread. "You should eat something, too."

"Over a day?" Lon whispered as he ate. "I didn't think Kaylen could hit that hard."

"She didn't have to, Lon. You passed out before she had a chance to hit you. I'm kind of glad you did it on your own. Father was in real trouble, and we both know Kaylen wouldn't have gone through with it."

"Is he all right?" Lon said as he tried to sit up, causing a surge of pain that coursed through his body.

"He's . . . recovering," Mellai answered quietly. "According to Kaylen, Father dropped to the ground as soon as you passed out."

"And?"

Mellai frowned at her brother. "The lower half of his left leg was trapped. When Father fell forward, his weight put a lot of strain on his knee before the dirt finally broke apart. He's going to have a bad limp for a really long time. Father's been in a lot of pain and Mother's been up taking care of him. They haven't slept much, which is why I'm sitting here talking to you instead of telling them you're awake."

"But he's alive?" Lon broke into tears. "I thought I'd killed him."

"So did Kaylen. I had felt something was terribly wrong. I was on my way up the hill when I heard her screaming for help. There really wasn't much I could've done to save him, but Father is stubborn. He was still breathing when I arrived. I forced Kaylen to leave you there and help me drag Father down the hill to our house. After we helped Mother put Father on their bed, we climbed up the hill again to get you. You know, it wasn't easy carrying you up here. I don't know why Mother wanted the healing rooms upstairs."

Lon's face twisted in agony as tears ran down his cheeks. "What kind of a son am I, Mellai? I suffocated Father to the edge of death. I wish I would just die. I'm not gaining any control, and every time I use this power, somebody gets hurt. How far does it have to go? How long until I kill someone?"

Mellai looked at her twin, her features drawn in concern. "Lon, you only reacted to an impossible situation. You didn't mean to injure him and you realized your mistake as soon as it happened. Besides, Father knew the risks when he decided to train you."

"I deserve death."

"You almost got it. Our connection was severed. For the first time I can remember, I felt nothing from you, Lon. Our bond wasn't restored until you just woke up. You were in as bad of a shape as Father—unconscious and barely alive."

"Is Father awake?"

"I doubt he's awake right now. It's the middle of the night. He did regain consciousness though, if that's what you're asking, after we put him in bed and Mother started working on his knee."

"Where's Kaylen?"

"Mother sent her home last night. She looked like a kicked puppy."

"She could've stayed." Lon said. "I wish she'd stayed."

"Scut doesn't know about your . . . condition. He wouldn't understand or allow her to spend the night. Kaylen had to lie to him about why you and Father didn't help milk the cows yesterday."

"What did she say?"

"You both got sick and Mother wouldn't allow anyone around you or let you leave. Don't worry though, Lon, I'll get her for you first thing in the morning."

Lon turned his head toward the dying glow of the fireplace and wondered how long it would be before he met his own death. When his eyelids became too heavy to fight, he drifted back to sleep.

✳ ✳ ✳ ✳ ✳

Lon inhaled the crisp morning air and welcomed the thick gray clouds hovering low in the sky. He was glad to be free of the house and wouldn't allow a potential snowstorm to darken his mood. As he neared Scut's fields, he caught sight of a dark figure outside his unfinished log house. He crept toward his house, expecting to find Braedr sabotaging it, but it was Kaylen. She was crouched outside the house, daubing the gaps between the logs with mud.

Lon stared at his betrothed with horror. His anger flared to see her performing such a dishonorable act and he ran to stop her.

"What are you doing?" he demanded in a hoarse whisper.

Kaylen gasped as she dropped the mud from her hand and fell against the house. When she saw it was Lon, her face showed both excitement and fear.

"Lon," she finally squeaked, "you're awake. I was afraid—"

"Answer my question," Lon cut in, struggling to keep his voice down. "What are you doing?"

Kaylen's breath caught in her throat and she was unable to respond. Tears flowed from her eyes.

"Are you working on my house? Of all the devious, insulting things you could ever do, you chose this?"

"Lon, please—"

Lon kicked a rock at the house. "I've been working like a mule the last six weeks! I've sacrificed everything, including my health. But what's the point when you don't even believe I can build a simple house? I might as well just tear it down and set it on fire. If any of the villagers found out what you've been doing—"

"They won't find out," Kaylen cried. "Lon, please. I was only trying to help you."

"Trying to help me?" Lon growled as his face turned red. "How is humiliating your future husband helpful?"

Lon's anger continued to build. He didn't care what her reasons were for doing it. He felt an all-around failure.

"If you can't trust me, if you have no confidence in me, where does that leave us? What hope do we have?"

True Sight filled Lon's vision as he finished speaking. He stood there clenching and unclenching his fists as energy continued to fill his vision. When Kaylen's glowing figure rushed forward and reached out to take his hand, Lon stepped back and jabbed his finger at her.

A blast of energy shot from Lon's fingertip and hit the side of the log house. Wood splintered as the building tilted sideways and crumbled to the ground with Kaylen caught in the destructive wave of energy. She flew through the air and hit one of the falling logs, dropping to the ground, motionless amidst the debris.

When Lon saw what he had done, his concern for her overpowered True Sight. The energy immediately vanished and he hurried to her side. She was still breathing, but her eyes were shut in a forced slumber and Lon couldn't wake her. He picked her up and carried her toward her home as Scut rushed to meet them halfway.

"I'm sorry, Scut," Lon said. "She was sitting next to our house and it collapsed over the top of her. I shouted for her to get out of the way, but it was too late."

Scut took his daughter from Lon. "Fetch your mother. Go!"

Lon turned and sprinted down the road as fast as his legs would carry him. When he reached his parents' house, he burst in and shouted for his mother. Shalán and Mellai ran out of their rooms in a panic.

"What's wrong?" Shalán asked.

"Kaylen's hurt . . . our house collapsed on her . . . she needs your help," Lon said between gasps for air. "She's at Scut's house."

Shalán eyed her son carefully, then returned to her room to change clothes. Lon heard her talking to Aron, but he couldn't understand what they said.

Mellai looked at Lon knowingly, but she didn't speak.

"Please, Mel," Lon pleaded. "Go with Mother. Tell Kaylen I'm sorry. I'm so sorry."

Mellai nodded and returned to her room while Lon stood in the doorway with his shoulders slumped. He stepped out of the way of his mother and sister when they left and closed the door.

"Come here, Lon," Aron called from the bedroom.

Lon took a deep breath and moped into his father's room.

Aron was lying on his back with his left leg elevated by a large quilt. His entire leg was wrapped tightly with linen, including the swollen knee. Lon winced, not only because he had caused the injury, but also from how helpless his father appeared.

"It's not as bad as it looks," Aron told him. "Your mother just wrapped my whole leg to keep the swelling down. The only injury is to the knee and I'm sure it will repair itself soon. I'll be back on my feet in no time."

"What do you need, Father?" Lon asked without emotion.

"I'd like to talk to you. Sit down, Son."

Lon sat stiffly on the edge of his parents' bed and looked at his father with a blank stare.

"What happened this morning?" Aron asked.

Lon clenched his jaw and looked away, too ashamed to tell his father what he had done.

"Take your time, Lon, and stay calm. I don't want you to lose control and bring the house down on top of us."

"That's just it," Lon said. Even to him, his voice sounded hollow and dead. "That's exactly what I did to Kaylen, the only person who's been able to keep me calm. I crushed her."

Lon sobbed until tears ceased to form in his eyes. His body shook with torrents of emotion.

"I need you to be more specific," Aron said when Lon quieted down.

Lon wrapped his arms around his stomach and rocked back and forth on the bed. "I lost control. She was only trying to help, but I didn't care. I lost control."

Aron said nothing.

"I found her daubing our house this morning," Lon continued. "I was so obsessed with my own pride that I refused to see reason. She tried to explain why she did it, but I didn't want to hear. I was so angry with her."

"With her?" Aron asked. "Or with yourself?"

Lon pondered the question. "Probably both. I've spent the past six weeks trying to prove my independence to everyone, but I always fall short. Kaylen couldn't even let me do the one thing I thought I was still capable of accomplishing by myself. I can't even build a house."

"What happened?"

"I summoned True Sight, Father, and knocked down the house. Kaylen tried to stop me, but she got caught in the blast."

"Did Scut see what happened?"

"I know he at least saw the house collapse from his field, but why does it matter? I've destroyed my life."

"That's exactly what I want to talk to you about, but not until you pull yourself out of your mud mind and start thinking clearly. If you won't listen to reason and speak rationally, I'm not going to try to help you."

Tears appeared in Lon's eyes again. "Do you really think that anything you tell me will help? We've tried everything, Father. What else is there?"

Aron stared at Lon, his face unreadable. It usually angered Lon that his father could remain so calm, but Lon was emotionally exhausted. He slumped and stared wearily at his father's injured knee. "I'm listening."

Aron shifted his weight forward and asked Lon to place another pillow behind his back so he could sit up. Lon helped him and returned to his spot at the foot of the bed, then Aron took a deep breath and let it out slowly before speaking.

"Lon, you're a grown man and I won't coddle you. Your situation is grave. Like you said, we've tried everything to help you, but without success. The truth is, there's nothing we can do, Lon. If you remain here in Pree and things continue as they have, you're likely going to hurt more people. You'll be lucky to live to see the spring. Your mother and I don't know much about Beholders, but we both recognize a doomed man when we see one."

Lon tasted bile, but swallowed hard to control his stomach as he repeated the key points of Aron's comments. "I'm a doomed man . . . there's nothing you can do for me . . . more people will get hurt . . . I'll die before I have a chance to raise a family."

"Those are the facts, Son."

Lon was getting used to the idea that he was going to die soon, but he didn't want to hurt anybody else. "Father, I have to leave. It's the only way everyone will be safe—especially Kaylen. I have to leave."

"A few bruises and a destroyed house won't change the way Kaylen feels about you."

"You weren't there," Lon countered. "You didn't see the way I yelled at her—the way I treated her. She'll never speak to me again, and I don't blame her for it."

"It sounds to me like you are the one who plans on never seeing her again."

Lon shrugged. "I wish the Jaeds would come and teach me how to control True Sight. I don't understand why they're ignoring me."

"I told you before that I believe Jaeds are only concerned with keeping the world's energy in balance. You must not be a notable threat."

"If no one can help me . . ." Lon started.

Aron shifted his body on the bed. "I said we can't help you, Lon. *We* doesn't include everybody."

Lon furrowed his brow and looked up at his father. "What do you mean? Where else can I find help?"

"Aside from the unlikely intervention of a Jaed, there is still one more option." Aron pushed himself forward and placed his hand on Lon's shoulder. "If anyone can help you, it would be the Rayders."

Chapter 12

Separation

"What?" Lon gasped as he pulled away from Aron. "Are you insane?"

"Give me a minute to explain."

"You already have. Rayders are our enemies, Father, remember? They won't help me—they can't help me."

"Lon, I—"

"Did Mother drug you? You're not thinking straight."

Aron slapped his hand down on the bed. "Do not demean me, Lon. I am your father."

Lon recoiled and resumed staring at Aron's injured knee.

Aron sat back against the pillows. "Most of the Rayders will probably know just as little as I do about Beholders. I'm talking about one Rayder in particular—a man named Omar Brickeden. He was a very close friend of mine and a respected Rayder scholar, which is important because the history of the Rayders is intertwined with the Beholders. If any living person can help you, it's him."

Lon took a deep breath and let it out slowly. He had a thousand reservations about his father's idea, but he knew he wouldn't be able to speak without offending him even more.

"This is the way I see it," Aron continued. "No matter where you end up, you're going to hurt the people around you before you die. Why not go to a place where hurting people can be put to the most advantage? There's always the possibility that you will learn how to control True

Sight, but if not, the only people you can hurt are the Rayders. If they kill you, you'll finally be free from your burden. There's no better way."

"And what about all of the hundreds of things that could go wrong with your plan, Father?"

"Unfortunately, there are no perfect plans in life that bring only good. You have to take the bad with the good. The most dangerous risk of living with the Rayders is that they might discover you're a Beholder. You'll be forced into the center of their politics. They'll view you as a weapon to be used against King Drogan. There's also the chance that Omar won't want to help you. He and I were very close, but my choice to leave was a disgrace. Also, the only way for you to contact Omar is to become a Rayder yourself. You'll have to be branded with the King's Cross and live as one of them."

Lon looked at his father. "How's your suggestion better than death?"

"Because you'll be doing it for Kaylen. If you succeed and learn how to control your power, then you can leave the Rayders, as I did, and return to Kaylen. The Rayders will hunt you, yes, but they'd have a hard time killing you with True Sight as your ally."

"Kaylen doesn't want me," Lon said as he stared at the floor.

"Stop moping," Aron snapped. "Lon, I can't tell you how many foolish things I've done that I thought would drive your mother away, but they didn't. Kaylen loves you fiercely and she understands what you're fighting. If what you say is true, that her injury was an accident, you don't need to worry. Give Kaylen some credit. After all, your mother forgave me for being a Rayder."

Lon stood and wandered to the open bedroom door. He placed his hand on the handle and let his head fall, then closed his eyes and took a long, slow breath. Aron watched him, waiting for his decision.

"All right, Father, tell me what to do."

✳   ✳   ✳   ✳   ✳

Shalán and Mellai hurried toward Pree. They staggered at the sight of Lon's collapsed log house, but continued past it to the Shaw house. Scut was standing in the doorway waving his long arms at them.

"In here, Shalán. Hurry!"

The two women followed Scut through his house and into Kaylen's room. She was lying on her bed breathing steadily, her eyes closed. Mellai sat down next to Kaylen while Shalán escorted Scut out the front door of the house.

"To maintain your daughter's privacy," she said before closing the door and returning to Kaylen's room.

"All right, Kaylen," Shalán said as she walked toward the bed, "tell us where you're hurt."

Kaylen sobbed and moved her hand over her heart. "Right here. How did you know I was awake?"

Shalán sat next to Mellai and took Kaylen's hand. "I've had plenty of experience with unconscious people, particularly during the last couple months. I don't blame you for pretending, though, especially since your father doesn't know Lon is a Beholder. Now let's hear it."

Kaylen put her head on Mellai's lap. "Lon was so angry with me . . . I didn't mean to hurt him. I just wanted to help."

Shalán gave Kaylen's hand a loving squeeze. "Take your time, dear. There's no hurry."

Kaylen wailed with renewed fervor.

Mellai shot Shalán an annoyed glance. "She'll cry forever if you allow her to, Mother. Come on, Kaylen, control yourself. We need to hear what happened." She shook her head as Kaylen hiccupped through her nose in an effort to stop crying.

Shalán looked at her daughter reprovingly before speaking gently to Kaylen. "What did you do?"

"I . . . I . . . I was working on the house."

Mellai and Shalán looked at each other in alarm. They both knew the traditions of Pree. As Lon's betrothed, Kaylen's choice to help with the house was the ultimate dishonor.

"What happened?" Mellai asked.

"He caught me . . . I tried to explain, but he was so angry. I couldn't calm him down."

"Did he hit you?"

Kaylen immediately responded. "Lon would never hurt me on purpose."

"What happened then?" Mellai asked impatiently.

"He summoned . . . it. I tried to calm him down, but he pointed at me and I was thrown against our house."

"Are you hurt," Shalán asked, "physically?"

"I have a headache and my back is sore."

"Sit up, let me take a look."

Kaylen leaned forward so Shalán could unfasten her dress.

"Oh, my," Shalán whispered after opening Kaylen's chemise to inspect her back.

Mellai leaned over and gasped at what she saw. The skin on Kaylen's back—usually smooth and flawless—was bright red and covered in light scratches. One spot just below her shoulder blade was deeply bruised and bleeding.

"Mellai, please heat me some water to make a salve," Shalán said.

Mellai leaped from the bed. "Kaylen, don't you dare feel bad for what you did this morning. If anyone needs to apologize, it's Lon. There's no excuse for what he did."

* * * * *

Aron shifted his weight again. *There's so much to tell him and there's no easy way to do this,* he thought as he watched his son.

"Lon, I know you're not a Rayder, but if you plan on joining them, I need to teach you how to act like one. It's best if I'm straight forward and don't soften anything. You have come of age and can make your own decisions, but right now you must let go of your pride and listen to me. Can you?"

Lon nodded, so Aron continued. "The most important thing you can do as a Rayder is follow orders. Rayders expect nothing less than perfect loyalty, and their punishments for violations of that loyalty are swift and severe. When you contact Omar, it must be done with careful discretion. If anyone thinks your behavior is suspicious, you'll endanger both of your lives. Perfect loyalty, Lon—that's your first and most important lesson. Do you understand?"

"Yes, Father."

"The next thing you need to know is that Rayders aren't nearly as ruthless and savage as our king make them to be. They're brutal and misguided, but there's a strong political hierarchy in the Exile. The Rayder commander, Rayben Goldhawk, functions as their king—and with just as much power. When he gives an order, it's considered law. If you disobey him, you are committing treason. He'll be the one who brands you with the King's Cross and swears you to loyalty. That's why the punishment for defecting from the Rayders is death. It's a violation of a personal commitment directly to their commander."

"Was Rayben the commander when you left?"

"Yes," Aron replied. "His name is used by the Rayders to create fear in Appernysians, and rightly so. He's not a man you want to trifle with."

Lon nodded, staring at the floor.

Aron sighed. "I don't want to discourage you, Lon. You just have to realize the significance of joining yourself with them, especially when you intend to desert them later."

"I understand."

"Good. Now, don't expect to find lean-to tents surrounding open fire pits in the Exile. The Rayders have had more than a thousand years to build up their territory. They have organized communities that are connected by a long road system. They've also built a large fortress city named Flagheim at the north end of their land.

"If circumstances haven't changed in the last twenty years, it's in Flagheim that you'll find Omar. He's a good man, Lon, but he's also very passionate about his people's history. Like most Rayders, he believes their banishment has long since paid for their ancestors' crimes. He hates King Drogan just as much as the rest of the Rayders, so you'll need to be sensitive to that."

Aron paused to observe his son. "I understand how you must be feeling, Lon. Our family is loyal to King Drogan. It will be really hard for you to be around so many people who hate him, but there's nothing you can or should do about it. Let them live their lives and you won't have any conflicts with them. If you defend the King, you'll be executed. Understand?"

Lon nodded absently to Aron's question.

Aron sat forward and placed his hand on Lon's shoulder again. "Look at me, Son."

Lon turned his head slowly and looked at his father. He looked emotionally exhausted and Aron could see the pain in his son's eyes.

"Don't be discouraged. I know it sounds overwhelming, but it will only take a moment in the larger scheme of things. Always remember why you're doing this. I know from my own experience with your mother that Kaylen will be your rising sun, offering you both direction and hope for each new day. Her memory will give you the strength you need." Aron paused, to smile at Lon. "It looks like depression doesn't trigger your power. Considering the path you're on, that's something to be extremely grateful for."

"Thanks, Father," Lon said. The corners of his mouth turned slightly upward.

Aron smacked Lon on his arm, then leaned back against the bed. "You need to understand more about the Rayder history in order to integrate into their society. I've given you pieces of information over the years, but let me see if I can tie it all together for you."

"I'd appreciate it. My head's spinning."

Aron laughed. "I know you've heard at least some of this history, but please be patient as I fill in the gaps. Rayders haven't always been called Rayders. They used to be called Taejans in the First Age. Most of them served as the Phoenijan, the elite guard of Appernysia. They were powerful and perfectly loyal to the King. They represented the honor that every Appernysian sought to obtain. From the Taejans came Beholders, wielders of True Sight and lieutenants over the Phoenijan guard. With ghraefs as their companions, Beholders ruled both the land and skies, but they never sought their own ambition. They served the king and selflessly protected Appernysia from the calahein. I often wonder what made the Taejans—and more specifically, the Beholders— so loyal to Appernysia's Kings. I can only assume they gained life-altering insight from the Jaeds. You don't find that sort of loyalty in our kingdom anymore."

"Wait a second," Lon interceded. "You're so caught up in your story that you've forgotten I don't understand half of what you're saying. I've heard of ghraefs and the calahein, but I don't know much about them."

Aron laughed. "I'm sorry for getting carried away like that. I'm no longer a Rayder, but I still love to tell their history."

"Obviously," Lon replied sarcastically.

"There are ghraef statues in Itorea, but I've never been there myself, so I'm not certain what they look like. I've heard they are massive beasts with feathered wings and an armored tail with a unique crystal on its tip. The stories say that real ghraefs were as big as a house and could destroy an entire army with one swipe of their tail. The details are probably embellished, but they still sound like remarkable creatures. Unfortunately, they disappeared at the end of the First Age when the Beholders were destroyed."

Lon lifted a questioning eyebrow. "With what I know now about the power of True Sight—which can't be much compared to what Beholders could do—I have a hard time understanding how the Beholders were destroyed."

"That's a really good point, but let me tell you more about the calahein and then we'll talk about the Beholders. The calahein were a ruthless horde of savage beasts and the bitter enemies of Appernysia. They plagued the northwestern region of the Tamadoras Mountains, and the Phoenijan were constantly battling to keep them out of Appernysia.

That's why the Taejans settled in the northwest of Appernysia—to create a barrier between the calahein and the rest of our kingdom.

"As the story goes—which you've heard many times—the calahein were getting too aggressive and the king was forced to send his army to exterminate them. It was the only way he could ensure the safety of his people. There was a long and ugly battle, during which many ghraefs and Beholders died, but Appernysia was ultimately victorious. The calahein were completely wiped out and their home city, Meridina, was destroyed."

"I've imagined that battle in my mind many times. It would have been amazing to see."

"Perhaps, but victory came at a dire cost. A lot of the Phoenijan died, too, and those who survived felt betrayed because the king honored the Beholders above the rest. A Phoenijan survivor named Bors Rayder was outraged at the disgrace. He rallied most of the remaining Phoenijan against the Beholders. They took the title Rayder and slaughtered any resisting Taejans and almost all of the Beholders and ghraefs."

"But I still don't understand," Lon said. "If the Beholders were so powerful, how were they so easily destroyed?"

"I asked Omar the same question," Aron replied. "He told me the Beholders wouldn't fight back against their fellow Taejans. With the exception of a few who fled, they allowed themselves to be destroyed."

"Why didn't all of the Beholders flee?"

"I don't know. Maybe they felt that if their own people wouldn't accept them, they had no reason left to live."

"And that's why the Rayders were banished."

"Exactly. The king exiled them north of the Zaga Ravine and stripped them of their honor. The role of the Phoenijan was dissolved and the First Age ended."

"What happened to the Beholders who fled?" Lon asked.

"Bors Rayder and his followers were bitter about their banishment. They blamed it on the Beholders. They hunted the remaining Beholders until they were all killed."

"That's a bit of a stretch—blaming their banishment on the Beholders."

"It seems that way, Lon, but we weren't there and don't know the full story. Even so, that was a long time ago. The Rayders believe that, even if they'd deserved banishment at that time, their sentence has long since been served."

"What is King Drogan's position on it?"

"The Rayders are still in the Exile, aren't they?" Aron replied. "That should answer your question. The Kings of Appernysia have probably passed down a similar tale and King Drogan feels just as strongly about his stance toward the Rayders as the Rayders do toward him."

"It sounds like an argument that could be resolved with a short letter and a little humility."

"Rayben Goldhawk and King Drogan are both proud men. They're great leaders, smothered in self-confidence—which is a critical characteristic of a good leader, but such a trait is also their greatest weakness, and often the cause of their own downfall."

"I just don't understand," Lon replied. "An apology seems like such a small thing to sacrifice for acceptance back into Appernysia, especially if the Rayders want it so badly."

"It shouldn't make any difference to you, Lon. You're not going to the Exile to resolve an age-old conflict. Forget their troubles and worry about your own. There are plenty of those for you to deal with."

"Alright."

"That's all I can think to tell you about the Rayders, Son. The rest is up to you."

* * * * *

As they sat together in silence, Lon pondered his father's counsel and mourned over his impending doom. The odds of surviving such an outrageous task were extremely slim, and he knew it. But Lon also knew there were no other options for him besides death. His father was right. If he wanted to spend his life with Kaylen, he would have to become a Rayder.

"When will you leave?" Aron asked.

"Immediately."

Aron's eyes widened. "Are you sure? Don't you want to say goodbye to your mother and sister . . . or Kaylen?"

"No, because they'll try to talk me out of it. I know they'll be angry at me, but leaving now is better than trying to explain myself."

"It's your choice," Aron answered. "I'll explain to them why you left, but I think the truth should be kept from the rest of the village."

"Agreed."

"What should I tell them? What's your excuse for leaving?"

Lon pondered over his father's question for quite some time before answering. "Even if I didn't need to join the Rayders, I probably would've left anyway because of what happened this morning. So, there's your excuse. I'm leaving because I'm ashamed of myself—because I can't build a house properly, but more importantly, because I have hurt the woman I love."

Aron nodded before posing another question. "How will you convince the Rayders to accept you and make you one of them?"

"You know these answers better than I do. Why are you asking me questions instead of giving me advice?"

"Because you are responsible for your own fate now, Master Lon. I can't keep spoon-feeding you after you leave Pree. Now, answer my question."

"I'll take Dawes and the swords of the five dead Rayders with me and return them to their families. They won't be happy to hear the Rayders are dead, but they'll appreciate the closure."

"That was a quick answer," Aron said suspiciously.

"Rayders or not, they're still humans, Father. They deserve to know."

"But they are still Rayders," Aron argued. Lon only shrugged in response, so his father continued. "You'll need a good excuse for having the swords in your possession. The Rayders might suspect you killed their owners. How and where did you find them and the horse?"

Lon thought hard for a minute, chewing on his lip. He didn't want to tell the Rayders where he'd come from—that would just endanger the village. Images of Trev's old maps came to mind and he screwed up his face, trying to remember every last detail.

"I was traveling along the trade route between . . . Réxura and the Perbeisea Forest, and ran into the aftermath of what must have been an ambush on the Rayders. They were all dead, beheaded and pinned to the trees by spears. I've always been sensitive to the Rayders, and the sight of such a merciless slaughter was more than I could handle. I pulled the dead men from the trees and, after unbelting their swords from their sides, I dug a hole and buried the bodies."

"That story would anger Rayben," Aron interceded. "Rayders are always burned. To bury them is to bury all memories of them, and that's considered a disrespectful act. Rayders obsess over their ancestry."

"Then I piled them together and burned—"

"That would dishonor their individuality."

"What else is there?" Lon replied in frustration. "I'll just remove their swords, leave them hanging there, and burn down the trees."

"That will work."

Lon stared at his father. "How can that be acceptable?"

"You honored their sacrifice by leaving them hanging, but also partially avenged their treatment by destroying the trees."

"That makes no sense."

"That's how Rayders think."

Lon shook his head. "Anyway, I immediately left the trade route and headed north in the direction of the Exile with the intent of joining the Rayders. I found Dawes on my way and knew, by the way he acted, that he was part of the Rayder party and had barely escaped his own execution. I calmed him down, named him Dawes, and took him with me on my journey north."

Aron sat forward. "Lon, what if you are ambushed—by Rayders or Appernysians?"

"I'd feel sorry for them," Lon answered without emotion. "I don't handle surprises very well—especially lately—and they'd probably get a little taste of my burden."

"That brings up two major problems. Why is using True Sight out there any less dangerous for you than it's been here? You might incapacitate or kill yourself. Second, what if one of your attackers survived? Your secret would be out. Everyone would know you're a Beholder."

Lon frowned at his father.

"I have a better suggestion for you, Son." Aron grabbed a leather pouch from the nightstand and handed it to Lon. "I don't need my powdered sedative anymore. Take it with you. If you're attacked, heave a handful of that stuff in their faces. They'll be incapacitated while you ride safely away. Only be careful not to throw it into the wind. It's extremely powerful."

"I know," Lon replied dryly and placed the pouch on the opposite side of the bed.

Aron pointed to a shelf in one corner of his room. "Hand me a piece of parchment and I'll draw a map showing you how to enter the Exile without getting caught. I'm glad to see you've already been perusing Trev's maps in the meeting hall. That knowledge will be invaluable to you."

Lon grabbed the parchment and a sliver of charcoal and handed them to his father. Aron sketched a quick map of Appernysia—including villages, cities and other major landmarks. When he was finished he turned the parchment toward Lon and placed the charcoal on a dense forest in the middle of the map.

"Once you reach the Perbeisea Forest, you'll have to be extra careful. Stay off the road and follow this path . . ." He drew a line between cities and watchtowers, through a barren marsh and over the jagged Dialorine Range. Aron looked up at his son. "Make sure to stock up on food and water before you enter the Gaurelic Waste. It's an ugly marshland, uninhabitable by humans and most animals—except for snakes and flies. The southern face of the Dialorine Range is also barren. You'll have to find a place to scale the mountains and cross through to their north side before you'll find any usable sources of water or food."

Lon shook his head. "That's impossible. I'm as good as dead."

"Don't be discouraged, Lon. You'd be surprised how many Rayders have managed to sneak through that area, myself included. And above all else, avoid Rayders on your way into the Exile. They'll kill you without question if they run into you in Appernysia."

"But they'll let me live if they catch me in the Exile?"

"Hopefully."

Lon threw his hands up in frustration and stood to leave.

"Sit down," Aron ordered.

"What?" Lon said as he returned to the bed, facing away from his father.

"You're going to need a lot more conviction than that if you hope to survive this trip. You haven't even started and you're already discouraged. Did you forget your reasons for deciding to do it?"

"No."

"Then stop feeling sorry for yourself and do what needs to be done. Your life depends on it."

Lon nodded as he continued to stare at the bedroom door.

"If you're riding Dawes and traveling quickly, you should be able to pass through the Gaurelic Waste and reach the top of the Dialorine Range within a day. There's vegetation at the base of the northern face."

Aron paused. "Are you paying attention?"

"Yes."

"I hope so. Two days without water, Lon. Don't forget. As long as you keep your head and don't lose your direction, you'll be fine. Dawes has traveled that path at least once, so he should be able to help you find a safe route."

Lon turned and looked at his father without expression. "If I make it to the Exile alive, I'll still have to convince the Rayders I want to join them. After that, I'll need to find Omar—if he's even still there—and *hope* he'll help me. If he does, I'll have to hide my true identity from the Rayders while Omar *tries* to train me, which may prove to be a complete waste of time. If by some miracle I accomplish all of that, I'll have to sneak back into Appernysia and hide for a year while the Rayders try to track me down and kill me for desertion. If I survive that year, I can finally return to Pree and marry Kaylen—if she's not already married to someone else."

"Yes," Aron answered. Lon could see it hurt him to be so blunt.

Lon rose from the bed and scratched at the back of his head as he breathed deeply through his nose. Aron didn't respond, despite Lon's obvious signs of frustration. Lon knew he was going to have to work through this one by himself. He stopped scratching his head and dropped both hands to his sides, taking deep breaths, before turning around to face his father.

"This has got to be the craziest plan I've ever heard and I'm almost certain I will fail," Lon said as he shook his head. "But it's our only plan and I have more than my own selfish reasons for leaving. Tarek Ascennor lives in the Exile, and he needs to know about his family. He needs to know that Myron died honorably."

"The other four Rayder swords are under my side of the bed," Aron said, pride radiating from his face. "There's also a stockpile of rations and other supplies. We learned in Roseiri to be ready to go at a moment's notice. Take the swords and anything else you need. Go, Son, and may the Jaeds watch over you."

As Lon thought of everything he had gained the past few years—respect, friendship, a trade, love—his chest throbbed in pain at losing it all. A tear crept from Lon's eye, but he quickly wiped it away, not wanting to appear any weaker. He rolled up the map, grabbed the swords and a box of packaged food from under the bed, then stood and opened the bedroom door.

"I'm going to leave Mother's pearl necklace on Mellai's bed. After all, it's rightfully Mellai's necklace anyway. I had planned to give Kaylen the necklace when we were married, but if for some reason Mellai decides to give it to her, please make sure Kaylen knows how much I love her."

"I'll pass along your message."

"Thanks, Father. Thank you for everything."

"Eat a hearty meal before you leave," Aron suggested as Lon stepped out of the bedroom and closed the door.

Lon proceeded to gather the necessary supplies for his long journey. An hour later, he left his parents' house with a full stomach and a thick woolen cloak hanging from his shoulders. He carried a bundle on his back stuffed with bread, cheese, and salted pork—as well as his new canvas tarp, hemp rope, leather gloves and extra clothes. One of the Rayder swords was belted to his waist, along with his father's pouch of powdered sedative, and he held the other four swords in his arms. His small one-handed hammer was also tucked into his belt. Lon thought about bringing his staff, but decided to leave it behind because it would be too awkward to carry while riding Dawes. However, he did attach his hunting bow and a quiver of arrows to the outside of his pack.

"It's almost as if the villagers knew I'd need this stuff," Lon had said to himself as he packed. He thought of the Jaeds and wondered if they had somehow influenced the villagers' decisions, but shook his head doubtfully. "Jaeds or not, I'm extremely grateful."

Lon walked to his donkey and tightened the rope, tethering it to the fence. "I'm leaving you and the cart behind for Father and Mother," he said as he patted its neck. "Be good to them."

Lon cut through the forest in the direction of Dawes's corral. When he arrived, Dawes was anxiously prancing around as if he knew what was happening. Lon calmed him and rigged him with his tack, including a whip and saddlebags, which he filled with the contents of his own pack. He used his rope to tie the four extra swords to the saddle between the cantle and skirt, then mounted Dawes. After glancing around to make sure he had everything with him, Lon guided him out of the corral to the road, and followed it north to the trail leading to his parents' property. He stopped there for only a moment before kicking Dawes into a canter.

Lon followed the road until he reached the south bridge, then rode down the embankment and traveled along the northern bank of the river.

If this route was good enough to hide the Rayders, he thought, *it will be good enough to hide me.*

He followed the Klanorean as it wound around the eastern edge of Pree, past the clearing where Aron found the Rayder camp, until the river brought him to the northern edge of the village. He dismounted Dawes and left him at the water's edge while he climbed Mellai's hill to look over the village. He could make out the Ramsey and Wellesly's families busy at work outside their silos. Lon strained his eyes for a last glimpse of Kaylen, knowing it was pointless. He couldn't even see Scut's house on the opposite side of the village.

Lon sighed and bid the village farewell, never expecting to see Pree again. As he rode north, the white flakes of winter's first snowstorm floated down from the sky.

"Perfect," Lon grumbled as he pulled his cloak around his shoulders.

Chapter 13
Fate

L on hugged the forest tree line, knowing that Roseiri was only twenty miles to the south. Although the night was unusually bright, the light of the full moon reflecting off the new-fallen snow, Lon still couldn't see the village through the darkness. He stayed alert, aware he might run across a hunting party trying to stockpile their venison stores before winter deepened.

Lon shook his head. Tracking deer in the snow had its advantages, but it also created more difficulties. The weeklong snowstorm had covered up all tracks and created an unnatural blanket of silence in the woods, making it difficult to sneak up on game. Even if Lon had wanted to hunt, it would have been impossible. Snares and ambushes were the only practical tactics, but both required Lon to remain in one spot—a luxury he couldn't afford.

He checked his saddlebags and sighed at his dwindling stock of food. Making it to the Rayder Exile was proving to be more difficult than he'd anticipated. Even so, Lon relished the sense of freedom he'd developed since leaving Pree. There were no boundaries, no limitations. He could do anything he wanted without fear of his father's disapproval. It was just him and Dawes.

"What do you think, Dawes?" Lon said as he peered into the darkness to his left. "Should we enter the dark, scary forest to find a shallower crossing, or get it over with now?"

Lon's excitement at being out on his own was overpowering. This wasn't the first time during his journey Lon had considered scaling the Vidarien Mountains, and perhaps even exploring the Forest of Blight on the other side. The terrifying rumors about those woods were so fantastical that Lon ached to see it for himself.

Such a rash decision never would have crossed Lon's mind before, but something strange had happened to him since leaving Pree. The burdens weighing him down had transformed into challenges and, in some cases, opportunities. Rather than brooding over his trials, Lon looked forward to conquering them. It was strange how much a change in scenery affected him.

The further he had traveled along the Vidarien Mountains, the more Lon's wanderlust pulled at him. On this occasion, as he contemplated how to cross the West River, his heart raced with excitement. Something in those woods called to him.

Lon clicked his heels against Dawes's sides and pulled his reins to the north. "We'll just take a peek. It won't take long."

Dawes blew out his breath and whinnied.

"Easy," Lon said, stroking Dawes's neck. "What're you trying to do, tell the whole forest we're here?" Dawes shuddered and tried to turn around, but Lon yanked on his reins. "C'mon. Stop fighting me."

Suddenly, Dawes froze. His eyes widened and rolled with fear. Lon turned his attention away from his horse and stared into the darkness. A wave of panic poured down his spine. Something was out there, watching them.

Taking care not to move too quickly, Lon grabbed his bow and strung it. He kept his eyes on the forest, watching for an attack. Once he had an arrow nocked, he wrapped the three first fingers of his left hand around the bowstring. "What's out there, Dawes?"

As if in response, two enormous blue eyes materialized in the darkness. They hovered high above the ground, calm but watchful, outlined by the shadowy figure of a massive beast. Lon's first instinct was to loose an arrow, but he fought the impulse. He only tightened his grip on the drawstring. The creature uttered a rumbling growl.

On an impulse, Lon lifted his hand from the bow. As foolish as it might seem, he believed this creature could be reasoned with. "Hold on a second. I'm just going to put this arrow back. That's all. Nice and slow." The blue eyes narrowed as Lon removed the arrow and returned it to his quiver. "Sorry to bother you," Lon continued, trying to remain calm. "We meant no harm. We're leaving, right, Dawes? No harm done."

Dawes backpedaled until they were bathed again in moonlight. Only then did he dare to turn and wade across the freezing river. Lon, on the other hand, continued to stare at the woods. The hovering eyes had long since disappeared, but Lon still searched for them between the trees. He never saw them again.

Once they had left the West River far behind, Lon finally relaxed and stowed his bow. Euphoria washed over him. "How about that, Dawes?" he said between laughs. "I've never seen anything like that before. Absolutely incredible. I won't forget that anytime soon, that's for sure."

As they continued quietly toward Réxura, Lon couldn't help but wonder if that creature was guarding something. He glanced over his shoulder once more. Was there something he wasn't allowed to see?

Chapter 14

New Horizons

Mellai wrapped her cloak around herself to shut out the cold afternoon air. She walked north along the main road of Pree, her feet crunching in the fresh snow with every step. It had been snowing every day since Lon left. Mellai privately wondered if winter had finally realized it was late and was trying to catch up before the end of November.

Mellai turned off the road and waved to Scut in his fields before pounding on the front door of his house. When nobody answered, she let herself in and slammed the door behind her.

"Are you still in bed?" she growled as she walked through the house.

"Yes," Kaylen whimpered from behind her bedroom door.

Mellai stopped outside her room and took a deep breath before twisting the handle and throwing the door open. "Kaylen, it's been a full week," she boomed. "That's seven days of your life wasted. I've been more than patient, but I've had enough. Get out of bed!"

"Why?" Kaylen asked pitifully as she snuggled the quilt Lon had received from Elora. He'd given it to Kaylen the day after his coming-of-age celebration. "There's no point."

"Yes, there is," Mellai fumed. "Unless you get out of bed and get dressed right now, I'll drag you out in your chemise and throw you into the hog trough."

"You wouldn't dare," Kaylen retorted with wide eyes.

Mellai's lips tightened. "You bet your dowry I will. You're acting like you are the only one who has lost someone, but Lon left me behind, too. I have plenty of my own pent-up frustration that's screaming to be let out."

Kaylen's lips formed a deep frown. She threw off the quilt and started putting on her day clothes. "I'm sorry, Mellai. I've been so wrapped up in my own misery that I never even thought you might be hurting, too."

Mellai bit her bottom lip to keep it from quivering, then turned and stormed out of the house. She slammed the front door shut, stomped through the snow, and leaned her arms and head on the fence. To distract herself, she focused on Lon. Although her sense of him was weakening every day, she could still feel his emotions when she concentrated. It took a moment for her to calm herself enough to allow Lon's feelings through, but all through the previous six days, the only feelings from him were excitement and anticipation.

"Is he really so glad to be away from us?" Mellai spat with disgust.

"He's still enjoying the freedom?" Kaylen said as she walked up and stood beside Mellai.

Mellai turned her head away and blew out a puff of air.

"Well," Kaylen continued as she choked back a sob, "at least it means he's still safe . . . and happy."

Mellai was unable to ignore her best friend's pain. She placed her arm around Kaylen's waist to comfort her. "Yes," she said quietly, "at least he's safe."

"What are we going to do?" Kaylen despaired. "I can't stay in this village without thinking about Lon. Every sight, every smell, every sound—everything reminds me of him. Worst of all, when I walk out the door, I have to stare at that." She pointed a shaking finger at the snow-covered pile of logs that was going to be her home. "How can I expect to move on with my life when I can't stop thinking about him?"

Mellai rolled her eyes. "This is the first time you've walked out your door since he left."

"I know, but do you understand what I mean?"

Mellai nodded.

The two of them stood together, silently watching the village. Aside from a dog playing in the fresh layers of snow in the village square, everybody west of the main road was inside keeping warm. Scut and Nybol were the only other people outside, busily caring for their livestock.

Mellai shivered as she followed the plumes of smoke billowing out of the chimneys. "It's too cold to stand around outside anymore. Let's go in."

"But you just got me outside," Kaylen complained. "I don't want to."

Mellai was about to argue, but something at the south end of the village caught her eye. A large flock of sparrows shot out of the woods surrounding Mellai's home and flew away to the west. Mellai strained her ears to hear the source of their panicked flight, but the thick snow muffled any sound that she might have heard.

"What do you think caused that?" she asked. "If I didn't know better, I'd guess Lon was back and playing around with True Sight."

"Birds only react that way from a large group of travelers," Kaylen replied absently, obviously wishing that Lon was back.

Mellai panicked. "Kaylen, what would travelers be doing in Pree? Nobody ever comes here. It could be Rayders."

Kaylen flinched at the possibility. "What . . . what should we do?"

"We need to warn everybody," Mellai urged.

"But your father said not to."

Mellai blew out her breath. "He isn't right about everything."

"What if it isn't Rayders, though? How will we explain ourselves?"

"Who else could it be?"

A gust of wind carried a chorus of braying donkeys to their ears. Kaylen's worried expression changed to excitement. "Rayders don't ride donkeys. Mellai, it's a caravan!"

*　　*　　*　　*　　*

No trading caravans had come to Pree for seven years. The caravan was a company of ten large, donkey-drawn wagons and fifteen families. Trev invited them to camp in the village square, and they were promptly surrounded by eager villagers.

Although the people of Pree could survive on their own, the trading caravans brought rare items, which couldn't be found in the village. The village women, Mellai and Kaylen included, perused carts full of oils, exotic perfumes, and expensive jewelry, while the men guarded their money purses. Children bombarded the trader of sweets with pleas for free samples—which were all politely declined.

The excitement eventually died down, wives began negotiating with their husbands. After an hour or so, the trading halted while the villagers prepared a feast for the traders. To pass the time, the tradesmen told stories to a captivated audience of children, and the veiled tradeswomen entertained with fast-paced songs and dances.

When the feast was finally prepared, Trev invited everyone into the meeting hall, but the tradesmen refused. They wanted to stay where they could watch their wagons, so the villagers moved the tables out into the snow. The adults ate while the children raced around, hurling snowballs at each other.

Mellai and her parents sat quietly at their own table with Kaylen. Shalán and Aron knew many of the tradesmen from their life in Roseiri and didn't want to draw attention to themselves.

"What news is there in Appernysia?" Trev asked the tradesmen as they ate. "A few of us just returned from Itorea, but everyone was too busy to talk with us."

"That's usually the case with Itoreans," a middle-aged man named Kutad replied. "The truth is, there's so much unrest right now that they were probably afraid you were one of King Drogan's spies."

"Spies?" Scut interceded. "Since when does our king need spies?"

"The Rayders have become more aggressive," Kutad replied. "Sightings have been reported all over the countryside. King Drogan set up patrols to catch them, and it sounds like he's having success. I heard many Rayders have been captured and imprisoned over the past couple of months."

"Do you think the Rayders are plannin' an attack?" Scut asked.

"Maybe," Kutad replied, "but I think the main reason they're here is because of the rumors. People are saying a Beholder is in Appernysia. The Rayders won't stand by and allow a Beholder to live unless he's one of them."

Mellai nodded absently. She had known about the rumors, but now she understood where they started—five years earlier on the night they left Roseiri. She dipped her head, feeling extra worried the tradesmen might recognize her.

Aron, who had recovered enough to leave the house with the aid of a crutch, placed his hand on Shalán's and locked eyes with Mellai and Kaylen. He mouthed the word *patrols* and shook his head. Mellai suddenly understood. Her father hadn't known about the patrols when he gave Lon his instructions, but there was nothing they could do.

"It's about time something was done about the Rayders," Delancy spat. "They're vicious savages who don't care about anyone but themselves. If I were king, I'd send my armies into the Exile and kill them all."

The surrounding villagers and most of the tradesmen agreed with Delancy, except for Kutad, who quietly sipped hot tea from his cup.

"Where do you travel next?" Trev asked the tradesmen.

"We just came from Humsco," Kutad answered. "We'd usually travel straight up to Roseiri from there, but we cut across the valley using the old trade road to visit your village first." He chuckled. "I guess we misjudged the weather. Anyway, Roseiri will be our last stop on the way back to Réxura."

Kutad's news sparked an idea in Mellai's head, but she held her tongue until the meal ended. When the men left to barter over goods while the women cleaned up, Mellai turned to Kaylen. "Let's go with them."

"With who?" Kaylen responded.

"The tradesmen. Let's go with them to Réxura."

In truth, Mellai had no intention of traveling all the way to Réxura. She wanted to see her grandparents, but she couldn't say so without someone in the village overhearing.

"Are you serious?" Kaylen questioned.

"Yes! This morning you told me everything you see makes you miserable, and the only thing about this village that keeps me happy is you. If we go together, neither of us will lose anything."

"That's a little harsh, don't you think?" Braedr said as he sat down at the table in front of them. "Nothing here makes you happy?"

"What do you want, Clawed?" Mellai said, eyeing his scarred face. It had been more than five weeks since their encounter on her hill. Braedr had healed, but deep grooves covered his face—permanent scars of Mellai's ruthless attack.

"Whoa," Braedr replied, "can't I say hello without getting attacked?"

"With you," Mellai continued, "it's never just hello. Go away, Clawed."

"All right, I'll ask. Why do you keep calling me Claude?"

Mellai laughed. "If you're not smart enough to figure it out yourself, you don't deserve to know."

Braedr's lips tightened. "I don't care what it means. Stop calling me that."

"Or what, Clawed?" Mellai sneered. "I'm not afraid of you."

"Maybe you should be," Braedr growled. "You don't have your brother here to step in and protect you anymore. The coward has run away. Don't worry, though. I'll pick up where he left off."

His gaze drifted to Kaylen as he finished speaking. She gasped as Braedr slowly licked his upper lip.

"If you don't leave right now," Mellai spat, "you'll regret it. I swear you'll never leave your house again after I'm done with you."

Braedr gave Mellai a sinister smile. "Your temper is going to get you in trouble, Mellai, along with that naughty mouth of yours. Tsk, tsk. I already told you once to control it."

"How about I help you with yours?" Kaylen shouted as she grabbed a half-empty cup of simmering hot tea off the table and threw it in his face. Mellai also seized the opportunity to flip the table over.

Braedr brought his hands to his face and wailed in a high-pitched scream as the table landed on top of him, burying him in the snow with the leftover food. Silence punctuated the village square. Everyone turned to see what happened.

Braedr crawled out from under the table and stood to face the women. His scarred face was bright red and his steaming clothes were spotted with scraps of food. He clenched his jaw, his eyes darting around, wild with anger. Even though the entire village was looking on, Mellai was suddenly terrified of what he might do.

One of the tradesmen's young daughters broke the silence with a giggle. A few more of the children joined in. Soon, the entire trading caravan was laughing at Braedr.

His pride was broken. Braedr fled from the village square at full speed and disappeared into his house. The tradesmen continued to laugh and a few of them even ventured to thank Mellai and Kaylen for the show. Hans and Ine offered their apologies for their son's behavior and quickly followed him to their house. During all of the excitement, Aron and Shalán continued to sit at their table as if nothing had happened.

Mellai turned to Kaylen. "I've never seen that side of you before."

"I'm just so wound up inside," Kaylen replied, her hands over her face. "I feel bad I let loose on Braedr. Bad things always seem to happen to him."

"It's his own fault," Mellai retorted. "He deserves everything he gets."

Scut was standing nearby and flipped the table back onto its legs. "Kaylen, I won't disagree with Mellai, but you were both still actin' out of line. We all know what he said and saw what he did. He'll get punished for it, but the punishment should be comin' from the village council, not the two of you."

Kaylen merely nodded.

"I hope that blabberin' moron gets a few more scars, treatin' my daughter that way. I oughtta . . ." Scut continued muttering as he walked away.

Mellai and Kaylen began cleaning the food and dishes off of the ground, but Trev interrupted them. "Mellai, may I please speak with you?"

Mellai stood and turned around to face him. "I didn't do anything wrong."

"I'm not here to talk to you about today. Would you please follow me?"

Mellai glanced at Kaylen with concern, then followed Trev as he led her toward Aron and Shalán.

"Master Aron," Trev said when they reached them, "may I please speak with you and your wife?"

Aron agreed and they followed Trev through the meeting hall and into the closed quarters of his house.

"May I offer you some of my wife's tea?" Trev asked.

"Forget the formalities and tell us what you need," Aron said.

"Very well," Trev agreed as he sat in a chair. "Please, sit down."

Once they were seated, Trev continued, "Let me first say, I'm terribly sorry about the disappearance of your son. Have you received any word from him since he left?"

"No," Aron replied, "and I don't expect to, either. He was very discouraged and wouldn't be consoled. That kind of dishonor usually follows a man the rest of his life."

Trev nodded and shifted in his seat. "I'm afraid we're about to lose another man from this village, but before action is taken, I want to verify the facts with you."

"What facts?" Mellai asked.

"Mellai," Aron interjected, "let us talk."

Mellai frowned and glared out the window.

"It's all right," Trev said. "She's actually the one who will have to do most of the talking."

Mellai ignored him and continued to stare out the window.

"Mellai, I need to confirm what happened during your previous encounter with Braedr."

She flinched at Trev's words and turned to look at her parents, but they looked as dumbfounded as she felt.

Mellai stumbled over her words. "I don't know . . . how did you . . . I mean, I . . ."

"One of Ramsey's sons—Tirk, I believe—was watching out for you the night you left Lon's coming-of-age celebration. It's no secret that he has an eye for you, but he's an honorable man and would never do anything to harm you. His intentions were pure."

Mellai nodded absently. She knew Tirk liked her, but she couldn't return his love. There wasn't anything necessarily wrong with him. She just didn't feel that way about him.

Trev continued, "Tirk stopped at the northern edge of his corn field, but when he saw Braedr walk up the road in your direction, he hopped the fence and followed Braedr to your tree. He was about a hundred yards away when Braedr attacked you."

"Attacked you?" Aron blurted out, struggling to stand. If it hadn't been for his knee, Mellai was sure he would have leaped out of his chair. "Mellai, is this true?"

"Yes, Father, but don't worry. He got all the punishment he deserved."

"What did he do to you?" Aron demanded.

Mellai didn't dare refuse to answer. "He insulted me, blocked my path when I tried to run away, then threw me up against the tree. He also covered my mouth so I couldn't scream."

Aron's face burned with rage. "That was over six weeks ago. Why haven't we heard about this before now?"

"Tirk is intimidated by Braedr," Trev replied with a mellow tone, "but what Braedr did to your daughter has been bothering him ever since it happened. Tirk had a long conversation about it with his mother last night and she convinced him to talk to me. He spent the morning telling me all about it."

Trev turned to Mellai. "He also told me what happened after Braedr pinned you against the tree."

"He did?" Mellai asked, worried that Tirk had seen Lon use True Sight.

"Oh, yes. Apparently Lon came looking for you and shouted at Braedr, which gave you a chance to . . . uh . . . incapacitate Braedr with your knee and attack him while he was lying on the ground. Tirk had intended to defend you from Braedr, but apparently his services weren't needed. He said Lon had to stop you from hurting Braedr. Is that correct?"

Mellai breathed out a sigh of relief. "Yes."

"You caused the gouges on his face?" Aron asked.

"Yes, Father, it was me. I had to clean his skin out from under my fingernails on the way back to the party."

Aron eyed his daughter carefully, then sat down again in his chair.

"No need to worry, Mellai," Trev said. "I'm only asking these things to make sure I know everything. I need to lead the village in a fair disciplinary council."

"A council?" Shalán asked.

"I'm afraid so. It's obvious from Braedr's behavior today that he feels no remorse for what he did. Action must be taken."

"When will the council be held?" Aron inquired.

"In two days. I'd like to wait until after the caravan has moved on. The tradesmen are anxious to get back home. They plan to leave tomorrow when all the bartering is done."

"Is that all?" Aron asked impatiently. "I need to get back."

Trev dismissed them and Mellai parted from her parents to search for Kaylen. She found her in the square, surrounded by three of the tradesmen's older sons. When Kaylen saw Mellai, she excused herself and hurried to Mellai's side.

Rather than tease her best friend, Mellai jumped straight into her news. "The village is holding a disciplinary council for Braedr in two days."

"What?"

Mellai quickly recounted her conversation with Trev before continuing, "Kaylen, I don't want to be here for that. The caravan is leaving tomorrow and I plan to go with them. I hope you'll come with me."

"I can't just leave my father behind by himself. Since my mother died, I'm all the family he has left."

"Let's go and ask him. There is no harm in that, is there?"

Without waiting for a response, Mellai left Kaylen and hurried to Scut's farm. Before Kaylen could stop her, she flagged Scut from his barn.

"Mellai," Kaylen pleaded when she caught up to her, "please, don't. Please."

"Hey there, Mellai," Scut said as he reached the fence. "What did Trev want? Was it concernin' your brother?"

Scut never spoke begrudgingly of Lon, despite Lon's offense to his daughter. For her part, Mellai suspected it was only because he didn't want to hurt Kaylen further with his snide comments.

Mellai leaned against the fence. "Braedr is going to be disciplined by the council."

"Ha! There you have it, Kaylen. I told you justice would catch up to him. When's it happenin'?"

"In two days," Mellai replied. "Trev wants to wait until the trading caravan leaves tomorrow before he takes action."

"Smart idea. There's no need to be wrappin' them nice folk up in our politics."

"I'm traveling with them to Réxura."

"That sounds just—" Scut faltered mid-sentence. "Wait now, are you serious? What about your family?"

"I know they'll understand. Ever since my brother left, this village has become a prison for me. I can't stay here anymore."

Scut nodded. "I understand, but are you sure you're not bein' rash? I know you don't know what's happened to your brother, and it'd be hard not to have some kind of closure, but are you really just usin' this as an excuse to go search for him?"

Mellai shrugged. "That's not why I'm leaving. I just need to find a new place where I can look around and enjoy the landscape without thinking of him—somewhere that I can start a new life."

"Makes sense," Scut said. "You can't expect someone to stick around a place that brings 'em nothin' but misery."

Mellai took a deep breath before responding. She chose her words carefully, knowing this would be her only chance.

"I've asked Kaylen to come with me, but she declined because you need her here, Master Scut."

Scut's eyes narrowed. He looked at his daughter with disapproval, but stopped short at the sight of her. Tears streamed down Kaylen's face.

Scut hugged his daughter over the top of the fence. "Go with Mellai. Aron's here every day to help me sort and bundle the feed. His knee's healin' fast, too. Soon he'll start helpin' me milk the cows again. Don't you worry about me, I'll manage here just fine."

"But, Father," Kaylen cried, "I can't leave you all alone."

"The only thing that hurts me worse than you leavin' is seein' you here unhappy," he responded with a forced smile. "I don't know if I've ever told you, but you're lookin' more like your mother every year. If she were here, she'd be wantin' you to go."

Kaylen buried her face into Scut's shoulder while he held her and stroked her hair. Mellai excused herself and walked to her house to talk with her own parents. Just as she had told Scut, she was sure they would let her go. If they had allowed Lon to join the Rayders, they would certainly support her going to Roseiri to live with her grandparents.

Mellai found her parents in the greenhouse packaging herbs they intended to trade. She shared her thoughts with them and was surprised at their reaction.

"We saw this coming a long time ago," Shalán commented as she worked. "You've never been content in Pree. Since your brother left, we knew you'd be close behind him."

"Thank you," Mellai said, overjoyed.

"Hold on," Aron added. "It's not as simple as just traveling to Roseiri and knocking on their door. You can't just show up and expect everything to be normal. Your grandparents don't even know where we've been the past five years. People will want an explanation. Many of them will remember what happened that night. If you return, you could endanger us all, including your grandparents."

Mellai frowned. "I didn't think of that. I suppose I could wear a veil like the rest of the tradeswomen, then only reveal myself to Grandmother and Grandfather. If they're angry and don't want me to stay, Kaylen and I will just continue with the caravan to Réxura."

"What if they do want you to stay?" Shalán asked. "Will you just hide in their house for the rest of your life?"

"Maybe, but they live at the northern edge of the village, so I could still help them outside without being recognized."

"Please be extra careful," Aron said. "Don't forget you're our only daughter. I also hope you'll find a way to let us know how you're doing, along with Lon's general state of mind. You're our only link to him. At least, we'll know he's alive."

"I promise to send word whenever I can."

Aron picked up their packaged supplies and hobbled to the door. "I'm taking the cart back to the square. I still have a couple of trades to finalize with Kutad. I'll talk with him and arrange for you and Kaylen to travel with their caravan tomorrow morning. Kutad and I were friends, so I'm sure he'll agree. Stay close to him while you're traveling, Mellai. The first year he came to Roseiri with the caravan, Kutad shared a good portion of his past with me. I see a lot of myself in him and I trust him completely. I know he'll keep you safe."

"Was he a Rayder?" Mellai asked.

"No, but he's had a lot of his own trials to work through. I admire him."

"What trials?"

Aron ignored her question and disappeared through the door.

Mellai blew out her breath. "Well, at least I'm used to living with people who have secrets."

Shalán smiled as she embraced Mellai and kissed her on the cheek. "We're all finished here. Come on. Let's go back to the house and I'll help you pack your things."

*　　*　　*　　*　　*

Mellai stood in the village square while the tradesmen packed their covered wagons and made last-minute exchanges. Her parents had already seen her off and returned home—at her own request—to avoid an overly emotional departure. Mellai kept glancing at the Shaw home, but Kaylen was nowhere to be seen.

As Mellai hugged herself to stay warm, she noticed Braedr standing in front of his house with his arms folded across his chest. He was too far away for Mellai to see his expression, but she could feel his eyes on her. Seconds turned into minutes as he continued to watch her. She finally dragged her bundle through the snow to Kutad's wagon and asked if she could place her things inside.

Kutad grabbed her bag and tossed it into his wagon, but not without noticing her distress. He followed her gaze and saw Braedr watching them.

"That man is why you want to escape this village, eh? Don't you worry about him anymore, Mellai. We'll be off within the hour, then you'll never lay eyes on him again."

Mellai thanked him and moved around to the other side of the wagon to hide from Braedr. As she did, Kaylen stepped out of her house with Scut behind her. He carried two very large sacks, and Kaylen had her own smaller bag. Mellai chuckled as the two of them walked toward her.

"Where do you think you're going to put all of that?" Mellai called when they were close enough to hear.

Kaylen blushed and ducked her head, but Scut replied unashamed. "I won't have her travelin' without extra clothes."

Kutad laughed heartily at the two of them, then took the bags from Scut and stowed them in the wagon. "Don't worry, friend. There's plenty enough room for a woman's comfort."

Scut thanked Kutad and turned to his daughter. He held her tightly for a moment, then walked away, wiping his eyes.

"I love you, Father," Kaylen called after him through her own tears.

Scut waved back, but didn't turn around.

"There's a man who loves his daughter," Kutad told Kaylen. "You're lucky to have such a father." He smiled. "My ladies, time for us to leave. I apologize I can't offer you a ride, but the donkeys are already pulling a heavy load. You'll have to walk beside the wagon with the rest of the caravan. The snow is deep, but we'll move slowly."

As the travelers finished up their final preparations, Mellai glanced back at the blacksmith shop. She sighed with relief when she saw Braedr had disappeared.

"What is it?" Kaylen asked.

"Nothing," Mellai replied. "I was starting to worry you'd changed your mind about coming."

Kaylen gave Mellai a reassuring smile, but Mellai saw a tinge of sadness.

Kutad cracked a whip in the air, then the two women joined the caravan as they turned north and left Pree behind.

*　　*　　*　　*　　*

It took four days for the caravan to reach Roseiri through the December snow. They followed the old trade road, which wound between the rolling prairies of Appernysia's Western Valley. As Aron requested, Mellai and Kaylen stayed close to Kutad, but they soon learned to trust the rest of the tradesmen as well.

Everyone was cheerful and light-hearted. They played music and sang as they traveled. When they camped at night, they circled the ten covered wagons around a large fire and placed all of the donkeys inside of the ring to protect them from roaming predators. The men and women would then take turns dancing around the flickering flames of the fire.

"Kaylen, I was talking with Kutad earlier today. He said Braedr was asking a bunch of questions before we left Pree."

Kaylen sat up. "What kind of questions?"

"How long do you think it will take you to get to Roseiri?" Mellai said in her best imitation of Braedr. "How long are you staying in Roseiri? Where will you travel next?"

"There's nothing odd about that. Half the village was asking the same thing."

Mellai wasn't convinced. She remembered the way Braedr watched her before they left; he probably already knew about the planned village council and was planning his own future.

Mellai searched the darkness outside their protective ring of wagons.

"Mellai?" Kaylen said.

Mellai forced smile. "Perhaps you're right."

As Roseiri came into view, she and Kaylen laughed freely with the rest of the caravan. By this time, the tension inside Mellai had disappeared.

Mellai took Kaylen aside. "I need to tell you something. I'm not going to Réxura. I'm staying in Roseiri with my grandparents."

Kaylen frowned, but she didn't look upset. "I thought you might, Mellai. After all, you haven't seen them in years."

"Will you stay with me?"

Kaylen looked toward Roseiri. "I've been thinking about it since we left Pree. I originally planned to stay with you, but these past few days have changed my mind. I enjoy being around other people."

"You like to be popular," Mellai said sarcastically.

"Call it what you want, but I've realized I'm happiest when I'm around people. I don't know if I can stay in another small village, especially if we have to hide in your grandparents' house."

Mellai worked it over in her mind. She couldn't expect Kaylen to stay with her in Roseiri—Kaylen had her own life to lead. "If you don't stay, will you help me find my grandparents when we get there?"

"Of course," Kaylen replied.

* * * * *

The sun was nearing the western horizon as the caravan drew close to Roseiri. Mellai found Kutad and spoke to him softly. "My name isn't safe in this village. I'll need another while we're here."

Kutad smiled. "Don't worry. You're with the greatest secret-keepers in all of Appernysia. Most people who travel with us are either running to or from something—and all of them have their secrets. We'll protect you."

Mellai thanked him profusely before adding, "It's also best if the villagers here assume Kaylen and I are part of your company. If someone recognizes us, I don't want to endanger anyone in Pree."

"Consider it done," Kutad replied as he pulled the donkeys to a halt. "Gather around, everyone!"

The rest of the caravan stopped their wagons and surrounded Kutad. "These women need our protection while in Roseiri," he said. "As most of you already know, the names Mellai and Marcs aren't safe in this village, so she'll be known as Linney instead. If anyone asks, we took her and Kaylen in when we stopped in Sylbie last winter, after their parents were killed by Rayders. Agreed?"

The tradesmen firmly assented and, after Mellai and Kaylen donned veils like the other women in the caravan, the company continued toward Roseiri.

"I hope Lon is safe," Kaylen whispered to Mellai as they walked.

Mellai was used to her best friend's constant thoughts of Lon. She released her emotions and searched for her twin's. "He's tense, but not in danger. It's been almost two weeks, so he's probably somewhere near the Perbeisea Forest."

"I hope he stays safe," Kaylen added, knowing the dangers he might face in that area.

"So do—" Mellai started to say, but stopped short as intense fear overwhelmed her. She gasped and dropped trembling to her knees.

"Mellai?" Kaylen screamed.

When Mellai's body stopped shaking, she shifted her weight back to sit on her heels. Kaylen continued to watch her.

"It's all right," Mellai said after taking a deep breath, "Lon had a very close encounter, but he got away."

"How do you know?" Kaylen asked.

"I just do."

A few of the other tradesmen, including Kutad, came running to see what happened. Mellai blamed it on a rat and apologized for the disturbance.

"Next time," Kutad responded as he shook his head, "you might consider climbing the wagon instead of falling to the ground. Falling only puts your face closer to the little rodent."

"Thanks for the advice," Mellai said.

Kutad smiled and everyone returned to their wagons to resume their course toward Roseiri.

"That wasn't a very good excuse, Mellai," Kaylen whispered.

"I had to think fast," Mellai snapped. "I'm a little distracted right now."

Kaylen grabbed Mellai's hand and stared at her. "Do you promise Lon is safe?"

"Yes, Kaylen. He's safe . . . for now."

Chapter 15

Narrow Escape

L on's eyes shot open.

The mid-afternoon sun still hung high in the sky. Light streaked through the leafless branches of the mighty Furwen Trees, towering more than six hundred feet over his head. He had entered the western edge of the Perbeisea Forest after sundown the previous night, traveling slowly through the dense shadows until, as sunrise drew near, he found a massive root to sleep under.

He was not alone. Snow crunched as someone—or something—lurked closer. Dawes's eyes opened wide in search of danger.

Lon crept out from beneath the root and peered around the tree. Three men appeared, stepping through the snow, using the staff-end of their halberds to keep their balance.

The man closest to Lon thrust his halberd into the snow and unsheathed his sword. The other two men did the same. They knew he was close.

Appernysian scouts, Lon thought. *They must have found my tracks entering the forest.*

Aron had warned him that trespassers in the Perbeisea Forest faced terrible punishments that would make them beg for death. Lon had no desire to see if his father's words were true.

He opened his leather pouch and filled both hands with the powdered sedative. If he let the scouts go, they'd follow him to the Gaurelic Waste. He had to incapacitate them, but he didn't want to hurt them.

Gathering his courage, Lon charged out from behind the tree, bearing down on the closest scout like an angry bear. The man only had time to turn his head toward Lon before his face was covered in white powder. He fell sideways as Lon continued to the next man.

The second scout swung his sword and Lon dropped to his side to avoid the sharpened steel. The scout raised his sword for another attack, but Lon flung the powder into his face. The scout's eyes unfocused and he, too, fell into the snow.

Lon reached into his pouch for another handful of powder, but it had emptied into the snow when he landed on his side.

He cursed as he looked for the white pile on the snow. He found it and packed it inside a large snowball as the third scout rushed toward him. Lon stood and hurled the snowball at the man's face, but the scout easily dodged it. Lon barely had time to draw his sword before the man reached him.

Better make this quick, Lon thought as he parried blow after blow, *or I'll summon True Sight for sure.*

The Appernysian scout thrust his sword at Lon, leaving his body unprotected. Lon sidestepped the attack, stabbed the man in his leg, then knocked the sword from his hand.

The man fell back. Lon flicked his opponent's sword away with his foot and sheathed his own sword.

"I don't wish to harm you," Lon said. "I just want to live."

The man stared at Lon's sword. He knew the scout saw the King's Cross etched into the pommel.

"You're a Rayder," the scout growled. "You deserve to die."

"Maybe I do," Lon answered as he walked to the previous two scouts, wiped a portion of the moist powder from their faces, and headed back toward the third, "but not by your hand."

"You can't stop me. Wound or not, I'll track you all the way to the Exile."

"Don't," Lon countered, then stepped on the man's chest and smeared the last of the powder under his nose. "I'm a bigger handful than your whole army could handle."

The man only managed to laugh twice before joining his comrades in a sudden loss of consciousness.

Lon hurried to Dawes and climbed into his saddle. "We got to move, Dawes." He kicked Dawes's sides. "They'll be awake soon, and right on our heels. We don't have much time."

Chapter 16

Bitter Reunion

When the caravan was about to enter Roseiri, Kaylen and Mellai both wrapped their veils around their faces.

"These will be perfect," Mellai commented as she fingered the delicate material. "Anyone here would easily recognize me if they got a good look at my face."

Roseiri consisted of two rows of houses, one running along each side of the deep West River. The old trade road intersected the village at the north bridge. From there, two dirt roads ran south along each bank of the river to another bridge at the south end of the village. Small irrigation canals spurred from the river like the legs of a centipede, dividing the villagers' properties and providing water for their crops.

As the caravan neared the north bridge, children half-bundled in their winter clothes ran to join the caravan, cheering as they followed the wagons. Mellai didn't need to ask to know that each of them was determined to be the first in line for sweets. She fought the temptation to look for her grandparents, knowing their home was just three houses away. She just needed to remain patient and stay hidden.

"I've never had so many people this excited to see me before," Mellai joked to Kaylen as she pulled her veil higher on her face. "Hopefully none of them recognize me."

Kaylen smiled at Mellai and waved at the growing crowd. "Oh, Linney, I just love children. I can't wait to have my own someday." Her voice faded and her hand dropped to her side.

Mellai's eyes softened as she watched her friend. She knew how complicated Kaylen's situation was. If Lon survived, it could still be years before he returned. Kaylen wouldn't start her own family for a long time, and there was a good chance it wouldn't be with Lon.

Mellai brought her hand to her chest and touched her mother's pearl necklace hidden under her clothes. She hadn't been sure what to do with the necklace when she and Kaylen left Pree, but as she stood there, witnessing Kaylen's sorrow, Mellai resolved to give it to her.

But now isn't the right time, she thought. *I'll give it to her tonight after things have settled down.*

As they stepped onto the bridge, Mellai unconsciously began counting the wooden planks under her feet.

Still seventy-four, Mellai mused once they were across, reminiscing about the wager she and Lon had made as children. She had won, and Lon had to do her chores for an entire month.

The tradesmen turned their carts off the north side of the road and formed a large half-circle in the snowy fields. The villagers had stopped on the road and watched the caravan, anticipation burning in their eyes.

"Why did they stop following us?" Kaylen whispered to Mellai.

"Just wait," Mellai replied.

When all of the wagons were in position, their coverings gave way and the younger women sprang out, dancing and twirling ribbons through the air while the men kept time with fiddles, fifes, and bodhrans.

Both Kaylen and Mellai began dancing with the other women. The villagers cheered and soon joined in the anticipated celebration. They piled wood in the middle of the circled wagons and started a roaring bonfire, which cast long shadows that frolicked across the snow in the failing light. Tables were brought and laden with casks of ale. Two villagers appeared carrying a large boar on a spit.

"We were wondering if you'd make your rounds this year," one of the villagers said as they set it over the fire. "We almost ate it without you." Its aroma soon filled the air.

Mellai forgot about her grandparents and laughed as she danced, enjoying the atmosphere of the celebration and a chance to relive her childhood. She had forgotten how much fun it was every year when the caravan had come to Roseiri. She allowed herself to be carried away in a wave of delightful memories until she finally had to sit down to catch her breath.

"It's nice to see you're still smiling," a familiar voice said next to her.

Mellai turned and was alarmed to find her grandmother sitting next to her. "Grandmother," she said breathlessly, "how did you—?"

"Oh, come now," her grandmother replied with a smile. "Did you really think five years and a silly veil could hide you from me?"

Mellai didn't respond. Her first instinct was to leap into her grandmother's arms and nuzzle into her shoulder. It wrent her heart to refrain, but she had no choice. All she could do was stare. Her grandmother looked the same, except for a few additional wrinkles on her face. Her silver hair sparkled in the firelight and tears filled her blue eyes as she reached out to embrace her granddaughter.

"Not here, Grandmother," Mellai said. She stood and backed away, a warning hand subtly raised. "I can't talk right now, but I'll find you tomorrow and explain everything. I promise."

Mellai sped to Kutad's wagon. She sat down behind the wheel on the opposite side of the fire, brought her knees to her chest, and folded her arms over the top of them. She took deep breaths as she looked into the darkness surrounding her, trying to sort out her feelings. They overwhelmed her as she noticed the tree in front of her, the same tree where she and Lon had played their last game of stick-stack.

Seeing her grandmother again reminded Mellai of Lon's curse. It was the reason her parents had forced them to leave Roseiri. It was the reason Lon was running to the Rayder Exile, and why Mellai and Kaylen left their parents in Pree. Mellai would never be allowed normal interactions with her grandparents, nor any of her childhood friends in Roseiri. So many emotions—too many for her to manage.

She buried her face into her arms and sobbed while the rest of the village danced merrily behind her.

✲   ✲   ✲   ✲   ✲

Mellai opened her eyes, awakened by the soft light of the sun creeping above the horizon. She reached her arms above her head and stretched, surprised at the soreness in her limbs, then sat up and observed the glowing countryside. She was in the same place where she hid herself the night before, with the exception of the thick buffalo hide wrapped around her. She realized she had cried herself to sleep and only partially remembered Kaylen waking her up to wrap her in the hide. Kaylen was still lying next to Mellai, peacefully sleeping like the rest of the members of their company.

Mellai decided to take advantage of the early hour and stood to sneak away. She had only taken a couple of steps, when she heard Kaylen's voice. "Do you want me to come with you?"

Mellai froze, then shook her head no.

"I understand," Kaylen whispered. "Your grandmother looked happy to see you last night. I'm sure your grandfather will feel the same way."

"I won't be long."

Mellai wrapped her veil around her face, crept out of camp, crossed over the main bridge, and turned north along the river's western bank. When she reached the third and final house, she stopped in front of it.

The house looked the same as it had five years earlier. The main structure was small—large enough to accommodate two people—with a larger expansion connected to the back. It was in that extension that Mellai's family spent the first twelve years of her life. A small greenhouse sat behind the house, followed by the long, narrow field her grandfather farmed.

Mellai took a deep breath and crept across the road to the front door. She knew the men in Roseiri, including her grandfather, would be awake tending to their fields by that hour. Just as she lifted her hand to knock, the front door swung open and her crying grandmother stepped out to envelope Mellai in her arms.

"Oh, how I've missed you," her grandmother said between sobs.

Mellai buried her head into her grandmother's shoulder and squeezed her back. "I've missed you, too, Grandmother—more than you can imagine."

When they were inside the house, Mellai removed her veil and paused to glance around the room. It was dark—lit only by a small candle on the table and the glowing coals in the fireplace. A small kettle hung over the coals, filling the room with a warm medicinal aroma Mellai knew too well.

"Where's Grandfather?" Mellai asked.

Her grandmother's face fell. "He's in bed. Your grandfather has been very ill for a few days now. I've done all I can for him, but nothing seems to do much good. It appears to be just a simple cold, but his body is getting too old to fight it off."

"Have you told him about me yet?"

"No. He sleeps most of the time because of the herbs I've been giving him."

Mellai sat on a chair next to her grandfather's bed. His breathing was steady, but shallow, his face careworn.

"Grandfather," she spoke softly as she took his hand in hers. "Grandfather, it's me, Mellai. I've come home."

Her grandfather's fingers pressed ever so slightly on Mellai's hand, but he gave no other response.

Mellai turned to her grandmother. "How long ago did you sedate him?"

"Just before you arrived. It should start to wear off around dinnertime. If you're still around, you can try talking to him then. Perhaps you'll have better luck."

Mellai turned back to her grandfather, still holding his hand. After a few minutes of silence, she leaned forward and gave him a gentle kiss on his forehead.

"Please fight this. I need you now more than ever."

Mellai cupped the side of her face with her grandfather's hand, then left the room with her grandmother.

"Your being here is greater than any medicine I can give him," her grandmother said as they left the room. "Your disappearance took a dreadful toll on him. He's missed you terribly."

Mellai nodded and sat herself at the table. "It wasn't easy for any of us." She paused. "You must be wondering where we've been and why I've come back, so why don't you just ask?"

Her grandmother's eyes leveled. "Mellai, we've been longing to hear from you for years. I'm not about to drive you away again by asking too many questions."

"I wish you would—ask me questions, I mean."

"I'll be more than happy to listen when you're ready to tell me," her grandmother answered, "but until then, I'll let the past stay where it is—in the past. Now that you're here, what are your plans? Will you be moving on with the trading caravan when they leave?"

Mellai looked at the floor and shifted her feet. "I . . . well, I was hoping . . ."

Smiling gently, her grandmother placed her hand on Mellai's cheek. "Of course, you can stay with us. You've been gone far too long and the villagers here will be happy to know you've returned."

"It isn't that simple, Grandmother," Mellai said as she pulled her grandmother's hand from her face. "Nobody can know I'm here. The risk is just too great. I'll have to stay hidden."

Mellai's grandmother looked carefully at her granddaughter, but did not pursue the subject. Instead, she leaned forward and gave her another hug.

"That means I get to keep you all to myself," she said as tears flowed down her face. "I'm sorry, Mellai, but I've been bottling up my feelings for too long, and now that they're finally coming out, there's no stopping them."

They held each other and cried until they were interrupted by a loud knock on the door. Mellai pulled away and looked around frantically for a place to hide.

"It's all right, Mellai," her grandmother reassured her. "It's just Theiss Arbogast. He volunteered to help us finish the harvest. We're a little behind because your grandfather has been sick. I know the snow came late this year, but it still caught us off guard. I hope we're able to save—"

"Theiss?" Mellai cut in. "He can't know I'm here. Nobody can know I'm here."

Her grandmother took Mellai by her shoulders. "Relax, Mellai. Everything will be just fine. Go in my bedroom and I'll see what Theiss needs."

Mellai hurried into the bedroom and closed the door; she hid herself in the darkest corner of the room. She heard her grandmother open the front door and speak with someone, but their voices were too low and muffled to understand.

A short time later, the front door closed and Mellai heard her grandmother's footsteps coming toward the room. The metal handle creaked as her grandmother unlatched it and poked her head into the room.

"He's gone, Mellai. Apparently the trading has started and he needed to go barter for his parents. It looks like we're going to have all morning to ourselves."

*   *   *   *   *

Kutad stopped Mellai as she wandered around the camp. "What are you looking for, Linney?"

"Have you seen Kaylen? I can't find her anywhere."

Kutad cocked his head to the side. "I haven't seen her all morning. I thought she was with you."

"No," Mellai answered, "I left her with the other women when I went to go visit my grandparents."

"I know. They said Kaylen followed you there."

"She never showed up."

Kutad frowned. "Come with me."

He hurried toward Mellai's grandmother's house with Mellai on his heels. While he searched out front, Mellai entered the house to question her grandmother.

"Any chance Kaylen stopped by here?"

"No," her grandmother replied. "Why?"

"She's missing. Apparently, she followed me here this morning, but no one has seen her since."

"I haven't—"

A loud knock on the door interrupted her. Mellai's grandmother opened the door and found Kutad on her doorstep.

"I think Kaylen's been taken."

"What?"

"There are obvious signs of a struggle by the river, and tracks lead away north. Is she in danger in this village?"

"No one here knows her. I can't imagine who would . . ." Mellai trailed off as a horrible thought struck her. "I knew he was up to something."

"Who?" her grandmother asked.

Mellai turned to Kutad. "Remember how Braedr was watching us when we left Pree—all the questions he asked you? The village was planning a disciplinary council for him the day after we left. He was either banished from Pree or fled before the council took place, but I'm almost certain he's here. He took Kaylen. I'm sure of it."

Kutad's eyes narrowed and he started back down the road at a quick pace with Mellai catching up from behind.

"Don't worry, Mellai," he said. "We'll find them both. We're more than just simple tradesmen. We don't survive our long travels across Appernysia every year because of luck. Rest assured Kaylen will be returned safely. Braedr will pay for this."

Chapter 17

Parting Ways

Kaylen grimaced. "Please, Braedr. I need to rest."

Braedr yanked on the rope tied to her wrists. With a cry of pain, Kaylen stumbled and fell. Before she could stand, he began dragging her forward by the rope.

"Stop!" Kaylen cried, her voice muffled by the snow pouring over her head. "Please!"

The wrenching ceased and she paused to catch her breath, digging the snow out of the top of her dress. She peered up at Braedr, who stood hovering over her with his fists clenched at his sides. He motioned for her to stand and she quickly obeyed, then they continued forward on their agonizing march up the mountain.

Kaylen kept her eyes down, afraid to look at her captor. He hadn't spoken more than a few words for two days, since he first grabbed her and threatened to break her legs. His silence was unnerving. She could see it in his eyes—sunken, bloodshot, and half obscured by his scowling brows.

Despite her fear, she didn't know how much longer she could continue. Her dress was torn, her wrists bruised and sore. She could feel that her knees and face were scabbed-over from repeated falls into the frozen snow.

Kaylen winced and glanced over her shoulder, silently praying the skies would remain clear long enough for someone to follow their trail. Her hopes of rescue withered with every passing hour.

Kaylen's condition continued to worsen as they pressed further into the forest. Braedr forced her forward at a brutal pace.

"It's getting dark," Kaylen pled. "I can't feel my feet."

He only tugged harder on the lead rope and grumbled, "Who's the fool now?"

As the sun began to set, they entered a small clearing high in the mountains. It was shaded by the snow-covered branches of towering oak and pine trees, leaving only a thin layer of snow on top of the pine needles and soggy leaves scattered across the ground. A deep river bordered the northern edge of the clearing, surging under scattered patches of ice. Its rushing waters muted the sounds of the forest. Under different circumstances, Kaylen would have loved the beauty surrounding her.

Braedr stopped walking, looked around the clearing, then led Kaylen to an aged oak with a large hollow high off the ground. He forced her onto her side at the base of the tree, brought her hands over her head, wrapped the rope around the trunk of the tree, and tied it to her ankles. Fearing the worst, Kaylen screamed and lashed out, trying to free herself. But Braedr grabbed her chin, glaring menacingly, and slowly shook his head in disapproval.

After making sure the rope was secure, Braedr threw Kaylen's cloak over her body, sat against another oak tree on the opposite side of the clearing, and stared at her. Kaylen's worried breath came out in short bursts, creating small clouds of mist in front of her that disappeared into the freezing mountain air. The sight of the mist reminded her of Lon. As she desperately tried to fight off the sleep that tugged at her mind and body, Kaylen wished he were there to protect her from Braedr.

Oh, Lon! she silently cried as Braedr's unmoving eyes continued to watch her.

✳   ✳   ✳   ✳   ✳

Mellai knelt next to Kutad's hunched figure and examined the ground. With the help of a handful of their fellow tradesmen, they had been pursuing Braedr relentlessly. She shivered in the mountain air as the temperature continued to drop. They had been able to move quickly because of the obvious tracks left by Kaylen and Braedr, but the sun had set two hours earlier. Although the moon was shining brightly in the cloudless sky, the mountain trees cast dappled shadows over the ground, making it difficult to follow the trail.

Kutad looked at Mellai. She knew they could easily miss a turn in the trail while tracking in the dark. It could take them hours in the wrong direction.

"I'll leave the choice to you," Kutad whispered to Mellai. "You understand the risks and I trust your judgment. Will we wait until morning or try to continue?"

Mellai bit her bottom lip in frustration, causing it to bleed. Either choice could prove disastrous for Kaylen.

Mellai decided to continue. "It would be pointless to stop now because I won't be able to sleep. Let's press forward, but we'll go slower so we don't miss their trail."

"So be it," Kutad replied. "Slowing down will improve our stealth, too. The tracks are fresh on the ground, which means we're getting close. I don't want to give ourselves away. It worries me to think of how Braedr would respond under such a circumstance."

Mellai agreed.

Their companions stood ready to follow as Kutad examined the trail one more time. When he stood to move on, a terrified scream filled the air. Mellai recognized Kaylen's voice and opened her mouth to respond, but Kutad threw his hand over her mouth to keep her quiet.

Mellai stared at him, eyes wide, and nodded. Kutad moved his hand from her mouth to grip his scimitar, which he slowly drew from the scabbard. The other four tradesmen also unsheathed their swords, then the six of them stole through the forest in the direction of Kaylen's screams.

* * * * *

Hours had passed since Braedr tied Kaylen to the tree, yet she continued to watch him across the dark clearing. Braedr hadn't moved in over an hour and appeared to have fallen asleep, but she didn't trust him and forced herself to stay awake.

Although they were deep in the Vidarien Mountains, an eerie silence filled the forest. An ominous feeling hung over the clearing. Kaylen felt something nearby, watching her, silencing the world around them. Even the wind had ceased to blow.

Kaylen allowed her eyes to drift from the still figure of Braedr as she scanned the clearing. She peered into the shadows and saw nothing, until her gaze returned to where Braedr sat. A vague silhouette towered over him, a deeper blackness against the night, accented by bright blue eyes the size of Kaylen's fists, hovering higher than a man's head, looking directly at her. Although Kaylen knew she should have been terrified, for a moment she felt only an uncanny sense of peace in its presence, until the beast uttered a low growl.

Kaylen's expected terror crashed in on her with a vengeance. With one swipe of its massive foreleg, the beast sent Braedr and the tree he was leaning against flying across the clearing toward the river. Kaylen screamed, flinching, when both Braedr and tree shattered the ice and vanished into the dark water.

When Kaylen looked back toward the beast, it had disappeared into the forest. She shouted for the creature to come back, but the only reply she received was from Kutad, who came rushing out of the woods moments later with a sword in his hand.

* * * * *

Kutad and Mellai tended to Kaylen while the other four tradesmen fanned out in search of Braedr. It wasn't until later, when Kaylen finally stopped crying, that they learned what had transpired. None of them had seen the beast or Braedr, nor did they find their tracks as they scoured the surrounding area. There was an obvious hole in the ground where the tree once stood, but the tradesmen found no other evidence a creature had been there.

"If Braedr fell into the river," Kutad said as he stared at the broken ice, "he's a dead man. Its current is quick and the freezing water will sap the life out of you in minutes. And if what you tell us is true, Braedr must have been badly injured. There's no chance he survived." He paused and glanced around. "I wonder what manner of beast would take an interest in saving your life, Kaylen, or have the strength to uproot a full-grown tree—though by all accounts, these mountains are full of strange and wonderful creatures."

"Whatever it was, it's about time something killed Braedr," Mellai stiffly replied. "That cretin finally got what he deserved."

The men in their company all agreed with Mellai, but Kaylen struggled with her feelings. The vision of his body flying helplessly through the air plagued her mind. Although she hated Braedr more than anything in Appernysia, somehow, she still thought nobody deserved such bad luck, not even Braedr.

After surviving two days without food or water, Kaylen needed a full day before she recovered enough to make the journey back to Roseiri. Even then, they had to move slowly, taking five days to return—and it couldn't have been a day later. They arrived early in the morning, before sunrise, and found the rest of the trading caravan completely packed up and ready to go in search of the rescuers.

There, waiting among the traders, Mellai's grandfather stood with Theiss Arbogast.

*   *   *   *   *

The morning sunlight revealed a subtle smile on her grandfather's face, but rather than approaching Mellai, he merely walked away, with Theiss following loyally behind him.

"You obviously love your family," Kutad said to Mellai as she watched her grandfather walk up the road. "Don't take them for granted. You never know what day will be your last with them."

Mellai looked up at Kutad and smiled at him. "We owe you our lives, Kutad. Without your help, Kaylen would—" Mellai's voice broke as she considered the possible ways she might finish her sentence.

"No need for life debts. You're part of our caravan and we have a responsibility to keep you safe. You're our family now."

Mellai's eyes filled with tears. She wrapped her arms around Kutad and buried her face in his chest. Kutad held her and patiently stroked her hair as she wept. When her trembling subsided, he kissed the top of her head and whispered into her ear.

"Stay with your grandparents, Mellai, but know you'll always have a home with us."

Mellai nodded and followed Kutad toward the caravan. They found Kaylen lying comfortably in a covered wagon, with young men standing guard. Mellai forced her way through the crowd until she was inside the wagon and sitting at her friend's side.

Kaylen's frostbitten feet were wrapped in cloth and two tradeswomen cleaned the cuts on her knees, hands, and face. When Kaylen noticed the tears in Mellai's eyes, she pulled her close and hugged her fiercely.

"It wasn't supposed to be this hard," Mellai said.

"I know," Kaylen replied softly, "but at least we're all safe again. Mellai, is Lon safe?"

"I don't know, Kaylen."

"Please try, Mellai. Please."

Mellai struggled to take deep breaths in an attempt to calm herself. Her body shook with hiccups for a few minutes after she stopped crying, but she eventually mastered her emotions and forced herself to relax. She expanded her conscience and felt for Lon. She found him alive, although he was exhausted. From what her father told her before they left Pree, Mellai guessed Lon must be nearing the end of his travels to the Rayder Exile.

"He's tired," Mellai told Kaylen, "very, very tired, but he's alive." She undid the clasp at the back of her neck and handed the pearl necklace to Kaylen. "This was my mother's. Lon wanted you to have it."

Kaylen carefully took the necklace. "Thank you, Mellai."

"Goodbye, Kaylen." Mellai didn't wait for Kaylen to respond. She climbed out of the wagon and hid herself behind a snow-covered bush to watch the caravan. Kutad poked his head in the wagon, then glanced around looking for Mellai. Mellai wanted to jump up and tell him goodbye, but she forced herself to stay hidden. Kutad placed a fist on his heart and bowed low in Mellai's direction, then returned to his own wagon and led the caravan out of Roseiri.

Chapter 18

Exile

L on peered through the dangling branches of a willow tree at the edge of the Weeping Forest, his hand on Dawes's shoulder. He had his cloak on to keep out the December cold, but it did little good as he stood knee-deep in the freezing marsh. Dawes pranced anxiously next to him.

"Easy," Lon said, patting Dawes on the neck. "If you keep splashing around like that, you're going to give away our hiding spot. Haven't we been through this before?"

Dawes's lips fluttered as he breathed out loudly and shook his thick mane in response, but he stopped fidgeting. Lon smiled at him and continued to scan the empty landscape. Ten miles to the southwest was Thorn, the Rayder watchtower on the north edge of the Zaga Ravine. It was a simple watchtower—conical, made of granite stone, twenty feet in diameter and sixty feet high.

Lon had learned in his childhood that at the end of the First Age, the king made the defeated Rayders build a stone bridge over the ravine, then forced them across it before tearing it down behind them. The Rayders—full of pride and scorn for the King—built Thorn out of the remains of the bridge on the north side of the ravine as a reminder of their separation from Appernysia; no Appernysian was allowed to cross onto their land.

A raised road ran northeast from Thorn, paralleling the Dialorine Range to the south. Marshlands and willow trees separated the mountains from the road, and Lon stood in the midst of them.

"Well, Dawes," Lon said as he pulled himself into the saddle, "that's the only path, and it must lead to their fortress. We might as well follow it."

Lon tapped his heels on Dawes's sides and he splashed away from Thorn and along the north line of the willow trees. Weary with hunger and thirst, Lon allowed his thoughts to wander as Dawes carried him.

Traveling through the Gaurelic Waste had been miserable, but Lon was grateful to be out of the mountains and away from the scores of dead bodies that littered their peaks. None of them had been Rayders. There weren't any obvious wounds on their bodies, either. They obviously hadn't died in battle. The only explanation he could think of was that, like himself, they had been Appernysians running to the Exile—only they hadn't made it.

But what were they running from? Lon pondered. *Is life really that miserable in Appernysia?*

Images of the corpses plagued him every time he closed his eyes, making his journey all the more grueling. Unfortunately, the northern face had provided little reprieve. Rayder patrols scoured the woods continually and Lon had to carefully dodge them on his way down the mountain. It had been nearly two days since he slept.

A low growl from Dawes forced Lon back into awareness. Two hundred yards in front of them stood ten warhorses, each carrying a soldier with a glaive in one hand and a diamond-shaped shield marked with the King's Cross in the other.

Lon instinctively allowed his left hand to drift to the pouch at his side only to discover that his mother's powder had run out. Moving his hand across his body to the hilt of his sword, he cursed his father for not telling him what to do once he was caught by the Rayders. He slowly pulled his sword out of its scabbard, intending to throw it to the ground, but the ten soldiers didn't give him a chance. They kicked their horses forward at a gallop.

Dawes whinnied and reared on his back legs in preparation to charge at the approaching Rayders.

"No, Dawes!" Lon shouted.

Dawes chomped the bit in his mouth and tossed his head impatiently, keeping his four legs on the ground. Lon dismounted and reached for the other four swords behind the saddle. He untied the bundle and held it under his right arm, while focusing his mind on staying calm—which came more easily than normal because of his exhaustion. If he summoned True Sight, all the sacrifices he'd made would have been a complete waste.

Lon took his own sword with his left hand and held it vertically in front of himself with the etched King's Cross symbol facing the soldiers. The soldiers were about fifty yards away, but Lon ignored his panic as he closed his eyes and bowed his head toward the ground. His ears pounded as the splashing of the galloping horses grew louder.

Just when Lon was certain he was about to die, the splashing ceased. He opened his eyes. The riders were only a few yards away, their glaives lowered—close enough that Lon could see their wide eyes looking past him. Lon turned and found Dawes standing directly behind him, his head hovering over Lon's right shoulder. He was as cool and steady as Lon. Lon smiled, but dared not move, worried he might startle the soldiers into another attack.

The man positioned at the front of the group raised his glaive. He had a short beard and long, blond hair pulled back at the base of his head. He had the King's Cross branded on his right temple. He examined Lon with a hardened face before speaking.

"Who are you, trespasser?"

"I am Lon . . . Shaw," he responded with a bow of his head, remembering his last name would be unsafe amongst the Rayders.

"Where have you come from?" the soldier asked.

"I'm a tradesman," Lon replied smoothly. "I have no home."

"Why are you here?"

"To become a Rayder."

The man eyed Lon thoughtfully, then handed his glaive to another soldier and dismounted. He stepped through the marsh toward Lon, carefully watching Dawes behind him.

"Don't worry about Dawes," Lon said. "He won't attack unless I command him to."

The soldier watched Dawes for a moment longer, then shifted his gaze to Lon. "Never before have I seen a horse so devoted to his master, nor so obedient. Have you raised him from a foal?"

Lon considered the question carefully before answering. "No, he was a Rayder's horse."

The soldier nodded. "You have spoken wisely, Lon Shaw. I know this horse. It belonged to a friend of mine, as did the sword you hold in your hand. Tell me, how did you come to obtain them?"

"I happened on the aftermath of a battle between your friend and King Drogan's scouts—"

"Do not speak of your king here unless you wish a quick death," the man interrupted.

"Can I say Appernysia?"

"Only when necessary."

"The Appernysian scouts must have ambushed your friend and his four companions. They had been beheaded and impaled on trees west of the Perbeisea Forest. I burned the trees down and abandoned my caravan to join you, with your comrades' swords as a token."

"You do not join yourself with anyone but our commander," the soldier interrupted again.

"Forgive me. I don't know your customs. I'm just a man who has grown tired of . . . Appernysia. I couldn't stand to live in a country where I was treated so unjustly."

"You will learn our ways soon enough, Lon Shaw," the soldier said. "How did you come across this horse?"

"I found him wandering the Taejan Plains on my way here. He seemed more than happy to return to the Exile. Dawes led me safely through the Dialorine Range."

"You call him Dawes?" the soldier commented. "If that is what you call him now, that will be his name. He seems happy enough with it. My name is Wade Arneson, and you will follow me to our commander. You may ride the horse, but I must relieve you of your weapons."

When he finished speaking, the nine other soldiers raised their glaives and positioned themselves at attention.

"As you wish," Lon said. He slid his sword into the bundle and handed it over, then watched Wade pull his bow and quiver from Dawes's saddle. "I've been riding a long time and I'm out of water. May I trouble you for a drink?"

After strapping Lon's belongings to his own saddle, he tossed a leather water skin to Lon.

"But that is against—" one of the other soldiers started to say.

"Silence yourself," Wade interrupted, "or I will."

The soldier moved his horse to the far left of the formation.

"Respect," Wade said in response to Lon's confused look. "Best you learn it quickly if you intend to join yourself with our commander."

Lon nodded and mounted Dawes. "Where do you want me to ride?"

"You will ride ten paces ahead of us, where I can keep my eyes on you. If you wish to earn my full trust, you must first earn the trust of our commander."

Lon nodded again and, by Wade's instruction, led the soldiers onto the raised road and northeast, in the direction of Flagheim.

As soon as Dawes climbed onto the snow-covered road, Lon noticed the ingenuity of the Rayders. When he had been south of the road, Lon was standing knee-deep in filthy marshlands, but the land north of the road appeared as though it would be lush and green during warmer months. Canals crisscrossed the countryside, all leading to culverts that drained under the road into the marshy southern lands. The Rayders had turned what used to be a miserable waste into a flourishing land.

"Where does the water go?" Lon asked at one point. "How do you keep the water down on the south side of the road?"

"There are culverts back by Thorn that drain into the ravine," Wade replied.

Lon smiled. *Genius.*

The closer Lon and his escorts drew to the fortress, the more inhabited the north lands became. There were farms similar to the ones in Pree. Large oak and birch trees, which Lon assumed must have been brought out of Appernysia in their infancy, were scattered across the countryside. He breathed in the crisp winter air, savoring the hints of alfalfa and corn.

They traveled all day without stopping, yet it wasn't until sundown that they reached the outer walls of Flagheim. For the most part, their course had been relatively flat, but the last hour took them up the long slope of a hill. It was at the top of the hill that Lon first caught sight of the Rayder fortress.

Flagheim stood in the center of an isolated valley surrounded by small hills. Unless a traveler stood on the crest of one of those hills, Flagheim would remain hidden from view. The first thing Lon noticed about the city was that, while looking down from the top of the hill, Flagheim's stonewalls formed the shape of the King's Cross. One wall encircled the entire city. Another high wall enclosed the central keep, and from it extended four others—one running in each of the four cardinal directions. They each connected to the perimeter wall and extended another fifty yards, ending at a one hundred-foot tall watchtower.

Lon and his escorts followed the road down the hill and to the angled, stone causeway. It was the only path leading to the gate through the thirty-foot perimeter wall. Four sentries emerged from the guardhouse and stood in attack position at the top of the causeway. Lon frowned, unsure of what he should do, but after only a few seconds the guards raised their weapons and stepped aside. Lon glanced back at Wade, who motioned for him to enter the city.

Chains rattled and an iron portcullis creaked as it slowly rose. By the time Lon reached it, the portcullis was just high enough for them to pass underneath its sharpened steel tips.

After Lon and the soldiers passed, the portcullis descended again; they now stood before a solid wooden gate fifteen feet ahead. Sensing danger, Lon instinctively grabbed for his sword before remembering he had given it to Wade.

I'm unarmed and under the escort of ten of their own soldiers, Lon thought. *They won't attack me. This is only a test of courage.*

He looked straight ahead, straightening his back and squaring his shoulders. Although he knew he was being watched through the arrow slits and murder holes spotting the surrounding walls, Lon remained calm, keeping his eyes forward.

After five minutes of uncomfortable silence, the gate in front of them swung open, allowing them to enter the snow-covered city. Lon clicked his tongue at Dawes as they moved out from under the wall.

Lon squinted in the brightness of the setting sun. When his eyes adjusted, he found himself in a large courtyard filled with people—young and old, male and female—all branded with the King's Cross. They didn't even glance in Lon's direction as they swarmed the snowy ground.

"Where do I go now?" Lon asked.

Wade whistled and motioned with his glaive. The man at the far left of Wade's column trotted forward in front of Lon.

"Thad will take you to see the commander," Wade said. "The rest of us will follow behind. Remember, Lon Shaw, if you attempt to run or fight, we will kill you without hesitation."

Lon nodded and followed Thad as they weaved their way through the city. Lon was surprised at the number of people who lived there. As in the courtyard, none of them paid any attention to him.

"Why won't anyone look at me?" Lon inquired.

"Because you are an infidel," Wade replied. "Unless you are marked with the Cross, you might as well be wind blowing through the trees. But do something to upset them and you will receive more attention than you'd like. I told you before, Lon Shaw—we do not take kindly to disrespect, especially when it comes from an infidel."

Lon breathed deeply. The strange customs of the Rayders seemed impractical to him, but to survive long enough to learn how to control his power, he would have to adapt to their ways.

By the time they reached the city's inner wall, the sun had completely set on Flagheim. It wasn't until then that Lon finally discovered how the Rayders gained admission without speaking. When the sentries barred their way under flickering torch light, Lon saw Thad tilt his head slightly to the left and touch the King's Cross on his right temple with the index and middle fingers of his right hand.

I bet that's what I was supposed to do when I ran into these guys in the swamp. Wouldn't have done me any good without the King's Cross brand, though.

The thought worried Lon, reminding him of how many sacrifices he would have to make to effectively pose as a Rayder. Although he wasn't looking forward to being branded with the King's Cross, what worried him most was that he might be sent on a mission into Appernysia, like the Rayders he and Myron had killed.

Lon's anxieties flared as they crossed through the inner gate and entered the bailey. It was well lit with scores of torches mounted on the surrounding walls. Their light reflected off the snow, revealing dozens of archers patrolling along the top of the wall and a towering keep straight ahead. Any of them would be able to kill Lon in an instant, not to mention the twenty fully-armored pikemen guarding the keep's entrance. They all watched Lon carefully, their hands tight on their weapons. Lon eyed them even more intently in return; this was going to be more difficult that he had imagined.

As Wade rode ahead to speak with the guards, Lon tried desperately to calm himself. "C'mon, Lon," he whispered harshly. "You made it all the way across Appernysia to lose control now?"

He knew he wasn't going to be able to stop himself from summoning True Sight without taking drastic measures. He scraped the edges of his leather pouch to catch any remaining powder under his fingernails before lightly sniffing them.

The effects of the powder immediately began pulling his senses away. He felt himself slumping forward in his saddle and then sideways, catching only a glimpse of the snow-covered cobblestones before he hit the ground.

*   *   *   *   *

When Lon regained consciousness, he was lying in the snow in the same spot he had fallen—his ten escorts standing in a tight box around him. Aside from Wade, they were all at attention facing the keep with torches in their hands.

"Stand up, Lon Shaw," Wade said indifferently.

The side of Lon's head throbbed, but he forced himself to his feet. When he turned to face the keep, he saw that the pikemen had split into two columns with their glaives held upright at their sides, a small path leading between them to the entrance.

Lon waivered for a moment before realizing that Dawes was no longer in the bailey. "Where's my horse?"

"He is in the stable," Wade replied. "We go now to my commander's throne room. I need not remind you that we are in the heart of Flagheim. If you try anything suspicious, Lon Shaw, we will kill you. If you keep your hands at your side and your head forward, you will arrive unharmed to meet Commander Rayben Goldhawk."

"What if he doesn't want me to join him?"

"We will kill you."

Lon straightened his shoulders as his escorts led him between the pikemen through the keep's front gate. The passageways inside the keep were extremely stuffy. Tiny arrow slits in the walls were the only source of fresh air.

Whether by standard, or because of the late hour, Lon encountered only a handful of men as they moved through the keep. These few men stepped aside at the sight of Lon's escort, then hurried away once they passed.

Although he was about to meet the man who would decide his destiny, Lon's exhaustion finally started to take hold. He fought his mind with every step, coaxing his leaden feet forward with promises of imminent rest. His eyes began to droop and his strength waned. Lon couldn't help but wonder if death had finally reached his door, considering how long he had gone without food, drink, or sleep.

One way or another, he told himself, *this will all be over soon.*

As the call of death's gentle release tugged at him, Lon began to think about whether he really wanted the commander to let him live. Just when he thought he couldn't take another step, they turned a corner and the doors of the throne room opened before him.

Lon almost cried out with joy at the sight of his journey's end. A tear escaped his eye, but he dared not move his hand to wipe it away, especially so close to the commander.

I bet a cough would get me killed here, Lon thought as the tear ran through his month-old beard and dropped from his chin.

Wade moved to the front and changed places with Thad. "You will stay behind me, Lon Shaw. You will not look my commander in the eye. You will only speak when an answer is requested of you. You will do what my commander asks without hesitation. If my commander receives you, I will show you to your quarters."

And if he doesn't receive me? Lon thought as he followed Wade past the sentries guarding the arched doorway and into the throne room.

Under different circumstances, Lon would have stopped to admire the architecture of the great hall. After being cramped in the tight quarters of the keep's passageways, the large hall created a tremendous sense of openness that allowed Lon to breathe deeply and freely. The granite stone walls were lined with burning torches, filling the hall with flickering light. A large fire also burned in the center of the room. Lon's eyes followed the smoke as it rose to the blackened ceiling high above, creeping along the peak before escaping through open windows on each side of the hall. The ceiling was supported by two rows of black marble pillars on each side of the hall, but Lon's eyes strayed to the two majestic columns at the far end. An intricate design of vinery was cut into the stone and spiraled around from the ceiling to the floor. They were separated by a polished black marble throne. Above it hung a ten-foot sculpture of the King's Cross, also carved out of black marble and secured to the neighboring pillars by thick chains.

Rayben Goldhawk sat upon his throne, dressed in a fine tunic of white cotton, partially covered by a blue velvet vest, and brown leather pants. A shining silver coronet rested upon his graying black hair. He sat forward in the throne, impatiently tapping his foot.

Lon diverted his eyes and noted two lines of armed pikemen spanning the length of the hall, creating a narrow passage between Lon and the commander. The pikemen stood facing the door, their eyes alert, looking straight forward. One false step and the last thing Lon would see was a wall of angry soldiers closing in around him.

As Wade led him across the hall, Lon swallowed hard and forced what little strength remained into his exhausted legs. Wade dropped to his knees ten paces from the throne. With both hands on the marble floor, he bowed low and touched his forehead to the ground. Lon copied Wade's movements and remained motionless until instructed to do otherwise.

"Stand, Lieutenant." Rayben spoke smoothly, his strong voice echoing through the hall.

Wade kissed the ground, then rose to his feet and stood at attention while Lon continued to kneel on the floor.

"This is the man your squad found wandering around in the Weeping Forest?" Rayben asked.

"Yes, my Commander."

"I would hardly call him a man, Lieutenant. He cannot be older than fifteen. You brought me from my bed chambers to show me this boy?"

Lon clenched his jaw in agitation, but he remained motionless.

"He showed admirable courage at our first encounter, my Commander," Wade answered as he handed Lon's sword to Rayben. "Although my entire squad charged him, he stood his ground and held this up for us to see."

"Whose blade is this?" Rayben asked.

"It belonged to Gil Baum," Wade replied.

"Did this boy kill him?"

"No, my Commander. He found the bodies of Gil and his squad near the Perbeisea Forest."

"Gil's squad . . ." Rayben said quietly, examining the sword, turning it over repeatedly in his hands. "They must have been on their way back."

"Do you think they discovered what they were searching for?" Wade asked. "Do you think he killed them?"

"We will never know," Rayben replied, then looked at Lon. "Stand, infidel."

Lon kissed the floor and stood on his feet, but kept his eyes cast down.

"What is your name?" the commander asked.

"Lon Shaw."

"Have you used this blade on another man, Lon Shaw?"

"Yes," Lon answered immediately, "to escape an Appernysian patrol on my way here."

"Did you kill anyone?"

"Yes," Lon lied, attempting to impress the commander. "Their scout."

"How did you escape capture?"

"On Gil Baum's horse," Lon answered, glad to have heard the name of Dawes's previous owner.

Rayben shifted his gaze to Wade, who nodded and spoke. "I told him the horse belonged to Gil, my Commander."

"Tell me, Lon Shaw. Why have you come to the Exile?" Rayben said as he turned his attention back to Lon.

"To join myself with you."

"Why?"

"Because I hate Appernysia and believe I'll be a valuable asset to your army."

"Why?"

"I've been a tradesmen my whole life. Over the past few years, I've seen the villagers' attitudes decay. The ki—I mean, the villagers—are being neglected. My own parents starved to death, sharing their rations with me to keep me alive. I once begged a band of Appernysian soldiers for help, but they spit on me and said it was exactly what I deserved. I've seen this same tragedy repeated across Appernysia as its economy worsened. I want no part of it anymore."

Rayben paused for a moment, then snapped his fingers. The guard closest to him pulled a dagger from his belt and handed it to the commander. Rayben flipped the blade over in his hand and, with one swift motion, flung the dagger at Lon's boot. It pierced the leather between two of Lon's toes and clanged loudly as it struck the polished stone floor. Lon didn't move—not even a flinch—an accomplishment he attributed to his complete exhaustion.

"Prove your dedication to me, Lon Shaw," the commander said.

Lon stared at the dagger, confused at the order he received. "Who do you want me to fight?"

Rayben laughed. "No one in this hall, Lon Shaw, unless you wish for a quick death."

Lon gritted his teeth again and breathed in deeply.

"Ah, so I see you do have some pride," Rayben said in response. "Good. I do not accept weaklings."

Lon raised his eyebrows, but he quickly brought them down, grateful to be staring at the floor. He wanted to ask what to do with the dagger, but held his tongue and waited for the commander to speak.

"Good," Rayben said after a few minutes of silence. "You also know when to keep your mouth shut. You will cut your left forearm until you believe you have proven your devotion to me. I will not tell you when to stop."

Lon reached down and pulled the dagger from his boot. Without a word, Wade and four of the guards placed themselves between Lon and their commander.

"Take care not to cut too deep," Rayben added. "You are no use to me with a maimed arm."

"I'm left-handed," Lon replied.

"Really?" Rayben answered with surprise. "I have met only a few of your kind. You may cut your right arm instead, if you prefer. I expect you to fail either way."

Lon ignored Rayben's insults. His thoughts drifted to his father as he rolled up his sleeve. Did Aron know Lon would have to do this? Had Lon seen similar scars on Aron's arm? He couldn't remember any, but either way, it didn't matter. Lon stood twenty-five feet from the leader of the Rayders in the center of his fortress. He had no choice.

Lon decided that even if Aron did know this was coming, it was a well-kept secret. To be branded with the King's Cross was horrible enough, but to mutilate oneself for an undecided amount of time was even worse. Lon was certain that, if he had known, his anxieties leading up to it would have caused him to summon True Sight. Surprise was good. He still had control of himself.

But how should I cut myself to prove my devotion to the commander?

He suspected most people would start at their wrist and cut lines up their forearm until they were unable to handle the pain. Lon also knew he would have to act like it didn't hurt. He didn't know if he could do it, especially without triggering True Sight.

Lon took deep, steady breaths and gripped the hilt of the dagger in his left hand. As he moved the blade toward his right forearm, he glanced at the King's Cross etched on the pommel, and a sudden idea came to mind. He shifted his grip and began carving a two-inch replica of the King's Cross into the top of his upper-forearm.

Carving a picture required more focus than just cutting lines through his skin. Lon hoped it would keep his mind off the pain just enough that he wouldn't summon True Sight. He knew carving the King's

Cross might anger Rayben because Lon hadn't yet earned it, but at the same time, it might also prove Lon's undeniable devotion. After all, it was only on his forearm, not his temple. It wasn't the true mark of a Rayder.

It hurt more than anything Lon had experienced before, but he was able to keep his composure through the entire ordeal and, to his delight, the image turned out very similar to the King's Cross—despite his blood getting in the way.

Rayben said nothing until Lon stopped carving, then told Lon to wipe the blood from his arm. Lon blotted away the blood with his left sleeve and revealed the King's Cross to the commander before it was smothered in red again.

Rayben stared at Lon's arm for a moment and looked at him thoughtfully. Lon dropped his arms to his sides and, although Wade warned him against it, returned the commander's gaze.

With a furious glare, Wade instantly drew his sword and made for Lon, obviously intending to punish him for his insolence.

"Halt," Rayben ordered.

Wade held his ground, his hand gripping the hilt of his sword.

Lon and the Rayder commander stared at each other in silence. Lon started to feel lightheaded as blood ran down his right arm and dripped from his fingertips. But he did not waver.

"Never before has an infidel dared to defy our laws so blatantly," Rayben finally said. "Do you know it means death to look me in the eyes as an outsider?"

"Yes," Lon answered.

"Yet you do it anyway? Why?"

"Because I value the chance to join myself with you more than my life. It's easy to recognize deceit in a man's eyes. What do you see in mine?"

Rayben brought his hand to his chin and rubbed it thoughtfully. "Is it for the same reason that you dare carve the Cross into your arm?"

"Yes," Lon replied as he dipped his head respectfully. "I am committed to becoming a Rayder. I'll die if I can't, whether by your hand or by my own."

Rayben's guarded expression turned to a slight smile. He stood and clapped his hands together. "I like you, Lon Shaw. Some of my men could learn from your show of courage. Wade will escort you out. If you prove your skill at arms, I will gladly accept you into my army. However, no amount of courage will protect you should you fail. I need fighting men, Lon Shaw."

Lon bowed his head as Wade motioned for him to follow. They traveled through the keep and out into the bailey before Wade spoke.

"You have impressed my Commander, Lon Shaw, but I do not like you. Your wanton disregard for our laws is both foolish and disrespectful."

Lon said nothing as Wade led him to a stable on the far side of the bailey.

"You will sleep here with your horse. Should you survive the night, I will take you to the training grounds at sunrise. I will be watching you tomorrow, Lon Shaw. I hope you give me a reason to kill you."

Lon bowed his head at Wade and entered the stables. It was as black as coal inside, but Dawes was easy to find. He danced around his stall as Lon approached. Lon found a loaf of stale bread next to a tall cup of water outside Dawes's stall, which he devoured before collapsing in the hay.

"Interesting people you've got here, Dawes," Lon said as he tore a piece of cloth from his tunic and tied it over the wound on his forearm. "If I don't freeze tonight, I might actually survive. All I have to do is prove that I know how to fight, then I can start searching for Omar. I can't believe I'm saying this, but Father's plan might actually work."

Chapter 19

Crossing Swords

A sharp pain in his ribs startled Lon out of sleep. It was still dark, but enough light crept through the stable doorway to reveal a man standing over him with a staff pointed at his chest. Surprised, Lon swept his leg under the intruder's, knocking him to the ground with a thud. Lon grabbed the staff, jumped on top of his attacker, and pressed the staff against the man's throat.

"I don't want to hurt you, but—" Lon started to say, but stopped short when he recognized Wade's face.

"Get off me," Wade croaked, the staff pressing his windpipe.

Lon hopped off Wade and offered his hand to help him up, but Wade ignored Lon's gesture, turning onto his side, gasping for air.

"I'm sorry, Wade. You startled me."

Wade took a few deep breaths before turning to address Lon. "I should have known better. I underestimated your fighting skills, Lon Shaw, but I do not forgive you. We will settle this on the training grounds today."

Lon nodded. "Are we going there now?"

"Yes," Wade answered, then stood and walked out of the stable. "We will leave immediately. Bring your horse."

"It's a wonder how these people can survive on such little sustenance," Lon grumbled as he saddled Dawes.

Dawes stomped his feet in the corner of his stall, alarmed by the confrontation. Lon spoke softly to him, reassuring him that they were

206 of Terron James

safe, until Dawes settled down enough for Lon to mount and ride out of the stable.

Wade and his nine comrades were waiting outside on their horses. Lon rode to the middle of their formation, after which they retraced their path out of the city. At the bottom of the stone causeway, they turned right and followed the outer wall around the perimeter of the city.

Lon flexed his sore forearm and licked his dry lips as they traveled, but dared not ask for a drink until after his weapons trial. He knew the Rayders despised insolence and weakness; to ask for a drink without being offered one would be a sign of both. He had only requested one the day before out of desperation. Wade would never give him a drink again.

The training grounds were located near the outer wall on the north end of Flagheim, in the middle of a large field. A tall palisade surrounded the grounds, punctuated by many wooden watchtowers that loomed around the perimeter, each with a dozen archers. A simple log house stood just outside the only gate in the palisade.

The center of the training grounds was littered with canvas tents of varying shapes and sizes. Although the sun was barely peeking over the eastern horizon, the grounds were bustling with activity, mostly in the open area between the tents and the perimeter wall. Men fought fiercely with each other, attacking and defending, practicing with an assortment of weapons. Those not fighting were busy lashing rope together—hundreds upon hundreds of feet long.

"What do we need so much rope for?" Lon asked.

The ten Rayders surrounding him glanced at each other, but none responded. After answering his questions so freely until now, their silence made Lon uneasy. He knew he had asked an important question, but he didn't dare press the issue.

"It looks like a prison camp," Lon observed instead, "except the prisoners have weapons."

"It is," Wade said. "Everyone not wearing body armor is a type of prisoner in this camp. They are all refugees from the south who have been accepted by my Commander. Until they prove their worth as a soldier, they will remain here under the careful watch of our weapons master, Tarek Ascennor. It will be Tarek who decides when you are truly ready to receive the Cross."

Lon's mind reeled at the mention of Tarek, but he refrained from asking more. Meeting Myron's son was a secondary priority. He first needed to find Omar. "Are all of these people really from App—I mean, from the south?" Lon said as he looked over the hundreds of unarmored men.

"Yes," Wade replied, "and more arrive every week."

Lon marveled that so many people were desperate enough to flee to the Rayders. Little did they know, they placed themselves into an even worse situation. "I have to admit, I'm surprised to see so many here."

Wade chuckled. "It's not a perfect kingdom. You know as well as the next man that people are starving and crime runs rampant through your cities. Most of these men's families are dead. In some cases, these men have abandoned their families for a better life here."

"I do, but still, I hadn't expected so many." Another thought came to Lon's mind. "Is it possible to prove your worth on your first day?"

"Rarely has anyone shown that level of skill. Our women could beat most of you."

As Lon watched the men in the training grounds more closely, he realized Wade was right. They fought aggressively—probably because they wanted to get out of the camp and run back to Appernysia—but they had almost no skill. They fumbled with their weapons and made awkward attacks that were easy to anticipate.

"Your kingdom is weak, Lon Shaw," Wade continued. "It grows weaker as each day passes. With every man who appears at our doorstep, Appernysia loses strength. It will not be long before we can take back our inheritance. Taeja may lie in ruins, but it will be ours again."

Lon nodded absently, still preoccupied with the lack of skill the Appernysian men displayed. "What'll happen after I prove my worth as a soldier?" he inquired.

"You should only expect to be humiliated today," Wade replied confidently. "If you ever prove your worth, you will return to our commander, receive the Cross, then fulfill whatever assignment my commander requires of you."

"Will I be sent into Appernysia, like Gil?"

"You are overconfident in your abilities, Lon Shaw. Worry about today. Your trial will be with me and I will not be caught off guard this time. Save our commander and Tarek, there is no one in the Exile as skilled as I."

Lon didn't respond.

They passed the log house outside the wooden gate and entered the grounds. As Lon and his escorts rode through, the sparring men stopped to stare at them. By the time they reached Tarek—who was observing an Appernysian spar with a Rayder on the opposite side of the grounds—the camp had grown quiet. Everyone was staring at him, wondering what kind of man required the guard of ten Rayders.

As Lon and his escort approached, the sparring Appernysian glanced toward Lon, distracted just enough that he failed to protect himself from the thrusting blade of his opponent. The sword pierced the man's stomach and he fell to the ground, grunting in anguish.

A bulky man in his early-twenties, stood nearby. He had broad shoulders, long red hair, and a thick beard that covered his face. Lon saw a hint of Myron in the man's brown eyes. He shook his head in disgust and motioned for the injured man to be taken away. The victorious Rayder wiped his blade on the arm of the bleeding man, then grabbed the same arm and dragged him through the mud toward the canvas tents. Lon wondered what the fate of the injured man would be, but he didn't ask.

Wade dismounted and faced the large man, who had turned toward them and crossed his arms. Wade touched the Cross on his right temple and tipped his head. "Good morning, Tarek."

"Spare me the formalities, Wade," Tarek said without returning the gesture. "You know better than to ride up in the middle of a sparring match. He was one of the best fighters in this camp. I was certain he'd join our commander's army today."

"Even if he had passed the trial," Wade replied, "he would not have lasted long. He is too easily distracted."

"Maybe," Tarek said, "but now we'll never know. He'll be dead by nightfall."

"Too bad," Wade answered with a brazen smile.

The two men stood staring at each other; neither of them flinched. Lon couldn't believe Wade's courage. Tarek's size alone was enough to intimidate Lon.

Lon dismounted Dawes and walked next to Wade. The other nine soldiers didn't strike, but they watched him closely with their hands on their swords.

"Meet Lon Shaw," Wade said, nodding in Lon's direction.

"I've come to prove my worth as a soldier," Lon said to Tarek with a bow. "I'm anxious to begin."

"I've already heard about you and what you did in front of our commander," Tarek answered without moving his eyes away from Wade. "Apparently it was enough to shake up the Lieutenant here. Nobody has ever needed ten escorts before."

"I do not trust him," Wade replied.

Tarek laughed and shook his head, then turned to Lon. "You're surprisingly confident and bold for a man so young. Are you really so anxious to bury yourself in a life of bloodshed?"

Lon was surprised to hear Tarek's candid response. Every Rayder Lon had met thus far was completely loyal to their commander, and treated the prospect of joining with him as an honor. Lon wondered if Tarek dared make such a comment because of his status and fighting skill, or if there was something more. Was there a part of Tarek that still clung to Pree and wondered what happened to his family there? Did he harbor a hidden grudge against the Rayders for being forced into their world? Would Tarek—if given the opportunity—leave the Rayders and return to Pree with Lon?

Tarek raised his eyebrow at Lon.

"Yes, I'm sure," Lon answered, realizing his silence was probably mistaken as hesitation. "I doubt bloodshed is the only reward of joining the commander's army."

"Maybe," Tarek answered, his arms still folded across his chest. "How old are you?"

"Seventeen."

"You're wiser than I'd expect for a man your age," Tarek commented. "Most men who come here are so anxious to leave Appernysia that they throw themselves at us without reservation. They don't take the time to consider the consequences."

Lon bowed his head in response.

"We'll begin with a short trial of weapons," Tarek continued. "If you fail, you'll remain inside these walls until you learn how to use them. You'll fight against someone who has already proven his skill, so look around and pick your opponent. It can be anyone marked with the Cross."

"Wade already volunteered to join me," Lon answered.

"Really?" Tarek glanced at Wade, who nodded in confirmation.

Tarek raised his eyebrows with surprise, then motioned for Lon to follow him to a rack full of various weapons. "Pick your weapon," he said loudly, then added softly for only Lon to hear, "Pick carefully. Wade intends to kill you in this match."

No wonder Wade answered all of my questions, Lon thought as he glanced over the array of weapons. Remembering his father's counsel, he turned to Wade. "What are you using, Lieutenant?"

"I need no other weapon than the sword at my side," Wade answered defiantly.

Lon glanced at the arming sword belted around Wade's waist, gauged its size and weight, then returned his gaze to the weapons on the rack. He ignored the heavy axes, maces, and two-handed swords, knowing that, aside from his inexperience with them, their weight would slow him down. Lon looked through an assortment of pole weapons and considered a glaive that looked well balanced and light, but he eventually chose an arming sword similar to the one he carried across Appernysia.

"Good choice," Tarek said quietly.

"What happens now?" Lon asked.

"It's simple," Tarek answered. "You'll face each other until I give a signal, then you'll fight until one of you surrenders or dies."

Lon closed his eyes and took a deep breath to calm himself. He knew the problems before him. Only once had Lon bested his father without summoning True Sight, yet before him stood a man determined not only to beat him, but to kill him. If Wade's claim to be a master was true, Lon couldn't hold back if he hoped to win. He would have to push himself to the limit of his abilities, and even that might not be enough.

Lon released the air from his lungs, then opened his eyes and whispered to himself, "For Kaylen."

Tarek glanced at Lon curiously, but said nothing as he led the Appernysian to stand in front of Wade. With the exception of his leather gloves and vambraces, Wade had removed all of his armor. Tarek stepped back to the edge of a tight circle of men who had formed around the two combatants.

Just as Tarek was about to signal the start of the match, Dawes panicked. With a frightened whinny, he bit down on the hair of a man standing in front of him and threw him out of the way, then kicked two other men behind him. Thad—the guard who had led them through Flagheim—unsheathed his sword and swung at the horse's neck, but Dawes dodged the attack and shouldered Thad's horse, knocking him out of the saddle.

"Wait!" Lon shouted as the other guards drew their swords.

Everyone paused to look at Lon, who dropped his sword and forced his way through the crowd until he reached the horse. Dawes was jittery, his eyes rolling wildly, but Lon grabbed his face and forced the horse to look at him.

"Relax, Dawes. We both need to stay calm if we're going to survive this."

Dawes squirmed and fought Lon, but eventually calmed down enough for Lon to return to his match. After Lon disappeared into the crowd, his guards positioned their horses so that Dawes was boxed between them. Dawes nickered at being boxed in, but he remained still.

Lon returned to his place opposite Wade and took another long, slow breath before picking up his sword. Wade sneered at him.

"Are you both ready?" Tarek asked from the perimeter of the circle, which had reformed around them.

Both men nodded.

"Begin!"

Lon stood motionless, focusing his thoughts. *I can't be aggressive, so I must fight defensively, but if I don't attack, I won't win. I have to trust my instincts. I have to—*

"Coward!" Wade taunted. "Are you so afraid to face me that you cower out of reach?"

—trust what my father taught me. I have to break his concentration. I have to . . . anger him.

Lon grinned with excitement. He suddenly realized that every time he lost control and summoned True Sight, he had become angry, frustrated, or worried. It never crossed his mind that he could use the same tactics to disable an opponent.

"Do not smile at me, infidel!" Wade shouted in anger. "You have no chance of beating me. I am Wade Arneson, descendant of an endless line of weapon masters!"

Lon gripped his sword and continued to smile at Wade. Soon his opponent would lose self-control and throw himself into combat, but Lon realized that Wade was still a skilled swordsman. Even when lashing out in anger, Wade would be difficult to beat.

Wade's face turned red with pure hatred. He spit at Lon and cursed him, his ancestors, and his descendants. His fury was so intense that Lon began doubting his tactic. He wondered if Rayders were so well trained that, even when blind with emotions, they were infallible in combat. Then he remembered his encounter in Pree. Gil's surprise at seeing a Beholder destroyed the Rayder's focus. He had been so anxious to capture a Beholder that he thought he could simply reach out and grab Lon.

Anger and surprise, Lon considered. *How can I surprise Wade, except through the use of True Sight?*

Wade finally rushed at him. Lon held out his sword, but Wade's blade was still inside its scabbard, making it difficult for Lon to predict the attack. When he was within striking range, Wade drew his sword with blinding speed and slashed upward in one fluid motion. Lon managed to parry the blow and sidestep Wade's charging shoulder, recognizing the attack as one of Aron's kill strokes.

The crowd surrounding them shouted enthusiastically, but he ignored them as he leaped forward to counterattack. They continued to exchange blows for what seemed like an eternity, neither one able to penetrate the other's defenses. Lon's shoulders ached, his arms felt like lead, and the scabbed wound on his right forearm cracked and bled, but he refused to yield. He struck at Wade with every improvisation he could muster, but Wade didn't falter and returned each blow with a counterattack.

Lon's concentration began breaking as frustration built up inside of him. He forgot his reasons for coming to the Exile, and became obsessed with beating Wade. Lon hacked, stabbed, and parried, but nothing availed him. He became so desperate and careless that, during one series of attacks, he left his right side exposed. Wade sliced down his abdomen.

The pain was excruciating. Lon curled over, grabbing his side and grimacing at Wade, who was smirking five paces in front of him.

"You are beaten, Lon Shaw," Wade said with a heaving chest. "Look at yourself. If you continue to fight, you will lose consciousness and die from loss of blood."

Lon glanced down to check the severity of the cut. His tunic and pants were already soaked with blood. Lon panicked and, much to his dismay, summoned True Sight. He kept his head down to hide his clouded eyes from the crowd, but watched Wade's glowing form through his peripheral vision.

"Drop your sword," Wade shouted in anger, "or I will kill you."

Lon wanted to obey Wade's command, but if he looked up to surrender, everyone would know he was a Beholder. The only way Lon knew how to remove True Sight was to either knock himself unconscious—which would be impossible to disguise from the judgmental Rayders—or use the energy that filled his body.

"I will not surrender," Lon barked as he tried to transfer the energy into his sword.

He wrapped both hands around his sword, which glowed with pulsing energy visible only to him. When Wade charged to attack, Lon silently plead for the Jaeds' help. He knew what he was about to attempt would either win the match or kill him. Should he miss, Lon would be completely defenseless against any counterattack. His timing had to be perfect.

Lon reared back with his sword and swung with all his might at Wade. Lon glanced up just in time to realize that his sword was aimed directly at Wade's head. Lon didn't intend to kill his opponent. He twisted the blade as it struck the side of Wade's head with a burst of light. Lon's eyes instantly cleared as Wade flipped sideways through the air until he landed motionless on his side.

Dumbfounded, the crowd grew silent. No one moved. No one spoke. Lon watched them for a moment, grateful for his cleared vision. He knelt down next to Wade to check for signs of life, but the loss of blood was taking its toll on him; his hands shook, and his head began to spin. Soon, he was joined by Tarek, who grabbed Wade's chin and turned it to inspect the side of his face.

"Amazing swordsmanship," Tarek commented. "You must have hit him perfectly with the flat of your blade. There isn't a scratch on his head. He'll have a serious headache when he wakes up, though. Poor thing," he ended with a small chuckle.

"Did I break his neck?" Lon asked, his voice low and weak. He was glad that Tarek—along with everyone else watching—had not seen the burst of light.

"Maybe," Tarek answered as he whistled for two soldiers, "but only time will tell."

Tarek instructed the soldiers to carry Wade back to his quarters in Flagheim, then turned his attention to Lon. "We better bandage up that wound before . . ."

Tarek's voice faded as darkness overtook Lon. He collapsed to the ground.

Chapter 20
New Beginning

Mellai sat up, startled awake by an overwhelming sense of anxiety and pain. It took her a moment to realize that the feelings weren't her own, but her brother's.

Her grandmother came bustling in from the bedroom, wrapped in a thick robe. "What's wrong?"

"I . . . I had a bad dream," Mellai responded. Her body shook as she worried over what had happened to Lon.

"Sweetheart, you're trembling," her grandmother said as she sat down next to her granddaughter, "I've never heard such an unnerving scream before. Do you want to talk about it?"

Mellai stared out the east window of their home at the glowing sunrise, hesitant to answer. She had been living with her grandparents for a week. They took her in and never asked for an explanation of her family's sudden disappearance or whereabouts. Mellai had been considering whether to tell them the truth about Lon and her family.

"I was screaming? I—" Mellai began, but was interrupted by the front door crashing open.

Theiss charged in, gardening hoe in hand, ready to start swinging. "Where is he?" he demanded as he scanned the room for trouble.

"It's nothing, Theiss," her grandmother answered, a little perplexed. "She just had a bad dream."

Allegna's words drew Theiss's attention to Mellai, whose face was partially hidden in the arms of her grandmother. He blanched. "Pardon me,

Allegna. I heard Linney screaming and . . . I apologize for barging in." Without another word, he ducked out of the house and closed the door.

"I'm sorry for the intrusion, Mellai," Allegna said as she stood up and looked through the back window. "That boy has a good heart. Should there be an intruder, I would have felt sorry for him. Theiss looked ready to grapple with a full grown bear."

Mellai joined her grandmother at the window and stared at the large field behind the house. Both her grandfather and Theiss were working nearby, removing the dead corn stalks and tomato plants and placing them in a large pile. Despite her apprehension for Lon, Mellai couldn't help but smile at the sight of Theiss vigorously ripping the corn stocks out of the ground.

"It'll take him a few days to recover from that," Mellai joked.

"Yes, it will," Allegna replied with a chuckle. "I doubt he's ever seen a woman in her nightgown before." They watched the men work for a short time before Allegna spoke again. "Are you feeling better?"

Mellai frowned. "Not really."

She realized that Lon's mind was completely at ease, which meant he was unconscious. Mellai was certain he had used True Sight. Had he revealed himself to the Rayders?

Allegna disappeared out of the room and returned with a leather satchel similar to Shalán's. Using a pot of hot water she had boiled for her husband, she made hot tea for Mellai.

"Drink this," she said as she handed a cup to her granddaughter. "It will help calm you."

Mellai took the cup and drank the tea slowly, enjoying how it warmed her body and soothed her nerves. When Mellai finished her tea, Allegna smiled and took the cup from her, cleaned it, and set it back on a shelf. Mellai watched her grandmother work. Her wrinkled hands handled the cup delicately.

"Don't your knuckles hurt?" Mellai asked with amazement. "You're still as nimble as I am."

"Oh, there's plenty of pain to deal with," Allegna replied, "but I have a special tea I drink every night. It deadens my joint pain so I can sleep. Your grandfather takes it, too. It lasts all night and a little bit into the morning, but by lunchtime we're both feeling our age again."

"I've noticed that Grandfather is a little hunched over and moves slower when he comes in for lunch, but I'd always thought it was fatigue. He works so hard."

"That doesn't help," Allegna laughed. "But the majority of our pain comes with our gray hair. You can't get as old as us without feeling the effects of it."

Mellai frowned again. She had never known anyone who lived to be older than seventy and her grandparents were well into their sixties. It bothered her that she missed the previous five years. There was so little time left for them to spend together. Mellai decided that regardless of the potential risks, her grandparents had the right to know what her family had gone through since they left Roseiri—especially everything within the last few months.

"Come sit with me, Grandmother. I have a story to tell you."

*　　*　　*　　*　　*

"That's quite a tale," Allegna said as she leaned back against the seat. "When your family disappeared that night, the only explanation I was left with came from the villagers. Their observations became so outlandish and fantastic I didn't know whom to believe. After a couple of days, people were saying that they saw you and Lon grow wings and carry your parents away into the clouds. That was, of course, ridiculous, but I still knew something unimaginable must have happened to create such a stir. I had no idea where you went."

"I know it won't change the past," Mellai said, "but I didn't want to leave. I've spent almost every waking moment hating my parents for making us go. Looking back, I feel horrible. They were just trying to protect our family, including you and Grandfather."

"We don't begrudge them. They did the best they could with a bad situation. I only wish they'd trusted us enough to tell us where you went. Anyway, the past is the past. You have returned, and that's what matters most."

"I'm surprised you're taking this so well."

"When you've heard what I've heard, the truth comes as quite a relief." Allegna sat forward. "So, about your dream this morning—do you think Lon is still in the Exile?"

"I think so . . . and maybe indefinitely. He was in terrible pain, Grandmother, and then . . . nothing. If he summoned True Sight and a Rayder saw his eyes, they'd know he's a Beholder. They'd never let him out of their sight. I mean, they'd see Lon as a valuable weapon against King Drogan. If Lon were caught, war would be inevitable."

"I fear war is coming, whether Lon is involved or not," Allegna responded. "King Drogan has been expanding his army; his scouts are constantly scouring the countryside. He claims it's to protect us from the Rayders, but I just don't know. I've grown very skeptical over the last few years."

Mellai stared at the floor and breathed out her frustration. "Did the world just become this crazy or was I simply ignorant of it before now? I feel like every day reveals more and more problems. I was living a happy, carefree life only a few years ago. Now, look at me. My parents are in hiding, and, although I've returned to Roseiri, I have to keep my identity a secret, too. My best friend has abandoned me for a trading caravan. My brother is a Beholder—*a Beholder!*—and most likely in the clutches of our kingdom's sworn enemy. Now King Drogan is preparing to go to war against them. Will life ever be simple again?"

"That's a complicated question, Mellai. Life will always present its challenges, but it only becomes as overwhelming as we allow it to be. Your grandfather and I have chosen to live a simple life. The world is complicated, yes, but don't allow it to overwhelm you. Focus on the things you can control and let everyone else worry about the rest."

"It sounds simple," Mellai grumbled, "but I can't ignore the world. My life is wrapped up in it."

"Perhaps, but you can still choose how it affects you. Take it one day at a time."

"Am I supposed to spend the rest of my life hiding who I am? I want a future with a husband and my own children. I want them to meet my parents. When will that ever become possible?"

A knock on the front door interrupted them, and Allegna stood to answer it.

"Go get your veil, Mellai," she whispered.

After Mellai disappeared into the bedroom, Allegna opened the door and found Theiss standing on the doorstep.

"Hello," he said timidly. "Your husband and I are taking a small break while he searches for a new hoe. I . . . uh . . . broke the one I was using. I volunteered to find a replacement, but your husband insisted I come visit with you instead."

"Did he?" Allegna said with a smile. "Well then, please come inside. Can I make you some tea?"

"No, thank you," Theiss answered as he removed his hat and stepped inside. "I'll only take a moment of your time. I want to apologize for my intrusion this morning. If Linney's still here, I'd like to ask for her forgiveness as well."

"Of course, she is," Allegna answered. "Have a seat while I go get her."

Allegna left Theiss alone in the front room and found Mellai in her bedroom, sitting stiffly on the bed with a scowl on her face.

"I can't talk to him," Mellai argued in a hoarse whisper. "He'll recognize me."

"Not if you hide your face, *Linney*," Allegna answered as she picked up the veil and handed it to her granddaughter. "Besides, the poor boy will never forgive himself until he apologizes to you."

Mellai glared at Allegna as she took the veil and wrapped it around her head. "I'm starting to feel like I'm back in Pree with my mother."

"Well, she *is* my daughter," Allegna said with a smile as she left the room.

Mellai reluctantly followed and found Theiss sitting in a chair. When they entered, he immediately stood and bowed politely.

"Good afternoon, Linney," he said.

Mellai glanced at her grandmother, unsure of how to answer.

"I . . . uh . . . well," he sputtered at her silence, "I want to apologize for my intrusion earlier. I didn't know that you were . . . uh . . . well . . . I thought you might be in trouble."

Mellai stared at Theiss. He was tall and fit—an inch or two taller than Lon—and his head was covered with blond hair, matted down from his hat. He wasn't handsome, or ugly, but the sincerity in his green eyes warmed Mellai's heart. Theiss was a good man. She knew it. He had been graciously taking care of her grandparents and, even when the rest of Roseiri refused, he volunteered to accompany her to find Kaylen. He was genuine and sincere.

Mellai turned and entered the kitchen. After wetting a dry cloth, she walked up to Theiss and began cleaning the dried dirt off his face. He blushed deeply.

"Uh . . . I . . . um . . ." he sputtered again.

"Yes?" Mellai answered, smiling behind her veil.

"Um . . . well, would you like to . . . uh . . . walk with me, Linney?"

"I'd like that."

Chapter 21

Ignorance

A cold gust of wind weaved through the gigantic trees and stung their faces. Aely, a girl Kaylen had met during her short stay in Réxura, growled as the wind fanned the pages of her book. Kaylen shivered and slid closer to Kutad. They had been traveling east for four days and were out of the mighty Perbeisea Forest.

"Thank you for taking us to Itorea, Kutad. You've been like a father to me," Kaylen said.

Kutad forced a smile as he cracked a whip at the team of donkeys pulling the wagon. He appreciated her compliments and the respect she showed him, but it hurt to be compared to her father. He'd become very fond of Kaylen, and although he knew she loved someone else, he still hoped he might win her over. Even with Aely along, he had thought the trip to Itorea would be a good opportunity to win Kaylen's heart.

"Are you sure you don't want to stay with our caravan?" Kutad asked. "We've all grown to love you. We'd be honored to keep you as part of our family."

"I feel the same way toward all of you," Kaylen replied, "but I can't spend the rest of my life wandering from place to place. I need a home where I can raise a family."

"Home can't be found in the soil," Kutad replied. "It's a place in your heart."

"We have different views of home, Kutad. I need to find a place where people can still find me." Her gaze turned north as she finished speaking.

"Are you sure Itorea is the best place?" Kutad asked Kaylen with a sideways glance at Aely. "No offense to your friend, but you don't know what kind of men live there. If you stay with us, there are many in our caravan who would love to raise a family with you."

"You know I've already given my heart to someone."

Her response stabbed at Kutad's heart, but he hid his feelings to protect hers. Kaylen was young and in love, while he was as old as her father. She didn't need the burden of his yearning.

"Is this man waiting for you in Itorea?"

"Yes," Kaylen lied. "I've told you this before. He serves in the King's Court. That's why I'm going with Aely. Her friends should be able to help me find him."

Kutad had his doubts about her story. According to Kaylen, her betrothed left three months earlier to secure a living in Itorea. He sent for Kaylen to join him once he started serving King Drogan. From Kutad's observations in Pree, Kaylen's father loved her deeply. A man like Scut wouldn't respect someone who abandoned his betrothed. The secrecy required in Roseiri and Kaylen's kidnapping also put doubts in Kutad's mind. Kaylen had spent the entire day crying after Mellai decided to remain in Roseiri, yet she was supposed to be traveling to live with the love of her life. She hadn't even shared his name. Too many questions. Too many doubts.

Kutad knew Kaylen was in love—no doubt about that—but he guessed she was secretly running away to be with him. Perhaps he had been banished from Pree, and that was the reason she wouldn't speak his name. Kutad mulled over the situation for a long time until he believed he had figured out Kaylen's secret.

Her lover is Mellai's relative, Kutad thought, *perhaps even her brother, Lon. He wasn't around when we were in Pree and I haven't heard Mellai speak his name once. But why would Kaylen leave to marry a man who had been banished, and why would Mellai approve of it, especially when he's her brother?*

"We're almost there," Kutad said to Kaylen. "We'll stay in Sylbie tonight, but within three or four days you'll be in the arms of your betrothed—no doubt the warmest place in Appernysia."

"Three or four days?" Kaylen questioned. "Why will it take so long to find him? I thought Itorea was an island off the coast of Sylbie."

"It is," Kutad laughed, "but that island is a hundred miles across. You have to travel fifty miles before you even reach the keep."

*   *   *   *   *

Kaylen's first sight of Sylbie came at dusk when Kutad drove their wagon out of the Perbeisea Forest. Even from ten miles away, the city's size should have impressed her, but it was dwarfed by the perimeter wall of Itorea, positioned farther and running as far as Kaylen could see.

She gasped. "Amazing."

"Aye," Kutad said, "and it's beyond that wall that you must travel, into the City of the King."

"How high is the wall?" Kaylen asked.

"Three hundred feet," Aely answered, closing her book.

"And fifty feet thick," Kutad added.

"How could anyone build a wall like that?" Kaylen said with bewilderment. "It would take centuries to finish."

"Yes, it would," Kutad answered, "if it wasn't done by Beholders. Those magic-wielding men conjured some impressive sorcery when they built Itorea. If you look hard, you can see the outline of different colored shapes on its walls. You'll see it better up close and in good daylight. There's more to that wall than just its height. Its beauty will give you something to think about for the rest of your life—and that's before you even pass under it. You're in for quite a surprise."

Under normal circumstances, Kaylen would have bubbled with excitement, but after Kutad's reference to Beholders, all traces of anticipation leaked away. Kaylen slumped back into her seat and folded her arms across her chest, wishing desperately that Lon were sitting next to her in the wagon.

Chapter 22
Branded

Night had settled over the Exile, but the great hall of Flagheim's keep shimmered under the glowing light of the torch-lined walls and the roaring bonfire. The room was packed with Rayders standing shoulder to shoulder. Commander Rayben Goldhawk sat upon his polished throne, quietly drumming the fingers of his right hand on the throne's arm.

The doors at the opposite end of the hall swung open and two columns of plate-armored soldiers filed in, their shields bearing the King's Cross. They marched to the bonfire in the middle of the room, then turned to face each other, drew their swords, and stood at attention.

Tarek entered the room next, followed by Lon, who had been primped and primed for the occasion. He had been washed and scrubbed from head to foot. His scraggly hair had been trimmed short and his beard shaved, save for a small tuft on his chin. He wore a plain silk tunic of pale blue, dark linen pants, and freshly-polished black leather boots. He walked with conviction, showing no signs of the trials he had endured over the last few weeks. Tarek led him between the soldiers to the crackling bonfire. Then Rayben stood and, descending from his throne, joined them in the center of the hall, the flames roaring between them.

"Why have you come, Tarek Ascennor?" the commander asked.

Tarek dipped his head and touched the King's Cross on his right temple. "My Commander, I have come to offer another soldier for your army."

"Is he worthy?"

"He has proven himself worthy in both courage and skill. I urge you to accept his service."

"Come forward, Lon Shaw."

Lon walked around the left side of the fire and stood in front of the Rayder commander.

"Turn your head and look on my throne," Rayben continued. "Do you swear fealty to me, that for the rest of your life you will obey my command immediately and without question?"

"I do," Lon lied.

"Do you swear to uphold our traditions and defend our land and people until death?"

"I do." *For now.*

"Do you swear to keep constant watch for the return of a Beholder and, should you find one, do everything in your power to bring him before me?"

Lon chuckled inwardly at the irony of Rayben's words. "I do."

Rayben pulled an iron rod out of the hot coals. On its tip was the tiny glowing symbol of the King's Cross. "I receive your service, having found you worthy to serve me as a Rayder. I mark you with the Cross as a token of my acceptance."

Lon eyed the branding iron and argued silently with himself. *There's no turning back after this. Are you sure this is what you want? All it would take is one false move toward the commander and your life would end, along with all your troubles.* He clenched his jaw and prepped himself for the branding. *But you're not doing this for yourself. This is for Kaylen.*

The branding took less than a second. Pain coursed through Lon's head when the red-hot iron seared the skin of his right temple, leaving an inch-wide brand of charred flesh. Lon's eyes watered, he fought back a cry of pain, but to his delight, he didn't summon True Sight. He had once again endured excruciating pain without losing control, but he had no clue how.

CHAPTER 22: BRANDED 227
Rayben tossed the iron rod aside and snapped his fingers. One of his guards brought him a sword and returned to his post.

"I present you with your chosen sword," Rayben said to Lon. "A three-foot, single-handed falchion."

Lon took the sword, a duplicate of his father's falchion. Although he had grown accustomed to the arming sword, a falchion would be a constant reminder of his end goal. After kissing the King's Cross etched into its pommel, he belted it around his waist, then bowed his head and touched the tender flesh of his right temple with two fingers of his right hand.

"How may I serve you, my Commander?"

"Come forward, Tarek Ascennor," Rayben said.

Tarek walked around the fire and placed himself next to Lon. "My Commander?"

"Behold," Rayben boomed as he raised his hands above his head, "the two greatest swordsmen under my rule."

The crowd of Rayders shouted and stomped their feet while the armored soldiers banged their sword hilts against their shields. Rayben let them celebrate briefly, then signaled for silence.

"I have an important task for both of you," he said loud enough for everyone to hear, "one of the most important tasks ever laid on our people since our banishment from Appernysia. I want the training grounds outside Flagheim purged of its Appernysian filth. Kill them all. I have no more time to waste on training those weakling runaways. From this point forward, the grounds will be used for a much more important task."

Tarek nodded while Lon stared in shock—too afraid to voice his opposition.

"I am issuing an order for all Rayder men to report to Flagheim," Rayben continued. "I need a strong army trained to fight against terrible odds. I now hold both of you responsible for that training. Tarek Ascennor, I hereby name you general over my full army. I place Lon Shaw in your keeping, to help train my army and ready them for battle."

Rayben turned his attention to the crowd. "No longer will I accept an Appernysian into the Exile. If any unmarked man, woman, or child is found within our borders, they must be killed on sight. A great task lies before us and I cannot afford to coddle refugees, some of which are no doubt spies.

"Taeja lies in ruins, uninhabited for over a millennium, but this shall be no more. Preparations to retake Taeja have already begun. Although there is still much that must be done to assure our triumph, I will no longer hide in the shadow of Appernysia. I will rule in the land that is rightfully mine. With the help of my new general, Tarek Ascennor, I will lead you all to triumph!"

Everyone cheered. Runners were immediately sent out to spread the commander's declaration. Extra wood was thrown in the fire and casks of mead and ale were opened. Smoke hovered in the rafters over the Rayders' euphoric celebration, yet Lon and Tarek stood motionless before their commander.

"Ah," Rayben said quietly, "I knew I had chosen wisely. The masses rejoice around you, yet you do not join them? Am I correct to assume you both wish to start immediately?"

"Yes, my Commander," Tarek replied. Lon didn't respond. He was still preoccupied with the extermination order and the daunting task of training Rayder soldiers.

"Very well," the commander continued. "I appreciate your loyalty, Lon Shaw, but I must ask you to wait here. Follow me to my personal chambers, General Tarek, and I will explain how I am going to take back Taeja."

Chapter 23

Old Acquaintance

The muffled sound of snapping bowstrings ricocheted across the snow-covered plains. Arrows whistled as they sliced through the air before falling down on their targets.

Lon folded his arms and glanced at Tarek beside him. "I'm impressed."

Tarek smirked. "That's because you keep forgetting who you're working with. These men are Rayders, not coddled 'Nysians."

A week had passed since Lon's branding. He and Tarek had spent every day training the Rayder men in archery. They started with close shots at bundled hay and had just advanced to moving targets.

"Still," Tarek continued as he watched a group of his men dart back and forth across the field, "it'll be nice when they get to shoot at real Appernysians with steel-tipped arrows."

An armored soldier fell sideways as a blunted arrow bounced off his helm.

"Kill shot," Lon muttered.

"It's funny," Tarek said. "When I first came to the Exile from Pree, the Rayders' steel helms had the Cross etched into them. They looked sharp, but I convinced our commander to take them off; they just made their heads a big target. Do you think we should put it back on? Our men would probably get a lot more kill shots that way."

"Probably not," Lon said with a laugh. "I've already got two targets scarred on me. That's more than enough."

Tarek shook his head and rubbed his left forearm. "I still can't believe you carved the Cross on your arm. I just sliced lines up mine and that was plenty to satisfy our commander. What were you thinking?"

"I'm not sure. Maybe I was feeling extra Rayder-ish that day."

Although Tarek had become a good friend in a short time, Lon hadn't told him of their connection through Pree. He hadn't decided whether it was safe to share anything with him. Only one person would know the full truth for sure, but Lon hadn't met him yet.

Dawes nickered nearby, drawing Lon's attention to a man riding hard from the outer wall of Flagheim. His head was down and he was urging his horse on with the flat of his sword.

Lon's hand drifted to the falchion belted around his waist. "Trouble?"

"Hardly," Tarek answered with a laugh. "That's our commander. He doesn't get out of Flagheim much, so when he does, he rides hard. He likes to feel the open air sting his face."

Lon squinted as the morning sunlight glinted off Rayben Goldhawk's silver coronet. "If he likes to ride outside Flagheim so much, why doesn't he? Does Rayder law bind him inside the keep?"

"It's just the safest place to be," Tarek answered before drawing a deep breath and turning to his men. "Rayders, our commander approaches."

Lieutenants echoed Tarek's decree, and in less than five seconds, over fifteen thousand Rayders were on their knees with their foreheads touching the snow.

Rayben wove between the soldiers to Dawes's side. "Rise, General Tarek. Follow me. Bring Lon with you."

They both kissed the snow, then stood and hurried to their horses. "After you, my Commander," Tarek said.

Without answering, Rayben kicked his horse and galloped back toward Flagheim. Tarek gave instructions to one of his lieutenants before he and Lon raced after the commander.

They were northwest of Flagheim, near the training grounds where Lon had bested Wade during his trial. Lon looked south, expecting to follow his commander around the outer wall to the main gate into the city, but Rayben continued straight toward the outer wall. When they came within fifty yards of the wall, a Rayder sentry whistled from atop the stone barrier. A small opening suddenly appeared in the smooth stone surface, allowing the three men access into the city.

A hidden postern gate, Lon mused to himself. *If Flagheim was under attack, Rayben and his guards could slip out unnoticed and ride to safety. I guess these Rayders don't consider themselves as invincible as they act.*

The Rayder commander led Tarek and Lon through the city and inner wall, where they left their horses with the stable boy before continuing into the keep. Lon struggled not to smile at the confusion on the faces of the men guarding the entrance into the keep. They were unused to having both a general and their commander in their midst, and didn't know whether to stand at attention, salute, or bow themselves to the ground as Tarek and Rayben walked by.

Rayben led them through the long passages of the keep, past the great hall, to a large wooden door. Rayben pounded on the door with his fist and, a moment later, a portly old man with thinning gray hair appeared.

"Come in, Rayben," the man said as he stepped aside.

Tarek winked at Lon and waited outside the door while Lon followed Rayben inside, wondering what sort of man could speak to the Rayder commander so casually. Lon had been warned by Tarek that anyone who called the commander by his given name wouldn't survive the day.

The size of the room was similar to the sitting area at Lon's house in Pree. A warm fire revealed a caged golden eagle in one corner and mounds of clutter everywhere else. Scattered tables were covered in parchment manuscripts and maps. Suddenly Lon realized where he was and his mind reeled.

"Good morning, Omar," Rayben replied. "I have brought you a new pupil in need of tutoring."

Omar Brickeden stared at Lon from under his bushy eyebrows. His eyes pierced Lon's. Lon shifted under his knowing gaze.

"This must be the famous Lon Shaw," Omar said as he continued to stare at the boy, "or perhaps I should say infamous. It is about time you bring him to me, Rayben. I have heard of his defiance to our laws and traditions."

"Bold, yes," Rayben interceded, "but not defiant. His confidence is what set my plan in motion."

Omar sat himself at a table and laced his fingers over his large belly. "That, I have also heard. Does this confidence make you capable of leading our commander's armies, Lon?"

"No," Lon answered. "I'm no leader. I'm overwhelmed just by the effort of training our men. We owe our success thus far to General Tarek."

"Good," Omar replied. "It looks like I might actually be able to teach you something. Appernysians have come here claiming loyalty, but listened to nothing I said. Are the bricks of your mind fired or malleable?"

"They're still dry dirt and straw. I came to the Exile seeking water and flame."

Omar tapped his thumbs together. "Wise, yet humble. You may leave us, Rayben. I'm sure you have far more pressing matters."

Rayben turned and exited the quarters. "Come, General Tarek," he said as he disappeared out of the room. "Back to your soldiers."

Tarek leaned in and grabbed the door handle. "Go easy on him, Omar. He's new around here." He winked at Lon again and pulled the door closed.

Omar sat forward and placed his interlocked hands on the table, his eyes fixed on Lon.

"Sit down, Lon. Tell me, since you entered the Exile two weeks ago, have you heard the name Aron Marcs?"

Lon's mind flinched as he took a chair, unsure of how to answer. *Why would he ask me that?* he debated with himself. *Is my father's history really so popular or does Omar suspect who I am?*

"No."

Omar's eyes narrowed. "Interesting."

"Why do you ask?"

"You remind me of him in many ways. I had the opportunity to raise him after his parents died."

"Really?" Lon asked, unable to constrain his curiosity. "How old was he when his parents died?"

The edge of Omar's lips curled up in a subtle smile. "He was only a young boy. Would you like to hear about his childhood?"

"Yes, please."

"Why?"

Lon clenched his jaw as he struggled to come up with a good lie. He had shown too much interest.

"I . . . just figured it must be important if you brought it up."

"You are lying to me, Lon . . . *Shaw*."

Lon's stomach lurched. He had no idea how to respond. His lying had finally trapped him in a corner and Omar knew it.

"Aron's life was a tragedy," Omar continued. "Much like you, he was wise and confident, with massive potential. But he chose to abandon the Rayders in his late twenties and hasn't been seen since, despite the efforts by our commander to track him down. I have often wondered what became of him and if he had any children."

Lon remained silent, not trusting himself to speak.

Omar grabbed a quill, dipped it in an ink vial, and began writing on a piece of parchment. "Why are you here, Lon Marcs?"

"Because I want to . . ." Lon started before fading into silence, realizing too late that Omar had called him by his real name.

Omar put down the quill and leaned back in his chair. "The truth is out, son of Aron. Now, why are you really here?"

"To join the Rayders," Lon answered earnestly.

"*That* I believe, but why?"

Lon stared at the floor, still unable to answer. The conversation was moving too fast and he was unsure of whether or not he could trust the scholar.

Omar sighed. "I see that I must take the first step. Very well. I admit I did not agree with your father's decision to marry Shalán, but I loved him and allowed him to run to Roseiri. Lies are not becoming of honorable men, Lon, but I have told my fair share to keep your father's secret. I love him now as much as I did when he left over twenty years ago. I would do anything for him, or his son."

A wave of relief overcame Lon as he realized Omar's true intentions. Despite his best efforts, tears filled Lon's eyes. If Omar knew Shalán's name and that she was from Roseiri, he had to be trustworthy.

"I understand the importance of a close friend with whom you can confide," Omar continued. "I expect General Tarek will become such a friend to you soon, but in the meantime, release your burden of secrecy. Tell me what brings you to the Exile, Lon."

Lon nodded as he took deep breaths to calm himself. "My parents raised me in Roseiri, but we've spent the past few years in Pree."

"I had considered that. Pree is where Rayben sent Gil Baum and his squad to look for a Beholder three months ago."

"Yes. They made it to Pree, but Tarek's father, Myron, ambushed them in the night and killed four of them before falling to Gil's sword."

"I have often wondered what became of Tarek's father. It is a pity he had to die." Omar rubbed his chin, deep in thought. "Rayben told me that you came to the Exile with five arming swords, not four. Aron used a falchion, so that means you acquired Gil's sword. What happened to Gil?"

"I killed him."

Omar frowned. "Another unfortunate death. He was a good man. However, I am glad you survived. I expect your father trained you how to fight?"

"Yes, but only after the Rayders showed up. The truth is, I only bested Gil by luck. He was distracted."

"Gil was an accomplished swordsman and not easily distracted. What caught his attention?"

Lon took a deep breath and sighed. "I'm the Beholder everyone has been talking about. I accidently did a little magic show in front of half the villagers in Roseiri, and my parents took our family away. That was five year ago. We've been hiding in Pree ever since." He anxiously eyed Omar, waiting for his reaction.

Omar pulled a piece of parchment from a stack and began writing on it with his quill. "Very interesting. I have many questions, but I want to stay on topic. Did you beat Gil using True Sight?"

"Not really. I didn't even know I was a Beholder until Gil told me so. Aside from what happened in Roseiri, I had never used my power before."

"What happened?"

"Gil tried to kill my twin sister, Mellai, and I instinctively used True Sight to throw her out of the way. That's what distracted Gil. He knew I was a Beholder and tried to grab me. I knocked him from his horse."

"Ah, so the rumors were true. You are a twin. Any other siblings?"

"No."

"So what brings a Beholder to the Exile? I know it would not have been an easy decision to make, especially with Aron as your father. Are you being pulled toward the roots of your ancestors?"

"In a way, yes, but let me explain. True Sight comes on sporadically. The only way I can make it go away is to pass out or use it. Even then, I have no idea how to control it and someone usually ends up hurt. To make things worse, I can feel it sucking life out of me every time it appears. Father said True Sight is killing me, and I have no idea why. That's why he started training me, hoping that by gaining more control over my body, I might learn to control True Sight. But it didn't work. He finally told me about you and your studies of the Beholder history. He said if anyone can help me, it's you."

Omar placed the quill on the table. "I will do what I can, but I need to see it first. Show me the power of True Sight, Lon."

"I can't. I don't know how to control it. It only comes when I am angry or afraid."

"If you want to learn how to control True Sight, the first step is learning how to summon it on your own terms."

"I have no idea how to do that."

"It shouldn't be too hard to figure out. Consider every time you have used True Sight. Think about what you've told me. When does it manifest itself?"

Lon thought for a moment before answering. "When I'm angry, hurt, or desperate."

Omar raised an eyebrow. "You have never used it when you are happy and well?"

"No . . ." Lon started, "Actually, just the first time in Roseiri. Mellai and I were playing a stick game and I was using True Sight to block a terrible windstorm from knocking the stack over. I didn't even know I was using it."

Omar nodded. "Then we will add intense concentration to the list of impetus. Think, Lon. What do they all have in common?"

Lon shook his head. "I've been thinking about this for three months. I don't know, Omar. That's why I'm here."

"I will help you with something so obvious this once," Omar said as he leaned back and laced his fingers over his belly again, "but only because of your turmoil over the past few months. You need to learn to decipher your own solutions in the future."

Lon leaned forward. "Thank you."

"Anger, pain, desperation, and deep concentration. They are all emotional byproducts of needing or wanting something. It is obvious that you feel deeply and passionately, Lon, so it is no surprise that whenever you felt you needed something so intensely, your mind summoned True Sight to help you accomplish it. Mellai was in danger, so you threw her off the road. You wanted to beat your sister at a game, so you manipulated your environment to help you win. What else?"

Lon thought of his confrontation with Kaylen, but suppressed the memory. "I used it a lot when I sparred with my father. I actually used it to beat Wade during my trial, too."

Omar nodded again. "Makes perfect sense. Concern for one's safety is a strong emotion. Do you see where I am going with this, Lon?"

Lon shrugged.

Omar tapped his thumbs together impatiently. "You wanted something and used True Sight to make it happen. Negative situations are not the only times when you can feel strong desires. Embrace your gift, Beholder. Yearn to use it instead of fighting it."

"How?"

"Close your eyes and concentrate. Remove your distracting thoughts and your desperation to survive. Think of the miracles you might perform using your power. Beholders built the entire city of Itorea through True Sight. What could you build?"

Lon's thoughts slipped back to Kaylen. "A house."

"Indeed, you could. Think of the time and energy you would save by doing so with True Sight instead of by manual labor. Do you want that?"

"Yes."

"Then let it happen. Make it happen. Take a slow breath and allow True Sight to come to you instead of forcing its way in."

Lon breathed deeply as he continued to think of Kaylen, but not of the pain he had caused her. He contemplated the problems that would have been avoided had he mastered True Sight in Pree—the exhaustion of cutting and hauling trees for his house, the frustration of his sparring sessions with Aron, the worry of accidentally summoning his power.

A smile crept onto Lon's face as he opened his mind and considered how easy life would have been. He felt True Sight slip into his mind and, for the first time, welcomed it. When he reopened his eyes, Omar's glowing figure was surrounded by the familiar haze of the world's energy.

"Fascinating," Omar said with excitement as he watched Lon's clouded eyes. "I have always wondered what it would look like."

"Now what?" Lon demanded. He could feel his mind slipping away as a sharp pain formed at the base of his skull. "I've summoned it before, but now is when I'm in danger. It's killing me as I speak, Omar."

"Do something with it," Omar answered. "Anything. Move the air, light a fire, grow hair back on my head."

"I can't," was the last thing Lon said before darkness overtook him.

* * * * *

Lon opened his eyes. He was hunched down in the same chair. Omar was in front of him, sifting through scrolls and scribbling feverishly on a manuscript. Lon licked his lips and tried to clear his dry throat.

Omar looked up from across the table and scratched at his nose with his thumb. "Good news, Lon. I know what is killing you."

Chapter 24

Itorea

Kaylen had been up most of the night, preoccupied with her thoughts. Despite her protests, Kutad had insisted she and Aely stay the night at an inn. She breathed out in frustration. The pale morning sun offered just enough light that she could see her warm breath as mist in the chilled air.

"Just another thing to remind me of Lon," she grumbled.

"Huh?" Aely replied groggily.

"Nothing," Kaylen answered. "I'm just getting ready to leave. You can go back to sleep."

Kaylen's thoughts had been roaming through her memories; she had cried through the entire night. She wept as she danced with Lon during his birthday celebration. Tears flowed as her betrothed battled his unwanted burden of True Sight. She sobbed at her last memory of him, where she disgraced him by helping him build their home. Kaylen didn't think about his reaction—how she was thrown through the air into their crumbling house. She knew Lon's actions were only a result of his overwhelming stress.

Kaylen threw off her blankets, wiped fresh tears from her eyes and started dressing.

"I'll talk with my friends today," Aely said as she pulled the blankets around herself. "Hopefully there's another opening for a handmaiden in the King's Court."

"Thank you, Aely. I'm sorry I've been lying to you about being engaged. I just didn't want Kutad to know I ran away from home."

Kaylen frowned, frustrated with the net of deceit she was weaving around herself. She hated lying, but it was the only solution she could think of to keep Lon's secret from everyone.

"I completely understand," Aely replied. "I don't get along with my family either. Last I heard they were down in Draege mining for gold." She hopped out of bed and gave Kaylen a tight hug. "I'll see you in a couple days."

*   *   *   *   *

Kutad was waiting outside the inn for Kaylen.

"Where did you sleep?" she asked.

"I found a stable to house my donkeys and stayed the night there," he answered. "I wanted to make sure nobody accidentally wandered off with them."

"Thank you again for your kindness," Kaylen said.

"Was Aely awake when you left your room?" Kutad asked, looking at the inn. "We have to travel a long distance today and I hope to leave soon."

"Yes, but Aely and I talked about it last night and decided we would just meet at the keep in a couple of days."

"I would be more than happy to take her to the keep."

"I know, but her friends are meeting her at the entrance to Itorea later today. I considered asking her if I could join them so you could return to Réxura, but I didn't want to intrude." *How am I going to keep track of all these lies?*

Kutad helped her into the wagon and handed her a cup of hot tea. "I know you're cold," he said as he climbed up next to her, "but don't drink it too fast. Sip it slowly and let it warm you."

Tightly-spaced two- and three-story buildings surrounded them. Because they had traveled through the city in darkness the previous night, Kaylen hadn't realized they reached the eastern edge of Sylbie, only two hundred yards from the banks of the Sylbien River.

Kutad turned the wagon south and followed the road a short distance until the buildings ended and Kaylen had an unobstructed view of the Sylbien River. The stunning view shocked her enough that she almost dropped her cup in her lap.

"It's gorgeous!" she said as she placed her hand on Kutad's forearm.

An enormous, white stone bridge arched across the half-mile Sylbien River, supported by five massive columns jutting out of the river. The bridge ended a short distance from the sheer shoreline of the opposite bank and a long wooden drawbridge spanned the gap, leading to the western gate of Itorea. The gate appeared to be only a small hole in Itorea's three hundred-foot perimeter wall. Massive flanking towers rose even higher on each side of the gate. Drum towers spotted the wall along its entire length; mighty watchtowers rose from behind the wall in sporadic intervals.

"How high are those watchtowers?" Kaylen asked.

"Five hundred feet," Kutad answered with a smile.

Kaylen shook her head. "Why? Didn't they think the wall was high enough?"

"I guess not," Kutad laughed.

Kaylen returned her gaze to the wall and squinted into the morning sunlight as it sparkled off the rippling surface of the river. A set of two enormous and beautifully-crafted crystals appeared on the face of the wall between every drum tower, each unique in design and painted in one of many vibrant colors. They sparkled in the morning light reflecting off the river.

In the space between the two flanking towers, two designs were divided by a thick web of carefully-trimmed green vinery that grew around the western gate and flared outward as it climbed to the top of the wall. To the left of the vinery was the bright red outline of a cube, and to the right was a purple pyramid.

Kaylen stared at the view, her mouth agape, completely awestruck by the harmonic grandeur before her.

Kutad glanced at her and smiled. "I wanted to explain this to you last night, but as you can see, it's beyond description."

"It's incredible," Kaylen nearly shouted. "Our village sends travelers here every year, but none of them ever told us it was this gorgeous."

"Maybe they also found themselves unable to describe it," Kutad said, "or perhaps they didn't want to share because they were afraid everyone would run away to come see it."

"I'm guessing it's the second," Kaylen responded, "but here I am. I'm about to cross onto the Fortress Island. If the city is even more spectacular inside, nothing is going to keep me from seeing it—not even a hundred armed Rayders."

"Lucky for the Rayders," Kutad laughed, "they won't be found here. They wouldn't dare attempt to enter Itorea with the King's Cross on their temples. The guards would discover and kill them before they crossed through the gate."

Kutad steered his donkeys to the bridge entrance. It was guarded by four proud soldiers adorned in shining plate armor and forest green cloaks. They each held a halberd upright in one hand, while the other hand rested on the pommel of a short sword. They didn't speak, but watched Kaylen and Kutad carefully as they drove their wagon onto the bridge. Soon the travelers joined a line of people heading into the city.

"It's really busy for this early in the morning," Kaylen observed.

"Aye," Kutad replied, "but mostly because everybody has been waiting for the drawbridge to be lowered. Itorea is a rich city, full of potential profit. Everyone wants a chance at it."

Small stone barriers ran along both edges of the wide bridge. Although Kutad kept the cart centered in the middle when people weren't passing in the opposite direction, Kaylen still felt herself growing more and more anxious as they ascended the arched bridge and the river seemed to fall away below them. The stone surface of the bridge looked icy. She was terrified the cart would slide sideways and plummet into the river.

It wasn't until after they reached the highest point of the bridge, arching one hundred feet in the air, that Kaylen realized it wasn't covered in ice.

"This bridge has no seams or mortar lines," Kaylen observed. "It's like it was carved from one huge boulder."

"Everything constructed by the Beholders is the same way," Kutad said, "even in the perimeter wall. I told you last night, Kaylen, this city was built by magic. No one could ever replicate what those wizards had accomplished here."

"What happened to the Beholders?" Kaylen asked, thinking of Lon. She had known the answer to her question since childhood, but she wondered how much the overall Appernysian population knew about their history. Kutad was a traveling man and must have picked up pieces of information as he crossed the kingdom. If anyone knew what the people believed, it was him.

"They were wiped out by the Rayders," Kutad answered. "I thought everyone in Appernysia knew that. I hadn't considered Pree, but I guess your village is in the outskirts of the kingdom."

"Pree's not my village anymore," Kaylen countered.

"Aye," Kutad replied sadly, "so you said."

He remained silent as they continued toward Itorea's gate until the people in front of them slowed to a stop. Kaylen stretched her neck and searched the front of the line, which started at the drawbridge. Guards were inspecting the crowd, throwing back hoods and removing hats from every person who passed.

"What are they doing?" Kaylen asked.

"Searching for Rayders," Kutad replied.

As they waited in the long line, Kaylen looked at the outer wall again. They had drawn close enough that she could see soldiers patrolling along the top and peering out from the side of ballistae mounted between the crenellations in the flanking towers. She spotted row upon row of arrow slits scattered across the upper half of the flanking towers, wondering how many soldiers were hidden in there as well.

Kaylen also realized what she originally believed to be painted outlines of crystals on the wall were actually combined columns of colored glass prisms. They had been skillfully fit together and embedded in the wall's stone surface to form marvelous shapes. Although the sun didn't shine through from the opposite side of the wall, the prisms captured the light off the water and reflected it back brilliantly. She wondered about the skill required to build them and the reasons behind it, but rather than bother Kutad with another question, she held her tongue.

When Kaylen and Kutad reached the front of the line, the guards made them get out of the wagon, which they searched thoroughly. The guard standing in front of Kaylen looked at both sides of her face, then rubbed both of her temples with his thumbs. Finding nothing, he signaled her to get back in the wagon. Kutad joined her and they continued forward toward the gate.

As they were passing over the drawbridge, Kaylen turned to Kutad. "I thought the Rayders were marked only on their right temple, so why do the guards check both sides?"

Kutad looked at Kaylen curiously. "That's true, but how did you know that when you didn't even know what happened to the Beholders?"

Kaylen panicked, realizing her mistake. She searched her brain for an answer. "Rayders appeared in Pree over a decade ago. They kidnapped a child and killed the rest of his family. Trev made sure we all knew what a Rayder looks like so something like that would never happen again."

Kutad's eyes unfocused as he stared past Kaylen, lost in his memories. "Kutad?"

He blinked and looked at Kaylen. "Pree and every other village in Appernysia," he said. "Those Rayders are sneakier than foxes. Anyway, to answer your question, they check both temples because many of the guards can't tell left from right."

Kaylen nodded absently and leaned back as they approached the fifty-foot archway leading through the curtain wall. A row of steel spikes protruded from the top of the arc directly above her, then again thirty feet further in.

"What are those?" she asked.

"Those are portcullises," Kutad answered. "They're massive iron gates that can be dropped at a moment's notice to block the way."

"How were they lifted up that high?"

"Beholders," Kutad replied. "Back then, they probably never considered the possibility that Beholders might not always be around. If one of those gates were to close, it would take at least a thousand soldiers and more rope than you can imagine to lift it up again. They always stay open now."

"But why are there two? Isn't one enough?"

Kutad smiled. "That's not all that blocks this gate." He pointed to two large gaps in the arching wall—one halfway between the portcullises and the other at the opposite end of the passageway. "One solid plank of wood is hiding inside each of those breaks in the stone. They were cut from a Furwen Tree in the Perbeisea Forest and can be pulled out to bar the way. They are two feet thick and sixty feet high. That's over a million pounds."

Kaylen's eyes grew wide. "Why didn't they cut it in half and put each half on hinges that could be swung open? Isn't that how normal gates work? It seems like they would be a lot easier to open that way."

"It would have only weakened the wall, and as I already said, it wasn't a big issue back then. They had Beholders to close the gate. Now they always remain open for the same reasons the portcullises are never closed."

"Doesn't that make Itorea vulnerable?"

"Not really. The draw bridges still offer a good defense, and even if an enemy ever got past them, all hope wouldn't be lost. The portcullises are much easier to drop than to lift. Just hit a lever with a big hammer and the portcullis falls down. I've never heard of them being closed since the Beholders were killed, though."

"This is madness," Kaylen said as she peered sideways through one of the gaps, finding only a solid piece of wood that looked like polished stone.

Kutad laughed. "Wait until we get through this wall and you see the city."

When the inside of Itorea came into view, Kaylen first noticed the aqueducts arching two hundred feet in the air over the city, supported by thick columns carved in the likeness of enormous winged beasts at the base. Further south the beasts spouted water from open jaws into a wide stone channel that ran parallel to the main road, which extended east into the middle of the city.

Kutad forced his wagon between the beggars that lined the polished stone road. "Blasted vagabonds," he shouted in frustration. "Why don't you make a living and stop preying on the hard work of others?"

Kutad turned southeast and followed the main road past shops, mills and smithies before they reached the closest statue three miles away. Kaylen hopped down from the wagon without waiting for Kutad's assistance and hurried to the stone column.

"I have to see it up close," she shouted, feeling a strange attraction toward the sculpture.

Its massive beast-like body was carved head-down, its wings folded in, and its head reared back to shoot a seven-foot column of water from its mouth and into the channel. A long, armored tail wound around the pillar and was tipped with a glistening yellow crystal. She placed her hand on the beast's paw and stared into its eyes.

"It's called a ghraef," Kutad said from behind her. "They were companions to the Beholders, but they disappeared when the Rayders revolted. They say these beasts were powerful and wise."

"I wonder if they had blue eyes," Kaylen said aloud as she fingered its long claws that dug into the pillar.

Realization struck Kutad and he placed his hand gently on Kaylen's shoulder. "Do you think a ghraef saved you from Braedr?"

"I don't know," Kaylen replied as she placed her other hand upon the ghraef's paw, "but I feel the same way looking at this sculpture as I did that night. I feel . . . safe."

"I feel something, too," Kutad said as he watched Kaylen gracefully trace the contours of the sculpture with her hands.

"Where is all this water coming from?" she asked as she stared at the ghraef's open mouth.

"It's pumped from the Nellis River, then pushed up huge stone pipes that feed troughs on top of the aqueducts. The aqueducts run parallel, but five miles apart from each other. There are also wells every five miles along each aqueduct."

"That's fascinating," Kaylen replied, "but why didn't they put a well here—and why are they just dumping the water out into the channel when it's needed for the wells?"

"See the big, green flags waving on top of the aqueducts? They're placed every five miles, so can you guess what they're marking?"

"The water outlets?" Kaylen answered.

"Exactly," Kutad said with a smile, "and there's a flag about a quarter-mile north of here, so there's no need for an outlet here. You also asked why this ghraef is spewing such a large amount of water into the channel. That's a little trickier to explain. Basically, the pumps that push the water up into the aqueduct system have to supply a constant stream to keep them full. When the water isn't getting used frequently, the aqueducts fill up and need somewhere to overflow."

"So this ghraef only shoots water out of his mouth when there isn't anybody drawing water out of the wells?"

"Technically, yes, but I've never seen the overflow stop running. The hand-pumps the watermen use to fill up their barrels aren't anywhere near the size of the pumps that fill up the aqueducts. Here's another piece of interesting information for you—the watermen are responsible for hauling water back and forth around the city. Itorea is the only place in Appernysia where a person can make their living by carting water around."

Kaylen stepped to the side so she could see down the length of the aqueduct. "How long are these?"

"Some run over twenty-five miles and the longer ones feed an irrigation system rather than just wells."

"That's a lot of water."

"Aye, and if you find the time, I suggest you visit one of the pump houses. The way the Beholders built this place is absolutely fascinating."

"Actually," Kaylen said slowly, "I was hoping you could show me a few of your favorite places here. I don't have to meet Aely for a couple days."

They spent the rest of the day touring the markets and shops in the northwest quadrant of Itorea's blade. According to Kutad, if someone were to view the entire island from high in the air—"perhaps upon the back of a ghraef," he added with a smile while explaining to Kaylen—Itorea would look like the head of a halberd.

Kaylen stared blankly at Kutad when he mentioned a halberd.

"The weapons the guards were holding at the bridge," Kutad said in response to Kaylen's expression, "those are halberds."

"I'm sorry," Kaylen replied. "I don't remember."

"Aye, I understand," Kutad said with a smile. "I wouldn't either if it had been the first time I saw Itorea's west gate. Let me show you." He traced the shape onto the wagon bench with his finger. "When someone refers to the blade of Itorea, they're referring to the big ax-shaped part of the island. Right now, we're near the very northwest corner—the tip of the blade. Another three hundred-foot wall runs down the center of the blade, which splits it in half, north to south. The water channel that runs from the west edge of Itorea to the keep splits it in half west to east, so the center wall and water channel together divide the blade into four quadrants. Make sense?"

"No," Kaylen said as she shook her head.

"Don't worry," he laughed, "you'll understand as soon as you see a map of Itorea. All you need to know for now is that you're in the northwest part of the blade—the only part of the island where the public is allowed. The high and mighty nobles hole themselves up inside their estates in the southwest quadrant. All of the land in the east half of the blade is reserved for the city's farms and livestock."

"This city feeds itself?" Kaylen asked with surprise.

"Aye," Kutad replied, "and very well, too. There are over five hundred and thirty square miles of farming and grazing land in the west half of the blade. The rich snobs south of here live mostly off their own land, so that just leaves this area and the eastern hook."

"What's in the hook?"

"The keep and its defenses fill up the west part of the hook, and the king's defensive army uses the east part."

Kaylen's eyes widened with surprise. "How big is the king's army?"

"At least seventy-five thousand at any given moment, but it's probably a lot bigger right now because of all the recruiting the King's been doing. Some of them are on patrols or guarding outlying cities and villages, but most of them are probably in Itorea right now."

She looked at Kutad. "How do you know all of this?"

Kutad purchased a bright-red apple from a merchant and handed it to Kaylen. "I've been around a long time and have talked to a lot of people. *Need an answer? Ask a tradesman!* Isn't that how the saying goes?"

Kaylen stopped her barrage of questions and bit into the apple, having had more than her fill of information to process for the day. The sun touched the top of the perimeter wall in the western sky, signaling the end of the day and reminding Kaylen that she had been so caught up in the excitement of discovery that she'd forgotten her hunger. The apple was the first thing she had eaten since that morning and she consumed it completely, core included.

"Thank you," she told Kutad when she finished swallowing the last bite, "but I'm going to need more than an apple for dinner."

"A great idea," Kutad agreed as he disappeared into the crowd and returned moments later holding a large sack.

"What's in the sack?" Kaylen asked.

"A surprise."

Kutad cracked the reins and turned his donkeys toward the north-west point of the island. A five hundred-foot watchtower stood in the narrow space of the angled perimeter walls, connected to the top of the nearby walls by two separate walkways. Kutad led his wagon under one of the walkways into the small triangular courtyard.

When they arrived at the very tip of the blade, Kutad hopped down and spoke quietly to one of the guards stationed there. After a moment, the guard nodded and Kutad returned with a big smile on his face.

"Can you handle a small climb before we eat?" he said to Kaylen.

"I guess, but what exactly are we climbing?"

"That." Kutad pointed to the three hundred-foot drum tower in front of them.

Kaylen had to lean her head back and look almost straight up to see the top. "Without eating first?" she asked skeptically.

"I promise it will be worth it."

Kutad extended a hand to help Kaylen out of the wagon. She breathed out doubtfully as she took it and climbed down.

Kutad grabbed the sack and led Kaylen to the base of the tower. The soldier handed Kutad a lit torch, opened a thick wooden door, and let them inside. The passageway was completely dark, but the light of the torch revealed a single staircase that wound upward around the outer edge of the tower. It was just wide enough that the two of them could walk side by side as they began their ascent.

Kutad pointed to tiny arrow slits that occasionally appeared in the wall. "These slits were placed this low in the tower mostly to provide a little air flow for whoever is inside. We're comfortable enough now because it's winter, but during summer months, when the air is hot and thick, a soldier could boil to death in his armor in here without any ventilation."

Kaylen only shook her head in response as she followed him. The muscles in her legs were already burning and her breath was staggered.

After five minutes they encountered another large wooden door on the outer wall.

"Please tell me we're at the top," Kaylen said breathlessly as she looked at the staircase that continued up the tower.

"Not yet," Kutad answered. "We're only two hundred feet up. This door leads into a large tunnel that runs inside the perimeter wall between the drum towers. There's another door on the other side of this tower that provides access into the other wall. Remember the aqueducts that carry water through the city? There are outlets leading out on top of them from inside these tunnels. If the outer walls were ever breached, archers could shoot down from atop the aqueducts. These doors can also be bolted shut from the inside to keep the enemy from doing the same thing."

"Water sounds nice," Kaylen muttered as she sat down on the stairs. "I'm a little light-headed and dizzy."

Kutad glanced up the staircase, then sat down next to Kaylen, opened the sack, and handed her a leather water skin and a large piece of bread. "Here. We're near the top, but we need to hurry if we want to reach it before the sun sets."

Kaylen took a long drink and a bite of the bread.

"If it were summer, I'd tell you the climb gets a little easier from here. The staircase moves to the center of the column, surrounded by defensive rooms full of arrow slits that ventilate the air more efficiently. The temperature would drop a few degrees up here."

Kaylen finished eating, then the two of them continued up the stairs and onto the central staircase. It was the same width and rose ten steps to an archway leading into the defensive rooms, then in the opposite direction another ten steps to the defensive room on the other side of the tower. It followed a similar pattern for the remaining one hundred feet of the tower. Kaylen and Kutad climbed for another five minutes before sunlight began to fill the passageway. When they finally emerged from the tower, Kaylen put her hand in front of her eyes and squinted under the intense light.

"Stay here until your eyes adjust," Kutad said as he placed his torch in a sconce on the wall and helped Kaylen sit at the top of the stairs.

She was sitting in the center of the tower, surrounded by its battlements. There were crenellations placed around the top of the stone wall, and inside each of them was a massive ballista.

"Why are those big crossbows aiming inside and outside of the city?" Kaylen asked.

"A big crossbow is a great way to explain a ballista," Kutad said with a smile. "The Beholders weren't ignorant enough to think this wall was impenetrable. If the curtain wall were breached, the soldiers could continue to defend Itorea from up here. Every tower in Itorea was built this way, including the flanking towers that guard the entrances."

Kaylen scrunched her eyebrows. "But they're pointing almost straight up. That seems silly. How do they angle them to shoot down?"

"It's actually very simple," Kutad explained. "See the long beam extending from the end of the ballista? It's connected to the ballista on a joint that allows it to pivot up and down. The soldiers use the beam to push the back-end of the ballista up, which angles the nose of the ballista down. Did I explain that all right?"

"I think so," Kaylen replied as she stood up and walked to the west side of the wall.

Stone steps allowed her to peer over the top of the crenellation. She shielded her eyes from the setting sun, which had dropped deep into the western horizon. Its light reflected off the snow-covered plains. Even from three hundred feet, the half-mile width of the river was still daunting as it split at Itorea's tip and continued past her along both sides of the city.

Despite the grand view, what amazed Kaylen the most was the Perbeisea Forest to the west. She had been impressed with the forest while traveling through it with Kutad, but she didn't fully appreciate the colossal size of its trees. Kaylen stood atop a three hundred-foot tower overlooking at least fifty miles of terrain in all directions, yet she still could only see the front line of trees bordering the eastern edge of the forest.

"How tall are those trees?"

"At least six hundred feet," Kutad answered. "To be honest, I was a little disappointed you didn't ask about them yesterday. I guess it's easy to take their size for granted when surrounded by so many of them, but the Furwen are amazing trees. They put the Beholders' best work to shame by comparison, don't you think?"

Kaylen nodded. "They're very impressive."

"It's more than just how they look. Do you understand how strong those trees have to be to hold themselves upright? Their timber is as solid as stone. That's why the gates of this city are made from one solid cut of their wood and only two feet thick. They don't need to be any thicker. It's actually somewhat funny. King Drogan protects the Perbeisea Forest by decree, but even if someone decided to disobey, he'd be hard-pressed just to get an ax through the bark."

"Then how were they cut for the gates?"

"Care to venture a guess?" Kutad replied with a smile. "Beholders. I wish they still existed. This city is full of wonders beyond our comprehension, and seeing those men use their power would be a marvelous site."

Kaylen sighed. Although she knew it was impossible to see, she followed the river north in the direction of the Rayder Exile. Lon was up there, desperately trying to learn how to control the overwhelming power Kutad seemed to envy so much. She wondered how her betrothed was doing and whether he was safe.

Kutad stood behind Kaylen and looked in the same direction. "He isn't here, is he?"

"Who?"

"Lon Marcs," Kutad said tenderly. "He's not in Itorea, is he?"

Kaylen said nothing as she took a deep breath and stared up the river.

"Did he join the Rayders?" Kutad continued.

"I don't know what to say," Kaylen answered after a short pause.

She could feel Kutad's eyes on the back of her head, probing for answers. He had been a true friend and she trusted him with her life, but she was still unsure of how to answer him, be it the truth or not. Something about him was still a mystery. Kaylen wasn't familiar with much beyond the borders of Pree, but Kutad still seemed to know too much about Itorea, even for a tradesmen. His knowledge of the city and its inner workings was especially thorough, and he knew all of their history, but what troubled her most was where they stood at that moment. Kaylen hadn't seen anyone but a soldier on top of that wall the entire day.

"How did you convince that soldier to let us up here?" Kaylen countered, trying to change the subject.

"I bribed him," Kutad answered quickly.

"Hmm." She turned around and folded her arms across her chest. "I think I'm not the only one keeping secrets. I was watching you, Kutad. Except for when he handed you the torch, you didn't come within two feet of him."

"Maybe I slipped him something then, or promised to pay him later."

"I doubt it," Kaylen said with a sniff. "Be honest with me, Kutad. You told me most of the people in your caravan are running from something, and that they all have their secrets. What's your secret, and what are you running from?"

Kutad's lips slowly formed a sincere smile. "You have a good memory, Kaylen. All right, let's be honest with each other. I'll share my past with you if you tell me about Lon. Is that fair?"

Chapter 25

Revelation

L on sat forward. "Are you serious? That's all it took?"

Omar nodded. "It was easy to figure out since I knew what to look for."

"What is it, then? How can I fix this?"

Omar took a moment to finish writing something on the parchment, then sat back and laced his fingers over his belly. "Have you ever butchered an animal, Lon?"

"Yes, lots of times. Why?"

"What's the very first thing you do?"

"I cut their neck and let them bleed out."

Omar smiled. "There's your answer."

Lon furrowed his brow. "Huh? I don't bleed when I use True Sight. What do you mean?"

"What happens when you cut their neck?" Omar continued.

"They die."

"Ah, so would you say that the blood is what keeps the animals alive?"

"I guess so, but I'm still confused."

Omar stared at Lon with annoying patience, like a parent waiting for a child to realize that one and one make two. "Think back to when you saved your sister's life. You threw her off the road with a blast of energy. Where did it come from?"

"Me . . ." Lon's eyes widened with understanding. "Wait a second . . . are you saying—"

"Yes," Omar interrupted. "You've been bleeding out your own energy, Lon. That's why you keep passing out. Your brain is trying to protect itself by taking control of your body. If you stop using True Sight, you stop killing yourself."

"That doesn't make any sense," Lon argued. "Why would I be fine when I use my power to create a huge energy blast, but then when I'm not even using it, I lose consciousness? Explain that to me."

"You need to be more specific," Omar replied, tapping his thumbs together.

"All right. The first time I remember using True Sight, I saw the haze of energy surrounding me, but I never used my power to do anything. I was just looking around. I always pass out in those circumstances, but when I actually do something with my power, like create the energy blast to save Mellai, I come away from it just fine. I don't get it."

"Ah," Omar said, nodding his head, "I understand. Let me see if we can discover an answer to your question." Omar sat forward and picked up his quill. "Start with what happens when you use True Sight. What do you see when it is upon you?"

Lon took a few minutes to describe the world through his eyes—the strange haze, the glowing people, the glowing trees and objects. "At first," Lon continued, "everything was just a big blur, but lately shapes have begun to emerge everywhere. The mist still fills the air, but objects have their own glow, too. Not just people, although they're definitely the brightest."

"Their own essence?" Omar asked.

"Yes, that's a good way of describing it."

"Fascinating." Omar hunched over and scribbled on the parchment. "And what about yourself? Have you ever noticed your own glowing essence?"

Lon shrugged. "I guess not. I've never really paid attention before."

"That explains it, then. Here is my theory, Lon. I know from history that Beholders are only capable of using their power while viewing the world with True Sight. That is how the original Rayders fought against the Beholders—they would watch for the Beholders' eyes to cloud over. By summoning your power, you link yourself to the surrounding world. The problem is that you have not understood what you see, or how to interact with it. Your body has its own energy supply—its own essence—but you did not know that it needed to be maintained and protected. When you summon True Sight, you remove the barriers that protect yourself from the surrounding world's energy. As I said before, you bleed out, in a manner of speaking."

"That part I understand, but what about—"

"I am about to explain," Omar interrupted again. "Just as you did not know you were leaking your essence into the world, I suspect you must have also pulled energy from somewhere to create the blasts; you did not use your own essence to perform the task. Then, because the need to use your power had passed, you stop viewing the world with True Sight."

"And I stop bleeding out my energy . . ."

"Precisely."

A smile formed on Lon's face. "So, I just have to figure out a way to protect my energy?"

"Yes," Omar agreed, "a way to keep a barrier between your essence and the rest of the world."

Lon laughed. "My father wasn't kidding. You're a genius, Omar."

"Summarize what you've learned so far," Omar continued, ignoring Lon's compliment.

Lon nodded. "All right. There are only two things, right? Wait, no, three things. My power is going to find a way to manifest itself, so I need to welcome it instead of fight it. That's the first one. Next would be . . . I summon True Sight through desire, which doesn't always have to be negative. Last is what you just taught me. I need to find a way to keep my own energy inside."

"Well done," Omar said. "Unfortunately, identifying the problem is always much easier than figuring out the solution. Obviously the third point is the most crucial, so we will start there. Any thoughts?"

Lon shook his head. "Not a clue."

Omar resumed scribbling on the parchment. After a few minutes of listening to the scholar's scratching quill, Lon began to doubt that Omar remembered someone else was in the room. "Omar?"

No response.

"Uh . . . Omar?" Lon said louder.

Omar glanced up at Lon through his thick eyebrows. "If I had any doubts before, they have jumped out the window. Your lack of patience proves that you are most definitely Aron's son."

Lon slumped. "I just want to know what you're thinking."

"I am thinking," Omar replied as he resumed writing on the parchment, "that this will take some time. Come back tomorrow. I have some ideas on how you can use your power without drawing out your own energy, but I need a day to ponder and clean up my quarters. I do not want you destroying any of my things while we are experimenting."

"All right," Lon replied with dismayed anticipation. "Should I get back to help Tarek?"

Omar stopped writing and looked up at Lon. "That sounded hesitant. Is there somewhere else you would rather be than helping General Tarek train our commander's army?"

Lon shifted in his seat. "Not really, but . . . well, yes."

Omar raised his eyebrows.

"Oh, no," Lon continued. "I just . . . it's been two weeks since I've been here and I can't stop thinking about Gil and his squad. Did they have families?"

"I see," Omar replied, setting down his quill. "Gil had a wife and three children. The other four were still young—parents and siblings, but no families of their own. Are you planning a visit?"

Lon shrugged. "I'd like to, but will our commander allow it? He seems passionate about training the men. I don't know if I'll be able to get away from that."

"There is no need," Omar said with a smile. "I tutor Flora's children regularly. I expect them to arrive within the hour."

"Flora?" Lon asked. "Gil's wife?"

Omar nodded. "You may wait here for them, but keep quiet. I have to think."

"Thank you," Lon replied enthusiastically. "I'll stay out of your way, I promise."

"Good. Go sit by the fireplace. I do not like people watching me while I work."

Lon wove his way through the piled clutter and sat in an upholstered chair by the hearth. As he stretched out his hands toward the flames, dread replaced his excitement. What was he thinking? He couldn't tell Flora the truth. How did he expect to make recompense? What could he say to comfort her?

He had only a few minutes to brainstorm until a soft knock came at the door. Omar answered it.

"Good morning, Flora," he said with a smile. "And good morning to you three, as well. Did you bring your brains with you today?"

Children's laughter filled the room. Lon's stomach lurched.

"Please, come in," Omar continued. "You three have a seat around the table. Flora, you have a visitor."

Lon stood as Flora entered the room. She was younger than he'd expected, at around thirty years old. Her long brown hair was pulled back in a tight bun, and she wore a purple cotton gown.

"Good morning," Lon said with a nod.

"Good morning," Flora replied, eyeing Omar. "What can I do for you?"

"Why don't you both step outside and talk," Omar interceded. "I don't want your conversation interrupting my lesson."

As soon as the door closed behind them, Flora jumped in. "If this is another match-making ploy concocted by Omar, I am not interested."

"Nor I," Lon replied, "That's not what this is."

"Forgive me," Flora replied. Her full cheeks blushed red and her brown eyes disappeared behind long eyelashes as she cast her gaze to the floor.

"Again, I understand completely. Too completely."

Flora glanced back up at him. "Pardon?"

"Even though you didn't know it," Lon continued, "our lives have been intertwined for months. I . . . I don't know what to say."

"Are you Lon Shaw?"

Lon's mouth hung open and his words caught in his throat. All he could do was nod.

Tears filled Flora's eyes and her bottom lip trembled.

"I'm so sorr—" he started.

Flora stepped forward and embraced Lon. He stood awkwardly with his arms out to the side, unsure of how to respond. Flora held him for a long time, her body shaking as she cried onto his shoulder, then she leaned back and kissed him tenderly on the cheek.

"Thank you," she whispered. "Thank you so much."

Lon remained speechless as she stared at her. How did she know him? Why had she thanked him?

"I placed my husband's sword on his side of our bed," Flora continued. "I keep it there at night to comfort me. Thank you for bringing it back to me."

"Who brought it to you?" Lon replied, finally making the connection.

"Omar did, just last week. He said a stalwart Appernysian man had returned it, after giving Gil a proper funeral. I heard you made quite an impression on our commander as well, Lon Shaw. Not many Appernysians have been accepted as Rayders. It is quite an honor."

"It's overwhelming," Lon replied. "I don't know why he chose me to train his soldiers."

Flora's eyes widened. "I had not heard that. You must have made a bigger impression than I thought, although it does not surprise me. Few men would dare travel across Appernysia with Rayder swords in tow. You are a valiant man, Lon Shaw."

Lon breathed out and scratched the back of his head. "This conversation was meant to be about you, not me. I wanted to ease the pain of your loss somehow. Will you take back Dawes?"

"Dawes?"

"I mean Gil's horse. I don't know his proper name."

Flora shook her head. "When I did not hear from Gil, we feared the worst," she responded through her tears, "but what worried me even more was that I would never find out what happened to him. Keep the horse as a reminder of how grateful I am to you." She kissed him on the other cheek and disappeared inside Omar's quarters before Lon could argue.

Lon made his way out of the keep with a heavier burden than when he first arrived in the Exile. He made a personal commitment to never allow Flora's family to suffer again, nor any other families of Rayders sent into Appernysia.

By the time Lon reached the bailey, an idea had formed in his mind—a solution to prevent others from suffering as Flora had. He climbed into his saddle, excited to relay the idea to Tarek.

No one will ever suffer like her again, Lon thought as he rode Dawes out of Flagheim. *The trick is convincing them to let me do it.*

* * * * *

"Did that come from Omar?" Tarek asked.

"No, it was my idea," Lon replied. "Why? Too far-fetched?"

"We'll have to see what our commander says. If it were up to me, though, we'd start today. It's a perfect training program. I don't know why someone didn't think of this before. Especially Omar. He's usually ten steps ahead of everyone."

"Maybe he already talked to our commander. We might just not know about it yet."

Tarek smacked Lon on the back. "Only one way to find out." He mounted his horse and galloped toward Flagheim.

"But I just came from there," Lon shouted after him. Tarek didn't respond, so Lon turned to the soldiers surrounding him. "Where's Lieutenant Wade?"

Wade Arneson pushed his way to the front. "What is it?"

"Sorry, Lieutenant, but I guess we're leaving again. Would you mind taking over?"

"It would be my pleasure," Wade said with a salute, then began shouting orders.

Lon mounted Dawes and looked over the soldiers, perplexed. Wade had acted strange toward him ever since their duel, as if Lon had earned more than just respect by beating him. But a salute? That was too much. Lon was just a trainer. He held no authority.

He kicked Dawes into a gallop and chased after Tarek, who had changed directions toward the Appernysian training grounds.

"Where are we going?" Lon asked once he caught up.

"This general is starving," Tarek replied, pounding on his own chest. "I need a fat slab of meat sitting in my belly before I go talking to our commander."

They rode to the entrance into the training grounds where Tarek's log house stood. While Tarek disappeared inside, Lon led Dawes into the training grounds. A thousand Appernysian slaves sat huddled together in the center. Some were weaving and sorting thick cords of rope, while others worked in large groups stacking massive piles of freshly cut timber. Rayder guards patrolled around the perimeter, whipping anyone who was working too slowly.

Lon bit his bottom lip, struggling to maintain control over his emotions. This brutality was his fault. Maybe he had been wrong. Either way, he couldn't stand to watch anymore.

Lon turned Dawes around and ran into Tarek. He was sitting on his horse a few paces back, holding a half-eaten hunk of something red and dripping.

"How long have you been there?" Lon asked.

"Long enough to know something's on your mind," Tarek replied. "Do you intend to talk about it?"

"Not today."

"It was the right choice, Lon," Tarek continued anyway. "If you hadn't suggested using them as slaves, our commander would have killed them all. Even for Appernysians, that would've been a huge waste. It's not their fault they can't fight."

Lon nodded, then gave Tarek a sour look. "Are you trying to make me throw up?"

"What, with this?" Tarek replied. He gnawed on the side of his food; red slime oozed into his beard.

Lon turned his head away. "Ugh. Can we go now?"

Tarek laughed and galloped south toward the Flagheim's main gate. Lon glanced at the nearby perimeter wall thinking how much time it would save to use the postern gate.

Apparently not even a general can use it, he thought as he grudgingly followed.

An hour later, as they approached the causeway leading into Flagheim, Lon eyed movement atop the surrounding hills. He glanced up in time to see a crowd of horsemen vanish over the other side.

"You see that?" Lon asked, pointing up the main road leading away from Flagheim.

Tarek followed Lon's finger. "What? I don't see anything."

"You're in charge of the patrols, right?"

"Yes."

Lon lowered his hand. "I just saw at least twenty horsemen crowded together up there. Is that normal?"

Tarek's lips tightened. "No, it's not." He kicked his horse hard and galloped to the main gate, shouting for the sentries to lock down the fortress and put archers on the walls, then rode back past Lon. "C'mon!"

They galloped up the road and topped the crest just in time to see the horsemen disappear south into the Weeping Forest. Lon searched the surrounding area. Further down the road he saw the gruesome aftermath of a battle. Horses and men were strewn over the road. Tarek and Lon scanned the carnage—fifteen Appernysian scouts and five Rayders. None were alive. Not even their horses.

Tarek clenched his jaw and pushed his horse into the swamp. "We got some hunting to do."

Lon followed after Tarek, struggling with his thoughts. What would he do if he found the Appernysians? They weren't his enemies. Would he allow Tarek to kill them? What if Tarek's life was threatened? What would he do then?

Despite the deep sludge, Tarek and Lon quickly made their way through the swamp and into the Weeping Forest. The Appernysians' were easy to follow. Wherever they rode, their horses cut a line through the dense moss floating on top of the water. Every few minutes Tarek would pause to listen for his prey. They were gaining on the Appernysians, but wouldn't reach them in the swamp.

"Why are we chasing after them?" Lon asked as they rode. "I know they killed a few Rayders, but they're running back to Appernysia. Why don't we just let them?"

Tarek pulled back on his horse's reins and stared at Lon. "Is it really that simple to you? Still have a special place in your heart for 'Nysians?"

"No," Lon lied, "but we're chasing after at least twenty scouts. That's tough odds, even for you."

"It's not about odds," Tarek replied. His tone was cool and icy. "They raided our land and murdered our brothers. It's our responsibility to avenge them. Besides, do you really think they'll stop there?"

Lon shrugged, not knowing what to say.

"They've been doing this for centuries, Lon, long before Rayders started retaliating. We were content to reestablish our lives in the Exile, but they wouldn't let us. The only way to stop this is to show the Appernysians who really has the power. They won't ever leave us alone. Get it?"

Lon only nodded.

"Where's your sense of honor?" Tarek spat as he resumed their pursuit.

Lon swallowed hard. Tarek's words contradicted everything he knew to be true. Had Appernysians really been sneaking into the Exile to slaughter Rayders? Lon fought the idea, but he couldn't ignore the logic. After all, Appernysians hated the Rayders as much as the Rayders hated them. But what about Aron? He grew up with the Rayders. He had to know all of this, but he still dissented.

Lon shook his head, his thoughts garbled. Nothing made sense.

It doesn't matter, Lon thought. *Who cares about Appernysia or the Rayders? I'm doing this for Kaylen.*

When they climbed out of the swampy forest, Tarek paused again. Lon brought his horse up next to the general and waited for instruction.

"They stopped running," Tarek said. He unsheathed his arming sword. "Keep your eyes open. I think we just rode into a trap."

Lon gripped his falchion and searched the forest, realizing his life was in real danger. He was branded with the King's Cross. No amount of pleading would save his life from the scouts. He would have to defend himself.

A crossbow bolt zipped through the trees at Tarek. He ducked under the projectile and slid to the ground, using his horse as a shield.

Lon baulked at the thought of using Dawes the same way. After everything his horse did for him, how could Lon throw his life away so easily? There was no other option. If he wanted to survive—with his horse—Lon would have to retreat.

But it was too late.

Another bolt flew from the forest, this time aimed at Lon. He leaned sideways and fell to the ground. By the time Lon regained his feet, twenty-five men were bearing down on him and Tarek. They were clothed in dark green cloaks and wore thick leather armor. Short swords gleamed in their hands.

"Wait for it," Tarek uttered from behind his horse.

Lon barely heard the order as panic overtook him. This was no duel. He had never fought so many opponents at once. He had no chance, but Dawes did.

Lon slapped his horse on the rump. "Get out of here, Dawes. You can't help me now."

Dawes reluctantly complied. As he retreated back into the swamp, Lon moved next to Tarek.

"All right, Lon," Tarek began, "when I give the order, we'll—" His voice caught when he turned and saw Lon's eyes, which had clouded over with True Sight. "What the—"

"I'll explain later," Lon cut in. "Let's survive this first." Although he had not purposefully summoned his power, Lon focused on Omar's counsel and welcomed its help. "I want you," he whispered to himself. "I need you."

Tarek scrunched his face and gave Lon a sideways glance. "Huh?"

Lon shook his head. "Never mind. You just do your thing and I'll do mine."

"Whatever," Tarek replied with a smirk. "You just do your thing far away from me."

Lon ignored him and concentrated on their position. Twenty-five men were attacking them in a half-circle. He and Tarek could rush to the outer edges to avoid being surrounded, but that would separate them from each other. That wouldn't work.

How can my power help? Lon asked himself. He thought through every circumstance where he had used True Sight. The only time he ever did something on purpose was when he had dueled with Wade. He had poured his energy into the sword to create a concussive blast.

"It has to work," Lon said as he grabbed a large rock from the ground with his left hand. He concentrated on pouring as much energy into the rock as possible. Soon it was pulsing with glowing light.

"What are you doing?" Tarek asked, his voice barely audible over the Appernysians, who were approaching fast.

Lon looked up from the rock and smiled. "Want to see a trick?"

He stepped out from behind Tarek's horse and hurled the rock at the scout in the middle of their arched formation. The rock hit him in the chest and exploded. Stone shards flew in every direction and a pulse of energy shot out in a wave. Most of the Appernysians fell to the ground, while those still on their feet looked around in confusion.

"Your turn," Lon said to Tarek, before collapsing to the ground.

* * * * *

When Lon regained consciousness, night had fallen. Snow-covered pine branches hung over him, orange from the glow of a nearby fire. Lon sat up, surprised to find himself wrapped in several dark green cloaks. Dawes stood nearby with another green cloak draped over his back.

Tarek sat on the other side of the fire. He twisted a long branch in the flames as he watched Lon.

"Please tell me I was only out a few hours," Lon said.

"Yes," Tarek replied. "You all right?"

Lon massaged the pain radiating from the base of his neck. "No, but I guess that's something to be grateful for."

"Good." Tarek pulled the branch out of the fire and pointed its burning tip at Lon. "We've got a long conversation ahead of us, you and me."

"Indeed," Lon agreed. "I've been trying to figure out how to tell you about this for two weeks. I guess fate made up my mind for me."

Tarek thrust the stick back into the hot coals. "So, spill it."

"I grew up in Roseiri," Lon started.

"I figured as much," Tarek commented. "That's where all the rumors lead back to."

Lon nodded. "I know, which was why my family moved to Pree five years ago. That's where I've been ever since, until I came here."

Tarek dropped the stick in the fire and leaned forward. "Did you—"

"I did," Lon interjected, "and he's one of the bravest men I've ever known. Myron saved my family's lives. He killed four of Gil's squad with his bare hands before Gil finally cut him down."

"What happened to Gil, then?" Tarek said. He lifted his hand and played with his red beard. "Did he run away?"

"No, Gil died. That one was my fault, but I didn't do it on purpose. He was trying to kill Mellai."

"Your twin?"

"Yes."

Tarek shook his head. "I don't place much value in rumors, but it sounds like yours were right on the mark—a seventeen-year-old boy from Roseiri with a twin sister. Weird."

"To say the least," Lon said. "I've tried so many times to tell you about your father. You deserve to know how he died. He was an honorable man."

Tarek leaned back and placed his interlocked hands on top of his head. "When the Rayders took me away from Pree, it took a long time for me to get over it. I pretended to want to be a Rayder, of course. It was the only way I could stay alive, but I never forgave that squad for what they did to my mother and brothers. I killed them all within the next two years, but it did little good. By then, I was converted to Rayder philosophy."

"What happened that day in Pree?" Lon said. "Had they plotted to abduct you?"

"They just planned to kill us all, but I guess I impressed them when I gave their squad leader a bloody nose."

"You punched him?"

Tarek smiled. "I grabbed his ears and smashed his face with my forehead."

Lon laughed.

"Seriously though, these guys are terribly misunderstood," Tarek continued, "and they're my kind of folks. Politics can be such a waste of time. Just pick a guy who can make decisions without asking everybody he knows first. That's why I like Commander Rayben. He gets things done."

"Why are you telling me this?"

Tarek stood up and walked around the fire. "I'm telling you this because I want you to understand what I mean when I say I feel sorry for my father. I'm glad he found peace, but killing those Rayders didn't help me at all. I'm one of them now." He sat down next to Lon. "The question is, what are you? Why are you here, Beholder?"

Lon grimaced. "Don't call me that. I'm not a Beholder. I've just been cursed with their power. Once Omar helps me figure out how to stop it from killing me, I'm out of here."

"I thought you might say that," Tarek replied. "You know, when it comes right down to it, I don't know if I'll be able to let you leave."

Lon nodded. "I thought you might say that. Sounds like we're at opposite ends of the stick. What now?"

"Let me ask you something," Tarek said. "What are you rushing back to? What's got you tied down to Appernysia?"

"Remember Kaylen Shaw?"

Tarek laughed. "Little Kaylen? Don't tell me you're married?"

"Engaged," Lon replied, then his face fell. "Or at least we used to be. I lost control and knocked our house down before I finished building it. Hurt Kaylen in the process, too. I ran away the same day without saying goodbye."

"Nothing's more powerful than love," Tarek commented, "which is why I stay as far away from it as I can. I have no interest in wearing a bride's bridle, if you know what I mean."

"That's your choice," Lon answered. "I'll never give up on Kaylen. I'd be dead if it wasn't for her."

"Which is why you chose her last name. Care to explain that one to me?"

Lon turned toward the fire and crossed his legs. "Might as well. I've already buried myself enough. My real last name is Marcs."

"As in Aron Marcs?"

"He's my father."

Tarek pulled his own green cloak tighter around himself. "That explains three things—why you came here, why Omar's helping you, and why you plan to leave. If Aron could do it, why not you, right?"

Lon just stared at the fire.

Tarek released a noisy breath. "Listen, you saved my life today. I owe you. Aside from that, I like you, Lon. I don't see eye to eye with many people around here. It's nice to have a friend."

Lon glanced at his general. "What are you saying?"

"What, do I have to spell it out for you? I thought Beholders were supposed to be smart." He paused to laugh at his own joke, then became very serious. "I'll keep your secrets, but you have to promise me something in return. Don't close your mind to the Rayders. That's all I ask."

Lon thought back through the previous two weeks and everything he'd learned about the Rayders, as well as the Appernysians. He wasn't convinced that the Rayders deserved to be back in Taeja, but things weren't nearly as black and white as he had thought.

He returned his gaze to the fire. "Agreed."

"Great," Tarek said with a grin, then moved to face Lon. "Now let me see you do that Beholder thing with your eyes again."

Chapter 26

Trading Secrets

Kaylen frowned. Her conversation with Kutad had turned back to Lon. *If Mellai were here, she'd absolutely refuse to tell . . . well, maybe not. Mellai knows Kutad and his dedication to our safety. Maybe she would trust him. If Kutad really cares about me, he'll feel the same way about Lon.*

"I'll tell you about Lon," Kaylen finally answered, "but I want you to go first."

"Fair enough," Kutad said. "How about we empty this ridiculously heavy sack and eat while we talk?" He helped Kaylen sit down on the stairs in front of the crenellation, then sat next to her and opened the burlap. "I hope this will be enough."

Kutad pulled out another loaf of golden-brown bread, a bottle of red wine, two pewter goblets, a large cheese wheel, and a roasted leg of mutton bound in leather.

"The meat will be a little cold, but it should still fill you up."

"I haven't eaten this well since I left Pree," Kaylen exclaimed. "It must have cost you a fortune."

"No price is too great for your happiness," Kutad replied as he poured wine into the goblets. "I hope you enjoy it."

They ate in silence for half of the meal before Kutad spoke. "I used to be in the king's army. I wasn't anyone special and only a few of my comrades knew me at that time, but I had been a soldier for many years and served the king valiantly."

"You were a soldier?" Kaylen said with surprise. "How did you end up as a tradesman?"

"Be patient. That's part of my big secret."

"Sorry."

Kutad smiled. "As a soldier, my duty was mostly here in Itorea. I helped maintain the peace of the city and took my turn on patrols. I spent a lot of my personal time in the Perbeisea Forest. It's a magnificent place and I felt duty-bound to protect the Furwen Trees from evildoers. My daughter and I lived happily in Itorea . . . until she died. Then, I decided it was time for me to leave. That was about ten years ago."

"I didn't know you had a daughter, Kutad. Can I ask how she died?"

Kutad sighed and drained his goblet of its wine. "She was killed by the high and mighty men of the Cavalier Crook."

"Cavalier Crook?"

"The southwest quadrant of Itorea's blade, where narcissistic men make the rules, but aren't subject to them."

"What happened?" Kaylen asked with concern.

"How she died was mostly an accident. She was taking a walk through one of the markets, but she was deaf and didn't hear the horses galloping up the road. She stepped in front of six men riding madly through the city with an important message for the king. They trampled her to death."

Kaylen placed her hands over her mouth and gasped.

"The men should've been more careful," Kutad continued, "but it was an important message about a group of Rayders who kidnapped a young boy from an outlying village and murdered the rest of his family. You told me a similar story about Pree while we were outside the gate, remember? Myron Ascennor used to be in the king's army with me before he moved to Pree."

Kaylen nodded, overwhelmed by the new information. She didn't know Myron had served in the army.

"The men didn't stop after they killed my Linney," Kutad continued, "but what really made me angry was that they never even came to pay respects." He filled his goblet and took another long drink. "I gave them a full month to return, but they failed to send a message. I demanded justice, but despite my pleas to King Drogan, I wasn't given an audience.

"I was outraged and decided to take the matter upon myself. I went into the Crook, to the front gates of each of their estates—but rather than face me, they hid behind their walls like cowards. I used every taunt and slander I could imagine, but nothing worked. I became angry and frustrated, enough that I eventually withdrew from the king's service altogether and joined the caravan.

"It was then that my name became popular among the soldiers. With the exception of a few loyal friends—like Jareth, the soldier that let us up here—they all say I've turned renegade, but I don't care. Why should I serve a king who didn't serve me? I know you've heard me speak out against the Rayders, but in all honesty, I've considered joining them on more than one occasion. They're savage and violent, but those characteristics can be just as readily found here. At least the Rayders understand the meaning of loyalty."

"How did your wife react to it?"

"Tayla died during childbirth two years after Linney was born."

Tears filled Kaylen's eyes. She took Kutad's hand and they sat together in silence for a long time before Kaylen dared to speak again. "I know it doesn't make any difference, but I can understand your pain. My mother died just a few years ago. Mellai would be honored to know you gave her your daughter's name."

Kutad only nodded.

"So, it's been a little over ten years since Linney died?"

"Yes."

"I feel terrible. If the men in our village had watched the Rayders more carefully, both Myron's family and your daughter might have been spared."

"Don't be ridiculous," Kutad countered. "It was just a run of bad luck."

Kaylen let go of Kutad's hand and sipped her wine slowly. "I'm glad you haven't fled to the Exile. According to Mellai's father, you'd have left a bad situation to join yourself with something even worse."

"And what would Aron know of such things?" Kutad answered.

Kaylen paused awkwardly. "I . . . thought you knew because you two are friends."

Kutad set down the goblet and lifted an eyebrow at her. "Knew what?"

As Kaylen struggled to find a response, Kutad chuckled. "He used to be a Rayder, didn't he?"

Kaylen nodded uncomfortably. "He was born a Rayder, but ran away to marry Shalán."

"That makes a lot of sense," Kutad said as he nodded slowly. "Lon abandoned you in Pree to restore his father's dishonor by becoming a Rayder himself."

"I don't blame you for thinking that," Kaylen said quietly, "but Lon didn't have a choice."

"No other choice? What's so important that your future husband had to disregard his promise to marry you just to become a Rayder?"

Kaylen set down her goblet, walked to the wall, and looked again toward the Exile. The five weeks since Lon left had been difficult for her, but the pain had become much harder to manage without Mellai around. She didn't need those kinds of comments from Kutad, but there was no one she could talk to about Lon. Her misery festered inside her like an ulcer and made every day more difficult. She had to find someone who would understand Lon's predicament. Someone she could trust. Someone who could keep a secret.

She looked back at Kutad. He was still sitting on the stone, cleaning up their meal.

He's a good friend of Lon's family, she debated with herself, *and he's been completely loyal to his promise to protect Mellai and me. He even went beyond what anyone expected of him and saved me in the mountains.*

Kaylen sat in front of Kutad and took both of his hands in hers. "I have something I want to tell you, but you might not like it. Can I trust you, Kutad?"

Kutad returned her gaze. "Of course, you can, Kaylen."

She took a deep breath. "Lon is a Beholder."

Kutad stared at her without speaking. Minutes passed without a word from either of them.

"Kutad?" she said anxiously. "Are you all right?"

He didn't respond. He just stared at her, as though she were a leper. The look on his face, as much as his silence, cut like a knife into Kaylen's heart.

Humiliated, she leaped to her feet and ran down the steps leading into the darkness of the tower. She struggled to pull the torch free of its sconce, but it wouldn't budge. She cursed the stubborn torch holder and dropped to the stairs, weeping openly.

Kutad appeared at the stairwell's entry carrying the burlap sack. He walked down the stairs and pulled the torch free.

"I'm sorry," he said as he handed the torch to Kaylen. "Your story was just so . . . shocking I didn't know what to say. Please forgive me."

"You didn't do anything wrong," Kaylen said as she wiped the tears from her eyes with her free hand. "If we switched places, I would have reacted the same way. It's just been so hard not having Lon around, and not being able to talk about him has made it a million times worse. I miss him, Kutad—so much it hurts."

Kaylen stood up and tediously walked down the tower stairs with Kutad beside her. She continued crying softly as they descended, but Kutad said nothing. It wasn't until they left the drum tower and were sitting in his wagon that he finally spoke.

"You don't have anywhere to stay in Itorea, do you?"

"No, I'm afraid not," she answered between hiccups. "But I'm still meeting Aely at the keep. Hopefully her friends will be able to find me a position there as a handmaiden."

"Let's find Aely and make sure that happens." He flicked the reins and the donkeys pulled the wagon along the road. "So, the rumors are true. A Beholder really has been born."

"It's not as wonderful as you might think. He has no control over his power and it's slowly killing him. That's why he had to go to the Rayders. If anyone would know how True Sight works, it would be them."

"True Sight," Kutad repeated with a smirk. "I think you've known a lot more than you've been pretending, Kaylen."

"I'm sorry."

"No need for an apology. You've been dealing with a lot, and I don't blame you for acting oblivious."

After a moment, Kutad spoke again. "I know why Lon joined the Rayders, but to throw himself at them without looking for alternatives—to just join with the King's sworn enemy—doesn't that seem rash? They might be able to teach him how to use his power, but only so they can use him as a weapon against Appernysia. You have to realize this."

"I know," Kaylen answered, "but it doesn't matter what anyone wants besides Lon. He doesn't want to use True Sight. He just wants to learn how to control it so that it doesn't kill him. I can't think of any other way Lon will be able to live a normal life."

"As soon as the Rayders find out he's a Beholder, they won't let him out of their sight. They'll never allow him to leave."

"That's why he's keeping it a secret. Aron had a close scholar-friend in the Exile. Lon is going to find him and ask for his help. We all know the scholar probably won't agree, but there's no other choice. Even if it doesn't work out, Lon won't be any worse off than he was when he left Pree. Unless he learns to control his power, he'll die no matter what."

Chapter 27
Choices

"Do not forget," Omar counseled as Lon shut the door to the scholar's quarters.

Tarek followed after Lon. "Don't forget what?"

"I'll tell you later," Lon replied, glancing up and down the corridor.

"Ah," Tarek said. "Something about that, huh?"

"Shut it," Lon argued. "Not here."

Tarek laughed. "Fine, fine. You can tell me tonight. In the meantime, let's get you all prettied up."

"Do I really have to do this?" Lon groaned. "It's not my celebration."

"No, but you're one of our commander's special guests. You've got to look your best."

"Looking good isn't my problem," Lon joked, then stopped to look at Tarek. "What are you hiding?"

"Nothing," Tarek said, bringing his empty palms up in front of himself.

"You know what I mean. Why did he invite me?"

"Where's your sense of pride, Lon?" Tarek grabbed Lon's shoulder and pushed him forward. He led Lon through Flagheim's keep to a room filled with bolts of colored material. Several women were in the room, including Flora Baum. They all paused when Tarek and Lon entered.

"Hello, Flora," Tarek said with a brazen smile.

"Good afternoon, General," Flora replied, then looked at Lon. "I've been waiting for you, Lon Shaw."

"I'll leave you two alone," Tarek said. He grinned knowingly at Lon, then winked and disappeared out the door.

"Sorry about that," Lon said to Flora. "He's been acting extra Tarek-ish today."

Flora smirked. "I could tell, but do not worry. We are all used to his unique behavior."

Lon laughed. "Unique, huh? That's an understatement. Anyway, what do you want me to do now?"

"We will take good care of you, Lon Shaw. No need to fret."

Flora and a few other women spent the next two hours measuring, cutting, and altering material around Lon. He left the room donned in an expensive blue velvet outfit that only Rayder officers wore. He felt even more awkward than before, peering out an arrow slit in the stonewall, gauging the position of the setting sun. Barely enough time.

Lon hurried through the corridors to the great hall. Two sentries nodded at him as he entered. Tarek and Omar were both inside, dressed in their own ceremonial clothing and seated near Rayben at a long rectangular table. Many other Rayders were present as well, all lieutenants in their commander's army.

Tarek waved Lon to a seat between him and Omar. "There you go, Lon. We'll keep you safe, don't worry."

Lon shook his head. Tarek's sarcasm was grating on his nerves.

Omar stood and called for everyone's attention. "Today we celebrate the unprecedented. On this day twenty-five years ago, Rayben Goldhawk took up the mantle as our commander. He has served us valiantly ever since. I drink in his honor."

Omar lifted a silver mug of ale to his lips and swallowed two large gulps. Everyone at the table did the same. In turn, they each stood and drank from their mugs to show their individual devotion to their commander.

"Remain standing, Lon Shaw," the commander said when Lon took his turn. Rayben rose out of his chair and walked around the table as he spoke. "As all of you know, we are lucky to have General

Tarek with us today. He is our greatest swordsman, but even he is not invincible. Your general would have died a month ago at the hands of an Appernysian ambush, had Lon not intervened. How many scouts did you say he killed?"

"Twenty-five, my Commander," Tarek replied.

"Twenty-five scouts," Rayben echoed, "who should have had the advantage of surprise. But they had not escaped Lon's sight. He charged into their midst and eliminated the threat before his general even had time to draw his sword."

Murmurs of approval rumbled from the lieutenants. Lon glanced at Tarek, angry about the embellished lie—Tarek had slain the rest of the scouts after Lon had passed out.

"It is this reason," Rayben continued, "along with his unmatched dedication to my soldiers the past two months, that I raise Lon Shaw into your fellowship. He has proven his tactical skill, his mastery of weapons, his loyalty to your general, and his devotion to me. Tonight, I make Lon Shaw my first lieutenant. Should General Tarek fall in battle, Lon will lead my forces—which is only fitting since Lon has been training them alongside General Tarek."

Cheers arose as everyone surrounding Lon hoisted their mugs into the air, while Lon watched their commander in a stupor.

Rayben returned to his seat at the head of the table. "I am also implementing one of Lieutenant Lon's ingenious ideas. I have taken a couple months to weigh the outcomes of such a program, but I believe only good will come from it."

The commander paused to take a long drink from his mug. "I have been sending an increased number of infiltration squads into Appernysia, but none have returned. I can only assume they were captured. Although I despise King Drogan, I would be foolish to ignore his intelligence. If I stop sending squads into Appernysia, he would notice. He would suspect an attack. Even if he captures every man we send into Appernysia, we must continue on as we now have to ensure that he does not discover our true intentions."

"You have our support in this, Rayben," Omar said.

"I appreciate that," Rayben replied, "but I am not resigned to purposefully send my men to Appernysian dungeons. This new plan—Lon's plan—will improve every Rayder's skill in stealth. I also believe it will strengthen their bond with each other. They will learn to trust one another and work together as a team. Most importantly, any Rayder wishing to join an infiltration squad must pass this program first."

"How can we help, my Commander?" Wade Arneson asked from further down the table. Enthusiasm radiated on his face.

"I would like to test it with all of you first before I introduce it to your men," Rayben answered. "Meet me here tomorrow for lunch and I will explain further. Be sure to dress warmly." He ripped a leg from a roasted turkey and nodded to Omar.

"Congratulations again to Lon," Omar continued. "May his honor bring glory to our commander. Now feast and enjoy yourselves. Rayben expects all of you to wake up tomorrow bloated and nursing a pounding headache."

Everyone laughed and filled their platters. Lon ate his own fill, but avoided the ales, not trusting his control of True Sight while under their influence. The celebration lasted for many hours. By the time Lon and Tarek left, Flagheim was shrouded in darkness.

"So, what did Omar want you to remember?" Tarek said when they reached his house by the training grounds. He slurred his words together clumsily. He'd obviously had too much to drink. "Thought I'd forget, didn't you?"

Lon shook his head. "It doesn't matter what I tell you tonight. You'll forget it all by morning."

"I didn't drink that much," Tarek argued. "I need my wits about me tomorrow when we introduce your special program. You're putting quite the twinkle in our commander's eye, aren't you?"

Tarek suddenly swung his fist at Lon, but missed and toppled off his horse. He hit the ground with a loud thud, then stood up and tried pulling himself back onto his saddle. "Lieutenant Lon," he mused as he fought to get his foot into the stirrup. "Catchy, isn't it?" He laughed.

"We're already here," Lon said. He dismounted and pulled Tarek through the front door.

"Get off me," Tarek growled once they were inside. "Beholder boy." He laughed again.

Lon grabbed his bedroll and laid it out in front of the fireplace. "What's with you?"

"Oh, I'm just fine, thank you very much," Tarek said. He walked by Lon and smacked him on the back of his head.

"Cut it out," Lon said. He unbuckled his falchion and threw it on the floor. "Seriously, Tarek, what's your problem?"

"The swords are off, are they?" Tarek spat as he tossed his own sword aside. "That's how it's going to be? All right, Lieutenant Lon, have at me."

Lon folded his arms across his chest. "You've got something on your mind. Spit it out."

Tarek spat on the floor. "Right here? Or did you want it closer?" He moved in front of Lon and spat on his boot, then lifted his chin to stare at Lon. "My problem, Beholder boy, is you and your lack of commitment. We shouldn't need programs to keep our brothers safe, not with you around. If our commander discovers you are a Beholder, he'd lead us into Appernysia tomorrow. What are you so afraid of? Don't want to help the Rayders?"

"You know that's not it," Lon argued. "You know how I feel about Rayben. I respect him."

Tarek backhanded Lon across the face. "Commander Rayben. Show him respect, First Lieutenant."

True Sight filled Lon's vision. His fists clenched at his sides as he glared at Tarek's glowing form. Despite his anger, Lon focused on maintaining a barrier between himself and the world's energy. He wouldn't allow himself to pass out in front of Tarek. Not again.

"I'm not doing this for any of you, Tarek, and I don't have to explain myself."

"Yes, you do," Tarek yelled, undaunted by Lon's clouded eyes. "You've got control of it now, Lon. You can go back home. Why haven't you?"

"I . . . I can't answer that."

"It's a simple question," Tarek spat. "Kaylen or the Rayders? Make a choice, or I'll make you make a choice."

"Get out of my way." Lon tried to step around Tarek.

Tarek blocked Lon's path. "You're not running away again. You're going to stay right here and figure this out."

"I'm warning you, Tarek." The energy surrounding Lon flared brightly, fighting to force its way into Lon's essence. "Back off."

"No."

Lon gave up. He released his barriers and allowed energy to fill him, then raised his left hand and threw Tarek against the ceiling with a concentrated stream of air.

"You want to know what Omar told me not to forget?" Lon growled as he held Tarek prisoner against the rafters. "I can't manipulate what I can't see. Guess what that means?"

Lon shut his eyes and listened as Tarek crashed to the floor. Opening his eyes again, he made for the door. He yanked at the door, but the knob was jammed. The room pressed in around him, demanding the same answer Tarek sought. Stifling. Suffocating. He had to escape. Lon placed both hands against the door and poured energy into it, then stepped back and kicked it hard. The wooden planks shot out in pieces.

"That's more like it," Tarek shouted as Lon fled into the snowy night.

Night Stalker

L on strained his ears for any sounds of movement as he lowered himself to the ground. Winter's biting cold had been replaced by spring's rain, leaving the ground wet and slimy. There were three hours until sunrise and the overcast sky muted all light from the moon and stars, making it almost impossible to see.

Lon had been slowly making his way through the forest since sundown. The other five members of his party were dead, leaving him to complete their mission alone. He knew his goal was only two hundred yards ahead, but he dared not move for fear of giving away his position. The forest was completely still, proof that Lon was surrounded by other men. It wasn't safe for him there.

These men are too good, Lon thought as he continued to listen. Not a sound reached his ears. *They're all around me. I can feel them.*

Lon closed his eyes, took a deep breath, and let it out slowly. When he reopened his eyes, flowing waves of energy filled the darkness of his sight, each cluster interacting differently in its element. The air bounced back and forth around him to the rhythm of a silent waltz, while the energy radiating from the nearby trees fluttered like a flag waving in a slight breeze. Lon smiled, still proud that he finally understood many of the subtle energy interactions around him.

He surveyed the area and found the bright outline of a man standing with his back against a tree, the particles in his body interacting so quickly and intensely that Lon couldn't distinguish between them.

The man held a sling in his hand and was frantically turning his head back and forth. Lon smirked at the man's fear and crept away in the opposite direction.

Lon hurried through the forest with renewed vigor that came from the clear vision of True Sight. He evaded five other men, all of which were watching from the cover of shrubs and brush. He even found a soldier high in the branches of a tree.

Coward, Lon thought as he slipped underneath him. *He knows he won't be able to see anyone from up there.*

Lon soon discovered the glowing light of a torch. He crept to the edge of the clearing just outside of the circle of light. The particles in the flickering fire battled with each other. They shot up and out of it like a volcano, dispersing into the surrounding air before being pulled back into the fray at its base. Lon watched the rotating energy with fascination, still unable to completely understand its behavior.

A broad-shouldered man stepped in front of the fire and blocked Lon's view of the torch. Lon shook his head, berating himself for being distracted, and brought his mind back to the task at hand. He glanced around and found the prize he sought—a glistening diamond the size of a man's fist.

The man heard and turned toward him.

"So it comes to this, does it?" said Tarek's familiar voice. "You snuck past my guards, but don't think I'll be so easily tricked, Lon. I'll kill you before you take this diamond." After placing a stone in his sling, Tarek spun it around with his right hand.

Lon smiled as he brought his left hand forward and aimed his palm toward Tarek. He focused on the leather sling, the air displaced by its spinning motion, and how it relayed to the pulsing energy radiating from his own hand. He carefully timed how fast the sling revolved. Just as it reached the top of its circular pattern, Lon forced a small ball of wind from his hand. It whipped through the air and struck the pocket of the sling, sending the rock and sling flying from Tarek's hand.

Tarek's eyes narrowed as he drew his sword and gripped it with both hands. "Too afraid to face me in a fair fight? I don't blame you—I'd hate to fight myself—but still, how can you live with such gutlessness?"

"Easy to say when you're holding a sword," Lon answered from the shadows. "I don't have anything but my fists."

"Not my problem," Tarek shouted back. "Stop hiding and face me like a true Rayder, if you can even call yourself one."

Tarek's words were followed by the voices of other men scattered in the woods, all coming to their general's aid. Unless Lon acted fast, the opportunity would pass. He brought both arms forward and faced his palms toward the clearing, pulling the air into his right hand and forcing it out his left. A small cyclone of wind formed in front of Lon, which he pushed toward Tarek. Leaves and dust were pulled into the cyclone and spewed from its top. Soon the entire clearing was obscured with dust, though not thick enough to stifle Tarek's fit of coughing.

When the dust finally settled, Tarek growled. Lon was strolling through the clearing just a few feet away from him. Tarek lunged to attack, but was caught by a mound of dirt Lon had formed around his right foot.

Lon laughed as he leaped onto a boulder, grabbed the diamond from its top, and tossed it playfully between his hands. "Tsk, tsk," he said as he winked one of his cloudy eyes. "You failed again, Tarek."

Tarek growled and yanked his foot out of the dirt pile, then slipped his sword back into his belt. Walking up to Lon, he squared his broad shoulders in front of his friend.

"Only against you, Brother," he said with a laugh as he grabbed Lon in a tight embrace.

"Not so tight," Lon gasped as he released True Sight. "I can't . . . breathe . . ."

Tarek let go and slapped him hard across the face. "Consider it payback for the dust cloud, the clump of dirt, and those eyes of yours—they still creep me out. You really ought to be more careful. Next time—"

Six men poured into the clearing and groaned when they found Lon holding the diamond.

"—I expect less mercy for the defenders," Tarek shouted as he glanced at Lon. "If the opportunity presented itself, you should have killed them—even if it meant five stripes for their incompetence."

Tarek brought his fingers to his mouth and whistled loudly. A few minutes later, they were joined by fourteen other men. Five of them wore helms made of thick leather, and the rest were wrapped in dark green cloaks.

"Stalkers by me," Lon commanded. "Who was killed tonight?"

The helmed men moved next to Lon and raised their hands.

"All of you?" Lon asked, trying to sound as disappointed as possible. "Tonight was a perfect opportunity, Rayders. The extra darkness should have given you plenty of cover and allowed you to slip by the defenders undetected. I can't recommend any of you to be infiltrators. If you still think you have what it takes, sign up for another Night Stalker challenge to prove yourself."

One of the men stepped forward. "But the rules say that as long as one stalker captures the diamond—"

"We make the rules," Lon shouted. "Unless you plan on taking your complaint to our commander, I suggest you bite your tongue."

The man stepped back and dipped his head. "Forgive me, Lieutenant. I spoke out of place."

Lon looked over the five men. "Don't expect that just because you're on my team, you'll automatically gain privileges or higher standing. I require proficiency from all of my men. I can't do everything myself."

"Yes, Lieutenant," the five men answered in unison.

"And competing against Lon's opposing team doesn't excuse you either." Tarek turned to his own group of men. "A defender must defend, regardless of who is attacking—and especially when the attackers are unarmed. We don't cower in hidden corners. We don't hide in trees. We are Rayder soldiers, men. We've been honored with bearing the

Cross. We represent our commander in every action, be it success or failure. Do not shame our name."

"Yes, General," the other fifteen men answered.

"Return to Flagheim," Tarek ordered. "As soon as you get back, all twenty of you will serve a double-shift cleaning our commander's great hall."

"Yes, General," the men shouted, then formed two columns, marching in double-time down the base of the Dialorine Range toward Flagheim.

Tarek pulled out his wooden sword and broke it in half over a rock. "A lot of good these things do defending against you. If you ask me, we should be using steel. It would give you a greater challenge."

Lon placed the diamond in a leather pouch hanging from his side. "I wouldn't stand a chance against a fully-armed Tarek—even if I used True Sight."

"Not true," Tarek argued. "Remember the first night we tried Night Stalker? You stomped on everyone, including our commander, and you didn't even use True Sight. You have incredible skills of stealth and evasion, Lieutenant Lon."

"Maybe, but using my power sure makes it a lot easier, especially on blackouts like tonight."

"Next time," Tarek said, "you might get caught. I know you're getting more skilled every day you spend with Omar, but to use True Sight so openly is dangerous. Be more careful, Lon. If anyone else found out you're a Beholder, Rayben would have all three of us executed. He may not act like it. He's always thinking about the rumors spreading through Appernysia—rumors about you. He wouldn't like it very much if he found out you had kept the truth from him."

"I won't get caught," Lon replied. "Even if I did, I couldn't be held prisoner."

"You're not that powerful yet. A squad of Rayders could easily take you down."

"I don't think so. But I don't plan to find out, either."

Tarek picked up the torch, then he and Lon started back in the same direction as the soldiers.

"I've got to be honest," Tarek said after a few minutes. "I still question your attitude."

"What do you mean?"

"I know it's been three months since you became a Rayder, but that's a really short time to completely change sides. You've gone from one extreme to the other, especially over the past month."

"I haven't changed sides," Lon replied. "I've changed perspective. I don't consider myself an enemy to Appernysia. I'm only staying to help our commander retake Taeja. After that, I have my own agenda to follow."

"And what agenda is that? Going to abandon us and run back to Kaylen?"

"Maybe eventually, but not before I make sure there is peace between our commander and King Drogan. I'm not helping to start a war. Every problem in the Exile and Appernysia exists because of the separation of Rayders and Appernysians; I want to eliminate it. I want to become a part of Appernysia again, like we used to be in the First Age. I want the Rayders to become Taejans—and maybe someday Phoenijans."

"Phoenijans?" Tarek said with a laugh. "King Drogan won't even let us stay in Taeja without a fight. There's no way he'd ever consider making Rayders his personal guard."

"I know," Lon replied. "That's why I don't want there to be any difference between Rayders and Appernysians anymore."

Tarek stopped and looked at Lon. "What would your family think of your plan? You've spent your whole life trying to prove yourself to your father. What would Aron say if you told him you wanted to bring the Rayders back to Appernysia?"

"I think he would be proud of me for trying to close the rift that separates us."

Tarek played with his red beard thoughtfully. "All right, say everything goes as you plan. We take back Taeja and, for some strange reason,

King Drogan lets us stay there. You know our commander is still going to harass the Appernysians. You'll just make it easier for him."

"Not if I can convince him to befriend other cities. If everything ends up how it used to be in the First Age, any man would be honored to join the Taejans. But this is all just speculation. The truth is there's no guessing what will happen once we retake Taeja. Our commander has been focusing on it for so long he won't know what to do with himself."

Tarek shook his head. "Lon, you're young and naive. The First Age ended a long time ago. I wish our future could end up that way, but it's not going to happen. You can't change a pattern that has been established for over a millennium."

"You're wrong," Lon countered. "You're our general, Tarek, and I'm a Beholder first lieutenant. If we work together, we can have a major influence on our commander and the rest of the Rayders."

Tarek laughed. "Oh, so now I'm part of your master plan? When did I get pulled into all of this?"

"Last night," Lon answered, "but you were too tired to remember."

Tarek slugged Lon in the arm. "If I don't remember it, then it never happened."

"We make quite the team, don't we?"

"But I still say you have the definite advantage. That took some skill to knock the sling out of my hand, and I thought the cyclone was going to swallow me whole. How do you do things like that?"

"I see the world's energies and how they interact with each other, then I manipulate them through my own personal energy."

"Sounds more like you're messing with evil spirits to me," Tarek said with a shiver, then stuck the torch in front of Lon's face. "Show me your eyes again."

"Leave me alone."

"Ah, c'mon," Tarek said eagerly with a hard slap on Lon's back. "Let me see you do it."

Lon stopped and sighed. "All right, but promise you'll stop bugging me after that?"

Tarek nodded and stood in front of Lon, who closed his eyes and focused his mind. Once he had drawn on True Sight, he opened his eyes and looked at Tarek.

"Amazing," Tarek said. "Now do some—"

Lon grabbed him and yanked him behind a nearby birch tree. Tarek immediately reached for a sword at his waist.

"See?" Tarek hissed as he waved his empty hand through the air. "Curse these wooden swords—I need steel."

Lon slapped his hand over Tarek's mouth and peeked around the trunk. A man sat on the large branch of an oak tree further down the hill. If Tarek hadn't convinced Lon to use True Sight, they would have missed him and might have been ambushed. Lon focused on the energy stirring inside the man's head.

"He's not a Rayder," Lon whispered to Tarek.

"You sure?"

"There'd be a dull spot next to his eye from the branded skin."

Tarek peeked around the other side of the tree. "Where is he?"

"About twenty paces straight ahead in that oak, staring to the right."

"Should I flank him?"

"Let me try something first."

Lon placed his right hand on the birch tree and peered around it again. The man hadn't moved. Lon focused on the energy creeping through the oak tree, distinguishing between the veins of water and the hardwood sections. Once he was able to separate the two in his mind, he curved his left hand toward the oak tree, pulling tiny portions of wood from the branch and transferring them into the birch with his right hand. The branch weakened and snapped, dropping the man ten feet to the ground with a thud.

"You're scary, you know that?" Tarek whispered and pounced on the man, who offered no resistance. "He's unconscious, and he's missing body parts."

Lon released True Sight and ran to Tarek's side. "Was it the fall?"

CHAPTER 28: NIGHT STALKER ✦ 291

"No," Tarek answered. He grabbed the man under his arms and lifted him onto his feet. "It must have happened weeks ago."

Lon examined the man. An old bandage tied off his severed arm about halfway down his left forearm.

"Looks painful," Lon said as he thought back to the night he was forced to cut his own forearm.

"I'm surprised he lived this long," Tarek added. "That bandage needs to be changed."

"Indeed." Lon grabbed the man's hair and pulled his head back. With a shout, he dropped the man's head and leaped back.

"What? Is he maimed?"

"Yes, but not recently . . ." Lon stepped forward and lifted the man's head again. "I can't believe it. This is Braedr Pulchria, Hans and Ine's son."

"What? No way. If this keeps up, soon everyone in Pree will be living in the Exile."

"Not my family," Lon countered.

Tarek didn't answer. Lon knew the comment was oiled straw his friend refused to throw a torch onto, no matter how tempting it appeared.

Tarek shook Braedr and slapped him repeatedly in an attempt to wake him up, but Braedr remained motionless.

"Why is he here?" Lon asked. "More importantly, what do we do with him? Rayben ordered the immediate execution of everyone not marked with the Cross."

"I know," Tarek answered. "Considering what Braedr did to your sister, do you wish him anything less?"

"I forgot I told you about that." Lon studied Braedr's pale face, imagining himself looking the same when he first entered the Exile. Lon felt a strange pang of sympathy for him, knowing Braedr had endured even harder trials than Lon on his journey. While logic said Braedr would become another bloodthirsty Rayder if he were allowed to live, Lon couldn't force himself to kill him. "Pick him up. We're taking him to your house."

"What's your plan?" Tarek replied as he threw Braedr over his shoulder.

"Find out what madness drove him here. I'd talk to him myself, but he hates me. He'll never give me an honest answer."

Tarek laughed, "An honest answer." They continued down the mountain at a quick pace. "Is that what you gave when you were first captured?"

"Shut it, Tarek."

"Fine, fine, I'll do what you ask, but it'll be difficult trying to get him to my house without being noticed by the patrols."

"You're their general. You don't have to give an explanation for your actions."

Tarek laughed. "You complain that Rayben abuses his power?"

"I swear I'll make Braedr a hundred pounds heavier if you don't shut your mouth."

Tarek continued his mocking laughs as they walked the rest of the way down the mountain to where their horses were tethered.

"Take him straight to your house, Tarek," Lon said as he untied Dawes and climbed into his saddle. "I'm going to talk with Omar."

"Send him my love," Tarek jeered as he threw Braedr over the front of his horse.

"Right," Lon replied, as he kicked Dawes and galloped away.

*   *   *   *   *

Lon didn't reach the outer walls of Flagheim until that afternoon. He rode Dawes quickly through the city until he crossed under the gate leading through the inner wall and into the bailey.

A stable boy ran into the courtyard and took Dawes's reins as Lon dismounted and headed into the keep. He ignored everyone as he made his way through the passages of the keep. After glancing in the great hall, he continued to Omar's quarters.

Lon straightened his clothes, then spit into his hand and ran it through his short hair. He knew his eyes were probably red and swollen from staying up all night, but there was little he could do about that. Once he felt he was presentable, he knocked softly on the door. Omar answered and invited Lon inside.

Omar flung his robes to the side as he sat down behind one of his tables. The chair groaned under his weight. "Where was I?" he said as he leaned back and rubbed the top of his bald head with his hand. "Oh, I remember!"

Omar picked up a quill and, after dipping it in a vial of ink, started writing. Lon stood at the other side of the table and patiently waited.

"What do you need, Lon?" Omar finally said.

"I'm in need of your counsel."

Omar stopped writing and looked up at him through his bushy gray eyebrows.

"Tarek and I found a man on our way back from Night Stalker this morning," Lon added.

"Was he an infidel?" Omar asked indifferently.

"Yes."

"Did he put up a fight?"

"No, he was unconscious."

"Did you leave him there?"

"No," Lon replied. "Tarek is taking him back to his home outside the training grounds."

"So, he must be more than just a common man."

"He was missing the lower half of his left forearm, making him weak and defenseless. It would have been a disgrace to kill him. More importantly, though, he's from Pree."

Rayben Goldhawk rose from behind a chair near the fireplace. "How do you know where this man is from if he was unconscious when you found him, and of what significance is Pree to you?"

Lon saluted Rayben. "Forgive me, my Commander. I'll excuse myself and leave you with Omar."

"Had I wished we be left alone, I would have instructed Omar to send you away when you knocked on the door. Answer me."

"Tarek was raised in Pree, my Commander. He recognized the man immediately." Lon pointed to a map hanging nearby. "Pree is in the opposite corner of Appernysia. If people are running to the Exile from that far away, things must be getting even worse in Appernysia."

"And?" Rayben said with a raised eyebrow.

Lon bowed his head. "I think it's time we execute your plan, my Commander."

"Perhaps it is, but preparations are not complete," Rayben said as he moved directly in front of Lon. "What is this man's name, Lon Shaw, and why did you allow him to live? I do not care what circumstance he was in when you found him. My order was to kill all free Appernysians on sight."

"His name is Braedr Pulchria," Lon answered, his mind racing for a safe way to answer the second half of Rayben's question. Despite his inward panic, however, Lon had become an expert liar since arriving at the Exile and maintained a calm appearance in front of the commander. "It must be a two-month journey from Pree to the Exile, and from the way Braedr's injury appears, he made half the trip with part of his arm missing. What he accomplished is no small feat. Judging from his motivation to get here, Braedr might have crucial information to share with us. Even if he doesn't, I still think a man like this would make a valuable addition to your army, my Commander."

Rayben folded his arms. "Is this the real reason you want to spare his life? Because Tarek knew him?"

"No, my Commander. Tarek hated Braedr," Lon lied, "enough that he laughed when he found him on the edge of death."

The commander furrowed his brow. "Why did you seek Omar's counsel instead of my own regarding this matter?"

"You've been busy making preparations, my Commander. I thought for a matter as trivial as this, it would be best to discuss it with Omar rather than to bother you."

Lon kept eye contact with the commander, knowing his reasoning wasn't the strongest, but hoping it was good enough to satisfy Rayben's curiosity.

"I find it interesting that you, of all people, would think such a thing," Rayben replied. "I keep forgetting how new you are to our culture, Lon Shaw. Sometimes I wonder if I made the best decision by making you a lieutenant, more specifically my first lieutenant."

"Forgive me, my Commander. If you wish, I'll gladly resign to rectify my mistake."

Rayben unfolded his arms and backhanded Lon across his face. "Omar and I have finished our conversation, but you will remain here for another lesson in our history. After that, you will return to Tarek's home and see what information this Braedr has for us. If you still think he would be an acceptable soldier, you will then bring him before me. Do not forget it is my decision to accept him, not yours. I do not want to hear of you making a mistake like this again."

"Yes, my Commander," Lon said, stepping aside to allow Rayben past.

Rayben turned to Omar. "Thank you for your insight, Omar. I will have the slaves test your design immediately."

"Glad to be of service, Rayben," Omar answered.

"I will put Braedr through the same trials you faced when you arrived in the Exile," Rayben said as he walked past Lon, "but I doubt he will live through it, especially with part of his arm missing."

After he disappeared down the corridor, Lon shut the door and turned to Omar. "We need some sort of signal to prevent that from happening again. I'm lucky I didn't share anything more."

"Yes, you are," Omar said as he continued writing on his manuscript. "I have warned you on many occasions that you need to be cautious before you talk about such things in this room. Perhaps now you will actually heed my advice. There is no need for a signal. Use common sense."

Lon sat down at the table across from Omar and spoke in a hushed voice. "Why does he do that, Omar? Why did he keep his presence here a secret?"

"Rayben is an untrusting man, which is why he is still alive and in command. History has taught us that plots always come from those closest to you. We have Bors Rayder to thank for establishing such a volatile leadership pattern. Rayben's continual caution has kept him commander for twenty-five years, more than twice as long as any of his predecessors."

"I wish he wouldn't treat me with distrust. I've served him faithfully for three months, obeying every order he gives me without hesitation."

Omar dropped his quill and looked at Lon. "It is his intuition that has led him to question your loyalty. Is he unjustified in doing so, Beholder?"

"I get it," Lon grumbled, "but I gained control over True Sight a while ago and I'm still here rather than back in Pree. That counts for something."

"Yes, it does," Omar said as he leaned back in his chair, "although it would benefit you to finalize your plans. You can be certain Kaylen won't marry you if you remain a Rayder. Your father taught you that."

"Does every conversation with you have to be a history lesson?"

Omar laced his fingers over his belly, which seemed to grow larger every week. "History is my life's passion. Would you have me cast away my true nature like a worn-out cloak and focus on something else?"

Lon rolled his eyes. "Will you ever drop the idea that I should reveal myself as a Beholder? I still have too much to learn."

Omar asked a different question, which Lon knew was to avoid another long and pointless argument. "What is the real reason for your visit?"

"I'm at the crossroad of a difficult decision," Lon answered with a sigh. "Everything I told Rayben is true, except for Tarek's opinion of Braedr. The guy is from Pree, but it's complicated. Braedr hates me more than he loves himself, mostly because I stole away Kaylen when I moved to Pree."

"Well, it appears he was unable to win her back after you left," Omar commented, "or he would not be here. That could be a stroke of good luck, should you decide to return to Pree."

"Maybe, but that's a decision for the future. What I have to decide now is whether or not to let him live. He's a terrible person, Omar, in many different ways. Now that he's here at the edge of death and completely at my mercy, I find myself feeling sorry for him. What should I do?"

Omar tapped his thumbs together. "Your decision to spare Braedr's life was merciful, but also short-sighted and dangerous."

"What do you mean?"

"What would happen if our commander discovered you came from Pree? What if he knew your real last name? Think how easy it would be for Braedr to share either, whether purposefully or not. You, Tarek, and everyone you know in Pree would be hunted if Rayben found out."

"That complicates things," Lon said as he slumped in his chair and blew out his breath. "I don't know how I missed that." He pondered the situation, then sat forward and shook his head. "I'm not worried about it, Omar. Say Braedr does talk, who would place his word over Tarek's and mine? Making such a claim against a general and first lieutenant would be an act of treason. Braedr would be put to death."

"Maybe so." Omar shrugged. "Follow your heart, Lon. Never have I read of a Beholder making a decision that led to his demise—aside from the fools who got overzealous with True Sight. According to my records, there is a ten-mile crater in the Forest of Blight from a Beholder's attempt to see how much energy he could hold inside himself."

"I know, Omar, you've told me many times. *If you try to manipulate too much energy through your body, you will blow yourself to pieces.* I've been careful. You don't need to worry."

"Do not forget my warning. One failed attempt could destroy all of Flagheim and everyone in it."

Chapter 29

History

O mar thumbed through a large pile of manuscripts. "Today I will teach you about the calahein."

"Why the calahein?" Lon asked. "They're extinct."

"Because I love history and I have been waiting for an opportunity like this for a long time," Omar said with an eager smile. "You were ordered by your commander to stay and listen to me, so you cannot leave."

Lon groaned as he slouched into his chair.

"The calahein lived in Meridina, a complex system of underground tunnels west of Taeja—on the opposite side of the Tamadoras Mountains. That entire area is a frozen tundra and accessible only through the Meridina Pass—or on the back of a ghraef."

"They were burrowers?" Lon asked as he sat up, intrigued. "What did they look like?"

Omar laughed at Lon's sudden interest and slid a piece of parchment across the table. "This is a drawing of the kelsh—the soldiers of the calahein. As you can see, the kelsh were large and muscular. They walked on two legs, standing about seven feet tall from head to foot. Like the ghraefs, their skin was thick and hard, and completely covered in fur. You might expect their fur to be white since they lived in an arctic climate, but they spent most of their time underground, so it was the color of leaves upon trees in late fall."

"It looks like its face was smashed in by a mace," Lon laughed.

"Laugh if you want to, but had you seen one of these in person, you would have wet yourself. Their eyes and snouts were small, but their senses were as refined as a ghraef's. They could see clearly in the deepest passages and smell your blood from miles away. Their ears could pick up the slightest sound. They could fit your entire head in their mouth and crush it like an egg. If you tried to run away, they would drop on all fours and easily catch you and skewer you with two fingers. Those claws were meant for tunneling, but they were also ideal for killing."

"What are these?" Lon asked as he pointed to spines that jutted out above their elbows and from the tops of their knees.

"Those," Omar answered, "along with the entire calahein race—are a mystery to me. Something cruel and bloodthirsty must have made them. Those spikes are part of their natural bone structure and can be used as terrible weapons."

Lon shivered as he imagined the terror of encountering such a beast. "Let's talk more about Meridina. They had lots of tunnels?"

Omar smiled. "More than you can imagine. Their underground city was layered on top of itself thousands of feet under the surface, making it easy to lose your sense of direction while inside it. In fact, a large portion of the men who died during the siege of Meridina were simply lost, not killed. Once they wandered down a passage, they were never heard from again."

"That makes no sense. How was the king sure the calahein were eliminated if people were getting lost down tunnels? Couldn't the calahein have hidden in deep passageways, too?"

"Excellent question. The king knew he had eliminated them for three reasons. First, they found the queen deep in Meridina, the sole producer of their entire offspring. The Beholders discovered that all kelsh and seith were spawned in eggs laid by this one queen that had been alive for thousands of years. She had grown too large to fit through their tunnels, so she remained trapped with nowhere to run. The remaining calahein rallied around their queen and fought desperately to protect her, but they were eventually defeated and their queen destroyed."

Lon furrowed his eyebrows in thought. "What were the other two reasons?"

"Even though it was obvious the last of the calahein had remained to protect their queen, the Beholders still traveled through every passageway and collapsed them. They found nothing in those tunnels besides dusty bones. That is the second reason, and the third is that the calahein never returned. They have not been seen again to this very day, and neither kelsh nor seith lived more than a hundred years. Without a queen to reproduce, any potential survivors would have died long ago."

"Interesting," Lon commented as he sat back in his chair. "You mentioned something called a seith. What were those?"

"Those were the great bane of ghraefs. Their basic anatomy was the same as the kelsh, although they were leaner and taller. They also had membranous wings that enabled them to fly. The seith were the only creatures in Appernysia or anywhere else that were dangerous to ghraefs. Do not misunderstand me. A ghraef would still win in a fair fight with a seith, but the seith did not fight fair. I expect that the seith were the reason that ghraefs decided to join forces with the Beholders in the first place."

"I'm starting to understand why the calahein were such a formidable threat to Appernysia, even with Beholders and ghraefs defending the kingdom."

"I am glad you do not think Beholders are invincible," Omar replied. "Hopefully that will keep you from doing anything too foolish. Which reminds me, I have a training exercise for you. It might help you learn to manipulate fire."

"Wait a second," Lon said as he sat forward and pointed to another piece of parchment. "What's that?"

Omar leaned forward to see what had caught Lon's attention. It was a tiny arcing symbol sketched in one corner of the manuscript, with claws and blades protruding from the arc. "Have I not told you about it?" Omar asked with surprise.

"I've never seen it before."

"That is the Beholder's Eye," Omar said as he thumbed through a separate pile of papers. "I am surprised you have not heard of it before now."

"Why?"

"Just like the King's Cross was originally tattooed on the right temple of the Phoenijan, the Beholder's Eye was tattooed around the left eye of all Beholders. Both were done with ink made from the blue petals of the Lynth flower."

Lon turned his head sideways, trying to imagine what it would look like on a person's face, until Omar pulled a sketch out of the pile of papers and placed it in front of him.

"Oh," Lon said as he stared at the picture of a blue Beholder's Eye wrapping around the left side of a man's face, "I get it now. It's a complicated design. Does it mean something?"

"Yes," Omar explained. "The two claws on the cheekbone represent the Beholders' companionship to the ghraefs. The blade on the forehead above his eyebrow should look familiar to you. It is the top blade found on the King's Cross and represents the Beholder's dedication to the Taejans and their king." He pointed to a line arching around the side of the eye, connecting the claws to the blade. "The five triangles extending from this arch represent the power of True Sight. All three elements are linked together to make a true Beholder."

Lon sat back in his chair and looked at Omar. "I have no intention of ever getting this tattoo."

Omar shrugged indifferently and gathered up the papers. "It is your choice to make. Would you like to hear about your new training exercise?"

"Yes."

"Now that you have learned how to protect your own energy by cycling particles from one hand to the other, I want to focus on more complex elements. To do this, you will need to learn how to safely absorb energy not only through one hand, but simultaneously through the surface of your entire body."

"Why my whole body?"

"Wind is easiest for you to manipulate because it is all around you. Solid matter like stones and dirt are manageable because they are constant and stable—"

"Oh, I meant to tell you," Lon interrupted, "I successfully removed the wood from a branch and transferred it into a different tree today. That's how we were able to capture Braedr without a struggle—although I'm not sure he was even conscious while sitting on that branch."

"You manipulated vegetation?" Omar asked. "How did you solve the water problem?"

"I just ignored the veins of water and focused on the hardwood sections. Once I was able to separate the two in my mind, it was actually easy."

"Did you interact with the water?"

"No."

"Good." Omar picked up his quill and wrote on a manuscript. "We do not want you forcing your own blood out of your body through a failed attempt." He finished writing, then leaned back in his chair. "Along with water, I have warned you against other dangerous interactions, such as fire."

"And don't forget about the floating energy blasts," Lon added, remembering the time he saved Mellai. "I have no idea how I did those."

"Neither do I," Omar replied. "I have searched my library and found many examples of Beholders doing things that were far beyond what I consider simple elemental control, but how they did it is beyond me. It appears we are just scratching the surface of your full potential as a Beholder, but we will just stick with the elements for now."

"Agreed."

"The difficulty with fire is that you cannot touch it to manipulate it—at least I think that is the case. You will have to do it from a safe distance."

"All right, so how do I make fire?" Lon asked.

"For any flame to stay ignited, it requires two things—air and something to burn. Both of those are easy to come by, but the difficult part is initially getting the fire started. You will face the same challenge. Let's approach this from a practical standpoint. In what ways can you start a fire?"

"A tinder box," Lon replied. "Or friction, if you're up to a challenge."

Omar smiled. "You are. You need to create friction between flammable objects. You could do this the ancient way, by rubbing sticks together, or you could do it using True Sight. If my estimations are correct, you will need to pull the dry material through your body and force it out your hands. While collecting it between your hands, you'll somehow need to create enough friction in it until it ignites. Once that happens, your task should become simpler. All you will need to do is keep a constant stream of flammable material pouring into the flame. "

Lon's eyes brightened.

"When you take a small stick out of a fire," Omar continued, "the flame burns out. Remember this simple rule. If you stop supplying fuel to your flame, it will extinguish and you will have to start all over again."

"So, by pulling this fuel through my whole body and pushing it out both hands, I could create a fireball floating in midair."

"Exactly. But be careful, anything you use for fuel will wither up and die, if it is not dead already. Pay attention to what you are burning."

"I just had an idea," Lon said, barely able to contain his excitement. "What if I could push the flammable material through one hand, and air through the other? Would it react like blowing on a fire?"

Omar nodded. "I had thought of that as well, but again, you must be careful. The brighter your flame burns, the more fuel you will need to supply. I expect you could use up an entire tree in no time at all."

"Amazing."

"For a third time, you still need to be extremely careful, Lon," Omar said with concern. "Aside from blowing yourself up, you might accidentally light a fire inside of yourself."

Lon summoned True Sight and looked at the flames flickering in the fireplace. All of the frenzied activity remained near the burning lumber, until the particles became so excited that they escaped as tongues of flame and dispersed into the air.

"Stop," Omar shouted. "There is parchment everywhere."

"I was just watching it," Lon said as he released True Sight.

"That is what you said when you killed my bird," Omar complained. "Which reminds me, you owe me another eagle."

"I know," Lon grumbled. Then he remembered what Omar had said at the beginning of their discussion. "How can I test your theory without killing myself?"

"Practice absorbing air through your body and releasing it through your hands first. Master that technique, then try it with matter. Then try both at the same time, one through each hand. Once you can do this, you will be ready to create fire."

"You've given me a lot to think about. Once I decide what to do with Braedr, I'll find a safe place and test it."

"Let me know what you discover," Omar said, as he once again picked up his quill.

Lon stood and opened the door out of Omar's chambers. "Thank you for your time, Omar. I'll return soon."

He closed the door and took only a few steps before he encountered Flora Baum and her three children.

"Good afternoon, Lieutenant," Flora said as she curtsied and touched the brand on her temple.

"Please," Lon said, "I've asked you before to call me Lon."

"It would dishonor you to do such a thing," Flora answered. "You have done so much for my family. I would not dare disgrace you, Lieutenant. You are a blessing to us, as well as the rest of our people. Children, come out and give Lieutenant Lon the respect he deserves."

Her eight- and six-year-old sons stepped out from behind their mother's skirt, bowed, and touched their brands, but the three-year-old girl just poked her head around the side and batted her eyelashes at Lon.

"Come on, Cortney," Flora urged gently.

The little girl bit her bottom lip and touched the King's Cross on her right temple with her fingers, then giggled and disappeared again behind her mother.

"You have strapping sons and a precious jewel hiding behind you," Lon said with a smile. "Are you on your way to study with Omar?"

"Yes, Lieutenant," Flora answered.

"You have excellent timing. I just left him and he seems to be in an especially good mood today. Study hard, children."

"Yes, Lieutenant," the two boys answered.

Lon smiled and dipped his head, then stepped aside to allow Flora and her children by.

"Thank you again for arranging these continued study sessions," Flora said with a curtsy, then escorted her children to Omar's door. As Lon continued down the hallway, he heard Flora bid her children farewell.

Lon grimaced and quickened his pace so Flora wouldn't catch up to him. Outside in the bailey, he found the stable boy waiting with Dawes, then rode out of Flagheim and toward Tarek's house.

* * * * *

"How long ago did you get here?" Lon asked Tarek, who was gnawing on a hunk of meat beside the unconscious Braedr.

"Not long," Tarek answered between bites. "Find out anything interesting from Omar?"

Lon smiled. "I think I'm on the edge of learning how to control fire."

"May the Jaeds protect me," Tarek exaggerated. "I swear to you Lon, if you singe one hair of my beard, I'll—"

"—finally start cooking your food long enough so that it doesn't bleed into your lap?" Lon interrupted, turning his attention to Braedr. "Have you checked his arm?"

"I thought I'd leave that to the expert."

Lon exhaled in frustration and stepped outside to get clean rags from Dawes's saddlebags. When Lon reentered, Tarek was kneeling on top of Braedr, who was struggling to sit up.

"Better hurry," Tarek said. "This man is getting a little fidgety."

Lon summoned True Sight and channeled the air around Braedr's face into an impenetrable barrier. Just as a closed pot would stifle the flame of a candle, Braedr was unable to breath the fresh air his body required. Lon had learned this tactic while sparing with his father, but had refined his skill by experimenting upon a squirrel. The key was to release the barrier as soon as the victim stopped moving, before they suffocated to death. The squirrel had not been so lucky.

Braedr's body panicked and he fought more aggressively, but Tarek was much larger. Braedr eventually passed out again.

"You little turd," Tarek said as he reared back to punch Braedr in the face, but Lon locked Tarek's hand in another pocket of air that kept him from swinging.

"Are you really going to beat an unconscious man?"

"He made me drop my meat," Tarek growled as he struggled to pull his hand free. "Let me go. I'll leave him be."

Lon released True Sight and unwrapped the dressing around Braedr's severed arm. The wound had healed into the layers of cloth touching Braedr's skin, so Lon had to rip them off.

"Good thing he's out," Tarek said as picked his food off the ground and resumed eating. "That'd hurt more than a hammer to your head."

"Indeed," Lon said as he cleaned the raw wound. "I wonder how this happened. His arm doesn't look like it was broken—just cut clean through."

"Maybe it was punishment for stealing," Tarek considered. "That might be why he ran away."

"From Pree?" Lon countered doubtfully. "It's a month's ride on horseback to reach the Exile from there. That's too long. This happened while he was on the road. I guess he could have been caught stealing somewhere else, but I don't know."

"Whatever happened," Tarek observed, "he keeps running from one beating to another. It serves him right. I hope there's a lot more to come."

"Tarek, you have the heart of a true Rayder," Lon said sarcastically.

"Thank you," Tarek replied before he shoved the rest of the meat into his mouth. "What's your plan with him?"

"He can't see me until we find out his story," Lon answered, then grabbed his falchion off the table and belted it around his waist. "You've changed enough over the past ten years that he shouldn't recognize you, so you stay here and question him. I'm going to check on the progress in the training grounds."

Tarek sat down and propped his feet up on a nearby stool. "Gladly. My arms were made for fighting, not building. You let me know when they're done with that thing, then I'll cross it and remind those 'Nysians why they fear us."

"Not everything has to end in violence. The goal is to sneak into Taeja."

"They're going to notice us sooner or later, then they'll come to drive us out. I look forward to that day."

Lon left Tarek's house and climbed into Dawes's saddle. I don't, he thought as he rode through the open gate.

The compound was filled with Appernysian men toiling under the brutal whips of Rayder taskmasters. In their midst was a drawbridge and its base frame, both under construction but nearly complete. It was made almost entirely of wood, with a few steel plates to secure the frame's key intersections. It was wide enough for five men to march through side by side. Once complete, the Rayders could transport the bridge without disassembling it.

Dawes carried Lon to the opposite side of the grounds where Appernysian blacksmiths labored to create tools and metal plates. He hopped down and picked up a steel wheel a foot in diameter and inwardly grooved around the circumference.

"What's this for?" he asked as he turned it over in his hands. "It's way too small to be a wheel for the base."

The blacksmith took the wheel from Lon and fit a large wooden beam through its center. "This will be attached to the top-rear cross-beam of the base, along with three similar models."

"Why?"

"For the ropes. You'll have to talk to your engineer about it. I'm only a blacksmith."

Lon dropped the wheel back onto the table and turned to leave. "Who's overseeing construction today?"

"I think it's Lieutenant Wade."

"Carry on," Lon said as he returned to Dawes and went in search of Wade.

Lon found him in the middle of the grounds yelling at men who were trying to lay planks the wrong direction. Wade noticed Lon ride up and leaped down from the bridge to greet him.

"Hail, Lieutenant Lon," Wade said with a salute. "To what do I owe the honor of your visit?"

"Good evening, Wade," Lon replied. "I wish you'd stop calling me that. We're the same rank."

"Not so," Wade disagreed. "You are first lieutenant, second in command to General Tarek. I owe you my allegiance."

Lon shook his head. "I overheard our commander talking to Omar today about new designs to our bridge. I assume you've received word of the improvements. Were they talking about the grooved wheels the blacksmith is constructing?"

"No, those were one of Omar's ideas from a few days ago. His new plan is to construct ground anchors that we can run the ropes underneath to minimize both the number of men and length of rope needed to lower the bridge. If you have a moment, I will show you what we will be doing."

"Of course," Lon replied as he dismounted and handed the reins to one of the taskmasters.

Wade led him to a pile of kindling and scrap wood. He knelt down in the dirt, grabbed a handful of sticks, and started forming a small model of one of the anchors.

"We will lay three logs on the ground, parallel to each other and about ten feet apart, then a large log perpendicularly over the top of them. This will create avenues where ropes can be run under the main log to the teams of men pulling them. We will then drive a set of two long wooden poles into the ground at intervals along the main log. They will crisscross over the top of the log in the shape of an X and secure it to the ground. There will be a lot of upward pull on the main log from the ropes running underneath it. We do not want the poles to pop out of the ground while we are in the middle of lowering the bridge, so we will put another log on top of the crisscrossed poles directly above the main log. We will lash it to the main log, and that should keep the poles from bending."

"Ingenious," Lon responded as he knelt down next to Wade. "Omar's a brilliant man."

"He is," Wade concurred. "If any of us were a Beholder, I would suspect him the most. His mind is full of ideas like this."

"Why would that make him the most likely candidate?"

Wade leaned closer to Lon and spoke in a low voice. "Because it is known among all Rayders that Beholders were very intelligent men who used their minds to control True Sight. The smarter the man, the greater his power. It is important you know this, Lieutenant."

"I already did," Lon said as he stood up. "Thanks for the update. I'll get out of your way."

"Always an honor, Lieutenant," Wade said with a salute, then returned to yelling at the Appernysian slaves.

Lon wandered toward Dawes, deep in his own thoughts. He knew the Rayders believed only men of high intelligence qualified to become Beholders. His father had told him the same thing many months before on the night Myron died. He didn't consider himself a particularly bright or intuitive man. Unlike Omar, who fed off new information and always had his nose in a manuscript, Lon hated studying. His history lessons with Omar were long and painful. If not for the potential wisdom that could help him better understand True Sight, Lon would have avoided them altogether.

Unfortunately, Lon realized he was only discovering a tiny portion of what Beholders were capable of—not where it came from or why certain people were chosen as Beholders. He knew the answer to a lot of *hows,* but the *whys* continued to evade him. *Why am I a Beholder? Why have the Jaeds chosen me? Why not my father or Omar?*

Lon mounted Dawes and turned him toward the gate leading out of the training grounds. Tarek was standing at the entrance waving his arm to catch Lon's attention. Lon kicked Dawes into a gallop.

"He's awake again," Tarek said as Lon rode up.

"Get anything out of him?"

"A little," Tarek answered. "He said a bunch of things you probably don't want to hear, but I also found out what happened to him."

"Tell me."

"It appears that life hasn't treated him well since you left Pree. He kept complaining about two devil women who ruined his life, and that he had to skip town to avoid an unjust council meeting. He said he was going to head straight for the Exile when he left Pree, but then the situation changed."

"Why wouldn't I want to hear that?" Lon asked with a furrowed brow.

Tarek scratched the back of his head and looked around uneasily. "Apparently, your sister and Kaylen left Pree at the same time with a trading caravan. Braedr followed them to Roseiri and kidnapped Kaylen—intending to bring her with him to the Exile."

Lon's eyes immediately clouded over with True Sight as he jumped off Dawes. "He's a dead man."

Tarek grabbed Lon's arm. "Hold up."

"Let go of me or you're next," Lon hissed through clenched teeth, his veiled eyes still focused on the house.

"There's more to the story. Why do you think he's missing part of his arm?"

Lon pulled his arm free from Tarek's grip and turned toward him. "What happened?"

"He said he forced Kaylen on a two-day march up the Vidarien Mountains. That second night, he tied her to a tree so he could get some sleep."

A gust of wind swirled around them. Lon was on the edge of losing complete control, but Tarek pressed on with his story. "His details got somewhat sketchy after that. He remembers hearing a loud crack and flying through the air. He thought he was dreaming until he landed in a river. Somehow he managed to pull himself out of the water downriver. It was then that he noticed part of his arm was missing. He doesn't know what happened to him."

"He's lying. That should've killed him."

"That's what I thought at first, but he must have gotten out of the water pretty quickly. Then he took off his tunic and made a tourniquet around his arm. He said he also had a few broken ribs on his left side, but there was little he could do for them. He fled to Roseiri, stole some warm clothes, then came straight here—stealing more food and supplies along the way."

"He left her tied to a tree?" Lon shouted, clenching his fists in rage. He shoved past Tarek and ran toward the house.

Tarek called for Lon to wait, but it was too late. Lon burst through the door. In the dark, the westering light shining into the house revealed Braedr lying on the floor, his face bruised, his right eye swollen shut. Blood trickled from his nose and the side of his mouth.

Lon drew his falchion and ordered him to stand up. Braedr didn't move, so Lon cut a deep gash across the man's right cheek.

"Stand up," Lon barked over Braedr's squealing, "or I'll cut off your other hand."

Braedr forced himself onto his feet and squinted into the sunlight at the shadow of Lon's body.

"Where are Kaylen and my sister?" Lon demanded.

"Stop," Braedr shouted. "I already told you, she's . . . wait . . . your sister? Lon?"

Lon placed his blade on Braedr's other cheek. "Answer me! Where are they?"

Braedr threw up his one good hand and cried. "They're fine. I saw Mellai and some tradesmen with Kaylen before I started down the mountain. They're both fine."

Lon lowered his sword. "Why did you take her from Roseiri? What was your intention?"

Braedr tightened his lips and flared his bloody nostrils at Lon. "To hurt you and your sister. You stole everything important to me. I lost Kaylen and became second best." He spat blood on the ground in front of Lon. "You're a curse. I sacrificed what little I had to start a new life with the Rayders, but even here, I can't get away from you."

"You never had Kaylen," Lon shouted as he pointed his sword at Braedr's chest.

Braedr's courage disappeared again. He whimpered and began crying once more.

Tarek entered the room behind Lon and placed his hand on his shoulder. "Let it go, Lon."

Lon's chest heaved as he stared at Braedr, but he nodded and released True Sight. Lon would keep Braedr alive, but not because of mercy. Even if he somehow survived the screening with Commander Rayben, Braedr would be killed during his weapons trial. There was no way he could beat a Rayder with half of his arm missing. He would die, and Lon could enjoy it from a distance.

"Tarek, tell our commander that I fully recommend Braedr becomes a Rayder. I can't think of a better way to teach him the true meaning of respect and honor."

"Yes, Lieutenant."

"Braedr also needs to learn what happens when grown men cry in the Exile. Please take a moment to acquaint him with our law, General."

"With pleasure."

"Tarek?" Braedr said hysterically. "Tarek Ascennor? It's me, Braedr Pulchria. You remember me, right?"

Chapter 30
Blooming Romance

Dear Mother,

I know writing you again is risky, but so much has happened in the four months since I last wrote. I also trust Theiss completely and know this letter will reach you safely. Thank you in advance for inviting him in again for some of your fantastic cooking.

Mother, you better hand the letter to Father because what I have to say will shock you. Theiss is still court-ing me. I know, even after four months. Just putting this down in words turns my cheeks pink. I'm sure you're as surprised as I still am, so let me explain.

There's little to do around here during the winter, but Theiss keeps finding random projects to do on the farm. I know it's an excuse to see me, and I can't say I don't enjoy having him around. We haven't had any arguments since he found out who I am. Actually, I think it has strengthened our friendship. He's unbelievably understanding and patient with me. He knows there's a reason I'm hiding my iden-tity, but he doesn't press me about it. The only thing

314 + Terron James

that doesn't seem like a dream is that he still doesn't know about Lon.

How are Hans and Ine doing? I feel terrible they had to find out about Braedr's death from my last letter.

Kaylen seems to be doing well since she left Roseiri. Kutad took her to Itorea and now she's working as a handmaiden in the King's Court with her new friend, Aely. She says she enjoys it there and loves living in such a busy place. She still hasn't made enough money to send a letter home to Pree, so she had Kutad give one to me instead. I included her letter. Will you please give it to Scut, so he'll know she's happy and safe?

Happy and safe. How ironic that Lon is the exact opposite. I've been even more worried about him lately. About a month ago something terrible happened to him. He was angrier than I've ever felt him before. Whatever happened did something to him. Ever since then, it feels like all the happiness has been drained out of him. He feels lost, torn, and empty. I wondered if he was thrown in jail or something, but I can't imagine the Rayders doing such a thing to a Beholder, even if they found out Lon was hiding it from them. Kaylen says she's been checking the dungeons in Itorea and Lon isn't there either. I can't understand what's happening to him, but I'll let you know if I feel any changes.

As for news regarding Appernysia, Kutad said the number of Rayder sightings has grown. People in

Réxura have become so angry about it that they have started rioting, but it sounds like King Drogan is more worried about the Rayders attacking than he is about his own subjects. Apparently, he thinks the Rayders are about to make a move against Appernysia. His growing army is ready to storm out of Itorea at a moment's notice. I hope they never have to. Not with Lon and Kaylen nearby. Kutad also said that creating such a large army has come at a great cost to our people. Our king has been reserving most of the Itorean crops and livestock for his soldiers, so there are hundreds of starving people living right under his nose. It seems like an impossible situation.

Sometimes I feel so overwhelmed by the problems around us. I know we're not completely immune to them, but I'm still glad we're in the outskirts. I also wish Kaylen and Lon were with us. I'm worried about them and pray every day they'll be watched over.

I wish I could send better news, but at least we know everyone is still alive. Grandmother and Grandfather asked me to send their love. They're taking great care of me. Grandfather likes to threaten Theiss that he'd better treat me like a princess, but they couldn't be more thrilled for us.

With all my love,
Mellai

Chapter 31
Conflicted

The blazing June sun drew sweat from Lon's brow as he sat atop Dawes. Wade rode at his side, while Thad and nine other Rayders filed behind on their horses. As a separate tactical squad, they could only watch as their commander, Tarek, and Omar directed the movements of the Appernysian slaves. After six months, the construction of the bridge and its base was finally complete. It had been secured together at the main joint, and now the slaves were pulling the bridge upright so it could be transported.

"It seems a lot bigger when it is angling into the air like that," Wade commented as he leaned his head back. They were positioned at the end of the bridge, where it was rising from the ground.

Lon didn't respond. He was watching the eighty slaves for any signs of fatigue or disorder. Four ropes were tied to the end of the four thousand-pound bridge. They ran the length of the bridge and over the top of the fifty-foot base. From there, they angled downward under a large ground brace, into the hands of the slaves.

The slaves had been divided into groups of twenty men. Each group pulled on a separate rope. Lon knew the weight per person should have been easy enough to manage, but he also knew if just one person slipped, it could create a ripple effect of disaster that would ultimately end in the bridge smashing to the ground and splintering to pieces.

Tarek and Rayben paced back and forth on each side of the line of men. They shouted, "Heave!" at regular intervals so the slaves would move the bridge together. Omar and three Appernysian slaves stood on a platform atop the base, where the ropes were being pulled over four steel grooved wheels. Omar continually turned his head back and forth, checking the structural integrity of the bridge and ropes. The beams in the base groaned under the crushing pressure of the ropes, but they held fast.

Only a handful of other Rayders were present. Leaders over their respective responsibilities—Vance Talbot, Captain of the Rayder cavalry; Warley Chatterton, lieutenant over siege weapons; Bryst Grayson, supply wagon overseer—were there with their most trusted soldiers. They were supervising the function of the bridge so they would fully understand what to expect once they reached Thorn. The rest of the Rayder army remained camped north of Flagheim in the same field where Tarek and Lon had been training them the previous six months.

The bridge slowly continued to rise. The angle of the ropes steepened until they stopped pivoting over the grooved wheels on the base and formed a straight line from the nose of the bridge to the ground brace. Lon watched carefully, knowing that the higher the bridge climbed, the harder the ropes would pull on the brace.

Although careful planning had been put into what they were doing, Lon still worried that the brace wouldn't stay anchored in the ground. He had already decided he would intervene to save the bridge from collapsing, even if it revealed him to the Exile.

"What use would air be against a slender rope or beam?" Omar had asked when Lon told him of his plan. "You will reveal your secret at the worst possible time. Everyone will know you are a Beholder, but more importantly, they will believe you to be a failure if you can't save the bridge. They will lose faith in you, Lon."

"I'll think of something," Lon had responded, but as he stood there evaluating his capabilities, he also started to doubt there was anything he could do.

Within ten minutes, the bridge was vertical and tied off in the center of the base. Lon shifted in his saddle and folded his arms. They had succeeded in the first step, but the difficulty wasn't over yet.

"Step two," Omar shouted from his platform.

The eighty exhausted Appernysian slaves were replaced by more than two hundred other slaves. Fifty positioned themselves at the front end of the base, while another hundred and fifty grabbed hold of ropes tied to the base's bottom. The remaining twenty picked up axes and hacked at long poles driven into the ground over the bottom beams of the base to hold it in position.

"Step three," Omar shouted once the poles were cut.

Lon held his breath. The slaves were attempting to pull the bridge backward out of the wheel holes. Lon was worried that, if the slaves didn't tip it over in the process, the six wheels wouldn't be strong enough to hold such a heavy load.

At first it appeared nothing was happening, but as the slaves pulled ever harder, the base slid along the ground and started to rise. Lon looked at the end of the bridge, one hundred and thirty feet in the air. To his surprise, it remained stable as the slaves moved the base completely out of the holes until it was resting on its six wheels.

"Step four," Omar shouted.

The slaves maintained their tension on their ropes while the fifty men at the front moved to the base's rear and sides. Under Tarek's command, they pushed the base toward the holes with all their strength. Despite their efforts, the bridge didn't budge because of the men still holding it back with the ropes. While Tarek whipped the fifty men and ordered them to keep pushing, Rayben instructed the others to slowly release the tension in their ropes. The bridge started moving gradually, sliding back down into the wheel holes until the base was resting again on the ground. The group of twenty slaves drove new poles into the ground at an angle over the base to secure it.

"Step five," Omar shouted.

The slaves moved away and the first eighty returned to their positions at the four ropes running from the top of the bridge and under the ground brace. They tightened the tension in their ropes and stood ready. Lieutenant Warley and two of his men stood at a ballista situated on one side of the base. They aimed the ballista in Lon's direction and loosed a heavy spear that had been tied to the end of a thick rope.

"Now it's our turn," Lon said.

"Do they really need our help, Lieutenant?" Wade asked.

Lon nodded. "Somebody has to pull the bridge. It won't tip forward by itself."

"But will four horses be enough?"

"We're about to find out."

The spear shot away from the front of the bridge and soared over the heads of Lon's squad until it stuck into the ground far behind them, leaving a long rope trail-arching overhead. As soon as the rope fell within his reach, Lon grabbed and secured it around the horn of Dawes's saddle. Wade and two of the other nine Rayders did the same. On Lon's order, they forced their horses away until the rope was tight against the front of the bridge. Their horses snorted and huffed as they strained against the resisting bridge, but it eventually tipped forward, at which point the eighty slaves behind the bridge pulled their ropes and slowly began lowering it.

Lon's squad unwound the rope from their saddles and dropped it to the ground.

"I am surprised that actually worked," Wade said with a smile.

The eighty slaves carefully lowered the bridge. When the ropes drew close to the elevated rear of the base, Omar and the three slaves slid the grooved wheels along the crossbeam and held them in place until the ropes curved over the top of them.

It took ten minutes for the bridge to lower safely to the ground. Both the Rayders and the Appernysians cheered at their success. Although serving as slaves to the Rayder commander, the Appernysians were never told of the extermination order issued six months earlier. They shouted Omar's name and begged him for a speech.

Lon and his squad galloped over to join the crowd as Commander Rayben Goldhawk climbed up the bridge's base. He stood in front of Omar on the platform and raised his hands high into the air. Once everyone was quiet, he stepped to the side and waved Omar forward.

"Make it short," Rayben whispered to Omar. "There is a lot of preparation still needed before we move out."

Omar stepped forward. "Fellow Rayders and Appernysians, you are part of a legacy that will usher in the Third Age. This trestle will abrogate the bulwark anciently proscribed to our ancestors, but it is dependent upon our aggregate endeavors. To serendipity!"

An uncomfortable silence descended on the crowd. Omar was a genius in many respects, but public speaking wasn't one of his strengths.

"Better get up there quick," Tarek said as he slapped Lon on the leg.

Lon dismounted and climbed the ladder to join Omar and Rayben on the platform. "With your permission, my Commander."

"Please," Rayben answered.

Lon stood next to Omar. "May I?"

Omar shrugged, so Lon turned to the crowd. "Omar Brickeden is a brilliant man. If this amazing structure isn't proof enough of that fact, then his speech is. Allow me to interpret his words. This bridge is going to remove the barriers that have been in place since our ancestors were exiled, but it will only succeed if everyone works together and follows our commander's plan. To luck and good fortune!"

The crowd cheered with renewed vigor.

Omar blew out his breath. "We are surrounded by dolts, Lon. We have lived so long in the Exile that everyone left in Appernysia has become dimwitted. How can we ever expect a Beholder to be born from men such as these?"

Ironic, Lon thought.

Rayben stepped forward and raised his hands above his head. "Omar is a respected man among all of us. Should I fall in the coming battle,

I have assigned him to take my place as acting commander until a tournament can be held. I have no doubt you will obey his orders as readily as you have mine."

Rayben paused and ran his hand along the platform railing. "This bridge, this magnificent bridge, is an important part of his legacy. It will span more than a thousand years of suppression and be the means of my retribution."

The commander unsheathed his sword and thrust its tip into the platform. "Behold! I name this bridge *Justice*!"

Omar nodded in approval as the crowd erupted again in celebration. Rayben stood smiling, then raised his hands once again for silence.

"In order to successfully execute my plan, precise timing will be necessary by every company. My army must be ready and in place to cross Justice immediately after she falls into position. General Tarek Ascennor, your foot soldiers will lead the army across Justice in four columns. How many men will you have?"

"Fourteen thousand, my Commander," Tarek responded with a salute.

"Excellent. Make sure they march double-time across the bridge."

"Yes, my Commander."

Rayben turned to the other three Rayders. "Lieutenant Warley Chatterton, you will drive your siege engines over Justice in a single column, followed by Bryst and his supply wagons. What will you bring to ensure our victory?"

"Ten trebuchets and fifteen ballistae, with enough projectiles to knock down Itorea's west gate, my Commander," Warley shouted.

"A brilliant comparison, but make sure you do not waste your munitions," Rayben counseled. "In battle, your supply can be quickly spent."

"Yes, my Commander."

"Captain Vance Talbot, you will bring your cavalry across Justice in a single column at the same time as Lieutenant Warley. How many knights will it take to protect our flanks and trample the enemy?"

"One thousand strong, my Commander," Vance answered.

"Do not push your horses too hard. We need them ready for battle when we reach Taeja."

"Yes, my Commander."

Rayben raised his hands in the air. "Rayders, we have planned for this moment for years. We will prevail, but it will not come without sacrifice. Many will die before the Appernysians are driven back. There is a good chance you will be counted among the dead. Return to your homes and say goodbye to your wives. We move out in four days."

Vance, Warley, Bryst, and their men walked out of the grounds cheerfully with arms wrapped around each other's shoulders. As they departed, Rayben addressed the slaves.

"Appernysians, you have proven yourselves valuable the past six months. We used less than a third of you today, but remember we will need all of your help to transport this bridge to Thorn. Once we get there, I want the same teams of men to perform the same tasks when we lower her."

Rayben glanced back at Omar, who nodded, then continued speaking. "There is one more task we need you to perform. You must create a ten-foot frame that will be attached to the underside of the bridge at her nose. The ground on the opposite side of the Zaga Ravine is not at the same elevation as our side, so we need a buffer to make sure Justice will rest securely on the opposite ridge. You have only four days to complete the frame, so work quickly and efficiently. I am relying on you."

Rayben pulled his long sword out of the platform, slid it into his scabbard, then spoke quietly to Lon. "Tell Tarek that if anyone slacks off, he is instructed to beat them bloody—even to death if that is what it takes to inspire the other slaves to work."

"I will, my Commander."

Rayben put his hand on Lon's shoulder. "You and your squad have until tomorrow morning, then you must ride out. Everything depends on your speed and stealth. The rest of us will travel to Thorn, but remain hidden behind the west edge of the Dialorine Range. As soon as my men see your signal, we will move in and drop the bridge. What have your scouts discovered?"

"As you already know, King Drogan has placed foot patrols along the Quint River to capture our infiltration teams."

"How often do the patrols change?"

"My reports say once every two weeks. I should arrive at the river just after their exchange."

"Are their numbers manageable?" Rayben asked. "Answer me truthfully."

"Yes, my Commander," Lon replied without emotion. "We'll reach the Quint and kill everyone on our way to Three Peaks. I'll meet you at Thorn within a week."

"Remember, Lon," Rayben added, "*time* is most important to me. As soon as you eliminate the patrols, it does not matter how hard you try to cover up your trail. The king will eventually find out we are in Appernysia. It will take my army three days to reach Taeja from Thorn and I need as much time as possible to prepare for his attack."

"My men will kill anyone who wanders close to Three Peaks," Lon said, "even after the relief patrols arrive. They'll be forced to send a runner back to Itorea to inform the king of our presence. You'll have two weeks in Taeja before his army arrives."

"Excellent, Lieutenant. Now go and rest. You have a long journey ahead of you."

Lon touched his temple and dipped his head. "Thank you, my Commander. I'll see you in a week."

"What's the update?" Tarek asked as Lon climbed down the ladder.

"Justice has to be ready in four days. If the slaves work too slow, our commander wants you to beat them into submission."

Tarek smiled with anticipation. "And what about you?"

"We leave tomorrow morning," Lon said loud enough that Wade and the rest of his squad could hear. "We'll leave from Tarek's house an hour before sunrise. Make sure your supplies are packed and your horses newly shod. And don't forget your cloaks."

"Yes, Lieutenant," the eleven men answered with a salute, then turned their horses and rode away.

As Lon climbed into Dawes's saddle, Omar shouted from the platform above. "Lon, meet me at Tarek's house."

Lon nodded and turned to Tarek. "You going to join us?"

"You two are about as interesting as a cow chewing its cud. I'll stick around here for awhile and make sure these 'Nysians get a good start on the bridge. Come get me when he leaves. I have something I want to give you before you go."

*　*　*　*　*

Lon entered Tarek's house and sat on a chair facing the empty fireplace, then proceeded to run a whetstone over the edge of his falchion while he waited. Once he was satisfied with the sharpness of the blade, he polished the full sword and scabbard with an oiled cloth and replaced the sword in its scabbard. Lon cleaned his sword every night before going to bed and it still shined like it just came from the blacksmith.

He relaxed in his chair and allowed his mind to wander. He knew the next couple of weeks were going to be difficult and dangerous, but he was far from worried. Nothing stirred his emotions anymore, not since Braedr arrived in the Exile. The news Braedr brought had placed a terrible strain on him.

As Kaylen's betrothed, he had a responsibility to protect her. That was his reason for leaving Pree in the first place, but he still felt like he should have been there to stop Braedr in Roseiri. Braedr deserved a punishment worse than death, which was why Lon convinced his commander to consider making Braedr a Rayder. Even if he survived, living under the strict rule of Rayben Goldhawk was the worst thing that could happen to a man like him.

To everyone's surprise, Braedr had succeeded in becoming a Rayder, but only through his cunning. During his weapons trial, the weapon he chose was his fist. His Rayder opponent laughed and threw down his own sword, then the two of them grappled with each other. Braedr had won.

Lon thought of the months he and Tarek had spent relentlessly training their army. He had initially resisted the nagging in his brain to help the Rayders, but slowly developed a sense of responsibility to them for placing so much trust in him.

Over time, Lon's feelings of responsibility grew to love. He saw the good in them that the rest of Appernysia ignored. He cared about them as much as they cared about him. Aside from his desire to reunite the Rayders with the Appernysians, Lon was certain that if Rayben's army failed in Taeja, King Drogan would move into the Exile and exterminate them, down to the last woman and child. Rayben's plan had to succeed. Lon needed to make sure of it.

Even so, Lon couldn't ignore the fact that he had promised his family and Kaylen that he would return as soon as possible. Was his responsibility to them greater than to the Rayders? He had decided the only way he could survive would be to bury his emotions. No more feeling, no more caring, only doing. Both the Rayders and his family needed him, but his family could wait. Life would become better for everyone in the end.

An hour passed with no sign of Omar, so Lon sat forward and looked around for something to pass the time. He noticed the stack of wood next to the fireplace; he hated the thought of lighting a fire in the stifling summer air, but he had nothing else to do. His supplies were already packed and he needed a fire to cook his food, so he placed himself next to the hearth and arranged three logs and a handful of kindling in it.

"Where's the tinder box?" Lon grumbled as he glanced around the cluttered room.

Tarek was always losing things. Lon had suggested more than once that Tarek at least straighten up the mess, but Tarek only laughed.

He was about to give up and return to his chair when he had an idea. He sat on his heels in front of the fireplace and closed his eyes to summon True Sight. When he reopened them, he immediately noticed particles of energy casually brawling with each other around the room. He had taken Omar's advice three months earlier and ignored his desire to create fire. Instead, he practiced absorbing energy into his entire body and transferring it out of his hands. It proved to be more difficult than he'd thought, so it took a long time before he mastered the skill. He still hadn't tried to create fire, for the same reason he hadn't returned to Pree—the Rayders needed him. If Lon wasn't around, whether because he returned home or killed himself trying to manipulate fire, the Rayders would die in their pursuit of Taeja.

As Lon stared into the dense cloud of potential heat that encompassed him, he abandoned reason for curiosity. He brought his hands together in front of his chest and spread his fingers apart like he was holding a large stone. After relaxing his eyes so he could focus on the energy surrounding him, Lon began drawing a stream of matter from the stacked wood into himself. When he felt his own supply grow, he brought it through his arms and out of the palms of his hands, trapping the matter in the small space between them.

The more energy Lon forced into the confined area, the more violent it became. Without notice, a tiny candle-sized flame ignited the timber and hovered between his hands. Lon laughed with excitement, but he wasn't satisfied. He continued forcing more fuel into his fire until the flame stopped flickering and transformed into a small sphere that spun around itself.

"I created fire," he whispered emphatically. "I actually created fire."

"Now do something constructive with it," Omar said from behind. He had entered the house unnoticed. "Place it on the logs."

"You should know better than to walk in on a guy holding fire in his hands," Lon joked.

"I have never had to worry about it until now," Omar said.

Lon concentrated harder and began forcing air into the mixture with his left hand. The flame swelled. He knew he could just move his hands over the top of the kindling, but that seemed too easy. He considered a couple of different options, but decided to force it out of his hands like he would a blast of wind.

As soon as Lon opened his hands toward the pile of wood, the fire shot out like a hot geyser springing from the ground—only it kept going. Lon kept forcing more air and fuel into the flame, still pulling from the logs stacked next to the hearth. A constant stream of fire poured from his palms and scorched the dry wood.

"Are you seeing this?" Lon shouted with exhilaration.

"Stop, Lon," Omar counseled. "You are losing control."

Lon realized the jet of flame had expanded. He could feel its heat warming his face, so he quickly shut his eyes and the flame was immediately extinguished. After waiting a few seconds, he reopened them and turned his palms upward to free his excess energy into the air. Once his personal supply became balanced, he released True Sight and looked into the fireplace. The pile of wood was gone. Three logs had burned to ashes in only ten seconds. Lon shook his head with astonishment, then noticed that half of the wood piled next to the hearth had shriveled into sticky ash, as well. "Look what happened to the wood I was channeling, Omar."

"As I suspected," Omar replied. "The remaining moisture in those logs dampened their remains."

"I'll have to remember that."

"That was quite a display of power," Omar continued, "but next time, do not lose yourself in the process. You were going to burn down the house . . . although it would not have bothered me." He regarded the filthy little room with unabashed disgust.

"What did you need to see me about?" Lon asked as he piled more wood into the fireplace.

"I want to talk to you about the next couple of weeks. There is a lot to think about, especially for you. I would like to have your full attention."

Lon stood and wiped Omar's chair clean with the back of his hand, also placing a nearby blanket over the seat.

"Please sit," Lon said as he grabbed another chair for himself. "Don't worry. That's my blanket, so it should be clean enough to sit on."

"Why do you keep a blanket in this room in the middle of summer?" Omar asked as he sat down.

"I sleep in front of the fire."

"I see." Omar leaned back in his chair and laced his fingers over his belly. "My first and most important question for you is whether you plan on using True Sight during your endeavors to help take back Taeja."

"Only if I have to," Lon answered.

"Then you should reveal your true identity now. Our Rayder brothers need to know they have a Beholder in their midst. It will give them courage."

"I think it would only make them lazy and overconfident," Lon countered. "I need my men to perform at their absolute best. Besides, I'm not ready to tell anyone about it yet."

"Why not?"

Lon blew out his breath in frustration. "Omar, we've had this conversation way too many times. I might already be in the middle of the Rayder society, but things would get much worse if everyone knew I'm a Beholder. I'd probably become a celebrity, but not everyone will think that's a good thing. Rayben might feel threatened by me. He might accuse me of trying to take his place as commander."

"Do you really think he will respond better if he sees you use True Sight in the middle of battle? In that circumstance, he might accuse you of intentionally deceiving him and have you executed."

"He'd die trying."

"Those are treasonous words, Lon. I am your mentor and have kept your secret these past six months, but I will not allow you to speak that way about our commander."

"If he tries to kill me after all I've done to help him, then he'd cease to be the man I swore to protect and obey."

They remained silent as the sun lowered into the sky, casting a vibrant glow that turned everything amber and purple. Lon knew he shouldn't have said those things to Omar. He tried to apologize many times, but his pride kept stopping him.

"Why do you bring this up now?" Lon finally asked.

Omar drummed his fingers on his belly. "Lon, I was very close with your father's family. As a younger man, Aron was a great pupil and dear friend of mine. He had so much potential, but he lost sight of the bigger picture when he met your mother."

Lon folded his arms across his chest. "Omar, you're tiptoeing along the edge of a very dangerous cliff."

"I will not speak ill of your mother," Omar answered with a toss of his hand. "I am sure that she is a wonderful person—she would have to be to raise a fine man like you. I am only pointing out that when Aron fell in love, he threw blinders over his head. I know because I saw it happen. I was leading his squad when he first met your mother. I have often pondered the irony of your choice to become a Rayder and help our commander, since your father chose the opposite decades ago. He forgot his duty as a Rayder, but more importantly, he forgot the reasons behind his duty. He was an only child of pureblood parents, who died when he was very young and left me to raise him. Aside from Aron, you are the only remaining Marcs who can carry on your family name."

Lon raised an eyebrow. "Where are you going with this?"

"When you first came to me, I took you under my wing not only because you are Aron's son, but also because of the strength in your bloodline. I saw the same qualities in you that I saw in your father. You have astonishing potential, Lon. Do not lose your perspective. Remember why you decided to stay in the Exile and fight for our commander."

Omar stood and walked to the door. "If you believe it is best to keep your gift of True Sight a secret, then I will support you in your decision. Please make absolutely certain it is the best choice, Beholder. Our people have been waiting a long, long time for this opportunity."

Omar slipped out the door, leaving Lon alone with his own thoughts to ponder.

Chapter 32
Truth and Sacrifice

Lon fell asleep as soon as his head hit the mat, but it felt like he had just closed his eyes when Tarek woke him up.

"Everyone's already here. They're waiting for you outside, sloth," Tarek growled as he kicked him. "Lieutenant or not, it's rude to keep a friend waiting . . . or leave him with Appernysians . . . or walk out on him when he specifically told you he had a gift for you."

Lon sat up and rubbed the sleep from his eyes. "I'm sorry, Tarek. It was a bad night."

"Good. You've been numb to the world for months. It's nice to see a little bit of the old Lon come back."

Lon chuckled. "Do you still want to give me your gift?"

"As a matter of fact, I do," Tarek said excitedly as he pulled Lon's pack onto his lap and undid the top flap. "I wasn't sure if I'd have a chance to talk to you this morning, so I stashed it with your stuff."

While Lon dressed, Tarek reached in the bag and pulled out a dark green cloak. It was different than the cloaks given to Lon and his squad. It was darker green and the material was more durable. It also had a silver pendant of a five-petal flower pinned under the seam of the hood.

"This cloak belonged to my father," Tarek said. "It was the only thing I got to bring when the Rayders took me from Pree—and only because I was wearing it at the time. It was Father's when he was part of the king's army."

"What's this?" Lon asked as he fingered the pendant.

"That's the Lynth Flower. It only grows in Itorea; it's the mark of an honored soldier. Father earned it when he intervened during an ugly tavern fight in Sylbie. He got stabbed six times in the chest by an outlaw before another soldier finally cut the man's head off. Father barely survived and was honorably discharged from the army. After he healed, he was awarded the pendant and a big pile of money for his bravery. Apparently, one of the king's closest friends was in that tavern and Father saved his life. Our family used the money to move to Pree, but I was only a baby then. I don't remember any of it."

Lon ran his hand over the smooth material. "I don't know what to say, Tarek. I had no idea Myron was a soldier, but it sheds a little light on how he was able to kill four Rayders all by himself. He must have been a true blademaster in his day."

"He taught me everything I know. Unfortunately, he was also really good at getting stuck in the middle of dangerous situations—except on the day I was kidnapped."

Lon smirked. "Sounds like you inherited that trait from him, too."

Tarek paused to take a slow breath, then continued. "If Father had to pick someone to take this cloak, it would be you. I hope it treats you as well as it did him. Well, I don't want you to get stabbed or anything, but if you take the cloak I want you to survive. Just take it!"

"I'm honored," Lon said as he carefully folded the cloak and placed it in the pack.

"I also made you something to eat while you ride." Tarek handed Lon a few sausage links. "A little overcooked if you ask me, but I wanted to make sure you'd eat them. You didn't get any dinner last night and you need good food in your stomach if you're going to survive your trip."

Lon took the food and headed for the door. "I meant to ask you yesterday, Tarek. How's Braedr doing?"

"You've never cared before. Why are you asking me now?"

"Just answer the question."

Lon had sorted through a lot of his feelings the night before. Although he had avoided interacting directly with Braedr since he arrived at the Exile, Lon couldn't help but admire Braedr's courage.

"Honestly," Tarek said, "he's become a skilled fighter these past four months. The other soldiers respect him. Our commander made him a lieutenant last week. Sorry I didn't tell you, but can you blame me?"

"No," Lon said, "Do you really think he's ready for that kind of responsibility?"

"I do, but I should warn you. Braedr is skilled in more than just swordsmanship. He is also very cunning and persuasive. If he decided to start a mutiny against our commander, many Rayders would join his side. That's partly why I suggested making him a lieutenant. I want to keep an eye on him."

"I'll feel better knowing you're around to watch him, General," Lon said as he stood at attention and touched his right temple with his fingers.

*   *   *   *   *

Lon and the other eleven members of his squad spent the first day traveling fifty miles southwest along the main road from Flagheim. All Rayders knew Rayben Goldhawk's plan, as well as the involvement of Lon's squad, so the twelve men were easily recognized as they traveled along the road.

Lon was offered many gifts, most of which he refused because he had nowhere to store them. The people waved and shouted gratitude and well wishes. The women bowed themselves before him with tears in their eyes. The older men, who were too old to serve in the army, stood proudly saluting him.

"Do not mind them, Lieutenant. They know your mission and need no response. They are honored enough to have the privilege of seeing your face."

"We're leaving a lot of people here unprotected," Lon replied quietly. "If we fail . . ."

"We will not fail," Wade answered.

They traveled fifty miles and spent that evening sharing a green pasture with a farmer's livestock. The hunched-over old man brought them a large meal of meat, bread, wine, and even stew when he saw them stopping in his fields. Lon accepted the offer, grateful that his men could save their personal supplies for an extra day. While they ate, Lon discovered that two of the old man's sons were part of the Rayder army he'd been training north of Flagheim.

"They are good men and skilled fighters who will defend Taeja until death takes them," the farmer said, "but it brings me great relief to know they will be fighting alongside you, Lieutenant. I know you will protect them."

Lon's thoughts buzzed inside his head when he tried to sleep that night, knowing that the families of more than fifteen thousand men were placing the same trust in their general and first lieutenant.

They rested well that night, though the next day introduced the first of many difficult trials. They crossed through the Weeping Forest and into the Dialorine Range without incident, but when the trees ceased and the trail through the jagged mountains narrowed, Thad's horse slipped on loose slate and toppled over the edge of a cliff. Thad was able to pull his legs free of the stirrups and roll backward out of the saddle, but the momentum of the horse's movement still forced him over the edge.

Lon and his squad turned around at the horse's cry and found Thad dangling near the top of the precipice, gripping a protruding rock with all his might. They pulled Thad to safety, but their problems were not over. His supplies were tied to the saddle of his horse, which was thrashing around on the sharp rocks forty feet below. They lashed their rope together and lowered Thad down. Grim faced and shaking, Thad slit the poor animal's throat and retrieved his supplies. By the time they pulled him up the cliff, an hour had passed.

We're going to be hard-pressed to keep our schedule if things like this keep happening, Lon thought as he looked at the remaining eleven horses.

They were close enough to the Exile that Thad could have walked back, but Lon knew the loss of a man like Thad would make their task harder once they reached the Quint River.

Lon made Thad share a horse with Dovan, the lightest man in their squad. Although Lon knew the decision would slow their progress, making Thad walk would slow it even more.

The rest of the day was uneventful. Lon's squad remained behind schedule as they wove their way through the complex maze of mountains. They were unable to reach the top of the pass by nightfall, and it was too dangerous to travel at night. They were forced to make camp on a narrow ledge with no shelter. A fire would have given away their position, so their evening meal consisted of small rations of cheese and dry bread.

When they finished eating and were about to pull out their bedrolls, a heavy eastern wind blew in a storm from the Asaras Sea. The mountainside disappeared under thick sheets of rain. Bolts of lightning streaked overhead and tore into the jagged rocks of the mountain. Sparks flew and the ground rumbled with every strike.

Rather than lie in saturated blankets, the squad dug their green cloaks from their packs and wrapped themselves as they gripped the reins of their panicked horses.

Dawes was the only horse that remained calm, seasoned by his previous trip into Appernysia. Lon sat against the rock wall next to him.

Wouldn't it be something if I could do that? he thought as he gazed up into the fury of nature.

The storm lasted most of the night. When the morning sun offered enough light that they could safely move on, the twelve men and their steeds had slept only a few hours. The men pulled themselves onto their horses and continued up the mountain, anxious to be out of the Dialorine Range. It wasn't until they neared the top that Lon realized no fresh bodies had joined the rotting corpses he had passed on his way into the Exile.

"A lot has changed in the past six months," Lon said. "Looks like everyone has stopped trying to run away from Appernysia."

"Or they're being prevented," Wade said. "They might know about our commander's extermination order, too."

When the squad reached the summit of the pass, they took little comfort from what they saw.

"You've got to be kidding me," Lon said as he surveyed the land below. Although the skies had cleared, the previous night's rain had flooded the already boggy plains of the Gaurelic Waste. Almost no dry land could be seen.

"Do we hold to our plans, Lieutenant?" Wade asked.

"Absolutely," Lon replied, regaining his composure. "Take the lead, Wade."

As Wade guided them down the south face of the mountain, Lon fell back to observe his men. They were exhausted—it was obvious from the way they hunched over in their saddles—but they were not discouraged. Their chins were up and their eyes looked forward. The arrangement between Thad and Dovan was also working surprisingly well. Instead of begrudging their circumstance and fighting over space on the back of Dovan's horse, they had become great friends and conversed cheerfully as they traveled.

These are good men, Lon thought as he watched them, then he spoke loudly so they all could hear. "It's an honor to have you with me, Rayders. With soldiers like you, I'm certain we'll see our task through safely and on schedule, but we must quicken our pace. We have hours to make up from yesterday."

The squad made their way swiftly down the mountain, reaching the edge of the Waste at midday. They stopped momentarily, resting their horses and eating a little in their saddles. Lon intended to spend as little time as possible in the Gaurelic Waste. Even on the murky bog's edge, they were overwhelmed by swarms of greedy mosquitoes.

"Keep moving," Lon said, urging Dawes into the sludge.

336 ◆ TERRON JAMES

His squad followed him west, along the southern base of the Dialorine Range.

"We just need to reach the Nellis," Lon said, trying to raise their morale. "Once we cross the river, this torment will end."

Unfortunately, the water was so high in the Waste that the horses could only trudge slowly. The mud almost touched the underside of their bellies—and the mosquitoes continued to multiply.

Precious time slipped away as they coaxed their horses forward, heavy and fatigued. Circumstances became so miserable that the men stopped trying to swat or shoo the mosquitoes, even when the bugs landed on their faces and speared the tender flesh of their eyelids.

Lon felt his patience waning. He considered using True Sight to create a barrier of air to protect them from the insects, but there was no way he could do it without being discovered.

Finally, one of the horses broke. Tarl gripped his saddle horn as his horse bucked and thrashed to get away from the mosquitoes, but so great was the steed's fit of hysteria that Tarl was thrown from its back and landed in the marsh.

"Move!" Lon shouted, but his warning did little good. Before Tarl had a chance to stand up, his horse toppled sideways and forced him under the water.

"Pull him out!" Lon ordered. "Hurry!"

Wade was the closest. He dismounted and clawed through the mud, but his efforts were fruitless. Tarl was too far away. When Tarl's body finally resurfaced, it was limp and void of life. They could only watch as the horse forced its way deeper into the waste.

Lon strung his bow and pulled an arrow from his quiver, knowing the horse would not survive. He took aim, ignoring the thick cloud of insects buzzing around him, and mercifully shot the horse through its heart. He stared with longing as the horse fell on its side and sank into the bog.

Wade continued toward Tarl's lifeless body.

"Leave him," Lon ordered. "He's too wet to burn here and we don't have time to carry him out."

Wade nodded and returned to his horse. "We cannot continue like this or we will all share Tarl's fate. I can see the same madness growing in Dax."

Lon agreed. Their situation was desperate. If something weren't done soon, none of them would survive.

"Form a tight circle," he ordered while he put his bow away.

"What is it, Lieutenant?" Wade asked.

Lon ignored him and closed his eyes, weighing his options. He had been training with these eleven men for many months. They knew everything about each other. They could predict each other's actions without a word. Not only were they his squad, they were his friends. He couldn't step back and watch them die, not while there was something he could do to prevent it.

The squad had been watching their leader, waiting for instruction. When Lon reopened his clouded eyes, they only gawked at him.

"Lieutenant—" Wade started, but fell silent when Lon created a large pocket of air around them to ward off the mosquitoes.

The men gasped as they watched the cloud of bugs thicken against the barrier. A Beholder—a living Beholder—had saved them. And not just any Beholder, but a Rayder lieutenant.

Wade was the first to break out of his stupor. "Praise the Jaeds!" he shouted as he unsheathed his sword and held it to the sky. "Our lieutenant is a Beholder!"

The other nine Rayders joined Wade in his celebration. They cheered, saluted, praised, and brandished their swords, while tears smeared their muddy cheeks. Pure joy filled their countenances, both from the desperately needed reprieve and for their lieutenant who offered the peace.

"We have to move out of the Waste," Lon shouted. "I can't hold this forever. Stay close, move quickly, and keep your voices down. There's no guarantee the Appernysians haven't wandered further north."

Although their bodies trembled with excitement, the squad obeyed Lon's order. They sheathed their swords and pressed forward as quickly as their horses could move while Lon stayed at the rear and shielded them.

The pocket of air was large, but Lon still worried his men would suffocate before they reached the Nellis River. He created temporary holes in the barrier to provide airflow, but closed them when the mosquitoes tried to enter. It was difficult, but he managed to keep most of the mosquitoes outside the barrier.

Lon could have maintained the process for a long time under normal circumstances, but his strength was fading. With the mosquitoes ravaging his exposed neck and ears, Lon could feel the blood trickling between his shoulder blades.

It only took a half-hour to traverse the rest of the Waste, but the deep, swift current of the Nellis River encumbered their course. They arrived at the north end of the river just downstream from where the Zaga Ravine ended in a high waterfall. It was the narrowest part of the Nellis and usually easy to cross, but it had also been flooded by the storm.

Lon cursed the weather as he stared at the green pastures on the opposite bank. His squad looked to him, but Lon knew he wouldn't be able to help them cross—even with True Sight.

"I'm sorry, but this is a problem I can't solve. We have to cross through it. This place looks as good as any. Wade, you'll go first. Once you're safely across, the rest of us will follow."

Wade drove his horse out of the protective air pocket and into the current. Dax was swift, but light. Lon believed if he made it safely across, the rest of them should be able to as well. The river wasn't as deep as it appeared, but it still moved fast. Dax's head disappeared under the water twice, but he eventually made it through.

"Now, the rest of you," Lon ordered as he released True Sight. The mosquitoes dove for them, but were thwarted as the horses splashed into the river. Lon followed last and nearly wept with relief as the thick mat of mosquitoes feasting on Dawes's hind quarters washed away.

Lon leaned forward and dipped his body under the water, reveling in the sensation of cool water running over his raw skin.

When Lon was halfway across, a large tree branch cracked and splashed into the water, sweeping down the river directly at Thad and Dovan. They kicked their horse and yelled frantically, but the overburdened horse couldn't move fast enough in the deep water.

Lon summoned True Sight and studied the branch. He locked onto its solid matter and held it motionless in the water, stopping it just two feet away from Thad and Dovan. Everyone stared at the motionless branch with wide eyes as the water gushed over it.

"Move!" Lon shouted to Thad and Dovan.

They blinked and kicked their horse forward again. When they were out of the way, Lon released True Sight and followed Dovan and Thad across until they were safe on dry ground.

Lon slid out of Dawes's saddle and dropped onto his face under the shade of a tree. He had lost a lot of blood while crossing the Gaurelic Waste. Dawes lowered himself beside Lon and munched wearily on the grass, seemingly as exhausted as his master.

"We'll camp here tonight," Lon said weakly. "Dawes and I need to rest."

The Rayders tethered their horses to the nearby trees, then gathered on the grass surrounding Lon.

Dovan bowed himself low before Lon. "Thank you, Lieutenant. We owe you our lives."

"As do the rest of us," Wade said. "None of us would have surv—"

He stopped short when he noticed the raw flesh on the back of Lon's neck and the blood seeping through the black hair covering Dawes's hindquarters.

"Elja," Wade shouted. "Grab as many wraps from our packs as you can carry. The rest of you, bring me your water skins. Move, men."

The Rayders hurried away while Wade kneeled down next to Lon. "Lieutenant, what happened? You protected us from the mosquitoes."

"Take care of Dawes first," Lon whispered as the world swirled around him. "He's a lot worse than I am."

While Lon watched Elja return and hover over Dawes, darkness closed in on him. Lon faintly heard Wade shout an order, then felt a cool sensation running down his neck as his eyes fluttered shut.

He was back in the heart of the Gaurelic Waste, standing waist-deep in the sludge. Kaylen hovered over the marsh in front of him, dressed in a beautiful white gown. She smiled and silently bade Lon to come to her. He clawed his way through the thick bog, all the while keeping his eyes focused on Kaylen. He was afraid that, should he lose sight of her, she would disappear forever. Before long, thick swarms of mosquitoes attacked him from every side, obscuring his view of her. Kaylen's smile turned to a worried frown, tears flowing from her eyes. Lon summoned True Sight and threw out torrents of wind in every direction to force the insects away, but with every blast twice as many returned. He reached his hands toward Kaylen as she disappeared behind the buzzing black cloud.

"Kaylen!"

Lon opened his eyes and jumped to his feet. It was late afternoon and he was standing in the grass where he had fainted. With the exception of Dawes, who was still sleeping next to him, Lon was alone. His squad and their horses were nowhere to be seen.

Lon drew his sword, thinking trouble had found them. The angled sun glared into his eyes. He summoned True Sight to better his vision and immediately noticed a man sitting high in a tree just a few feet away.

It was Dovan. His eyes were wide with fright as he looked at his first lieutenant. Lon gave him a hand signal they had established to ask for signs of danger, but Dovan didn't respond with his own sign. Instead, he cocked his head to the side.

"Are you awake, Lieutenant?"

"Of course I am," Lon whispered. "Where is everybody?"

Dovan eyed Lon for a moment, then smiled. "It is all right," he shouted. "He is awake. It is safe to come out."

Lon looked around in confusion as other members of his squad appeared from behind nearby trees. Wade, who had hidden behind the tree sheltering Dawes, placed himself in front of Lon and saluted.

"What's going on?" Lon asked as he slid his falchion back into its scabbard and released True Sight.

"You must have been asleep, Lieutenant," Wade replied, "but with your eyes wide open. You were shouting and throwing out gusts of wind in every direction. The horses were spooked and bolted north, so I sent Preton and Elja after them. The rest of us took shelter behind the trees."

Lon couldn't help but smile as Dovan swung down from the lowest branch and landed lightly on his feet.

"You climbed a tree to escape the wind?" Lon asked.

"I like trees," Dovan answered. "I feel safer in their branches than I do in Flagheim."

Lon shook his head and laughed. "Only you could say that, Dovan. You're so skinny you could fly if we tied feathers to your arms."

Lon scratched at the back of his itchy neck, but recoiled at the tenderness of his skin.

Wade frowned. "Your neck is very swollen, Lieutenant. Forgive us, but we used all of our supplies to treat Dawes. I assumed you would prefer it that way."

Lon nodded. "How long have I been asleep?"

"Only an hour, Lieutenant," Wade answered. "We still have a couple hours before it will be dark enough for us to continue south. You should rest more."

"I'm fine," Lon replied, "but you men should sleep if you can."

"After what you just did?" Wade laughed. "Not likely, Lieutenant. I do agree that we could all use a bit of relaxation, though. We should at least sit down to rest our muscles. Maybe someone could even tell us a story about their past." Wade sat down and watched Lon out of the corner of his eye.

Lon sat next to Dawes. "Did you sedate him?" he asked as he stroked the horse's neck.

"No, Lieutenant," Wade answered. "He fell asleep shortly after you. Do not worry. He is breathing normally. He will awaken as healthy and strong as ever."

The other Rayders joined Wade on the grass and watched their lieutenant patiently. Lon became annoyed with their unspoken expectations.

"I get it. Wait until Preton and Elja get back. I don't want to explain twice."

Lars, the oldest of the squad, spoke up. "While we wait, Lieutenant, will you tell us about Kaylen? We all heard you shouting her name. Was she a lover of yours?"

Lon looked over the Gaurelic Waste. His dream had been so real—so terrifying—but he didn't know what to think. He still loved Kaylen, but he hadn't heard any news of her since Braedr arrived. He didn't even know if she still loved him. Even if she still waited for him, what was the meaning behind his dream? Was he really driving her further away by helping the Rayders? Would she still be around after he fulfilled his responsibilities to the Rayders? Should he write to her, explaining his decision to stay? Would she understand?

"Lieutenant?" Wade asked.

Lon blinked and looked back at his men. "We were engaged, but I lost her. That's all I'll say, for now."

With the exception of Lars, the Rayders seemed satisfied with Lon's answer and none of them pressed him. Lon lowered himself onto his back to wait for Preton and Elja.

Before long, everyone fell asleep except Lon and Wade. They sat huddled together, speaking in hushed voices.

"I can see the pain and conflict behind your eyes," Wade said. "You are only seventeen, a young age to have experienced so much. I admire how well you have handled everything. You are a good man, Lieutenant—a man worth serving without question. The fact that you are a Beholder is proof enough, not to mention everything else you have done to serve our cause. Since I was a little boy, I have been taught that all Beholders were upstanding men, stalwart and true to themselves and everyone around them. You have proven these teachings to be true. As a Beholder, your decision to keep your true identity a secret had to be for good reasons. I do not question it."

Lon didn't answer, unsure of how to respond to such devotion.

Elja and Preton returned with the horses within half an hour, but by then Lon was the only one left awake. He allowed them to rest until the sun dropped below the horizon, then woke Wade and had him prepare the squad. Dawes, who had awoken when the rest of the horses returned, was bright-eyed, prancing around eagerly.

"Easy, Dawes," Lon tried to soothe him. "We've still got another day before we reach the patrols. Save your strength."

After donning Myron's cloak—taking special care to keep it off his tender neck—Lon climbed into the saddle and was soon joined by the rest of his squad, each wrapped in their own cloaks. Dawes paced back and forth in front of them as Lon spoke.

"Rayders, all of your training has been in preparation for this moment. We're about to move into Appernysian territory. Three days ago, my scouts reported there were fifty men patrolling the Quint River. These men are armed soldiers who have successfully captured every infiltration team we've sent into Appernysia for the last six months. They're talented and know the lay of the land. We're outnumbered and heading into a trap, but our enemies don't know what's coming for them. It is us who will spring the trap."

Lon studied each man. Their bodies were tired, but their minds alert. "Of over fifteen thousand soldiers, our commander and I selected you specifically for this task. You are our finest soldiers."

Lon paused to search their faces. Pride glowed in their eyes.

"We have about fifty miles to cross tonight under the cover of darkness," Lon continued. "Stay along the shoreline where the trees are thickest. I still plan to stop about five miles from the Quint River, but as I've said many times, the patrols may have spread out further. Stay on guard."

Lon took a slow breath before continuing. "Some of you might think, because I'm a Beholder, this will be a simple task. You're wrong. I can't do everything, which is why I've kept my talents hidden until now. Move and work together as we've practiced."

The men nodded in unison.

"I'm not ready to reveal myself to the rest of the Rayders," Lon continued. "I want all of you to swear on your honor that you'll keep my secret."

"Yes, Lieutenant," the men shouted together as they kissed their fingers, then moving them to the King's Cross on their temples.

"Keene, you'll take the lead with Dovan and Thad. If we meet an Appernysian tonight, kill him and save his horse. Thad will need it."

"Yes, Lieutenant," the three men said.

"Wade and I will guard our rear," Lon added. "Move out and keep your eyes open for an ambush."

The squad formed a single column on their horses, moving south through the trees lining the Nellis River's western bank. They ate a quick meal while riding, then strung their bows and nocked their arrows. No one spoke as they stole through the darkness.

They reached their destination without incident and decided to camp in a dense grove of trees as the sun peaked above the eastern horizon. They rotated shifts every three hours until sunset. Lon took the first watch. As darkness began to fall, Lon gathered them to plan their attack.

"Elja and Preton will stay here with our horses while the rest of us spread out and travel in pairs to where the Quint joins the Nellis. Dovan, Channer, and Keene—cross with me to the southern bank. The rest of you will stay on the northern shore. We'll fan out and sweep through the trees together on our way up the river. Don't allow anyone to escape."

Wade smiled. "That will not be a problem, Lieutenant."

"Perhaps not, Wade, but don't forget we have to cover forty-five miles in two nights. Bring only your weapons and stay light on your feet. Keep your sling handy and your bow strung, but don't use them unless you have no other choice. Always try for the silent kill first."

Wade shifted on his horse. "Forgive me, Lieutenant, but do you doubt our abilities?"

"Tarl's death leaves only nine of us to eliminate their fifty. We'll need to be extremely cautious. Stealth is our greatest ally, Rayders. Remember your Night Stalker training. All of you have personally captured the diamond, so you've already proven you can defy impossible odds."

Lon motioned to Dovan and Thad. "You will lead each group as our eyes and ears."

Everyone separated to gear up and say goodbye to their horses. Lon took his bow and quiver from Dawes's saddle and slung them over his shoulder. Dawes stared anxiously at his master, as though he knew they might not meet again.

"Don't worry, Dawes," Lon said as he stroked Dawes's neck. "I'll be back before you know it."

Dawes shook his mane and bit playfully at Lon's hair. Lon laughed and slapped Dawes on the shoulder before returning to his squad.

The other members of the squad were armed the same as Lon. They were all expert marksmen with their bows, but some also developed an attachment to the sling during their training. They felt more confident while carrying it and a small pouch of smooth rocks at their sides.

Everyone stood at attention, waiting for Lon's order while he watched the sun slowly disappear. The sky flared brightly from yellow to orange, then darkened from purple to dark blue.

After the first star appeared in the night sky, Lon turned to his men. "Move out, and may the Jaeds watch over us."

Chapter 33

Three Peaks

D ovan and Thad bolted ahead with Lon and the other six close behind. They moved swiftly through the trees, ducking from shadow to shadow. They regrouped at the Quint River, again encountering no Appernysian soldiers.

Lon second-guessed his plan as he stared at the opposite bank fifty yards away. The river had been less than half that width when he crossed it on his way to the Exile six months earlier.

"I don't like this," he hissed to Wade. "Look at the opposite bank, how it cuts down into the water. They dug it up. This river has been intentionally widened, and it's too easy to cross. We haven't seen a single Appernysian, but they're out there, waiting for a man foolish enough to leave the cover of the trees."

"What is your order, Lieutenant?" Wade whispered.

"Ready your bows and stay hidden. I'll cross alone. Remember, these patrols are set up to capture Rayders—not kill them—so don't just shoot at anything that moves. I'll try to draw them out so you'll have a clear shot. If any survive or try to escape, I'll take care of them. I'll signal you when it's safe to send my three men across."

"But, Lieutenant—" Wade started, stopping short when the moonlight reflected off Lon's eyes dimmed as they clouded over.

"These 'Nysians don't know what they've gotten themselves into," Lon said.

Wade pulled his bow from his shoulder and passed Lon's order to the rest of the squad. Nik and Riyen, the most skilled archers, climbed separate trees to obtain a better vantage point.

Lon removed his bow and quiver, then pulled his hood over his head, covering part of his face. "Remember, wait until everyone is exposed. They won't fight back until they know we're a threat. I'll make the first move."

Lon hunched over and lifted one shoulder as if injured, then limped out of the forest and into the water while gasping for air. He made it halfway to the southern bank before he heard the first Appernysian.

"Identify yourself," the Appernysian soldier shouted from behind a tree on the southern bank.

Lon only coughed and wheezed as he continued forward.

"Who is that?" another man shouted from the same direction.

"An imposter. Shoot him."

"Are you insane? What if he's one of our own men?"

"Why won't he identify himself?"

Lon fell forward into the water with a loud splash, thrashed around, then pushed himself up on his hands and knees as he faked another fit of coughing.

"He's hurt," a third Appernysian soldier shouted. He ran out of the southern forest and into the water toward Lon. Two more soldiers also appeared, but they stopped on the southern riverbank, anxiously looking around.

"Come back," one of them shouted. "You're falling into our own trap."

"Help me," Lon whispered as he glanced around from under his hood.

Light buzzed brightly inside the three men. They were the only soldiers Lon could see with True Sight. He waited until his rescuer was two steps away, then drew his falchion and slashed upward across the man's chest.

The man screamed as Lon sheathed his sword and grabbed him by the front of his tunic. Lon held him upright as a protective barrier between himself and the other two Appernysians, who aimed their bows frantically in Lon's direction.

Two arrows whistled over Lon's head from behind and pierced the Appernysians' hearts. Both men released their arrows as they fell backward to the ground. Lon's human shield grunted as one arrow struck him between the shoulders while the other arrow whizzed past their heads.

Lon looked into the face of the man he was holding. The Appernysian's eyes widened and his lips parted as if to speak, but only his final breath escaped as he slumped lifelessly under Lon's grip.

Dovan, Channer, and Keene splashed through the water past Lon to the southern bank to search for more soldiers. Lon ignored them as he watched the man in his hands. Lon hadn't anticipated what True Sight would reveal when a man died. It shocked him.

The bright energy which filled the soldier didn't fade and disperse as Lon expected. Instead, it shifted out of the dead body and hovered behind in the same shape. It seemed to stare back at Lon for a moment before vanishing suddenly. Lon blinked and looked at the southern bank to see the same thing happen to the other two men lying in the mud.

Lon released True Sight and stared at the dead soldier in his hands. The body's listless eyes were glazed over—looking past Lon—and his limp arms hung at his sides. Blood seeped through his clothes and drained into the river. There was no life left in him, only an empty shell.

I killed another man, Lon thought, *only this time he wasn't attacking me. He was trying to help me, and I slaughtered him.*

Lon turned his head to the left and ground his teeth, but found no comfort as he watched a dark trail of blood run downriver from his victim.

I'm a murderer.

"Lieutenant," Wade called quietly from behind him, "we need you over here. Quick."

Lon carried the dead Appernysian through the river and placed him amongst the trees on the northern bank. "What do you want, Wade?"

he asked impatiently to disguise his anguish. "My men are waiting for me on the southern bank."

Wade stepped to the side and pointed at Lars, who was flat on the ground with the feathered end of an arrow jutting out of his abdomen. "Lieutenant, you are a Beholder. If there is anything that can be done for him, I know it will come from you."

Lon evaluated Lars' condition, but he had no idea how to heal a wound with True Sight, or if it was even possible.

"I'll do what I can," Lon lied. "Join my men, Wade, then the seven of you continue up the river. We don't have time to delay. I'll catch up with you as soon as I can."

Wade saluted and dashed across the river while Thad, Nik, and Riyen stood staring at Lars.

"Save him, Beholder," Thad pleaded.

"Go," Lon ordered.

They fanned out and disappeared up the river.

Lon knelt and put his hand on Lars' shoulder. "Hold on, Rayder."

Lars smiled weakly. "You cannot fool me, Lieutenant. I see the despair in your eyes. I am a dead man."

Lon's pride broke. He released True Sight and slumped. "I'm sorry, Brother. I've failed you."

"Why are you here when the rest of your men need you?"

"You need . . . someone." Lon shook his head in frustration. "Honestly, Lars, I can't do it anymore. I murdered someone tonight. I can't kill again."

Lars placed his hand over Lon's and gripped it. "No one enjoys killing, but eventually you realize it is a personal sacrifice you must make for a greater purpose. These men have to die, Lieutenant."

"Have you killed before?"

Lars shifted and took a painful breath. "Yes—in a manner of speaking. When I was thirteen, I stumbled across a young couple in the wild. They were children of two pureblood families who had been feuding for generations. Their parents had forbidden them to see each other. I did not want to be the cause of their deaths, so I kept their secret. A few weeks later, Sévart and Geila ran away together."

Lars gasped and clenched his jaw in pain before continuing. "They were captured within six months and brought back with the news that Geila had born a child in the wilderness. She had killed the baby because of shame, but that did them little good. They were both publicly executed for their fornication. Had I told someone my secret when I first saw them, it would have saved their child. I should have done what was necessary for the greater good."

"That was a long time ago. You're almost fifty now."

"And glad I won't have to endure fifty-one."

Lon turned around and sat on the ground. The sound of Lars's forced breathing echoed in his ears.

"I've been a mess the past nine months," Lon said above the sound of the river. "I can't seem to figure out who I am or what I want. I miss my old life. I miss . . ."

Lon grabbed a rock and hurled it into the river.

"Lieutenant, if you are looking for someone to confide in, I am the perfect candidate. I will be dead before I have a chance to tell anyone what you say."

Lon looked left and stared at the moonlight sparkling off the rippling water of the Quint. "It's Kaylen. I hurt her, Lars, then left without saying goodbye. I haven't talked to her since. My heart tells me to find her and make amends. At the same time, I have a deep responsibility to the Rayders. I can't abandon you and the rest of my men."

"No, you cannot," Lars agreed, "nor are you doing anything different than the rest of us. We have also left our wives and families behind to serve our commander. You have made the right choice, Lieutenant. Do not doubt your decision."

Lon looked back at the Rayder. Sweat clung to Lars's face and the moonlight made shadows of his sunken eyes.

"What about your family?" Lon asked. "What will I tell them if I return? That I judged poorly and caused your death by a stray arrow?"

"You will tell them I died honorably serving my lieutenant. There is no greater honor than to die for you. You are a Beholder—the first of this Age. . ." Lars drew a pained breath. "The Jaeds must have great and important things planned for you . . . I am certain of it. Trust your heart, Lieutenant. Trust the Jaeds. . ."

Lars didn't say anything else. Lon watched over him as he slipped away. He didn't groan, cough, or spasm like Myron had. He simply laid his head back and stared up into the sky, smiling.

Lon summoned True Sight and once again saw bright energy shift out of Lars and stare back at him.

"What do you want from me, Jaeds?" Lon shouted as Lars's essence vanished. "Why did you give me this curse?" Lon cast his eyes around wildly. "Where are you? Why won't you show yourselves?"

The only answer was an eerie silence that permeated the darkened woods. Nothing appeared. Nothing spoke.

"If you won't answer me, then don't judge my decisions. I'll choose my own destiny until you decide to intervene."

Lon spit on the ground, then stood and ran up the river's northern bank.

* * * * *

Lon glanced at the dead bodies he passed, watching for a familiar face to appear, but none of them bore the mark of the Cross. By the time he overtook Thad, Nik, and Riyen, they had already traveled ten miles upriver. More importantly, his men were alive and uninjured.

Lon instructed Thad to continue in the lead while he took the rear guard. He was amazed at how quickly his squad traveled, especially in silence. Occasionally the shadow of a fellow Rayder would appear on the opposite bank, signaling the position of Wade's men and the number they had killed since their last update.

They don't even need my help, Lon thought.

He was both proud and relieved to make such an observation—proud that his men were prepared and focused, and relieved he didn't need to participate in the killing. Although he was determined to defend his men if necessary, Lon was still shaken from his own encounter.

As dawn approached, Lon signaled his men to halt for the day. Each group huddled together in dense foliage while they ate and slept. The Appernysian patrols didn't move during the day. They were active only at night when the Rayders would normally try to sneak past.

Although Lon's men were exhausted the next night, they pressed up the river. The Appernysian patrols thinned as the squad traveled further west. Due mostly to Lon and True Sight, they ensured no one slipped by unnoticed.

They were three miles from the base of Three Peaks when the sun peeked over the eastern horizon. Their combined kills totaled forty-eight Appernysian men.

Lon knew there was a good chance they had eliminated all patrols, but he still watched the terrain carefully. He was about to call for his men when he noticed a man positioned high in a pine tree. His green cloak hid him from the rest of the squad, his glowing form aiming a crossbow at Thad.

Lon knew a flying crossbow bolt would be too difficult to deflect. Half panicked, he focused on the ground and ripped the tree up by its roots.

The Appernysian let go of his crossbow and grabbed around the trunk to keep from falling. Nik and Riyen noticed his movement. Each shot an arrow in the Appernysian's direction, piercing his leg and forearm. The enemy lost his grip and tumbled from the falling tree until he landed hard on the ground.

Thad was there waiting for him. He picked the man up and placed the edge of his sword against his throat, ignoring the falling tree as it crashed next to him.

"Wait," Lon called as he released True Sight and ran to meet Thad.

Along with the two arrows sticking out of him, the man's leg was severely broken—the bone protruding through the skin of his left thigh—but he ignored the pain as he pleaded for his life.

"I have two little girls and a pregnant wife with no other family to care for them. They'll starve and die. Please, have mercy."

Lon signaled Nik to notify Wade, then turned to the Appernysian. "How many more of you are there between here and Three Peaks?"

"I'm the last man, my Lord," the man whimpered. "I was posted here as a lookout. The rest of our patrols are further east. Please don't kill me. My wife—"

"How many men are at Three Peaks?" Lon interrupted.

"Two per peak and an outpost at the mountain's base. I have two little—"

"How many men are in the outpost?"

"Five, my Lord," the man cried in anguish. "Three horses. Please."

"Make it quick and as painless as possible," Lon said to Thad, then turned and ran after Nik in the opposite direction of the terrified Appernysian soldier.

"Please, my Lord," the man screamed. "My unborn child . . ."

Lon tried to ignore the desperate plea coursing through the air. He didn't want to kill the man, but they couldn't bring him along as a prisoner. If they released him, he would die anyway. There was no other choice.

"Bring everyone to the north side of the river," Lon called to Dovan, who stood on the opposite bank. "We just eliminated the last of the patrols."

Dovan nodded and disappeared into the shadows of the trees, then reappeared with Wade, Keene, and Channer.

"What happened to your head?" Lon asked when he saw blood trickling down the side of Channer's face.

"He tripped over a root and nearly took his head off with his own sword," Keene answered laughing.

Channer punched Keene hard in the face and wrapped his hand around the grip of his sword.

"Enough," Wade ordered. "These two have been like this for half the night, Beholder. It is a miracle they are both still alive—mostly because I want to kill them myself."

Lon couldn't stop himself from smiling. Channer and Keene were cousins and very close friends, but they had an interesting way of showing it.

"All right, cut it out," Lon said to the cousins as Thad and Riyen appeared. "We're extremely fortunate, men. I'm glad to see all of you alive and well. You've proven once again that you're our best."

Lon lifted his hand and pointed west in the direction of Three Peaks. "We were able to extract some crucial information from the last Appernysian we found. There are five men in the outpost at the base of Three Peaks and two men on each peak."

"That is all?" Wade asked. "Compared to the past two days, taking Three Peaks should be easy."

"Agreed. Elja and Preton should be here shortly with our horses. We'll sleep here until tomorrow night. I hoped there would be eight of you to take Three Peaks, but Tarl and Lars have left us."

The squad cast their eyes down.

"What should we do about Lars's body, Lieutenant?" Wade asked instead.

"I know it goes against our tradition, but as with Tarl, we have to leave Lars unburned. The enemy will be watching for any signals from our direction. A fire large enough to burn a body might catch their attention. Also, we still need to take Three Peaks. There's no time to go back." Lon leaned against a nearby tree. "You know the plan. Two of you per peak. Wade and I will wait for your signal while Elja and Preton hold your horses here."

Lon looked back through the trees at the morning light. "You've accomplished the impossible by traveling so far in so little time, but it's been a long night and we're all exhausted. I want everybody to sleep. Keep your cloaks on and your hoods over the Cross, just in case. Channer—bandage that gash before you lie down. I don't want a maggot making its new home in the cut while you sleep."

* * * * *

Elja and Preton arrived two hours after Lon and his men fell asleep. They had been traveling behind at a safe distance so the horses wouldn't give away their position. When they had encountered Lars's corpse along the way, they released his horse before continuing upriver to convene with their Rayder brothers.

"I realize it's our tradition to free the horse of our fallen brothers," Lon said, "but that was a foolish thing to do. Thad needed a new horse, preferably a Rayder horse."

"Forgive us," Preton said, his head bowed.

"Allow me to go back for the horse," Elja pleaded. "I will return by nightfall."

Lon shook his head. "We don't have the time for backtracking or foolish decisions. Use your heads."

Amidst more apologizing from Elja and Preton, there was a brief, but heartfelt reunion between the men and their horses. Eventually, everyone drifted back to sleep. Except Lon. He climbed into Dawes's saddle and rode north to the edge of the trees, where Three Peaks was plainly visible.

The solitary mountain was completely devoid of vegetation. It looked as though it was pieced together by giant layers of red and gray rocks that had chipped away slowly since before the First Age. A thick layer of loose rubble surrounded its base. From there, the mountain climbed half a mile into the sky. He also knew a small lake situated at its north-eastern base, from which the Quint River flowed.

There was only one pathway up the mountain—a long trail of switchbacks in a narrow cavity starting near the outpost. It climbed fifteen hundred feet to where the three separate peaks met at a small gap. From there, the path split into three different sets of switchbacks that continued to the top of each peak. The mountain was too steep and jagged to climb; the squad would have to use the switchbacks and trust that they wouldn't be spotted.

"I hadn't realized how difficult this will be," Lon said to Dawes as he looked at the hundred-foot stone pillars on top of the peaks. "We're lucky there are only two men manning each crest."

Dawes snorted and tossed his head. Lon patted the horse's neck as he rode back into the trees. "Never a challenge too difficult for you, eh, Dawes? Let's go get some rest."

* * * * *

Because the switchbacks up Three Peaks started at the outpost, Lon sent all six men to capture it while he and Wade rode their horses in a wide circle around the eastern face of the mountain. Preton and Elja were once again left to guard the horses. After Three Peaks was secured, they would take the horses to the outpost for the rest of the squad, then ride after Lon and Wade.

As they rode, Wade noticed Lon glance at the outpost. "Do not worry, Lieutenant. You have trained your men well. They will not fail you."

"I know," Lon replied. "We're just at the most critical point of our mission. A simple spark to oiled wood is all it would take to ruin everything. If those signal fires on top of the peaks are lit . . ."

"That will not happen, Beholder. The Jaeds are watching over us—just look at the sky."

Lon looked up and realized that a thick layer of clouds had moved in, obscuring the moon and stars. The realization warmed Lon's heart. He and Wade rode confidently around Three Peaks to a point north of its base and waited for the signal.

* * * * *

Thad and Dovan snuck up the main switchback, the other four Rayders following close behind them. They had dispatched the Appernysian men at the outpost by means of a simple ambush—the Appernysians were all dead before any of them knew danger was afoot—then moved up the trail at an unrelenting pace. It was a grueling march, but none of them complained as they climbed further up Three Peaks to the triple fork. From there, they divided into their teams and continued up the separate paths.

Channer drew his sword and took point while Nik followed with an arrow nocked onto his bow. They scaled the northern peak and discovered one man sitting on its tip trying to survey the land through the darkness. The hundred-foot pillar was nearby with a steep staircase spiraling around its circumference to the top, where a massive pile of oiled wood covered its entire fifty-foot diameter.

"Hey," the man called, "come take a look at this."

Another soldier opened the door of a small guardhouse and rubbed his eyes. "This better be important or I'm going to knock you off the mountain. I just got to sleep."

"I think I saw something moving around the base of our mountain."

The second man stood next to the first and squinted into the darkness. "I don't know what you're looking at. I can't see a—"

Channer's sword cut the guardsman's sentence short while an arrow from Nik prevented the other soldier from responding. Channer ran into the guardhouse and lit a torch from the coals in the fireplace, then stood motionless outside while he watched the other two peaks. A small glow pierced the darkness from the southwest crest, signaling that Dovan and Thad had also neutralized their peak, but there was still no signal from Keene and Riyen.

Minutes passed as Channer and Nik anxiously watched the southeast peak.

"Hurry, Cousin," Channer whispered while Nik paced back and forth behind him.

A small light finally appeared. It moved quickly across the crest and was climbing up around the pillar's staircase.

"Shoot him, Riyen!" Nik shouted pointlessly into the darkness, knowing it didn't matter who heard him if the beacon was lit. "Shoot him!"

When the torchlight almost reached the top of the pillar, it fell straight down to the rocks below.

Nik breathed out a loud sigh of relief as the torch was lifted up and held motionless.

"That was way too close," Channer said as he ran to a ballista stationed next to the stone pillar. "Time to signal the Lieutenants."

Nik helped Channer crank back the arms of the ballista and armed it with an oiled spear from a nearby barrel.

Nik lit the spear with the torch, after which Channer yanked hard on the release rope. The spear flew from the ballista, leaving a glowing trail of firelight as it arched through the air toward the barren northern base of Three Peaks.

Chapter 34

Final Sprint

The Taejan Plains, the land north of the Vidarien Mountains and west of the Nellis River, were flat and boring to ride through. Tall stalks of yellow wild grass covered the ground, dotted here and there with small clusters of juniper trees. All clouds from the previous night had disappeared by morning, so there was no barrier to lessen the heat of the sun.

Lon was exhausted and becoming ever more irritable. He wondered why such a dry and barren land appealed so much to the Rayders. The further they rode, the more his attention wavered. He caught himself falling asleep in the saddle more than once. Lon tried talking with Wade to keep his mind occupied, but the thudding hooves of the horses made it almost impossible to carry on a conversation.

As the day progressed, the heat increased. Fluttering vapors radiated off the ground. Lon became so fatigued that he began thinking he was looking at the world through True Sight. When he caught himself trying to manipulate the heat without using his power, Lon decided it was time to stop. He searched for a place to rest and found a larger cluster of juniper trees ahead of them.

Lon grabbed Dawes's reins and directed him toward the oasis. A small pool of water floated on the sand, covered in a thin film of dust. Lon brushed it aside before plunging his entire head into the cool water and drinking with heavy gulps. Dawes stood breathing heavily for a moment, before dipping his head and drinking. Wade and Dax arrived shortly after and joined them at the water hole. After riding hard for five hours, they all welcomed the respite.

Lon sat back against one of the trees and surveyed the northeastern horizon. He could see the Dialorine Range clearly, including where it tapered off at its western edge. He squinted his eyes in an attempt to see the watchtower, Thorn, at the western base, but it was still beyond his sight.

"We are probably about thirty miles from Thorn." Wade commented. "If we cannot see the watchtower from here, there is no way they can see us. We will need to travel at least another ten miles before there is any chance of being noticed."

Lon glanced up at the sky. "We can't continue in this heat. We'll rest here until dusk, then we'll go on."

Wade plopped down next to Lon. "We should probably take turns watching so we do not sleep longer than necessary."

"Do you really think you can stay awake?"

"No."

Lon positioned himself on the ground so that the sun would be in his eyes within a few hours.

"Problem solved," he said to Wade, closing his eyes.

Lon's plan worked as he intended. Five hours later, the sun glared red through his eyelids and forced him to wake. Lon felt refreshed enough that he could ride the last thirty miles without a problem. They ate a hurried meal, filled their water skins, and rode north.

When they were fifteen miles from the Zaga Ravine, Lon and Wade began riding in a wide, crisscrossing pattern to signal their commander that the patrols had been slain and Three Peaks was under Rayder control.

At first it seemed as though they were still too far away to be seen by the lookouts in Thorn, but soon the great bridge Justice appeared from behind the Dialorine Range, jutting into the sky twice as high as the watchtower.

Lon and Wade shouted exultantly and slowed to a canter, knowing it would still take a few hours before Justice would be ready to lower.

The Appernysian slaves had to move the bridge into the pre-dug wheel ruts, secure her base to the ground, construct the ground brace and run the four ropes underneath it. They wouldn't finish until after sunset, and Lon knew Omar wouldn't allow the bridge to be lowered in darkness. Lon and Wade had until morning before their services would be required again.

"I hope Elja and Preton arrive before morning," Wade commented as they straightened their course. "It is going to be a high-stress day tomorrow for our commander. If he has to wait for them before the bridge can be lowered—"

"They'll be here," Lon said.

*   *   *   *   *

Lon and Wade reached the southern edge of the Zaga Ravine within two hours. They positioned themselves next to the remains of the crumbling stone bridge and waited.

Nearly a thousand slaves accompanied Justice on its journey. The slaves continually rotated positions to pull and push the bridge along the last stretch of the road. The Rayder army followed behind, led by fourteen thousand foot soldiers clad in steel breastplates, each wielding a glaive and an elongated diamond shield bearing the bright blue emblem of the King's Cross. An arming sword and large quiver of arrows hung from each soldier's sides, and a longbow was slung across each of their backs. They marched in four columns that ran for nearly two miles along the road. A mile-long trail of a thousand similarly-armed knights rode their horses in two columns on the grass west of the footmen. The siege weapons and supply wagons brought up the rear.

It was an awesome sight to behold. Lon and Tarek had trained these men hard for six months to become masters of sword, bow, and spear. They could serve in whatever capacity was required of them. Lon stared proudly as the westering sun glinted off their glaives and shields. He knew they would triumph.

"All this weaponry and armor would bankrupt Appernysia ten times over," Lon said.

"Our people, as well," Wade replied, "if we had not spent the last twelve-hundred years saving and stockpiling. We have been preparing for this day for a very long time."

Lon nodded. "Best to expect Appernysia has been, too."

Soon Justice was in place and the necessary ropes were lashed to her. Omar, Rayben, and Tarek trotted to the front and dismounted. Omar climbed the ladder onto the platform at the top of the bridge's base. Rayben and Tarek removed steel-lined plates that had been placed over the six wheel ruts until the bridge was moved into position.

"Step four," Omar shouted.

Most of the slaves moved away from the bridge, while the remainder either picked up the ropes trailing behind the base or stayed at the base's rear and sides. Just as they had practiced, the bridge was pushed forward into the wheel holes until the base was resting on the ground.

Lon breathed a sigh of relief. If Justice had tipped over and shattered, the deaths of Tarl and Lars would have been for naught. Omar continued shouting instructions to the slaves from his sixty-foot platform while Rayben and Tarek remounted their horses and rode to the northern edge of the ravine.

"Well met, Lieutenant," Rayben called to Lon.

"My Commander," Lon replied with a salute.

"Updates?" the commander asked.

"Success. Preton and Elja will be here soon."

"Excellent," Rayben said. "Find some shade and rest. We will lower Justice at sunrise."

"Yes, my Commander."

Rayben turned his horse and rode back to observe the slaves, but Tarek remained with an obvious question on his face.

"Two dead," Lon shouted across the chasm. "Tarl in the Waste and Lars at the Quint."

Tarek bowed his head and saluted to honor the fallen men, then looked back at Lon. "I'm glad you're alive, Brother. I'll talk to you tomorrow when we don't have to shout across this stupid gorge."

They saluted each other, then Tarek rode back to join his soldiers.

"Tomorrow." Lon mumbled as he dismounted and pulled a large piece of salted pork from his saddlebag. "Seven months ago, it seemed like an eternity away."

"Agreed," Wade said as he also dismounted. "I have been looking forward to tomorrow for my entire life."

✳   ✳   ✳   ✳   ✳

Elja and Preton arrived two hours after sundown. They rejoiced to see Justice intact and ready to be lowered.

"How's the rest of our squad?" Lon asked when their celebrations had ended.

"All is well," Preton replied, "except Keene is still angry at himself. He tripped on the way up Three Peaks and gave away his and Riyen's position. While Keene engaged with one of the soldiers on the peak, the other ran up the stone pillar with a torch. Riyen barely shot him down before he lit the signal fire."

"Anyone injured?"

"Funny you should ask," Elja said with a smile. "When Keene slipped, he gashed his head open on his own sword. It wasn't a serious cut, but now he has a wound to match Channer's."

Wade laughed. "Channer will never let him forget that."

Preton nodded and continued with his report. "Once we saw you both ride away, we convened back at the outpost. Dovan, Channer, and Keene stayed there with their three horses, while Thad, Nik, and Riyen rode their horses up to each crest of Three Peaks to keep watch on the Taejan Plains. They will signal us if there is any trouble."

Lon looked south toward Three Peaks. He couldn't see it in the darkness, but he knew the mountain would only be a small dot at the edge of the horizon. If the beacons on top of the peaks were lit, they would be easy to see—even from sixty miles away. In daylight, the smoke would rise into the sky, and at night the mountain would glow red. It comforted Lon to know he had men on Three Peaks, but even more, three of the most stalwart Rayders he ever met. Their army wouldn't be ambushed without warning.

Chapter 35

Chaos

Kaylen sat up in her bed, startled awake by loud bells clanging from the top of the keep. She threw on a robe and ran out of her room. Soldiers ran up and down the long corridor, paying no attention to Kaylen or the rest of the confused servants.

"What's going on?" Kaylen asked Aely, who was standing outside the neighboring door.

"I'm not sure," Aely said, rubbing her eyes. "That's the emergency alarm. Are we under attack?"

Kaylen tried to stop a passing soldier to ask him, but he pushed her aside and ordered her out of his way.

"That was Sátta," Aely said. "He's normally very nice to me. Something really bad must be happening. What should we do?"

Kaylen closed her door and grabbed Aely's hand. "We're going to follow him."

They ran through the hallway after Sátta, dodging between soldiers until they finally found one shouting from the top of a crate.

". . . two nights ago. They've murdered your fathers and brothers and are marching their army into our lands as I speak. King Drogan won't tolerate their impudence. All soldiers report outside immediately for further instru—"

"What's going on?" Kaylen interrupted as she took hold of the soldier's arm.

"The Rayders murdered our patrols at the Quint River and took control of Three Peaks," he replied as he pulled his arm free.

Aely cupped her hands over her mouth. "The Rayders are in Appernysia?"

"It appears so," Kaylen answered as she stepped out of the way of a group of soldiers running past. "Who brought the report?" she asked the same man.

"Zaxton arrived this morning," he replied, his impatience obviously growing, "on a stolen Rayder's horse. He was the only survivor at the Quint."

"What can we do to help?"

"Stay out of our way," he growled.

Kaylen took Aely's hand and started back up the hallway. "Best we do as he says."

As the two women headed back to their rooms, the soldier resumed his shouting. "We go to war. They may have the rumored Beholder, but we have our unshakable courage. Beholder or not, we'll remind the Rayders why they're not welcome, and drive them back into the Exile. Our king . . ."

Kaylen dropped Aely's hand and stopped in the middle of the hallway, oblivious to the curses from the men dodging around her. Her bottom lip quivered and a tear rolled down her cheek as the reality of what the man said sunk into her heart.

"Kaylen, what's wrong?" Aely asked.

Kaylen burst into tears. She ignored Aely's calls as she sprinted down the hallway, locked herself in her room, and fell on her bed.

"Oh, Lon," Kaylen cried into her pillow. "How could you?"

She didn't want to believe that Lon could have turned traitor, yet deep inside, she knew it to be true. Her body shook as waves of torment swept over her. Her one true love had abandoned her to serve the Rayders. Lon had betrayed Appernysia. He had betrayed her. He had betrayed his family.

Kaylen's last thought stuck in her head. She clenched her jaw and forced herself to stop crying, then grabbed a bottle of ink, a quill, and a piece of parchment from a nearby stool. Her hands shook as she uncorked the bottle and dipped her quill into the ink. After taking a deep breath, she touched the tip of the quill to the parchment.

Dear Mellai . . .

Chapter 36

Justice

Lon breathed the morning air as he sat upon Dawes. Wade, Elja, and Preton were next to him on their own horses. Together, they watched the northern bank of the Zaga Ravine.

All preparations for Justice were complete and the army had lined up behind the slaves. Rayben and Omar stood on the platform—Omar making final inspections of the bridge and riggings, while Rayben shouted to the soldiers.

"As soon as Justice is lowered, move quickly across at a fast march. Keep moving until General Tarek tells you to stop. We need to get everyone across as quickly as possible. The slaves will cross in the middle of the foot soldiers, then the rest of you will follow."

"Do you know why our commander is bringing the slaves?" Wade asked Lon.

"I'm not sure," Lon answered. "My guess is that he'll use them to bargain for the release of our own men. Even if that's not the reason, it's still not safe to leave them alone in the Exile."

Wade nodded. "Good point, Lieutenant."

They watched as Rayben climbed down the ladder and took his position next to the ground brace, opposite Tarek. Eighty slaves gripped their ropes and waited for Omar's order. Warley Chatterton stood ready next to his ballista with two Rayders at his side.

"Step five," Omar shouted.

Warley shot the spear over Lon's head. The four of them wrapped the connected rope around the horns of their saddles and moved their horses back until the bridge tipped forward.

"Heave," Rayben shouted to the eighty slaves, who pulled their ropes and held the bridge suspended at a slight angle in the air.

"Lower," Rayben shouted again.

The four lines of slaves moved forward toward the ground brace, making sure to move together at a constant speed to keep Justice from twisting in the air. The bridge slowly lowered toward the southern edge of the Zaga Ravine, where Lon and his three men waited.

"There's nothing to worry about, Lieutenant," Wade said confidently. "You can—"

Suddenly, twenty slaves on Rayben's side let go of their rope and charged at the commander. He was caught unaware for what must have been the first time in his life. Tarek and the front line of foot soldiers rushed to his defense, while Rayben fought for his life. Seven slaves died by Rayben's sword, more limbs were severed, but the Appernysian numbers were too great. Before the Rayders could reach their commander, Rayben was overwhelmed by the slaves and stabbed with his own sword.

Justice twisted in the air from the unbalanced force.

Although Tarek alone killed the twenty slaves who murdered Rayben, the sight of the commander lying there, a sword sticking out of his chest, spurred the next row of slaves to action. They also released their rope and charged at Tarek, who tightened his lips and rushed into the crowd, killing every man who came within his sword's reach until the Rayder foot soldiers arrived to protect him.

Justice twisted even further; the steel joint connecting the bridge to its base groaned.

"Move to the opposite rope," Omar ordered the two remaining rows of Appernysians, who fought desperately to keep the bridge aloft. "Move—"

Omar stopped short as the three Appernysians on his platform ambushed him. Omar head-butted the first and threw him over the side, then cracked the heads of the remaining two together.

"Move now or Justice will crumble," Omar shouted to the remaining slaves as he kicked the two men off the platform.

The closest row of Appernysians let go and sprawled for the next rope, but they weren't quick enough. The twenty remaining slaves were unable to keep the bridge aloft by themselves and the weight of Justice jerked them forward. Those who didn't let go were pulled into the ground brace and crushed to death.

Lon's mind froze as he watched the bridge falling toward him. They had failed. The bridge was going to break in half and there was nothing he could do about it. Lars, Tarl, and their commander had all died for nothing.

"Save Justice, Beholder," Wade shouted, breaking Lon out of his stupor.

Lon summoned True Sight and hurled as much wind as he could muster out of his left hand at the underside of the falling bridge. He clenched his jaw and grunted as he tried to pull more and more energy through his right hand to increase the force of the wind, but the bridge continued to fall.

"This isn't enough," Lon shouted. "I can't save it."

"Please, Lon," Wade begged. "For our commander."

Lon switched tactics. He absorbed energy through his entire body and threw air at the bridge with both hands.

"Stop!" Lon shouted at Justice as energy coursed through him.

Lon was going to fail, just as he had repeatedly done in Pree. The Rayders would continue to be outcasts. He would be too ashamed to stay with them, or return home to Kaylen. He would be completely alone.

The bridge was now within twenty feet of the ground.

"No!" Lon growled. Suddenly, he felt a strange sensation overwhelm him. A large sphere of glowing energy flew from his hands and exploded under the bridge. Along with their horses, Lon and his three companions were thrown by the force of the blast as Justice crashed to the ground.

Lon smacked into the remains of the old stone bridge. Dust encompassed him as he struggled to remain alert. He glanced up and saw Justice sitting safely on top of the ledge in front of him, its ten-foot frame crumbled underneath.

"I did it," Lon whispered with astonishment, "but how?"

Waves of terrified screaming pierced Lon's ears from the opposite side of the ravine. He stood and rushed across Justice in time to see Captain Vance Talbot and his knights slaughtering the Appernysian slaves. The Rayders showed no mercy—not even to the men who had tried to save the bridge.

Lon shouted for them to stop, but his voice vanished into the wretched cries of the defenseless slaves. He summoned True Sight and was about to intervene, but Tarek jumped in front of him.

"Our commander ordered this with his dying breath," Tarek said heavily. "I don't agree with it either, but you can't stop them. Look at their eyes, Lon. They're bloodthirsty for revenge."

Lon released True Sight and watched the carnage. Helpless Appernysian men darted around the clearing in search of safety, only to be cut down by a Rayder glaive or sword. Lon had never seen so much blood; his stomach squirmed.

"I don't understand why the slaves revolted," Tarek continued. "They were proud of their accomplishments in the Exile. Why would they sabotage their own creation?"

"There were only twenty of them at first," Lon answered, "and they probably had this planned from the start. Half of them still tried to help us."

Lon flinched as he watched a slave throw himself into the ravine to escape a charging Rayder knight. "Is this the cause I was born to defend—the murder of a thousand defenseless slaves?"

"War breeds death. You can't save everybody, even as a Beholder."

Lon turned away from the merciless slaughter and stared over the ravine. "Rayben is dead?"

Tarek nodded.

"We'll move our soldiers across, Tarek. We still have a schedule to keep and I won't abandon my men at Three Peaks."

*   *   *   *   *

Try as he might, Tarek couldn't bring the knights under control—partly because Vance obviously didn't consider himself subject to Tarek's authority anymore. Vance and his knights rode over the dead slaves repeatedly, trampling the Appernysians into the dust and mangling their corpses.

Only Omar, by dint of his position as the interim commander, commanded enough respect to bring them to heel. He cupped his hands around his mouth and shouted at Vance from his elevated platform, ordering the captain to stop his men and move to their position behind the foot soldiers. Vance obeyed only after hewing the head from another dead Appernysian.

Tarek placed Rayben's body in a wagon, then everyone rushed across Justice. As acting commander, Omar took his place at the front of the Rayder soldiers and led them on their march toward Taeja.

Lon soon discovered his actions had gone unnoticed. The Rayders attributed the bridge's survival to the frame built under its nose, believing that it had absorbed the impact.

As the Rayders traveled southwest through the Taejan Plains, Wade quietly updated Tarek and Omar on what had happened during their squad's journey to Three Peaks—including Lon's uses of True Sight.

When Wade finished, Omar turned to Elja and Preton. "I know what our customs suggest, but it was unwise for you to leave Lars's horse with his dead body for more than Thad's need of a new mount. If the horse wanders south and is spotted by the king's men, it will most certainly raise questions. You may have cut days off our preparation time in Taeja. We will have to start building our defenses the instant we arrive."

The men turned their horses to ride with the other knights, but Omar called them back. "One unwise decision does not negate the many other things you have accomplished for our commander. Learn from your mistakes and do not repeat them again."

Omar looked at Lon. "Your squad knows your secret, but perhaps we should tell the rest of the men, so they will stop giving me praise I do not deserve. You are the true hero, Lon. You alone preserved Justice."

Lon ignored Omar and rode away.

"He's very conflicted, my Commander," Tarek told Omar. "I don't envy the turmoil he's facing, even if it meant I could use True Sight."

Omar only frowned in response.

The Rayders' journey to Taeja was long and uneventful, although everyone kept one eye on the unlit beacons atop Three Peaks. They traveled fifteen miles the first day, then twenty-five miles each of the following two days.

Dovan greeted them in the afternoon of the third day as the Rayders passed the west side of Three Peaks.

"We've seen nothing since we took the mountain," Dovan told Tarek, saluting. "You have a clear path for the remaining thirty miles to Taeja. You will be within its borders by the end of tomorrow."

He glanced around in confusion as he finished speaking. "Where is our commander?"

"He fell victim to a slave revolt," Omar replied.

Dovan flinched, then set his shoulders. "I hope you killed every last one of them."

"We did," Omar replied as he cast a weary glance toward Lon, who still rode apart from them.

Dovan saluted and turned his horse toward Three Peaks. "I need to get back before Channer and Keene kill each other. May the Jaeds watch over you, my Commander."

"And you," Omar answered.

By the end of that day, the ruins of Taeja were just visible on the horizon. The Rayders celebrated that night with song and dance. Although Omar ordered the men to stay sober, Bryst Grayson still guarded the wagons of ale and mead with a drawn sword until everyone quieted down and dropped off to sleep.

Lon continued to keep himself aloof from his men. Images of the massacre at Thorn kept creeping into his mind, turning his stomach. He wandered around by himself that night, staring *into the bright stars in search of answers.*

Those Appernysians were good men who came to the Exile seeking refuge, he thought, *but all we gave them was slavery and death.*

Lon wiped fresh tears from his eyes and ground his teeth together. "What am I supposed to do?"

"You could start by talking to a friend," Tarek answered from behind.

Lon drew his falchion halfway out of its scabbard before he realized who it was. "Go away, Tarek. I didn't leave because I'm looking for a friend."

"Then what are you looking for?" Tarek responded. "If you want answers, you're not going to find them out here by yourself."

"What do you want me to say?" Lon hissed. "When Lars died by the Quint, I swore to follow my own path until the Jaeds made their will known to me, but it isn't that easy. I don't even know what I want anymore. I don't know what's right."

"Makes perfect sense," Tarek answered. "You're not the only one who's had to work through a personal crisis. How do you think I felt after I was kidnapped? I was only eleven and my family had been murdered in front of me. I didn't know how to deal with it anymore than you do with this. The only way I survived was to endure life one minute at a time. If I was hungry, I ate. If I was thirsty, I drank. When I had to pee, I found a tree. If someone made me angry, I pummeled them. One minute at a time, Lon—it's the only way to get through Rayder life. Our soldiers need their lieutenant back. We trained these men. I can't lead them into battle by myself."

Lon turned his head to look at his friend. "Do you still think fighting against King Drogan is the best decision, Tarek? Maybe we should've tried diplomacy before we barged into Appernysia uninvited."

Tarek laughed. "Nice idea, but you know letters and presents wouldn't do any good. Their hatred has been festering for generations upon generations. The only way we'll take Taeja back is to fight for it—and if you ask me, it's about time."

Lon smiled. "Always looking for a brawl, aren't you?"

"Always," Tarek answered as he slapped Lon on the back. "Now how about you join us?"

"All right," Lon said. Turning, he followed Tarek back into camp.

Omar, Wade, Elja, and Preton were sitting in a tight circle staring at the glow of a small fire. They smiled when they saw Lon return with Tarek.

"Welcome back, Lieutenant," Wade said as he saluted.

Preton leaned forward. "Our commander tells us you can create fire. Is it true?"

Lon raised an eyebrow at Omar, who merely lifted his shoulders. "Yes, it's true. But I can't control it very well. It's still too dangerous to use."

"Amazing," Preton said excitedly as he watched the flames dance across the blackened logs.

"Your men tell me you have sworn them to secrecy," Omar said to Lon.

"That's correct," Lon answered, "but I would rather not talk about it tonight."

"Very well," Omar replied. "I will not even ask how you saved Justice."

Lon groaned and shook his head.

Elja threw another log into the fire. "Can you believe we are only a day away from Taeja? It makes me want to sing!"

"Then sing," Tarek encouraged.

"Come on," Preton urged, "sing."

Elja chuckled and stood up. "Fine, but no complaints. You asked me to do this." He cleared his throat, took a deep breath, and began.

Plains of Taeja, sweetest home, land of beauty, free to roam,
From the peaks come rivers long, with pride and glory rush along;
To stunning falls that splash in foam,
Then through our cities gently comb,
And out to sea they make their course,
The uncontrolled and living source;
Of life or death to those who dare to build a ship and venture there,
But why seek danger out at sea, when Taeja's near to make you free?

Phoenijan guard, proud and strong, always fight to right the wrong;
Wise Beholder, mighty ghraef, by claw and blade do keep us safe,
Blessed light from glorious Jaed, the grand design of Taeja made,
Underground we force beneath the wretched kelsh and flying seith;
Calahein, the vile snake, upon our shields will surely break!

Come to me, be not afraid, a shining glade that will not fade,
Taejan lands, hold steadfast, I come to you, my home at last.

Silence overtook the camp as Elja's clear voice rang brightly through the air. When he finished, no one spoke. A sense of peace settled on them. Like the Rayders of old, they were men destined for war, men destined to win.

* * * * *

The next morning, the Rayder camp started for Taeja with a boost in their morale. Elja's song sank deep into their hearts. Everyone was eager to stand on Taejan soil. The soldiers marched double-time to close the twenty-five mile gap.

It took seven hours before they reached the outlying buildings of the city the next afternoon. A hush fell over the army as they stared at the crumbling stone towers and roads. Large gaps separated the stone remains, where wood buildings once stood. Lon could feel the enthusiasm draining from the Rayders, so with Omar's permission, he dismounted and scrambled up to the top of a large structure to address the men.

"Rayders, these lands have been abandoned for over a millennium, but don't be dismayed. We will rebuild this city. We will resurrect its glory and preserve it with our lives. Look at the ground on which you stand. Today you're no longer Rayders. Today you are Taejans, home at last!"

The men cheered and banged their shields with their glaives as they spread Lon's words to those who were out of hearing range.

"There's much to do here," Lon continued. "We must first beat off the vile snake that seeks to destroy us. Rather than the calahein, whom our ancestors destroyed in the First Age, a new threat has arisen. My fellow Taejans, our own king seeks to drive us from this land."

The soldiers glanced around at each other with confusion.

"You heard me correctly," Lon continued. "I said *our* king. We must stop ignoring who we are—what's in our blood. From our race came the Phoenijan—the elite guard of Appernysia. We haven't come here to destroy this kingdom. We only wish to retake what is rightly ours. Should that require the defeat of King Drogan and his armies, so be it. Appernysia is our home. Let us make it a place worthy of our allegiance."

Tarek moved his horse closer to Lon's stone platform. "Uh, Lon?" he said, eyeing the nearby Rayders. "You sure this is a good time?"

Lon ignored him. "We've trained together a long time in preparation for the coming battle. If the king sends his entire army—which I'm sure he will—we'll be heavily outnumbered. Every Appernysian soldier you kill will be replaced by four more. Don't let down your guard, and don't expect any mercy. Every man here knows what to do, so let's move to the eastern edge of this city and prepare for war! Even to our death!"

There was no cheer. Lon had spoken words that were difficult for many to accept. Some, like Bryst Grayson, muttered disagreement under their breath. Others stared at the ground and shifted the weight between their feet.

"Interesting speech," Omar told Lon after he returned to Dawes's saddle. "I think you made enemies today, First Lieutenant."

"Unbelievable," Tarek fumed. "If we didn't have a battle to prepare for, I'd whip you for insubordination and lock you in chains. What are you trying to do, start a fight before the 'Nysians even get here?"

"I meant every word I said, Tarek. What did everyone expect? Did they think we'd simply move into Taeja and build our own private empire on Appernysian soil? We're Taejans, Omar, which means we are also Appernysians."

"I do not need to be lectured on the history of our people," Omar replied. "I side with Tarek. Your words should have been reserved until after we drive the king's army back."

"They wouldn't like it then, either," Lon countered. "Best they heard it now before they get ideas of what'll happen here."

Lon looked over the men accompanying him. Wade held his chin high, his loyalty unshaken. Elja looked troubled, and Preton stared at Lon unblinking with a furrowed brow.

At least one enemy already, Lon thought as he turned away, *and from my own squad.*

They led the soldiers around the eastern perimeter of Taeja and began building fortifications. Tarek and Omar rode through the Rayder ranks with Elja and Preton, showing them where to dig trenches and set up defenses. Warley Chatterton moved the siege weapons behind the line of soldiers and oversaw the construction of the trebuchets. Vance Talbot and his knights accompanied Bryst Grayson as he moved the supply wagons deeper into the city to a more defensible position.

Lon sat upon Dawes, apart from the soldiers, and surveyed the city. There were no walls protecting Taeja—only half-crumbled towers scattered throughout the land. During his lessons with Omar, Lon had learned that the Phoenijan were all expert fighters. Whenever the Phoenijan saw the beacons of Three Peaks burning, they immediately rode out to battle, with their Beholder lieutenants flying above upon ghraefs.

"Walls were only barriers that impeded the ability to quickly rally their men to battle," Omar had said. "Besides, the Phoenijan needed no walls when Beholders were around to wield the earth into any form their need dictated."

Lon watched his soldiers digging trenches and constructing defenses out of spare lumber. He considered helping them with True Sight; he felt a sense of urgency to finish, especially after Omar's comment about Lars's horse wandering around the Quint River. For all he knew, the king's army was already on its way.

These men have been shocked enough today, Lon thought as he decided against using his power, *and I'm still not ready.*

He turned Dawes around to face Wade, who was sitting on his horse with his hand on his sword. "What is it, Wade?"

"You have my loyalty, Lieutenant," Wade said, "but not everyone here feels the same way. I have committed myself to your safety. With your permission, I would like to stay with you as your guard."

"I'm honored," Lon answered as he looked back over the Rayders. Many of them stole quick glances at him as they worked. "I hope they'll trust me again by the end of this battle."

"As do I," Wade agreed.

Chapter 37

Dawn of a Beholder

Despite the glaring July sun, the Rayders worked diligently to construct their defenses. A deep trench was dug in a wide arc around the eastern perimeter of the city. Three narrow land-bridges spanned the trench at wide intervals. It was across these that Omar intended to route the opposing army, thus keeping the King's superior numbers from overwhelming the Rayders.

Fifteen ballistae were scattered along the trench's inner edge, which was lined with sharpened poles angled to discourage a cavalry charge. Two large barrels of steel-tipped spears accompanied each ballista—terrifying munitions that could be shot more than a thousand feet. One hundred feet further back stood ten trebuchets, each positioned next to a pile of large stones. A wagon full of oil casks was placed a safe distance behind each trebuchet. The casks would be lit and hurled nearly twice as far as the ballistae could shoot. Both the ballistae and trebuchets were protected by eight-foot wooden walls.

That night, the Rayders held a large ceremony for their fallen commander and burned Rayben Goldhawk's body. It was an emotional funeral and Lon kept to himself that night. Even though Omar was acting commander, Rayben needed to be replaced officially by means of a tournament. All Rayder men were allowed to participate in the tournament, but Lon knew there were three strong candidates for commander.

Omar was a born Rayder. He was Rayben's closest friend and a reputable scholar. He was chosen by Rayben as acting commander. Lon respected Omar and knew he would serve honorably, but Omar was older than most of them. Even if Omar survived the battle with Appernysia and somehow won the tournament, he would probably die soon from old age.

Lon knew he and Tarek were the other two contenders. They were both powerful soldiers and strong leaders, but they were also adopted Rayders. Tarek was light-hearted and casual—qualities that wouldn't fit the role of a commander. Lon sighed. Even if he wanted to be the next commander, his inexperience and speech the day before had rattled a lot of the Rayders' trust in him.

At the end of their second day in Taeja, fire and billowing smoke appeared atop Three Peaks. The next morning, the remaining six members of Lon's squad arrived, bearing grave news.

"The Appernysian army approaches from Sylbie," Thad said, "but it is much larger than our commander anticipated. There must be at least a hundred thousand of them. They will be here in three days."

"How's that possible?" Lon asked.

"Remember all the men who fled to the Exile?" Omar asked. "King Drogan has been conscripting heavily over the past few months and they were running from it."

Lon breathed out in frustration. "That's almost seven soldiers to every one of ours. What do you think, Tarek?"

Tarek only laughed.

"I don't even know why I asked you," Lon said as he turned back to Omar. "How about you, my Commander?"

"Their extra twenty-five thousand men will not make any difference to us," Omar replied, "as long as our defenses hold. We will continue to cut them down as they sift through the trenches. However, a little extra help would be nice."

Lon shook his head. "I know what you're thinking and the answer is still no. I won't use True Sight. I'm not going to give our men false hope that a Beholder has come to save them."

"But is that not exactly what you are doing?" Omar asked. "You have come to us—from the least likely of places."

"No," Lon shouted. "I didn't run to the Exile to liberate the Rayders from their oppression. I'm not your savior." What strengthened Lon's resolve was what he couldn't express, not even to Tarek. He didn't want to be a Rayder soldier, nor an Appernysian soldier. Most of all, he didn't want to be a Beholder. He just wanted everybody to get along so he could go back to his simple life in Pree.

His squad stood watching Lon as he breathed through his clenched teeth, then Omar turned to them. "Spread the word that we have three days until the enemy arrives. Remind them that courage is what will see us through to victory. Do not sow seeds of doubt."

✳   ✳   ✳   ✳   ✳

The next three days passed slowly for the Rayders. They finished constructing their defenses. All they had left to do was wait.

At the end of the first day, a dust cloud filled the eastern sky, but the approaching army was still too far away to see. Vance requested permission to send scouts to watch their advancement, but Omar denied his request.

"Lieutenant Lon's squad has learned all we need to know from watching them at Three Peaks. Preserve your knights' energy, Captain. They will need it for the coming fight."

The dust cloud grew thicker and darker throughout the second day. Finally, just before sunset, a long line of soldiers could be seen in the distance. The horizon glowed from the Appernysian fires that night.

When Lon woke up the next morning, the Appernysians were within ten miles.

"They must have marched during the night," Wade commented to Lon.

"Obviously," Lon replied, "but now they'll be tired. That gives us another advantage."

The Rayder soldiers, each protected by shining breastplates and helms, took up positions along the inner rim of the trench a few feet behind the ballistae. The foot soldiers placed their glaives and shields on the ground, their longbows strung, their arrows nocked. Warley's men armed the siege weapons, while Vance and his knights sat clustered upon their horses behind the trebuchets—out of range of the Appernysian archers.

Lon, Omar, and Tarek positioned themselves in front of the center land bridge, along with the remaining nine members of Lon's squad. They now donned full plate armor delivered by Bryst in one of his wagons. Each of them held a glaive and shield, their swords belted tightly around their waists.

Lon turned and glanced over the soldiers behind the battlements. They looked proud and confident, ready to die for Taeja. At the very front of the line stood Braedr Pulchria. He was the only foot soldier not holding a bow, but he was fully armed and ready to fight. He gripped his arming sword in his right hand and a shield had been lashed to his left forearm. Lon dipped his head at Braedr, who touched his fingers to the Cross on his temple.

Lon drew his falchion and raised it high into the air. "For Taeja!"

"For Taeja!" the men shouted in response.

"Nice," Tarek teased as Lon turned back around.

"Shut it," Lon replied.

For the next four hours, they watched the Appernysian army close the distance until they finally stopped a mile away. A small group of armored horsemen, bearing a dark green banner marked with the head of a halberd, rode out from the center of the army and stopped a half-mile away.

"I guess they want to talk," Tarek said as he kicked his horse in the sides. The twelve of them rode out to meet the envoy.

"What can we do for you?" Tarek asked with a smile.

"You aren't welcome here, traitors," one of the opposing men replied. "You can leave now with your lives or stay and die."

"Where is your king?" Omar asked. "Is he too much a coward to speak with us?"

"Where's your Beholder?" the man countered.

"Beholder?" Omar answered smoothly. "If we had a Beholder, we would have skipped over Taeja and headed straight for Itorea."

The man smiled. "You can't fool us. We have credible information a Beholder is living among you."

"If that information excuses your retreat," Omar said, "then believe what you want. Now leave us be. You abandoned this land."

"We didn't abandon it," the man replied. "We destroyed it. We stopped the rivers and tore down the buildings, but it was the treachery of your ancestors that truly desecrated it. No one is welcome here."

"This is our home, our rightful inheritance," Omar continued. "We will die defending it."

"So be it," the man said, then turned and rode away with his envoy.

"Quick responses," Tarek commented as they galloped back to their battlements.

"In all honesty, we have no Beholder," Omar stated. "Lon has no intention of using his gift."

Lon shook his head and blew out his breath. "You're never going to let it go, are you, Omar? I'll tell you what—I'll let you fight up here without having to worry about me."

Lon kicked Dawes hard and galloped to the southern land bridge and positioned himself behind the trebuchets.

✳ ✳ ✳ ✳ ✳

Once back to their battlements, Tarek and the rest of Lon's squad dismounted and dispersed themselves among the other foot soldiers at the center land bridge. Omar led their horses back to the cavalry.

Tension filled the Taejan Plains while both armies faced each other. An hour passed before the Appernysians began their assault. Five thousand peasant men filtered through the ranks of the soldiers and slowly made their way toward the Rayder battlements. They were armed with hammers, axes, and war scythes. Every third man carried a small round shield made of wood.

Tarek cursed King Drogan. "These aren't soldiers. They'll all die before they even reach our battlements."

The peasants continued forward at a slow pace. When they closed within a half-mile, Warley stepped forward. "Put one stone in the middle of them."

The center trebuchet flung a large boulder high into the air toward the approaching peasants. They shouted in fear and split their ranks in half. The rock struck a boulder and shattered. Tiny chips of rock whizzed through the air and struck many of the fleeing peasants.

Warley turned back to the team operating the trebuchet. "Excellent shot, Rayders."

What little courage the peasants displayed instantly disintegrated. They retreated back toward the Appernysian line. Tarek watched with horror as a volley of crossbow bolts erupted from the opposing line and landed in the midst of the peasants, who fled back to the center of the field.

"Cowards," Tarek shouted with disgust, along with many of his men.

Suddenly Lon burst through the lines, galloping fiercely toward the stranded Appernysian peasants.

"Please don't tell me he intends to fight their entire army by himself," Tarek said to Wade, who stood anxiously witnessing the scene before them.

The peasants scattered when they saw Lon approaching until he drew up in their midst. "Fellow Appernysians," he called. "King Drogan has abandoned you, but I will not! Join us, and I promise you the protection of the Taejans."

The peasants stopped running and looked back and forth between the two armies.

Lon dismounted Dawes and tossed his glaive to the nearest peasant. "I was once living in Appernysia, but fled to the Exile for protection. They welcomed me, even made me one of their leaders. Don't be afraid. You have my word that you will be protected."

The peasants exchanged glances with each other. A few joined Lon at his side, followed by a few more. Soon, all of them—more than five thousand—were walking with Lon toward the Rayders, although some more willingly than others.

A furious cry erupted from the Appernysian line and a mass of light cavalry charged forward.

"Run," Lon shouted as he leaped into Dawes's saddle. "Hurry!"

"Captain, protect your lieutenant," Tarek shouted to Vance and his knights, but Vance ignored Tarek's order.

"Your general has given you an order, Captain," Omar said. He was sitting on his horse next to Vance.

"I will not obey a command that contradicts what our real commander would have me do," Vance spat. "His last request was to slaughter all Appernysians. If Commander Rayben was still alive, he would have executed Lon for his actions."

"Is that your final decision?" Omar asked calmly.

"Yes. I refuse to protect a corrupt Appernysian-lover. You may be acting commander, but not even you can convince me otherwise."

With one smooth motion, Omar drew his sword and lopped Vance's head from his shoulders. Vance's body shuddered and tumbled out of his saddle.

"Forward!" Omar called as he kicked his own horse into a gallop.

*　　*　　*　　*　　*

The Rayder steeds, powerful beasts bred for speed and trained for combat, were quickly closing in on the fleeing peasants. As they rode, the Rayder knights slipped their glaives into leather loops on the side of their saddles and pulled their composite bows from their backs.

After sliding their shields up their arms, the Rayders each nocked an arrow and released a deadly volley at the opposing horsemen, striking nearly half of them to the ground. The Appernysian peasants watched with awe as the Rayder cavalry slid their bows over their shoulders and retrieved their glaives just in time to engage the remaining horsemen.

"Keep running," Lon shouted to the peasants as he turned Dawes around to help.

Omar and his knights finished off the rest of the Appernysian horsemen, with the exception of one man who fled back toward the Appernysian line. Lon grabbed his own bow and took aim. He loosed an arrow that soared more than two hundred and fifty yards, striking the man at the base of his neck. He keeled over and fell out of his saddle while his horse galloped madly through the front line of Appernysians.

Lon replaced his bow and escorted the Appernysian peasants over the trench and behind the line of trebuchets. Omar and his knights followed on their heels.

"Stay here," Lon called to the peasants, "and don't do anything foolish. This isn't your battle."

The peasants consented and sat on their weapons between Warley's men and Omar's knights. Lon dismounted, reclaimed his glaive from the peasant, and walked to the front line to stand between Tarek and Wade.

"Welcome back, Lieutenant," Wade said.

"You've been saying that a lot lately, Wade," Tarek inserted. "Think Lon will stick around this time?"

Lon smacked the flat side of his glaive against Tarek's helm. "Watch it."

Tarek laughed and whapped Lon on the back.

Appernysian horses were galloping around the plains. "Look at that," Tarek called. "Even their mounts are glad to be free of them." The men around him burst into laughter.

"Nice," Lon said.

Another hour passed before the Appernysians renewed their assault against the Rayders. Long lines of pikemen—thousands strong—advanced onto the field, each clad in chain mail, dark green cloaks, and a large wall shield that protected nearly their entire bodies. Behind each line of pikemen came soldiers wielding armor-piercing crossbows.

"Finally," Tarek shouted. "Now, for the real fight."

The soldiers marched over the dead peasants and their fallen knights, stopping a half-mile away to regroup. They spread out and formed into small mixed battalions, then continued toward the Rayders' defenses.

Warley waited until they were well within the trebuchets' range, then ordered his men to throw burning casks at the enemy. Large fireballs flew from the ten trebuchets, soaring over the plains and breaking open to send gallons of flaming oil onto the Appernysian formations, but they appeared undaunted, pressing forward through the flames.

When the enemy closed within a thousand feet, Warley ordered the ballistae teams to bombard them with steel-tipped spears. The Appernysians ducked behind their shields as the massive bolts zipped through the air. The heavy spears pierced the shields like paper, impaling the unsuspecting soldiers behind. The men broke into a frantic run toward the Rayder line until they were within range, then loosed a deadly barrage from their crossbows.

The siege teams hid behind their wooden barricades while the Rayder footmen picked up their shields and formed a tight wall of steel over their heads. Scattered screams echoed through their ranks as bolts slipped through the gaps, but most of the Rayders remained unharmed.

When the hail of bolts ended, the Rayders dropped their shields and released their own volley in retaliation. The sky darkened with black-feathered arrows that rained down on the Appernysian soldiers as they tried to span their crossbows. The Appernysians fell by the hundreds, but still they came on.

Warley's siege weapons ripped great holes in the Appernysian lines, but each hole was quickly filled in by more Appernysians while wave after wave of bolts continued to pour down on the Rayder defenses.

The dwindling gap between the two armies filled with approaching Appernysian soldiers and still more poured in from behind. The Rayder siege munitions were running low and the footmen's quivers nearly empty.

As he reached for his last shaft, Lon surveyed the battlefield. Large catapults were creeping up behind the lines of pikemen, escorted by thousands of mounted knights.

Lon loosed his final arrow and turned to Tarek. "If those catapults get within range, our defenses will be useless. We can't stay here or we'll be trapped and obliterated."

"What do you suggest?" Tarek shouted over the noise.

Lon smirked. He dropped his bow, then picked up his shield and glaive.

"You're crazy," Tarek said with a laugh as he did the same thing, then together they charged across the trench.

"Rally to our general," Braedr called from behind and chased after them.

The Rayder footmen picked up their glaives and shields and followed Tarek and Lon over the land bridges toward their enemy.

"Keep the enemy's heads down," Warley shouted to his men.

The Rayder ballistae unloaded their remaining spears into the Appernysians until Lon and Tarek reached the first line of pikemen. They were soon joined by their brothers-in-arms, and together they wreaked havoc along the front line. The Appernysians faltered as the Rayder carnage pressed deeper into the Appernysian ranks.

Lon dropped his shield and swung his glaive around with blinding speed, dodging and parrying, cutting down all who opposed him. He glanced at Tarek, who was wielding his sword and shield with devastation.

"I thought they'd offer some sort of challenge," Tarek boasted when he noticed Lon looking at him.

Lon leaned his head back to catch his breath. It was then that he saw three fiery casks soaring over the plains. They were falling directly at him and would kill hundreds of Rayder and Appernysian men. Tarek also noticed, but didn't attempt to flee, knowing it would be pointless.

In an instant, Lon surveyed the carnage strewn across the battle-field. He remembered what True Sight had revealed from the man he killed at the Quint River. As Lon imagined the bright essence of the dead hovering above thousands of fallen bodies, the words of his father whispered from the back of his mind.

Wise men will embrace correction while the foolish stubbornly cling to their pride.

"Get behind me," he shouted to Tarek as he summoned True Sight and stepped forward, spinning his glaive rapidly over his head and pouring as much energy into it as possible.

Tarek dove backward as Lon twisted his body in a full circle and swung the glaive toward the Appernysians. Lon intended to deflect the casks with his glowing weapon, but a beam of invisible energy shot from its tip, flaring from the ground upward. The fires enveloping the casks were extinguished, then the casks themselves shattered as they struck the sweeping energy shield.

Everyone near Lon was thrown backward by the impenetrable shield. They flew over their own comrades in a massive wave. The oily cloud, settling over the battle in a fine mist, spread through the air until it reached a small fire smoldering in the dry grass. The fire surged through the mist, causing a concussive explosion that knocked everyone within a hundred-foot diameter to the ground, while those unfortunate enough to be within thirty feet were cooked in their armor.

An eerie silence broke out as both armies gawked at the explosion, then widened their eyes when huge pillars of dirt slowly rose out of the ground in front of Lon and formed a solid staircase leading to an earthen platform high in the air.

Lon picked up his shield and started up the stairs. An Appernysian soldier shot a bolt at Lon, but he easily deflected it with his shield and softened the ground underneath the man's feet. The soldiers surrounding the man jumped back in alarm as he sank waist deep into the soil. Lon continued climbing the stairs.

Another flurry of bolts flew toward Lon from his left. He lifted his left hand and grabbed hold of their wooden shafts with True Sight, stopping them mid-flight. Everyone stared in awe as ten armor-piercing bolts hovered motionless in the air. Lon shattered them and swept them aside before continuing up the stairs.

When Lon reached the elevated platform, he dropped his shield, brought his hands together in front of himself, and summoned a fireball the size of his head. "This fight ends now," he shouted as he raised the flame above his head. "Return to Itorea at once or, by my honor, I will incinerate your entire army."

The Appernysian soldiers surrounding Lon exchanged worried glances. They gazed at him in wonder until the sound of galloping hooves broke the silence. It was the same man who had led the Appernysian envoy before the battle—their general, Lon assumed. He thundered up from his place by the catapults and halted a few yards off.

"The fool has placed himself on a platform," the Appernysian general shouted when he drew close to Lon. "Kill him!"

Lon opened his palms and shot a flame in the man's direction. The general's horse reared up on its hind legs as the grass in front of them burst into flame.

"I said move," Lon shouted again. He focused on the energy leaving his mouth, capturing and projecting it across the mile-wide battlefield like an eagle strafing the ground. "Go home and leave us in peace."

Lon's power overwhelmed the Appernysians. No one moved or spoke as they watched him—the first Beholder in twelve hundred years—until their general turned his horse around and galloped away.

The Appernysian soldiers gaped as their general abandoned them. Lon saw their fear and, to force their decision, projected another flame into the grass and slowly moved it closer to their front lines. The Appernysians watched the approaching column of fire for only a few seconds before they started to back away.

Lon continued to force their retreat until the entire field was cleared, then lifted the trapped Appernysian soldier from his earthen prison. As he watched the soldier sprint away after his comrades, Lon marveled over what he had accomplished. Never before had he crafted permanent pillars of dirt. He never knew he was capable of such a thing. His ability to stop and shatter the crossbow bolts in mid-air was even more astounding. Everything had happened so fast. His reactions were not planned, but instinctual. His speed, precision, and power were overwhelming. For a brief moment, Lon felt like he had finally been allowed a glimpse of his true potential as a Beholder.

He released True Sight and turned around. The Rayders stood motionless, watching him. As Lon descended the earthen stairs, his squad and Tarek all dropped to one knee, saluting him.

Lon watched with wide eyes as the entire Rayder army followed their example and bowed in unison before Lon—all except Braedr, who stood clenching his sword, fury burning in his eyes.

"Blessing of the Jaeds," Omar boomed from the midst of them. "Hail, Beholder."

"Hail, Beholder," the Rayders echoed.

Lon ignored Braedr and walked between his men, swelling with pride over their victory. He couldn't help noticing that not a single person looked up at him. Why? Were they afraid? Angry? Confused?

Lon buried his uncertainty deep within himself as he climbed onto Dawes and lifted his eyes. Before him knelt thousands of the finest soldiers in the world, all awaiting his command. Rising behind them, the scattered ruins of his ancestors summoned him. His tasks were far from complete. He closed his eyes and breathed deeply, then clicked his tongue and rode toward the heart of Taeja—his new home.

Chapter 38
True Sight

M ellai wiped away her tears and picked up the letter from
Kaylen. She took a deep breath and read the last paragraph
one more time.

> *The truth is this whole letter has been a big waste of*
> *parchment. I'm just trying to delay the real reason*
> *I started writing this in the first place. The Rayders*
> *have attacked Appernysia. Tonight, Aely and I*
> *watched as King Drogan's army ran up and down*
> *the hallways in preparation for battle. They're going*
> *to start their march to Taeja tomorrow morning*
> *and force the Rayders back to the Exile, but for you*
> *and your family the situation is much worse. King*
> *Drogan believes a Beholder is leading the Rayders*
> *against us. I'm sorry, Mellai, but your brother has*
> *betrayed us all.*
>
> *I wish I wasn't the one who had to tell you this. Please*
> *forgive me.*
>
> *Kaylen*

By the time Kutad delivered the letter to Mellai, the Appernysian army had already returned to Itorea—miserable, dejected, having lost the battle and failed their king. Only then had Kutad dared to pass along Kaylen's lamentable news.

"I had to know that what she said was true," he told Mellai. "This letter carries too much weight to be handled lightly."

He confirmed what Kaylen suspected. A Beholder had led the Rayders against the king's army and used True Sight to drive them back from Taeja. The end of July brought with it the end of the Rayder banishment.

"But what good is any army against a Beholder?" Kutad commented. "They say he wielded a power so terrible that our general fled in the middle of battle, abandoning his men to the Rayders."

Mellai ran away that same day, crying as she wandered north into the Vidarien Mountains. After two days with no rest, she ended up in the same clearing where she had rescued Kaylen the previous winter. As she stared at the hollowed tree, she dropped to the ground and cried herself to sleep.

The next morning, Mellai read the letter again, hoping that somehow its message would change, but she knew deep inside Kaylen's words were true. It couldn't have been an easy decision for Lon—she had felt his turmoil over the previous months—but in the end he chose wrong. The Rayders were the enemy! They had killed Myron's family. They had tried to kill her. Lon had been so valiant the day he saved her life, but everything had changed after that.

Mellai knew going to the Exile had saved her brother, at least partially. Lon had obviously learned how to control True Sight—it was the only way he could have driven Appernysia's entire army back to Itorea—but he made the wrong choice when he decided to help the Rayders instead of returning home. Thousands of innocent lives were taken; he would have to answer for them. She would make sure of it.

Even through Mellai's connection to Lon, she could not comprehend how Lon could have become so deceived. Were the Rayders really so convincing that her brother forgot everything their father told him? Did he forget what happened to Myron's family? Did he forget why he left in the first place? Did he forget about Kaylen?

Wait. Was it really Lon who led the Rayders to Taeja? Or was there another Beholder?

She shook her head, crumpled up the letter and threw it to the ground. *Don't be foolish*, she thought. *There is no other Beholder.*

She leaned against the tree, weeping violently, her body shaking with torment.

"What happened to you, Lon?" she screamed to the sky. "We had a plan!"

When Mellai squeezed her eyes shut to force out her tears, a bright light suddenly pierced her eyelids. She turned her head away in pain, blinking rapidly in an attempt to clear her vision. Her eyes felt as though they were covered in a layer of film that blurred her vision. A sudden terror seized her—had she gone blind?

"You are not blind," an ethereal voice sounded in her ears. "In fact, you will see the world more clearly now than ever before."

Mellai threw her hand up as a shield and squinted into the bright light. "Who are you?" she demanded.

"Do not be afraid. My name is Llen. I am a Jaed."

"A Jaed? Why . . . why are you here?"

"The balance of the world's energy has shifted, Mellai," Llen replied. "Appernysia needs you."

Glossary

<u>Pronunciation Guide:</u>

\ā\ *as* **a** *in ape*	\ər\ *as* **er** *in person*	\th\ *as* **th** *in thin*
\a\ *as* **a** *in apple*	\ī\ *as* **i** *in ice*	\ū\ *as* **u** *in union*
\ä\ *as* **o** *in hop*	\i\ *as* **i** *in hit*	\uh\ *as* **u** *in bug*
\ch\ *as* **ch** *in chip*	\ō\ *as* **o** *in go*	\ü\ *as* **oo** *in loot*
\ē\ *as* **ea** *in easy*	\qu\ *as* **qu** *in quiet*	\ů\ *as* **oo** *in foot*
\e\ *as* **e** *in bet*	\sh\ *as* **sh** *in shop*	\zh\ *as* **si** *in vision*

Aely – (ā´-lē) new friend of Kaylen Shaw.

Allegna Ovann – (uh-leg´-nuh | ō´-van) wife to Dhargon Ovann; mother of Shalán Marcs.

Appernysia – (a-pər-nē´-zhuh) the kingdom in which this story is set, established at the beginning of the First Age.

Aron Marcs – (ä´-ruhn | märks´) husband to Shalán Marcs and father of Lon and Mellai Marcs.

Beholder – a person with True Sight who can manipulate the world's energy.

Beholder's Eye – the tattoo surrounding the left eye of Beholders.

Bors Rayder – (bōrz´ | rā´-dər) a Taejan who led the Phoenijan rebellion against the king and Beholders at the end of the First Age; all Taejans who followed him took the title of Rayder.

Braedr Pulchria – (brā´-dər | půl´-krē-uh) son to Hans and Ine Pulchria; raised in Pree.

Bryst Grayson – (brist´ | grā´-suhn) Rayder supply wagon overseer.

calahein – (ca´-luh-hīn) ancient enemy of Appernysia; exterminated from their home in Meridina near the end of the First Age; composed of kelsh, seith, and one queen.

Cavalier Crook – the southwestern quadrant of Itorea that houses the city's nobles.

Channer – (chan´-ər) member of a twelve-Rayder tactical squad; cousin to Keene.

Coel – (kōl´) village leatherworker in Pree.

coming of age – an important transition from adolescence to adulthood in Pree, enabling a person to participate in village councils, start their own trade, build their own home, and marry and start a family; age fifteen for girls and age seventeen for boys.

Cortney Baum – (kōrt´-nē | bäm´) young Rayder daughter of Gil and Flora Baum.

Dawes – (däz´) Rayder horse previously owned by Gil Baum.

Delancy Reed – (de-lan´-sē | rēd´) village brewer in Pree; father to Sonela Reed.

Dhargon Ovann – (där´-guhn | ō´-van) husband to Allegna Ovann; father of Shalán Marcs.

Dovan – (dō´-ven) member of a twelve-Rayder tactical squad.

Drake – (drāk´) a member of Gil Baum's Rayder squad.

Edis Ascennor – (ē´-dis | uh-se´-nōr) deceased wife of Myron Ascennor.

Elja – (el´-zhuh) member of a twelve-Rayder tactical squad.

Elora – (ē-lōr´-uh) village alfalfa farmer in Pree; widow with four sons.

First Age – the time period which began when Appernysia was first settled; ended after the Rayder revolution and banishment to the Exile; reference Second Age.

Flagheim – (flag´-hīm) fortress city of the Rayders; located in the Exile about thirty miles north of the Dialorine Range.

Flora Baum – (flōr´-uh | bäm´) Rayder widow of Gil Baum; mother of Cortney Baum and two older sons.

Furwen Tree – (fər´-wen) a massive tree with wood as hard as stone, grows over six hundred feet tall; located in the Perbeisea Forest.

Geila – (gā´-luh) young pureblood Rayder woman executed for fornication with Sévart; gave birth to a child in the wilderness.

ghraef – (grāf´) a large beast with thick, hardened skin that is covered in fur and an armored tail with a unique crystal on its tip; served as companions to Beholders, but disappeared after the end of the First Age.

Gil Baum – (gil´ | bäm´) the deceased Rayder husband to Flora Baum.

Hadon – (hā´-duhn) village farmer of wheat and oats in Pree, along with Landon.

Hans Pulchria – (hänz´ | pŭl´-krē-uh) village blacksmith in Pree; husband of Ine Pulchria and father of Braedr Pulchria.

Ine Pulchria – (īn´ | pŭl´-krē-uh) mother of Braedr Pulchria and wife of Hans Pulchria, the village blacksmith in Pree.

Itorea – (ī-tōr´-ē-uh) the capital of the Kingdom of Appernysia; also known as the Fortress Island or City of the King.

Jaed – (jād´) an ethereal being; regulates the balance of the world's energy; only visible by Beholders.

Jareth – (jer´-eth) soldier in the Appernysian army; friend of Kutad.

Justice – a Rayder bridge.

Kaylen Shaw – (kā´-len | shä´) girlfriend of Lon Marcs and daughter of Scut Shaw.

Keene – (kēn´) member of a twelve-Rayder tactical squad; cousin to Channer.

kelsh – (kelsh´) the ground troops of the calahein.

King's Court – an entity consisting of the seat of government and the royal household.

King Drogan – (drō´-gen) current king of Appernysia.

King's Cross – branded into the right temple of all Rayders; in the First Age, it was tattooed into the right temple of the Phoenijan from the blue petals of the Lynth Flower.

Kutad – (kü-täd´) leader of the Appernysian trading caravan.

Landon – (lan´-duhn) village farmer of wheat and oats in Pree, along with Hadon.

Lars – (lärz´) member of a twelve-Rayder tactical squad; oldest member of the squad.

Linney – (lin´-ē) deceased daughter of Kutad; the name Mellai Marcs uses to disguise herself while in Roseiri.

Llen – (len´) a Jaed.

Lon Marcs – (län´ | märks´) twin brother of Mellai Marcs and son of Aron and Shalán Marcs.

Lon Shaw – (län´ | shä´) nickname used by Lon Marcs.

Lynth Flower – (linth´) a rare blue flower that grows only in Itorea; its petals were used to tattoo Beholders and Phoenijan in the First Age; replicated as a silver pendant that is given to honored soldiers in Appernysia.

Mellai Marcs – (mel-ī´ | märks´) twin sister to Lon Marcs and daughter of Aron and Shalán Marcs; also known as Mel.

Meridina – (mer-i-dē´-nuh) underground city of the calahein; destroyed near the end of the First Age.

Myron Ascennor – (mī´-ruhn | uh-se´-nōr) prior village delegate of Pree until his family was murdered by Rayders and his youngest son, Tarek, disappeared; has wandered Pree alone ever since.

Night Stalker – a tactical game created by the Rayders to test their stealth and skill; one team of five men tries to capture a diamond from a separate team of fifteen men without detection.

Nik – (nik´) member of a twelve-Rayder tactical squad.

Nybol – (nī´-bōl) village sheep and goat herder in Pree.

Old Trade Route – abandoned trade road in Appernysia that runs from Humsco to Pree before returning to Roseiri; reference Trade Route.

Omar Brickeden – (ō´-mar | bri´-ke-den) respected Rayder scholar.

Perbeisea Forest – (per-bā´-zhuh) sacred woods located west of Itorea; made up of Furwen Trees.

Phoenijan – (fēn´-i-zhan) elite guard of Appernysia in the First Age; composed completely of Taejans and led by Beholder lieutenants; after the Rayder revolt at the end of the First Age, the role of the Phoenijan was dissolved.

Pree – (prē´) a small village located in the southwestern corner of the Western Valley in Appernysia, 5 miles east of the Tamadoras Mountains.

Preton – (pre´-tuhn) member of a twelve-Rayder tactical squad.

Ramsey – (ram´-zē) village farmer of vegetables and fruits in Pree, along with Wellesly; father of Tirk.

Rayben Goldhawk – (rā´-ben) current Rayder commander.

Rayder – (rā´-dər) title acquired when the Phoenijan followed Bors Rayder in a revolution against their king and the Beholders at the end of the First Age.

Rayder Commander – leader of the Rayders; functions similarly to the king of Appernysia.

Rayder Exile – the land north of the Zaga Ravine and the Dialorine Range; where the Rayders were banished at the end of the First Age.

Réxura – (rex´-ər-uh) a major trade city located at the eastern tip of the Vidarien Mountains.

Riyen – (rī´-yen) member of a twelve-Rayder tactical squad.

Roseiri – (rōs-ēr´-ē) a village located twenty miles south of the Vidarien Mountains, along the West River; home to Dhargon and Allegna Ovann.

Sátta – (sä´-tuh) soldier in the Appernysian army; friend to Aely.

Scut Shaw – (scüt´ | shä´) village dairy farmer in Pree; father of Kaylen Shaw.

Second Age – the current time period in the story which has been in existence for one thousand two hundred years.

seith – (sēth´) flying calahein; great bane of the ghraefs.

Sévart – (sā´-värt) young pureblood Rayder man executed for fornication with Geila.

Shalán Marcs – (shuh-län´) wife to Aron Marcs and mother of Lon and Mellai Marcs; village healer in Pree.

Sonela Reed – (suh-ne´-luh | rēd´) daughter of Delancy Reed.

Sylbie – (sil´-bē) large city that handles shipments from Réxura to Itorea; located at the connecting fork of the Sylbien River and Prime River.

Taeja – (tā´-zhuh) ruined city in the Taejan Plains; home to the Taejans and Beholders in the First Age.

Taejan – (tā´-zhuhn) title of the Rayders before their revolution at the end of the First Age; from the Taejans came the Phoenijan and Beholders.

Taejan Plains – (tā´-zhuhn) the northwestern region of Appernysia between the Tamadoras Mountains and the Nellis River.

Tarek Ascennor – (ter´-ek | uh-se´-nōr) son of Myron Ascennor; went missing when the rest of his family was murdered by Rayders.

Tarl – (tärl´) member of a twelve-Rayder tactical squad.

Tayla – (tā´-luh) deceased wife of Kutad.

Thad – (thad´) member of a twelve-Rayder tactical squad.

Theiss Arbogast – (tīs´ | ar´-bō-gast) young man who lives in the village of Roseiri.

Thorn – a conical watchtower situated north of the Zaga Ravine

Three Peaks – solitary watchtower mountain located in the Taejan Plains.

Tirk – (tərk´) son of Ramsey, one of the village farmers of vegetables and fruits in Pree.

Trade Route – trade road that extends from Itorea to Pree, then circles around the Western Valley of Appernysia; reference Old Trade Route.

Trev Rowley – (trev´ | rō´-lē) current village delegate in Pree.

True Sight – the ability of a man to see the world's energy.

Vance Talbot – (vans´ | tal´-buht) captain of the Rayder cavalry.

Wade Arneson – (wād´ | ar´-ne-suhn) member of a twelve-Rayder tactical squad; Rayder Lieutenant.

Warley Chatterton – (war´-lē | cha´-ter-tuhn) Rayder lieutenant over siege weapons.

Weeping Forest – a boggy forest of weeping willow trees situated at the northern base of the Dialorine Range.

Wellesly – (wel´-es-lē) village farmer of vegetables and fruits in Pree, along with Ramsey.

Western Valley – the southwestern region of Appernysia between the Tamadoras Mountains and the Pearl River.

Zaga Ravine – (zä´-guh) a deep gorge that extends from the Tamadoras Mountains to the western tip of the Dialorine Range; marks the northern edge of the Kingdom of Appernysia.

Zaxton – (zax´-tuhn) Appernysian scout at the Quint River.

About The Author

Born in the wrong age, Terron James continually fantasizes of shining steel, majestic stone architecture, thundering cavalry rushes, and opportunities to prove his honor. Under the direction of his queen, Terron labors diligently in his kingdom, striving to prepare an inheritance worthy of his five heirs.

When he finally graduated from the University of Utah with his English BA, Terron had become besties with most of the English department staff, as well as the employees of Brio, who make a wicked cup of hot chocolate.

Terron currently resides in Tooele, UT. His dream is to capture every sunset with his wife, fingers interlocked, the reflection of his soul in her brown eyes, and the ocean surf rolling over their bare feet.

Terron is a junior high English teacher at Excelsior Academy and a former Tooele Chapter president of the League of Utah Writers.

Visit www.TerronJames.com

CPSIA information can be obtained
at www.ICGtesting.com
Printed in the USA
FSHW011526091219
64892FS